MW00713865

TURKEY RANCH
ROAD RAGE

PAULA BOYD

Diomo
Books

Diomo Books
Hot Springs, AR
www.diomobooks.com

Chapter One

Springtime in the Rockies is just plain gorgeous, but don't tell anyone. There's a foot of new snow on the ground, but I could sit outside on my deck naked if I wanted to. I don't do that sort of thing much after that incident involving the bird feeder and the meter reader, but I could if I wanted to. So, instead of working on my winter tan, I was sitting at my desk putting the finishing touches on a feature story about a friend of mine here in the mountains who has a book coming out this month. I do a variety of freelance jobs to supplement my income, which otherwise comes solely from a card company I sold a few years ago. For the most part, it means I do not have to live in a box under a bridge while I do what I enjoy. What can I say, I got lucky.

Feeling warm and fuzzy and satisfied with life in general, I ended the article and started to log on to the Internet to send it to the newspaper that had agreed to pay me for it. The ringing of the telephone stopped me.

As I grabbed the receiver, I turned my chair to look out the window at the unbelievably blue sky, a deep vivid blue that I've never seen anywhere but here in the mountains. Some days—actually a lot of days—it's just too blue to be real, too good to be true, and it always makes me thankful I live here rather than someplace else.

"Hello," I said, my voice lilting upward in a cheerful happy tone.

"Jolene, it's Jerry."

Zing. My sky-blue musings flew out the window for a variety of reasons, not the least of which was the deep timbre of Jerry Don Parker's voice. Jerry, AKA Sheriff Parker of Bowman County, Texas, and I had been communicating quite a bit lately—and quite pleasantly, I might add—but not in the middle of a work day. That was my first clue that this was not a personal call. The second was the weary resignation in his usually seductive voice as he said, "It's about your mother."

Oh, lovely, wasn't it always. Just as my ugly thoughts were queuing up for a fast-forward replay of Lucille history, a stab of real fear punched the pause button. The woman is in her seventies after all. "Is she okay?"

"Relatively speaking, I suppose."

Jerry's voice was not one of compassion, as if preparing to deliver the ultimate of bad news, but rather a weary tone heavy with disillusionment, distress and *déjà vu*, and I got the message loud and clear. "What has she done this time?"

"I'm sorry, Jolene, but she's in jail."

Jail. Behind bars. Oh, my.

Okay, we all know I was not shocked. I quit being shocked about such things several months ago when my mother officially became insane. Well, maybe she's not really insane, in technical and clinical terms, but from where I sit she is plainly nuts. I leaned back in my chair, closed my eyes and rubbed my lids, a futile gesture usually practiced when my mother is actually in front of me. I've yet to make her—or me—magically disappear, but somehow it's comforting to know that you can blink the world away for a few seconds. A very few. "All right, let's hear it."

"We had no choice but to arrest her and her friends."

You expect me to be surprised, what? "And?"

"Fritz tried to post her bail the minute after he booked her, but she didn't take too kindly to any of it."

No, I bet she didn't, particularly from Fritz Harper, who was, last I'd heard, my mother's latest squeeze. He was also a semi-retired deputy who worked for Jerry, my old high school sweetheart and would-be lover. Would be, that is, if we weren't distracted by my mother's determination to get herself arrested, or the various murdering crazies running loose spoiling things. That we're seven hundred miles apart wasn't helping much either. One bad thought led to another, and before I knew it the big screen version of *Terminator 73: Lucille on the Loose* was playing wildly in my head. "Who'd she kill?"

"No one was hurt," Jerry said tentatively. "But there's a county maintenance truck with a bullet in the radiator, at least that's the only one we've found so far. Bullet, that is."

I groaned, but asked the obvious anyway. "Why did she shoot a county truck?"

"You knew about the picket line, right?"

Wrong. I knew nothing about anything, and in particular, nothing about a picket line. "As in protesters with signs and things?"

"Exactly. They set up out on the north end of Turkey Ranch Road where the county was doing some right-of-way work."

The mental geography was fairly easy in that Jerry Don Parker and I had spent quite a bit of our teenage days in that area. Turkey Ranch Road went past the old Little Ranch, which had several access roads up to oil wells that were perfect for star gazing. Dedicated students that we were, we went out there several times a week to map constellations for extra credit. I might not be able to locate more than six constellations, but I knew exactly where Turkey Ranch Road was, and it wasn't very far from my mother's house. That answered nothing about why she was out there causing trouble, however. "Okay, Jerry, I don't have a clue about what's going on. Tell me."

"It's about the RV park that's going in."

"RV park?"

"I'm not sure of all the details myself, but the rumor is that about two thousand acres at the edge of Kickapoo are going to be turned into a camping park of some sort."

A park? With camping? In Kickapoo? Why? "Oh, geez, this doesn't have anything to do with the new falls, does it?"

"Well, yeah," he said, a sort of "duh" tone in his voice. "Redwater's getting a lot of tourist traffic now. People that would have just passed through are making this a stopover. The waterfall is a nice tourist attraction."

I suppose it was that, relatively speaking, since the only other tourist attraction around town was the four-story medical building out off the bypass that was affectionately known as "the tower." I did not say these things aloud as I've noticed that Jerry Don seems to kind of like the place and does not find my little observations and witty commentaries particularly humorous.

It was yet another of the insurmountable gulfs between us, maybe even harder to overcome than the distance factor. "So, let me get this straight. Mother isn't happy about this so-called park and was protesting. She got a little carried away, whipped out her concealed weapon and maimed a radiator. Am I close?"

"Yes, generally speaking, I guess. But the county guys were just mowing the grass, not actually starting on the park. Gifford Geller's nephew Gus had just parked the truck on the shoulder and walked across the road when she shot it. He's making noise about attempted murder, but we only charged her with destruction of public property."

I took a deep breath and willed away all the pesky questions that were flitting through my mind. The details of what happened and why were irrelevant. What mattered was how I was going to get myself uninvolved with it. "Okay, listen, Jerry," I said, a plan forming as I spoke. For all my faults, I can make decisions fast and firm when I have to. "I'll call Mother and tell her to control herself. You just take my VISA number and pay her fine, or bail, or whatever. As long as it's under five grand, I should be okay. Just free her and haul her home. I'll handle it from there."

"I can't."

"Excuse me?"

"She refuses to leave, Jolene," he said, sort of pitiful-like. "She even tried to assault Fritz when he went to get her then told us to arrest her for that too. We're in a tough place here."

I let another little groan slip out before I caught myself. I knew exactly where this was headed, and I wasn't going for it, not no-way, not no-how. My mother was a grown woman and could very well take care of herself. Besides, she tended to get even more Lucille-ish when I got involved; therefore, it was my civic duty to stay out of the mess. (Rationalization is as handy as denial and I am free and loose with both.) "I'm not coming down there, Jerry. At some point, I need to do some actual work here and make some money so I can keep my house."

"Jolene..."

There was a definite pleading tone to his voice that I would have preferred to hear in a very different context—one that didn't involve my mother. "I can't."

"If Fritz can't make her see reason, you're the only one who can. She's a seventy-year-old woman and she doesn't need to be staying here at the jail. It's not good for her, and it's not good for me either."

For him? Oh, now we were getting somewhere. Mr. Sheriff's concerns extended past the usual pain-in-the-butt Lucille issues. "PR worries, eh?"

He hemmed and hawed for a second then said, "Well, yes. She called up the newspaper and one of the radio stations before we took her cell phone away."

I wasn't sure which of these details was most amusing, the fact that she'd called the media or that they'd let her keep a phone to do it with. "Well, Jerry, it sounds like you've got a real problem there."

"She's your mother," he snapped back, adding an accusatory tone to be sure I got the message.

"I was switched at birth."

"Jolene…"

"Look, Jerry, what do you want me to say? Just treat her like you would any other vicious criminal who'd done the same thing and move along."

"It's not that simple." He sighed, heavily. "Your mother and her friends have been writing letters to a whole lot of people, such as every member of the city councils of both Redwater Falls and Kickapoo."

"Okay, nothing illegal about that."

"These were threatening letters," he said. "Some have appeared in the Redwater paper."

Public threats. Yes, that was bad, likely very bad, but I couldn't acknowledge it or I'd find myself heading south before I could even utter the words "please God, not again." "Well, Jerry, I think that's great that she's trying to do things to get somebody to pay attention to that park problem. Granted, shooting a county maintenance truck was a bad call, but the rest seems perfectly legal and civic-minded even. Did I mention that I also have American Express?"

"In her letters," he said, deftly avoiding my attempts to buy my way out of this mess," she promised, and I quote, 'to take out every last scum sucker involved in such a stupid idea'."

Oh boy. My stomach gurgled and I reached for a couple of antacid tablets. I lie to myself, saying I keep the bottle on my desk because the calcium is good for me and I am dutiful about watching my health. The truth is my consumption of stomach mints is tied less to concerns about healthy bones and more to phone calls to, from or about my mother. I crunched up the tablets then washed them down with a swig of Dr Pepper. This, of course, created an instant volcanic eruption of foam, which went both up and down my available airways. I covered the receiver with my hand while I swallowed, sputtered and coughed, listening to Jerry detail my mother's most recent activist activities. As he talked, I automatically grabbed the bottle again and ingested another three hundred percent of my daily-recommended dosage of calcium carbonate. I did not swig anything during or after, but I choked just the same.

"Furthermore," he continued, "she said that her daughter was a 'hot shot' reporter in Denver with connections and that heads were going to roll. She said Jolene Jackson knew people and she wouldn't let a 'bunch of thugs' ruin her mother's home. She hinted at mob ties and hit men as well. I can fax you the articles if you'd like."

No, I would not like. Not even a little. Hit men? Rolling heads? Damn. The scar on my arm began to twitch then escalated to throbbing spasms. It had been about eight months since a would-be killer's bullet had ripped through the flesh and bone just below my shoulder. The wound had healed remarkable well, considering, but it still provided a major punch of physical pain to go along with flashbacks and panic attacks that even thinking of having to go back to Kickapoo, Texas brought on. Like now.

As a last ditch effort, I decided to look for a situational loophole, one that would keep me seven hundred miles away from the reality of it, whatever "it" was this time. I rubbed my arm and took deep calming breaths. I could do this; I just needed more to work with. "Just exactly how is this park going to ruin my mother's home?"

"She thinks they're going to put the campers right behind her house."

"Well, are they?"

"I guess it's possible. The land goes all the way to her house, Jolene, you know that."

Meaning, yes. That familiar sick feeling balled up in my stomach and the sound of gunshots exploded inside my head. There are no words to describe how badly I did not want to go to Texas or deal with anymore lunatics, which in my experience were generally well-armed lunatics. And the first pistol-packing lunatic to deal with was my mother. I could easily envision Lucille Jackson leaning over her back fence, blowing holes in Airstreams and Winnebagoes. I could see it, but I sure couldn't stop it. Palpitations thumped an irregular cadence on my breastbone. "My mother is going to do whatever she pleases whether I'm there or not," I said as firmly and unemotionally as I could. "You know that."

"Well, we have to do something," Jerry grumbled. "It's getting ugly around here, and your mother is the instigator of most of it. Her spacey group has already been pegged as a bunch of militants because of their threats, which is bad enough, but then the environmentalists showed up and started talking animal rights. Well, that upset some church ladies, who were real quick to tell them that God had given man, not animals, dominion over the land. Obliged to enforce this holy directive, they began vigorously protesting the protesters, and well, it became rather complicated. Surely you saw it on the news."

No, surely I had not. The knots in my stomach wrenched a little tighter. "Look, Jerry, I haven't watched the news, I haven't read the paper, and more importantly I haven't talked to my mother in almost two weeks. I don't know anything about what's going on down there."

"Well, Jolene, it's like this. I've got several mobs of people with picket signs marching outside my window right this minute." He paused and took a deep breath, letting it out slowly. "Half of them are waving Bibles and the other half are dressed up like horned toads."

Huh? Apparently I needed a sign myself so I'd know what the hell he was talking about. "Horned toads? Horny toads? Those spiked frog-lizard things we used to torture as children?"

"Exactly."

"Why, dare I ask, are people wearing lizard suits outside the county jail?"

"I told you, they're protesting. I have to give them credit though," he said, the dark cloud lifting from his voice, lightening it to almost a chuckle. "They know how to set a stage. A pretty girl in a cage wearing body paint and foam lizard parts is hard to ignore." He coughed a little, probably getting all choked up just thinking about it. "She's attracting a lot of attention."

Obviously. "I'm guessing she's one of your environmentalist protesters."

"It appears that way."

As I wondered about the naked lizard impersonator, Jerry went on to give me the gory details of the militant wildlife group my mother had embraced along with a few highlights of their tactics. I'd never heard of AAC (All Animals Count), but it sounded like a standard "save the wildlife by burning down the condos" kind of group. I couldn't imagine my mother giving a rat's rear about the plight of a spiked lizard, but I could very well imagine that she'd go Rambo over something a little more personal, like campers behind the azaleas.

Indeed, I could see my militia-minded mother quite clearly, her hair pristinely coifed, eyebrows and lips freshly painted, clusters of purple balls dangling from her earlobes, her glittery bespangled sweatshirt crisscrossed with bandoliers, and an automatic weapon in each hand, the purple nail polish of her trigger fingers providing a lovely contrast to the gray-green gunmetal. Laugh if you will, but Lucille Jackson is a card-carrying member of the NRA, has both a concealed weapon and a legal permit for the same, is fond of laser sights and has a lifetime membership to the Redwater Falls Gun Club. In fact, I would only be mildly surprised to learn that she has a box of AK-47s stuffed under her bed, and the surprising part would be that they were under her bed rather than on a display rack above it.

Okay, maybe I'm exaggerating a little, but only a little. I don't really know what all the woman is capable of. I've found out more about my mother in the last few months than in the entire rest of my life combined. It has made me both jaded and wary. During this same time period I have also learned to trust my gut. So, regardless of what my guilt-trained mind might say—like, "you really should go, she's your mother"—my wiser inner warning system screamed "Are you stupid!"

When Jerry finished regaling me with things I'd rather not know, I reiterated my position on the situation. "I said I'd pay her fine, Jerry, or whatever, but there is no reason for me to drive down there to do it. My VISA number is—"

"You don't have a choice."

"Oh, yes, I do," I said, the scar tissue in my upper arm twitched and throbbed. "I'm not the woman's babysitter or her legal guardian."

"You will be if I get her declared incapable of caring for herself."

A cold chill swept up my spine. Would he do that? Could he do that? Or, was he just threatening me to get his own way, assuming I wouldn't know one way or another, which I did not. "You can't do that."

"I can. I don't want to, but I can."

"Blackmail does not endear you to me, Sheriff Parker."

"Oh, now, Jolene," he said, his voice softening to a cajoling rumble, dipping into that tone that makes my brain turn to mush. "Once you get here everything will settle right down. If your mother isn't stirring up the AAC people, they'll leave and everything will get back to normal in no time."

"Fat chance," I grumbled.

First of all, nothing about Kickapoo, Texas resembled my idea of normal. Ever. Second of all, what sounded mildly eccentric over the phone had a nasty habit of transmuting into wildly deranged when you had to face it in person. And thirdly, but not leastly, my mother was not only in the middle of the current mayhem, she was the ringleader of it.

For not the first time, or the fiftieth time for that matter, I wondered exactly why I'd been born to Lucille Jackson. What grave past-life crime had I committed to warrant this kind of punishment? Some soul-searching theories propose that we choose the circumstances of our birth and parents so as to overcome particular challenges in this lifetime. That these specific circumstances will help us evolve into more enlightened beings.

It's kind of a neat theory until you really think about it. I mean really think about it. *I asked for this?*

Since there wasn't a New Age theory yet devised that could explain my mother and make me like it, I was rethinking my stance on the whole Satan-is-out-to-get-you thing when Jerry cleared his throat to remind me he was still on the line. "So when do you think you'll get here?"

Before I could come up with a clever variation of "when Hell freezes over," I heard a series of loud pops, like the *rat-a-tat-tat* of a string of firecrackers. Or bullets. Then, a thundering boom followed by what sounded like one of my favorite four letter expletives sputtering from the usually sterile-mouthed sheriff. "Get down here, Jolene." *Boom.* "Now!"

Click.

The phone had gone dead so I tossed the receiver into the cradle, wondering exactly what I'd just heard. A worried sheriff for sure, but what else? Bullets? Bombs?

Not in Kickapoo.

Of course, in Kickapoo.

After running the myriad possibilities through my ever-ready mental visual system, I determined that any slim chance of avoiding a trip to Texas had exploded right along with that loud boom on the other end of the phone. The only remaining question was how to get there. I usually drive. I always drive. I'm about an hour and a half from Denver International, and Kickapoo is two and a half hours from the Dallas-Fort Worth Airport. Add in wait times and car rental time and I can be at the Texas border. So why was I even thinking about flying? And what were the odds that I could get on a plane at my convenience that wouldn't require me to take out a second mortgage?

Since I had to log on to the Internet anyway to send the article—and assure that Dr Pepper money would be forthcoming—I decided to investigate one of the online ticket getters.

I'll spare you the lengthy details of the process, but if you've never bid for a plane ticket online, do not do so unless you *really* want to buy the ticket. Who'd have guessed my $168 random roundtrip figure would actually get me a seat on a jet to Dallas at the last minute? Not me, that's for sure. Thanks to my eager fingers and ever-willing credit card number, I had about five hours to get myself seated and buckled aboard a southbound plane. Translated to real time, I had maybe an hour to get my house in order, throw some clothes in a bag and get out the door.

Yes, I am insane, and it is clearly an inherited trait.

Chapter
Two

T hanks to the friendly skies and a peppy rented Toyota—
which cost more than what I'd get for that one lousy article—I arrived at the Bowman County jail a few minutes
before ten that night.

The courthouse, where the Sheriff's Department resides,
was dark, but I made my way around to the back. The main
door was indeed open, but the secondary door where Jerry let
himself in and out was locked, probably always was, now that
I thought about it. Still, if I could avoid explaining myself to
whoever was manning the front desk, all the better. I knocked,
hard, until I saw a figure moving toward the small window.
I wasn't even a little surprised to see Deputy Leroy Harper
eyeing me through the square re-enforced glass in the door. I
waved and tried to smile.

Leroy pushed open the door, nearly knocking me down.
"What in the hell are you doing here?"

I didn't take offense as he sounded shocked, not homicidal as in previous episodes. Furthermore, I had asked myself
that same question so many times that it had kind of lost its
impact. "I didn't have a choice, Leroy. You have my mother.
Remember?"

He shooed me inside and slammed the vault-like door
behind me. "Well, yeah, Jerry told us you were coming, but I
don't know how you got here this fast." He paused, propping
his hands on his hips, which is no easy feat considering the
width of his waistline. "Jerry called you not nine hours ago.
You'd had to drive a hunnerd the whole way. That's speeding,
even in Colorado and New Mexico. How many tickets did you
get? I'm not fixin' any tickets. No can do."

And did I ask such a thing? "No tickets, Leroy," I said, trying to ward off all the usual thoughts that inflict me at this particular moment in time, meaning the point where I really realize where I am and that I apparently don't speak the same language as the natives. "I flew in to Dallas and rented a car. I obeyed the speed limit" mostly "and broke no other laws that I am aware of. Where's my mother?"

"Oh." He sounded a little disappointed. "Lucille's in the back office. We were just about to watch the news."

The jailer and the jailee were watching the news. In the back office. Some big crisis we had here. Glad I'd rushed right down.

We headed down the hallway, homing in on the sound of the ten o'clock news behind door number three. The door was cracked open so I peeked inside to get feel for Lucille's state of mind—the unrehearsed version. She sat in a chair in front of the television, sipping a cup of coffee, legs crossed, gold glittered slipper swinging, and a not a wrinkle in her purple pantsuit. Clearly, she was neither traumatized nor in need of rescuing. "Well, fancy meeting you here."

She jerked around in her chair, very nearly spilling her coffee then leaped to her feet. "Jolene!" Yes, she sounded more stricken than thrilled. Imagine that. With her dark and frosty blonde hair (yet another new color) piled high, dangly purple ball earrings, matching acrylic fingernails, gold bangle bracelets and professionally applied cosmetics, she looked quite stunning. And darned nervous. Guilty even.

I smiled. "Surprise!"

She was not amused and frowned to prove it. Setting her Styrofoam coffee cup on the desk, she tried to cover her shock and dismay. "My Lord, Jolene, how on earth did you get here so fast?" She checked her watch, trying—poorly I might add—to pretend interest in my travel abilities. "Jerry Don called you not nine hours ago."

Apparently, there had been a lot of clock watching going on, my potential arrival time having been precisely calculated. My showing up sooner rather than later was both unexpected and unappreciated by the damsel in supposed distress. I could only guess at what theatrical display she'd had planned for my arrival tomorrow. I had deliberately not called Jerry on my way in, hoping I could surprise him. But not wanting to be overly surprised myself, I'd also wanted to get a feel for what I had to deal with, which was why I'd stopped at the courthouse first. With the shocked—and somewhat guilty—reactions I was receiving from Lucille and Leroy, I figured I'd done exactly the right thing. I repeated my flight and car arrangements, which seemed to mildly impress her, at least the part about my great concern over her awful, awful situation. I wrapped my arm around her shoulders and gave her a little daughterly squeeze. The hugging thing is not a natural and normal exchange between my mother and me so she was rightfully wary, eyeing me nervously, like she was waiting for the axe to fall. I kept one hand on her shoulder while I said to Leroy, "What do I have to do to get her out of here?"

Leroy glanced at Lucille and shrugged. "Jerry Don says she can go. She just don't want to."

Lucille twirled out from under my arm, spun to face me and straightened her shoulders. "Don't you start with me, Jolene," she said, waggling a finger for emphasis. "Things went real well today, but I'm not leaving here until I've made my point."

"And what point would that be? What, exactly, went 'real well' today, Mother? Was that the attempted murder of the county maintenance truck or the fiasco at the courthouse? What was it that I heard blow up?"

Lucille's eyes darted to the TV hanging from the ceiling in the corner. She pointed to a chair beneath the TV and suggested I sit there. I didn't. Neither did she.

Leroy, however, hitched up his pants and settled himself in the chair behind the desk. "'If I hadn't been watching what they were doing, I'd have thought terrorists were trying to blow up the courthouse. Those cans sounded like bombs when they went off."

"Cans?"

"Yeah, aerosols. The AAC people had parked an old camper trailer out in front of the courthouse then started painting their animal slogans and things on it. The costumed toads was supposed to act like they was dying then throw firecrackers at the camper. Didn't go real well though. There was some kind of scuffle and—"

"And the idiots caught the grass on fire," Lucille snapped, "right beside the pile of spray paint cans. Must have been fumes or something because the flames just shot up and those cans started jumping like popcorn. I've never seen such a thing in my life."

"It sure was something," Leroy agreed, adding a whistle to his punctuate his amazement. "Them cans was exploding like rainbow hand grenades. Made the most awful mess you ever did see," he continued, his chins jiggling with the telling. "Paint went splattering all over everything, including the protesters. Nobody really got hurt though, so that was good."

"It wasn't good enough for the TV people," Lucille groused, stomping a golden slipper to emphasize her irritation. "Oh, the local stations came by for a few minutes then played their little ten second clips on the six o'clock news, but that won't get us noticed in Decatur much less Dallas. We need the big guns out here." She glanced at the TV again. "They better be showing something again this evening, even one of those little snippets that flashes by like a blink, or I'll be calling them, that's what I'll be doing."

No sooner had she uttered the words than said snippet popped onto the screen. Larry grabbed the remote and turned up the volume.

The segment was indeed short, and after I saw the actual scene, it didn't seem like much of an event at all. It looked like there were maybe forty people, including law enforcement, lizard people and Bible wavers. The camera made a quick pan of the naked lizard girl Jerry had eagerly told me about then lingered on the camper for a second longer. All in all, the clip was twelve seconds, tops, with voice-over.

"Now, isn't that just the most pitiful coverage of a news story that you ever did see?" Lucille stood with her arms crossed, glaring and grumbling at the TV. "If they'd had even a lick of sense they'd have come inside the jail house and asked me about the people trying to steal my home, that's what. But there was not one word about it. Not one. Pitiful, I tell you, just pitiful."

I slumped down in the chair beneath the TV and sighed. I had so many questions, but it seemed best to start as much at the beginning as I could—at least the beginning of today's reason for me being in the Bowman County sheriff's office. "Speaking of pitiful, exactly what were you thinking when you opened fire on the county maintenance truck?"

Lucille clamped her lips shut and lifted her chin. "I don't know that it was necessarily my bullet that hit the radiator. They were out there mowing, and it could have just as easily been a rock that flew up and hit it. You know very well that laser sight isn't worth a darn out in the sun."

Oh, I'd heard that sorry excuse before, the laser in the sun, not the flying rock. My mother is a crackerjack shot and she doesn't need a squiggly red dot to get the job done either. Even though it was a question that pretty much answered itself, I asked, "Who else was armed?"

She shrugged and inspected her nearly inch-long purple nails. "Most of us were, I guess."

Now, this statement was both said and taken with the greatest of seriousness. Carrying a gun in Texas is part of one's civic duty, right up there with saluting the flag and knowing all the words to "The Yellow Rose of Texas." I glanced at Leroy. "How many of them were there?"

"Enough, that's how many," she said, her voice building in passion and volume. "They're not going to sneak around and do things behind my back like I don't know what they're up to. I'm going to stop that stupid camper city. Some of us care what happens to our homes and we're doing something about it."

"Yes, we're all real clear that you're doing something about it." I turned to Leroy. "So, do you have any official membership numbers on this subversive group?"

Leroy shuffled his feet and scratched his head. "The toad people?"

"She means us, Leroy, SPASI," Lucille said, tipping her nose in the air. "The Smart People Against Stupid Ideas."

I sorted out the acronym in my head, wondering how long it had taken them to come up with *that.* "So, Leroy, how big is this group, and who else was arrested besides space cadet number one here?"

Lucille glared and snorted then stomped over to her chair and sat down.

16

"Oh, just the three of them," Leroy said, but that was from the morning incident. Nobody was arrested at the rally."

I wondered why no one got nailed for the courthouse fiasco, but I did not wonder about who he meant by the "three of them." He meant Mother and her two very best friends in the whole world, to use her words, Merline Campbell and Agnes Riddles. I also wondered about the "friends" terminology since Lucille and Merline were eternally locked in a fashion/coiffure competition that bordered on guerilla warfare. Agnes has tried to mediate, but despite her best efforts the two still managed to one-up each other until Merline sported six pounds of sparkling spangles on her sweatshirt and Lucille had glowing pink hair. I couldn't decide if uniting them against the park was a good thing or not.

"Miz Campbell and Miz Riddles posted their bonds right away," Leroy added, hesitantly, glancing between me and the mother ship. "Miz Jackson didn't want to do that."

"I told them to go on home," Lucille said magnanimously, hand to her chest, like she was ready to recite the pledge. "It's my house and I'm the one that should suffer most for the cause."

Somehow I didn't quite equate this with some of your bigger causes, like say women's rights over their own bodies, equal pay for equal work, or even save the whales. But then I wasn't the one about to have campers lining up for the dump station in view of my back porch either "How long has this park thing been going on?"

"I've seen people prowling around over there for months now," Lucille said, snatching her cup from the desk. "Out behind my fence, poking around my yard and peeping in my windows. That's just flat trespassing." She sipped the coffee and sighed. "I should have kept your dad's deer rifle, that's what I should have done. I could have gotten them with that."

Yes, meaning that she *hadn't* gotten them with what she *had* used. Her handgun is not a long distance weapon, thank God. I sighed and rubbed my eyes again just for the drill. It had yet to change anything, but a moment of melodramatic martyrdom made me feel a little better. "What were they doing behind the house? Staking out camper pads? Counting horny toads? Drilling for oil, what?"

Her head snapped up. "Why'd you say that?"

"Say what?"

"They're up to no good, that's what they're up to." Lucille set her jaw and her narrowed her eyes darted this way and that. "Right there behind my back fence."

I know that look and it never bodes well. Never. So, what had triggered it? Camper pads and lizards were not new on the conversational menu, but my offhand comment about drilling for oil was. Suspicion bubbled up like Jed's Texas tea. "What have you seen back there? Trucks, equipment, what?"

More eye darting and brow furrowing. "Yes, well, there were trucks out there, yes, mostly pickups. They had lots of lights too, and one bigger truck with a shiny silver pole on it. I tried to take pictures but you couldn't tell anything, I don't know what they're doing but they're up to no good, that's for sure."

"Tell me about the truck with the pole."

"It was making all kinds of racket," she huffed. "It rattled my walls, that's what it did. I thought we were having earth-quakes." She reached for her cup again and sipped, but her arm was shaking as she did so. "Just made me so mad I could spit."

As we all know, Mother does not spit, but she was indeed mad. But why was she *that* mad? "You know, I hate to say it, but it is Bob Little's land and he can do whatever he wants on it."

She slammed the cup down, hopped up and paced. "They can *not* do anything they want. My property is there too and I have rights. I'm not stupid or senile either like that idiot Gifford Geller seems to think, telling me they were putting in a water well. Why the jackass thought I'd believe that when there's city water right in front of my house, I don't know, but I just played dumb and let him think I'd bought his pack of lies. He's about as worthless a county commissioner as there is."

"Now, Miz Jackson," Leroy said, "The commissioner—"

"Shut up, Leroy, you know as well as I do that he's got his dirty hands in this. Same with that Gilbert Moore who's been out there. He'll tell you one thing one time and then something entirely different the next, and then when you call him on it, he tries to make it out like you're the one who's crazy. Well, I'm not crazy, and he's a big fat liar." She stopped and stomped her gold sparkled foot. "They think they can just come in here and do whatever they want to, and they most certainly cannot. I've let them know that real plain, and if they mess with me, I'll do it again."

I had no doubts of that. "So how long has this been going on?"

"Probably about six weeks. Three days of having my dishes rattling in the cabinets and my coffee splashing out of my cup just sitting on the table was all I could stand. I tried talking nice to them about it and then I gave them a what-for, but they wouldn't stop. Agnes talked me out of shooting them, but as you can very well see I am not getting any good press this way so I sure hate it that I didn't blast them when I had the chance." Seeing the look of disbelief that was apparently on my face, she added, "Well, I wouldn't have killed any of them, Jolene. I was only going to wound a few."

"Oh, well, in that case..." I said, sighing dramatically because really, that's all you can do. "Anyway, why is Bob Little—"

"Oh, Bobby can be such an idiot sometimes." She gave a dismissive wave. "He got himself in way over his head, and before he knew what he was doing, well, here we are. To be so smart about some things he sure is dumb as a post about others."

Ditto for me or I wouldn't be sitting in the Bowman County Jail having this conversation. "Let's go back to the house so you can show me what's been going on first hand. Show me where the trucks were, that sort of thing."

"I told you I'm not leaving."

"Who knows," I said, deciding to dangle a little bait, "maybe if we leave right now you can catch somebody out there in the mesquites and shoot him."

She cut her eyes toward me. "You're just saying that."

"Fine, you stay here and I'll go knock on Mr. Little's door myself and have him tell me what's going on."

Lucille eyed me again, frowning and chewing her lip. After another glare, a huff and a pointed scowl, she sat back down and crossed her legs. "You can do what you want, I suppose, but it would be a complete waste of time," she said, her glittery slipper twitching like it was on fire. "He won't talk to anybody anymore."

"Even you?"

She huffed again and folded her hands in her lap. "He hasn't been himself lately."

"Well, guess what, I don't care. I had to rush down here because you're in jail yet again for committing a felony and somebody is going to tell me something that makes some kind of sense."

"I'll have you know that Jerry Don only wrote me up for a misdemeanor."

Leroy nodded in agreement. "But then she wouldn't leave. That's why he called you. He thought she'd listen to you."

"Right, because that always worked so well before." I leaned an elbow on the armrest of my own chair and propped my cheek in my palm. "I have no idea what to do, none."

"There is something you can do," she said, responding to a statement I hadn't realized I'd said aloud. "Since you're here, you might as well write one of your stories about what all's going on, me being in dire straits, penned up in jail like a common criminal and such, and send it to the paper. That'll get some attention. If you do a good job, it might even make the wire service."

"That's not how it works. And even if it did, I wouldn't write articles about family. It's a conflict of interest." It also isn't smart since I'm kind of particular about printing the truth, and as best I could tell, there wasn't much of that to be had here from Her Highness, and what was true wouldn't reflect that well on her, and therefore me. Nope, not something I was getting dragged into. Ever. "No way."

"Good grief, Jolene, you act like it's some big deal to write up a simple story. How hard can it be to tell what the scumbags are up to and why everybody in their right minds should rally and stop them? Shouldn't take you over ten minutes."

Ten minutes. Did she think I was that good, or that what I do for a living takes such little skill and effort that it can be accomplished instantly? Don't answer that. "No."

She hopped up and began to pace yet again. "Well, we need some national coverage, and a story in that Denver paper would surely get some kind of attention."

Yes, surely it would. Not the kind she'd want, but it would get attention. "No."

"I called CNN and the girl who answered the phone said they'd send a whole crew out immediately. She was real sweet about it, even offered to send Barbara Walters. I thought that was real nice of them, but I said I hated for her to have to drop her big celebrity interviews for it. I guess I shouldn't have been so thoughtful since whoever their next in line was, Harry King I think was his name, certainly didn't bother to show up. I know if Barbara had been given the assignment she'd have been here in no time."

I gritted my teeth and kind of smiled. No way did any of that need to be clarified, rectified or even discussed, especially by me.

Lucille stopped in front of Leroy's desk and tapped her nails then proceeded onward as if I were in complete agreement, not to mention cahoots, with her. "An interview from the jail cell is what we need though. And where is CBS? I called them too, and that Fox station. You'd think with the kinds of things they have on that channel they'd have jumped at the chance to be in on a real hot story like this one."

"Um, excuse me, Media Queen—"

"Not now, Jolene, I'm thinking." Lucille continued to march around the small room. Two steps, stomp, spin, two steps, stomp, spin. "Okay here's what we do. They just hauled in some drunks and a gas thief a little while ago. I'll get in the jail room beside them. The kindly sweet grandmother behind bars for a cause. It's a good angle, and since the TV people aren't doing anything to speak of we'll just have to make do with what we've got. We'll get some photos first then worry about what we're going to write later. Run get your camera, Jolene."

"What? We have covered this already. No. I'm not taking photos because I am not a photographer. I am not writing a story about you because I am your daughter and no one would print it." That wasn't the only reason I wasn't writing a story for her, or even the best reason, but it was one that should register since her main goal was scoring column inches. "This is your deal, not mine. I am here because... Why *am* I here?"

"Hey, Jolene," Leroy said, rubbing his chin as if in deep thought. "I've got a camera out at the house that you can use."

Had either of them even noticed I'd already said this wasn't going to happen? "We really don't need a camera, Leroy." Particularly since the only kind of camera Leroy Harper was capable of handling was the Polaroid variety. "Thanks anyway."

"It's a real good one. Nikon with three lenses, filters and flash, all the bells and whistles. Do my own digital work too."

What did he just say? Leroy Harper knew how to use a real camera? And he did say "digital work," as in computer? Was that some kind of joke? "Really?"

"Leroy may be a jackass, but he's a fine photographer," Lucille added, sounding like she really meant it—the fine photographer part, the jackass is a given. "You know, we could have him do one of his artsy portrait things, where the lighting and such gives the subject, that'd be me, a haunting quality." She tipped her chin upward with a long nail and gazed at the ceiling, trying to look wistful, perhaps. "Why, if it was done right, it might not even need your story."

Oh, please. That tactic is lame and I quit falling for it when I was ten.

"Miz Jackson, you're gonna make me blush," Leroy said before I could comment. He ducked his head and shuffled his feet. "I'm not all that good."

"Leroy's got his faults, I'll grant you," she said, dismissing me with a wave of her hand. "But he takes awful good pictures." She sucked in a dramatic breath. "Oh, I just know he could do wonderful things with this setting. And with me." Unbridled glee bubbled up like a thirteen-year-old wannabe model. "You know he's won all kinds of awards. Some of his pictures are even hanging in the Redwater Falls Art Gallery too. Now, wouldn't that be something!"

Leroy? An award-winning photographer? With his work in an art gallery? I waited for the punch line, but it never came, and they both just stared at me as if I should be ecstatic that Leroy was ready to save the day. I wasn't, of course. Having the otherwise inept on-duty deputy sheriff take photographs of the supposedly incarcerated and imperiled grandmother, the prints of which might just be hanging in an art gallery someday, was about three miles past ridiculous. For this part of the country, however, it was darned near perfect.

"Well, get moving, Leroy," Lucille said, shooing her hands at him. "We have to strike while the iron's hot."

Before I could throw out a more helpful cliché, like "stop or I'll shoot," Leroy's beige-uniformed bulk was thundering for the door, his buggy eyes blinking with excitement. "Won't take me over fifteen minutes. If the phone rings, just answer 'Bowman County Sheriff's Department' and take a message."

He was looking at me. "Oh, no, I'm not answering the phone, Leroy, and there's really no point to—"

"Dispatch is down the hall and Larry's on duty up front. It should be pretty quiet back here." He paused and jammed his meaty fingers into his shirt pocket." Just in case, here's my card." He jogged back and tossed it on the desk. "Call me on my mobile if it's an emergency or something."

"Wait!"

The door slammed and within seconds a siren howled to life. I just shook my head and sighed. Lucille, however, took the blaring squeal as a call to arms and began digging in her handbag. "I suppose I should try to make myself look a little bedraggled for the shoot, get the sympathy vote. Or maybe neat but forlorn would be better. Hmmm. Well-heeled but put upon? It's very important we get the right tone. What do you think?"

What did I think? My opinion was about as important to my mother as it was to Leroy's vacated chair, and we both knew it. The chair, however, wasn't going to force me to carry on a conversation with it. So, I got up and walked around behind the desk and settled myself into the spongy brown vinyl. Oh, sure, I could fight it. I could stomp and scream and rant and physically drag her from the jail. Maybe. Or, I could just take a little nap and let nature run its course. There were no good options, trust me. "You just do whatever makes you happy, Mother. That is indeed why we are all here."

Lucille ignored my sarcasm and set her mini-tackle box of make-up on the desk and snapped it open. "I think I'll use Ash Rose on my lids and Driftwood above, kind of heavy, to give a sunken look. Hollow out the cheeks with a bronze blush, and add a touch of Merlot Bisque lip liner. Yes, that should do it. Elegant, but haunted." She grabbed the case and turned to the door. "I'll be in the ladies room."

For two hours.

I smiled and nodded, and was just lifting my feet to prop them on the desk when the inevitable occurred. Yes, the stupid phone rang. By the third ring, I figured letting it go unanswered would be worse than picking it up, so I cleared my throat and gave it my best fake TV cop voice. "Bowman County Sheriff's Department."

"Who is this?"

Uh oh. The caller might not recognize me, but I sure recognized him. Unfortunately, the voice of the man I dream about was not so dreamy at the moment. However, it didn't seem like he had recognized me, and if we could keep it that way it would eliminate a whole bunch of explaining. I tried to lower my voice about six octaves and speak native. "Hello? Sheriff's Department. Help you?"

"Who—Jo, Jolene?" Dream boy's voice ended with an incredulous tone. "Is that you?"

So much for fooling Mr. Sheriff. "Oh, hi, Jerry, didn't recognize you at first." Yes, it was just as lame as it sounds.

"What are you doing there? Where's Leroy?" He said it with a decidedly accusatory tone, as if there'd been a takeover of the office or something equally awful. "What's going on? Is something wrong?"

Well, yeah, there was always something wrong around here. Relatively speaking, however, the fact that Leroy had sped away with siren wailing to get his camera, to take pictures of an inmate for a publicity stunt, was really not that out of the ordinary, probably. "Everything's fine. Leroy just had to step out for a minute, and I told him I'd answer the phone if it rang. He should be back any second." Or twenty minutes, but who was counting.

"What are you doing here? I wasn't expecting you until tomorrow."

Yes, apparently no one was. And, it did not escape my notice that his order of concern was first and foremost for his office. After that, his concerns regarding me were more along the lines of suspiciousness. He seemed somewhat confused and distressed—as opposed to surprised and happy—by my early arrival. It was getting to feel like everyone had planned to have a nice relaxing evening and rest up for when Jolene arrived the next day so they'd be at the top of their game to make her life a living hell. Well, too late.

I explained, for the third time, that I had managed to fly to Dallas and rent a car. He didn't sound as impressed as he did relieved, and again, my heart did not go pitty-pat.

"So you're going to take her home then," he said, relaying exactly what was relieving him.

Rather than get personal about things—which I darned well wanted to do in a not so pretty way—I said, "Tough situation you've got here, Jerry. She's determined to stay and make a martyr of herself. Not having much luck changing her mind about it, but I'm working on it," by serving as a witness to her photo shoot by your deputy photographer. "As soon as Leroy gets back," and takes the jail pictures, "I'm hoping we can head on out to Kickapoo," eventually, possibly. "It's been a long day and I'm ready to get to bed."

"That would be best," he said with a heavy sigh that ended in something that halfway sounded like a growl. "When can I see you?" His voice had dipped into that tone that sends shivers through me in ways best left to the imagination. "I've really missed you."

I hadn't seen it coming and my reaction was instantaneous and intense. Dammit. I both love and hate the fact that he can do that to me. Forget touch, all he has to do is shift his tone of voice, utter a few choice words, give me a certain look or even just breathe on me, and I'm, well, um, let's just say in sort of a puddle. Yes, it is pathetic. "You know where I am," I said, in an inviting tone that a deaf man couldn't miss. Then, through the fog in my brain, it occurred to me that having him run right over might not be a great plan. I sincerely doubted that either of us would find the experience satisfying—or even pleasant. Before I could start backing myself out of that corner, I realized that he wasn't exactly spewing forth with a breathy "I'll be right there, baby" reply.

"I can't right now." Another pause. "I've got the kids tonight."

Ah, the kids. Jerry's children are in elementary school, mine are in college. He is in the middle of parenting hell and I'm down to only periodic dips into the fiery flames. It is not a good fit. "That's okay," I said, as cheerfully as I could, considering. "I'll be out at Mother's tomorrow if you want to drop by sometime after the kids go to school."

"Tomorrow then, at nine?" he said, sounding a little disappointed himself.

"Sounds great." Okay, great was pushing it just a tad. Great would be seeing him somewhere other than Kickapoo, Texas, and without my mother or his kids.

"See you then." His voice rippled through me yet again, but before I could fully enjoy it, he said, "Tell Leroy to call when he gets back." He was back to his official sheriff voice. "I need to talk to him. Immediately."

"He's not in trouble, is he?"

Jerry paused for a few long seconds. "I don't know, Jolene, is he?"

Not as much as he was going to be, I feared. "As far as I know, everything is just fine." It wasn't a lie. Technically, things were basically still as fine as they were before I got here. "Yep, just fine."

Mr. Sheriff muttered something about "we'll see," and after I hung up, I felt neither warm nor tingly anymore—nor at ease. Fine was out of the question. I'd been in town, what, an hour? And in that short time, how many situations with the potential for seriously bad trouble had formulated? A lot, that's how many.

Right on cue, ground zero for the trouble came bouncing back into the office, looking like she'd just been to a Mary Kay makeover party. I didn't see a single hair out of place, not to mention a crooked eyebrow or lip line. "Well, Mother, if you're going for the 'poor pitiful me' look, you better go give it another shot."

"No," Lucille said, patting her plastered-in-place hair. "I decided to just be me and look my best. I'm going to tell it like it is, and if they don't like it well, too bad. I'm not backing down and they're not ruining my life."

In truth I couldn't argue with her about not wanting a parade of trailers, complete with TVs, boom boxes, generators and screaming kids out behind the back fence. Whether they were really going to put them on her back doorstep, I didn't know. But I did know one thing for sure, if they weren't already, the parks people were going to be real sorry they messed with Lucille Jackson. We all were. I leaned back in Leroy's chair again and propped my feet on his desk. "Okay, Mother, tell me about SPASI."

I pilfered a legal pad from Leroy's desk and took as many notes as I could while Lucille rambled. Only one who has had the misfortune of interviewing Lucille Jackson can truly appreciate the effort involved to keep from hurling yourself through the nearest plate glass window during the task. Nevertheless, I emerged from the soliloquy with a few facts and a plethora of local—and pointless—trivia.

The fact that Agnes' recently neutered cat had clawed a hole in the window screen and run off the night before the protest didn't seem like a pertinent detail. Ditto the fact that Merline had bought a new rhinestone-covered denim jacket—that was just plain tacky—at the factory outlet store in Mineral Wells to wear in the picket line because she wanted to look good when the news people came out and filmed the protest, which she did not, look good, that is, according to Lucille.

What I did learn that seemed semi-fact-based was that SPASI was formed over a glass of iced tea and a hamburger at the DQ, thus the limited thought given to the name. It was, however, as Mother pointed out, a good generic name that could be used in the future as there were always stupid ideas that needed stopping. Who could argue with that?

She swore she had nothing at all to do with the AAC people showing up. In fact, the head space cadet seemed kind of worried that the out-of-towners might steal her activist glory. Worse still, apparently, was that Ethel Fossy—AKA that damned Bony Butt who didn't give a hoot about the town or anybody in it—had lost her ever-lovin' mind, and not in a way that benefitted Lucille. And just because she was a member of the Church of Christ, it sure didn't mean that she was the only one going to heaven, because she was not. By God. Bony Butt's Bible waving and preaching at the AAC people seemed to be a sore spot as well, although it was hard to tell exactly why. There was also a mention of Ethel climbing right into the very hotbed of sin she'd been preaching against, so to speak, but it was hard to follow. What was clear, however, was that the whole thing was just a sorry state of affairs, that's what it was. (Paraphrasing Lucille is almost as tedious as interviewing her.)

When my mother starts talking, there are so many layers of angst propagated by the details that it's hard to know where to start. Not starting at all would be the best plan, but that never seemed to work out that well for me.

Bony Butt, as Mother was happy to call her, at least behind her back, was Lucille's rival in a weird religious/female competition sort of way. Basically, Ethel'd had a thing for Mother's last boyfriend, the aforementioned now-dead mayor. Take a liberal dose of religious fanaticism, mix with politics, add a boatload of jealously, rampant adultery and multi-level coveting, and make up your own story. It can't be half as ridiculous as what I lived through the last few times I've been in this state. A shudder rippled through me. Surely to God not again.

I don't know when she quit talking or when I quit writing, but I was staring blankly at the wall when the sheriff's department back door opened and Leroy came thundering in. "Man, oh man, I'm sorry I took so long," he said, huffing and puffing. "Couldn't find the right set of filters, and then the batteries in the flash were bad. Anyway, here it is."

He patted a large gray padded suitcase-like thing, then opened it up and began assembling the appropriate lenses and flash. This was professional grade gear and I couldn't help but be impressed. I'd kind of been expecting your basic digital camera, kind of like I owned myself and only halfway knew how to operate. It was not.

Leroy and I have developed a tentative truce of late, and while it was kind of weird, I preferred it to the serious head butting and round robin sniping of previous visits. Trying to keep him from killing me hadn't been that much fun either. But Leroy really did seem to know his camera business.

"Okay, Miz Jackson," Leroy said. "Where do you want your picture made?"

"Well, let's start in the jail cell, the one next to the drunks, with me looking forlorn. Then we can do a couple of portrait types in the office just in case." She held out her wrists. "Cuff me, Leroy."

Lovely. I propped my elbows on the desk and buried my face in my hands, which apparently evolved into a nap because the next thing I knew, I was jumping out of my skin—and the chair—hitting my knee on the desk, yelping, and hearing a shrill "Wake up, Jolene," and not necessarily in that order.

Lucille had her always-ominous black purse over her elbow, a small overnight bag in the other hand and a glint in her eye. "Let's go. I'd prefer to stay here as a statement to the cause, but since you've made such a fuss about me going home tonight, I suppose I don't have much choice."

Oh, please. If I hadn't been busy rubbing the throb from my knee and trying not to appear scraped from the ceiling, I'd have rolled my eyes at her lame attempt to pawn off her mind-change on me. As it was, all I could manage was a disgruntled "fine."

"Leroy's going to bring the prints out to the house in the morning for me to look over. We're also going to take some more shots there. We've decided to go for one of those heart-wrenching photo documentary things. That'll get some attention."

We could all bet on that. And I wanted no part of it. "Sounds perfect."

Chapter Three

Morning dawned entirely too early. Nevertheless I was up watching Lucille ham it up for the camera. Photographer Leroy stood about ten yards away, on the far side of the house, getting a shot that showed the would-be parkland behind Lucille's house. He had light meters and filters and lenses and, strange as it was to say, he looked like a pro.

Mother Dearest's behavior, on the other hand, was leaning more toward goofy. She had cleverly, or so she thought, chained herself to the front porch post. I had no intentions of pointing out that no one was trying to drag her off of said porch or park campers on it, although it might have added a touch of real emotion to the pictures as she tried to get herself unchained to whack me for saying so.

I glanced at my watch. "Better finish up. Jerry should be here any minute."

"Yeah," Leroy agreed, a little more readily than expected. "He sure asked a lot of questions when he called back last night. I didn't tell him about any of this though. I'm not on the clock anyway right now."

Oh, shit, I'd forgotten to tell him to call. "I'm sorry, Leroy. He told me to tell you to call and I forgot." I had no good excuse, except for my mother and the complete ridiculousness of the bizarre situation I found myself in that seemed to suck out all my brain cells. "I'll tell him it was my fault when he gets here."

"It's okay. I think he kind of understood."

Why didn't that make me feel better?

"I need to get going anyway because I've got to get these on the computer to see if they need any work before I print. Dad's working the desk for me until I get back." He glanced at Lucille, but she turned up her nose, apparently still holding a grudge against Fritz for something. "He'd sure like it if you gave him a call, Miz Jackson. He's been real down in the mouth since you two had words."

Lucille lifted her chin even higher and sniffed haughtily. "If you all are through with me, I believe I'll go make a fresh pot of coffee for Jerry Don."

After she'd gone inside, I walked over to where Leroy stood, repacking his camera case. "Seriously, Leroy, I hate to butt in, but are you sure you should be doing this? Doesn't this sort of qualify as one of those pesky conflict of interest issues that a deputy sheriff probably ought to avoid?" At all costs.

"Huh?"

"Taking these kinds of pictures, of someone charged with a crime. Since you're the one who kind of charged her with the crime, it could be a bit of a conflict."

"Nah, I've done it before. The gallery people think it's kind of neat that I'm in law enforcement and take photos inside the jail. Think it gives me insight into the human condition. I don't usually have people in the pictures, but they say you can still feel them there. They really like that."

Wow. Big words in a big sentence. Scary. And how had it come to this anyway, chatting amicably with Leroy Harper? It was unnatural and unsettling, to say the least. Almost made me wish for the good old days when he breathed fire and looked ready to behead me. *That,* I understood. I didn't know what to make of this version of Leroy that sounded halfway coherent at times, and it made me wary.

"Jerry says it's okay as long as I'm off the clock and don't take pictures of crime scenes. Besides, Lucille's already paid her fine and paid to replace the radiator, including labor charges, so it wasn't like she was really an inmate."

Was that so? Sheriff Blackmail and I would be discussing many things at length. Jerry Don Parker's propensity for letting Lucille off the hook for all her crap wasn't helping anyone, especially me. I didn't come down here for my health. It never helps my health to come down here. I get headaches, I shake and twitch, and I feel like I'm going to throw up. A lot. And that's before I've even seen my mother. The ludicrousness of this particular situation triggered all the above and was even pushing me toward bitchy, which is shocking, I know. Whatever the case, it was long past the time for some scared straight tactics—for both of them, all of them.

"So, what you're really saying, Leroy, is that the caption and byline under the picture you want published in the paper would go something like this: 'Deputy Sheriff Leroy Harper photographs park protester Lucille Jackson pretending to be locked in the Bowman County Jail. Ms. Jackson had been arrested earlier in the day for shooting a county maintenance truck that was mowing grass on the right-of-way near the planned park site. When released by the sheriff's department, she refused to leave the jail where Harper befriended her. Over a cup of coffee and the evening news, they devised this photo shoot to bring attention to Lucille's plight and to give new meaning to serve and protect.' Or something like that."

He frowned, beads of sweat popping out on his brow. He shifted from foot to foot and scratched his head, all apparently important steps in his thinking process. "That doesn't sound good at all."

You think? I just shrugged at him. It was his call.

After a little more mental processing and fidgeting, the latter still being indicative of the former, Deputy Leroy Harper snatched up his camera case and headed toward his truck. "Tell Miz Jackson I'll get back to her."

"I'll do that."

☉ ☉ ☉

As it turned out, there was no need for Leroy to rush off to avoid his boss since Jerry Don Parker did not arrive as arranged at nine-thirty. He also didn't arrive at ten-thirty, and he did not call either. By the time eleven rolled around, I was not a happy camper, to borrow an unfortunate phrase. By noon, I was vacillating between seriously worried and seriously pissed.

Mother had been on the phone a good part of the morning, making strategy calls to Merline and Agnes, but she assured me that both Jerry and Leroy had her cell phone number. They also had mine. In fact, the entire Bowman County Sheriff's department had every number available for both of us, and had used them all on a number of occasions. They knew how to reach us.

I had wasted most of my time sitting out on the front porch or staring over the back fence. I had several vivid memories rooted in that mesquite field, mostly ones where I found myself lying in a patch of red hot dirt and thorny goatheads after my pony "Dino-mite" flung me off and left me for dead. My dad loved me, really he did, but buying a horse named after an explosive material for a girl with the riding skills of a rock is a recipe for disaster. The next horse was no better, but he was bigger—a lot bigger. He was about sixteen hands tall and named Echo, probably because once he took off all you heard was the echo of his hoof beats across the prairie. I covered a lot of ground on or because of ol' Echo. And it wasn't all mesquite patches or perfectly flat either. There were a few real trees amongst the scrub. Echo loved those. He could scrape me off on a low hanging branch without ever breaking stride. He was good at finding ravines too. Well, maybe it had only been a drainage ditch, but he'd jumped it multiple times, leaping through the air like a Lipizzaner. I have no idea how I stayed in the saddle for that or for the race through the pump jacks and storage tanks that followed. I just remember being grateful that he hadn't bucked me off in the salt flats. My mother had convinced me that the crusty white stuff would eat the skin off my hands and I'd be left with only bones if I touched it. Ah, those were the days.

I had just stepped back up on the porch to go inside when my mother rushed out the door.

"Jolene! You'll never guess what happened! Get in here. Right now!" She spun and hurried back inside. "It's on the news. Hurry!"

I followed, but got there in time to only hear a teaser on the weather, about three minutes of local news, four commercials and a brief interview with some idiotic author promoting a mystery novel as if anyone cared. After another commercial, however, we were visually whisked back to the breaking news.

"See there," Lucille said, pointing at the TV with a long nail. "That's why Jerry Don couldn't come. Leroy either. It looks like a bomb went off."

It is a fine art, listening to my mother and the news at the same time, but I have honed this skill to razor sharp precision. Thusly, I was able to figure out—all at the same time—that somebody had tried to blow up what used to be known as Vetterman Brothers Feed and Seed. Vetterman's Feed, Tack and Computer Store didn't have the same ring to it, but the times they were a changing, even in Bowman County. It was also noted that Mr. Sheriff was on the scene and handling the crisis personally. As the onsite reporter relayed more of the facts and less of the excitement, it became clear that the only things actually "blown to bits" were some bags of rabbit chow and horse feed. Eyewitness accounts described how the bags just exploded, spraying livestock pellets like buckshot. No one was injured but some poultry was still unaccounted for.

I glanced at my mother, who was suspiciously quiet during this big event. No gasping, no "see there," nothing. In fact, she was slumped down in her velvet wingback chair with a frown on her face, a meaningful frown, and I didn't like it one little bit. As I pondered exactly what it all might mean, the reporter on the scene gave me a nice big hint. It seems that the feed store bomber had left a note: Animals are people too! Free the chickens!

I looked back at my mother. "Free the chickens?"

"Chicks. Baby chicks." She stared at the TV, scowling. "Vetterman always has a pen full of them this time of year."

"Well, now, just when did you get interested in what's in stock at the feed and seed?"

"They sell computers and fancy boots now too, catering to the hobby ranchers and such."

I indulged myself in a brief but multi-purposed eye-rolling. "Unless Vetterman stocks Mary Kay Cosmetics between the chickens and the hard drives I can't imagine how you'd know about any of this."

Lucille hopped up from her chair and made a dash for the kitchen. "I had nothing to do with it, Jolene, if that's what you're thinking."

Of course that's what I was thinking. "Not so fast there, spacey lady," I said, following on her heels. "Just how hooked up is your little group with the chicken bombers?"

"They didn't bomb the chickens, Jolene." Lucille fiddled with some dishes in the sink then moved on to the refrigerator. "The AAC people are a little quirky, but they mean well."

"Quirky?" I leaned against the doorway and crossed my arms. "They tried to blow up a feed store to free chickens. That's more than quirky. Somebody could have been seriously injured."

"They meant well."

"You knew they were going to do this." It was not a question.

Lucille shook her head firmly. "No, ma'am, I did not. I know their group likes to send messages to people and companies who exploit those who can't help themselves."

"That'd be the chickens."

Lucille huffed and propped a hand on her hip. "And the horny toads. That's why they're here, Jolene. Haven't you been paying attention?"

"Ah, yes, the horny toads. I'd love to hear your explanation for that one right after you tell me how you're not an accomplice in a bombing—a pathetic excuse for a bombing, but a bombing nonetheless. Blowing up feed stores is against the law, Mother. A real no-no. Somebody's going to jail."

"Don't you get smart with me, Missy." She snapped her nose upward again. "Nobody knows exactly what happened or how so don't you start thinking you do. I certainly had nothing to do with it. I was here with you all morning. Never stepped foot off the place."

That was true in terms of a physical alibi, of course, but that's all it was. "Oh, you're involved, and we both know it. How deep you're in is what I don't know."

"I didn't invite those AAC people here," Mother Accomplice snapped back. "They just showed up." She grabbed a dishtowel from the drawer and wiped the counter out of habit. "They're not from around here, and I made allowances for that, but quite frankly, some of them are just plain peculiar."

Look who's talking. I uncrossed my arms, sighed, heavily and grabbed my keys and billfold from the kitchen table. "I assume if I head down the main street of Bowman City I'll find the Feed, Tack and Computer Store."

Lucille nodded begrudgingly. "Won't be much of a story left by the time you get there. It's twenty minutes at least. Everybody will probably be gone by then. Be better to just write a story about me from here. That's really the bigger issue anyway."

"I'm going to the feed store." And there will be no story writing. "Because you know, and I know, that exploding paint cans in front of the courthouse and rabbit chow raining down Main Street are connected to you because these things always are. And this time, Mother, I am going to find out what's going on and put a stop to it before the actual shooting begins. Although that's technically not possible since bullets have already been flying. They were your bullets, of course, and we all know—"

"You made your point, Jolene." Lucille flung the towel down and mashed her lips into thin little painted lines. She managed to mutter something I was better off not hearing then ended with a quite audible "I'll get my purse."

"Oh, I don't think so. You're not going anywhere. You are not to leave the house. Do not even think of leaving the house. Leaving the house is not an option. You are to stay inside the house."

One must be explicit when giving Lucille directives as she is taking meticulous mental notes as well as drawing loopholes in them at the same time. "Do not open the doors and do not answer the phone. Phones. Don't make any calls from any phone. Or hand signals from the window." I did not add this last directive facetiously. She's done it. As more flashes of the things my mother has done—and her perfectly illogical rationalizations for doing them—flashed through my head with big red warning lights, I revised her orders. "On second thought, why don't you just go to your room and stay there until I get back. Pull the shades, turn off the lights. Take a nap."

Lucille took these directives fairly well, or either she wasn't listening. Yes, my vote too. A closer look told me her face was now in thinking mode rather than teeth-gnashing mode. It was not necessarily an improvement. "The leader goes by the name of Tiger," she volunteered, clicking her inch long nails together. "That bunch he has around him acts like he's the Second Coming or something, swarming him like a bunch of gnats, ready to cater to his every whim, and all he does is stand there and stare."

"Ah, the Great Horned Toad Messiah."

Lucille scowled. "That's not funny."

"You know, it really kind of is, and I'd like to see it firsthand."

"Well, you won't be laughing when you've got Ol' Bony Butt after you."

"Surely with all the other heathens in town, I'm far enough down her 'come to Jesus' list to avoid too much grief."

"I don't know why you say ugly things like that; you most certainly did not learn blasphemy in my home." Lucille stared at me, grinding her teeth, chewing around for the very best words. "I'll tell you one thing, Ethel may have herself convinced that Bobcat's got the hots for her, but I know better, carrying on like teenagers in front of the whole town. It's just sickening, that's what it is."

Say what? I tossed my purse and keys back on the table. "You want to explain that? Start with Bobcat."

Lucille propped herself against the cabinets, her fingers click-ety-clacking on the counter. "He's Tiger's second in command and Ethel Fossy has latched on to him like a tick," she said, her voice escalating in both volume and speed. "She seems to think he's interested in her, but he most certainly is not… interested in her in *that* way. Not really. Any idiot can see what's going on. He's just using her and she's acting like a fool. Why, he's twelve years younger than she is. Just because she started dying her hair and painting herself up like a rodeo clown, which I'm just sure is mortal sin, especially at that narrow-minded church she goes to, does not change the fact that she looks old enough to be his mother. She keeps it up and I'm going to tell her that he came after me first but I had more sense than to just fall for some fool who's only looking for a piece of tail, and why on earth he'd want that piece is just beyond me."

Oh, there were apparently so many, many things that were beyond me, and the list grew every time my mother opened her mouth. Realizing my jaw had fallen open, I shut mine.

"And that's another thing," Lucille said, oblivious to the fact that I was not enjoying her senior sex story time. "That hussy hypocrite's been talking dirty about me behind my back all this time, preaching at me, calling me names—you remember all that slut business—and now look at her. Look who's acting dirty now! Why, I ought to give her some of her own medicine, that's what I ought to do."

"Alright, enough," I said, stopping her before she worked herself—or me—into a stroke. "Let's take this one trauma at a time."

Lucille grabbed the dishtowel again and slapped it against the counter. "There is no trauma here, Jolene, and I have nothing further to say about that holier-than-thou lying, hypocritical, cheap, painted-face slut. She can hop into bed with every one of them for all I care, and she probably already has. Just a little bit of attention and all of a sudden she's one of those sex groupies."

Sex groupies? Religious fanatic Ethel Fossy, a sex groupie? Now that pushed the bounds of plausibility, even for Kickapoo. But, speaking of groupies, "What happened to Velma Brotherton? I thought she and Ethel were joined at the hip. How does she fit into this?"

"She doesn't." Lucille snorted in a highly undignified manner. "When Bony Butt started following around after these newcomers like a slobbering blind sheep, Velma high-tailed it back to California. Everybody had just figured they were like Jerry Don's ex-wife, but now that Ethel's run off with a man hippie, it makes you wonder. I've read that some people like both, they call it bisexual." She waved her hand to dismiss the topic. "Whatever the case, she's sure whoring it up and preaching hellfire all at the same time."

If even a fraction of my mother's tale could be believed, the potential that Ethel had been sucked into some weird cult was very real. "Messiahs, brainwashing and Grandma Gone Wild. Please tell me religion is not involved here."

Lucille puffed out her chest. "Not real religion. Not like the Methodists, of course, or the Baptists for that matter, even though they're always squabbling about who's the best kind of Baptist or even Ethel's Church of Christ with their weird thinking. Do you know that her very own pastor held a special prayer meeting for her, and there's talk around town of trying to buy her an exorcism? Nobody's sure if there's a Christian way to do that sort of thing or if it's just for Catholics and witches, but they're checking into it."

I didn't say anything because frankly I was still processing the exorcism criteria. And then Lucille opened the refrigerator and nabbed a bottle of water, something I had never in my entire life seen her do before. She twisted off the top, took a long swig and kept talking. "I was glad for the help from the AAC people at first, thinking they were good Christians and all, but now I think it's just some kind of cult. They're all real secretive and peculiar acting. I wouldn't be surprised to find out they're all on mind control drugs. They're a weird bunch. And that's another thing, Ethel Fossy has to be blind as a bat and dumb as a doorknob, because if she'd been paying any attention at all she would have realized that those men darned sure brought their own women with them in that van. Girls, really, about your age, following those old men around like sheep, why I've never seen such a thing. I suppose they're hopped up on drugs or maybe hypnosis. They brought in a van full of kids too, but they were just a bunch of dopers that would holler and protest about anything. I sure couldn't make any sense out of them, but the reporters seemed real impressed so I didn't fuss."

Resisting all my natural urges to sigh, rub my face and bang my head against the wall, I said, "Okay, so the main players are Tiger, the leader, and Bobcat the second in command, both old hippie types, and some forty-ish women. Two women?"

Lucille nodded. "The snooty dark-haired one is Iris. Always wears black like Cat Woman and acts like she's the Queen of Sheba. I was trying to be friendly and make conversation with her, and she just looked down her nose at me like she'd just as soon shoot me as not, and then she walked right off without saying a single word. I've never seen somebody so rude in all my life. Hateful hussy. She marched herself right over to Tiger and started talking about me. I know she did because I saw her lips move just a little bit, like a ventriloquist. Merline and Agnes thought she was probably just talking dirty to him or making plans for later. They think she looks like one of those dominator women who carries around handcuffs and such in her purse. I never did see her with a purse myself so I couldn't say, but it wouldn't surprise me any."

You'd think at this point I'd be somewhat accustomed to this sort of thing from my mother, but I am not. The best I can do is reel my brain past the deeply disturbing conjecture and cast about in a new pond for some glimmer of a pertinent fact. "What about the other woman? Tell me about her."

"Lily. She's younger than stuck-up Iris, probably in her thirties, although it's hard to tell with how she carries on. Blabbers all the time about nothing, flitting around in her long hippie skirts and sandals, playing with her braids like she's a schoolgirl. They're all real strange, I'll tell you that."

Yes, well, strange was relative. And while there may have been some bits of relevant information in Mother Dearest's ramblings, but I did not have the wherewithal to ferret them out at the moment. I pushed away from the edge of the door and said, "Okay, here's where we are. I'm going to the current crime scene for a first person view of the festivities, and you are going to spend your time in solitary confinement, figuring out how to get yourself out of this mess."

"There is no mess, Jolene. I haven't done anything wrong. And even if I have, er, had, whatever, well, you're not in charge of me. I'm telling you, I was not involved in any of it."

"I believe this is where we started this conversation. And yes, you were, I just don't know the details yet."

Lucille snorted and lifted her chin. "Fine then, you just run along and see what dirt you can dig up on me. There isn't any, of course, but you go on and have a good time trying. I have plenty of things to do right here."

Oh, I just bet she did. Red flags and blue flashing lights accompanied the warning bells in my head this time, forcing me to face a reality I really wanted to ignore. I couldn't leave her alone. Regardless of what orders I gave, she still had unfettered access to a phone, a Buick and a 9mm handgun. There were no good outcomes from that scenario. None. "Change of plans. Get in the car."

"What! All this fuss about locking me away in my own house and now you just up and order me to get in the car? Why, I don't even know if I want to go now," she said, reaching for her purse on the table. "That little rental car of yours is awfully small."

"Hold on there. You can take the purse, but the gun stays here."

Lucille made a good effort at registering shock and outrage, but she moved on to snarling rather quickly. "I can take my gun anywhere I want. I have a permit."

"I don't care."

She glared for a few seconds, weighing her options. Finally, she flung open the black bag, fumbled around inside, pulled out the gun case and set it on the table. "This really hurts me, Jolene."

"We're taking the Buick. Get in the car."

Chapter
Four

I chose the paved road to Bowman City, and fourteen minutes
after we'd passed the Kickapoo city limit sign we were there.
To her credit, Lucille had kept her mouth shut most of the
way, a whoop escaping only at the crest of a really big hill. And
not from fear either. She was having a ball. My mother's idea of
fun has apparently changed significantly in the last few years.
Months, even.

As I'd expected, the road into the crime scene was blocked.
Also as expected, I knew the deputy directing traffic. I pulled
up and rolled down my window. "Hey, Leroy, getting things
finished up here?"

"Hey, Jolene, Miz Jackson," Leroy said, bobbing his head at
us and snickering. "I'm a packin'. That's something."

Huh? I looked at Leroy and then at my mother, who was not
so surreptitiously shaking her head at Leroy.

"Best license plate in the county, maybe even the state," he
said. "I kick myself every day for not thinking about it first."

Lucille waved a dismissive hand at me. "It's just one of
those 'Keep Texas Wild' license plates with a horny toad on it,"
she said. "That's all. I support protecting the horny toads, you
know."

"Yes, I know." After a few seconds, I finally caught up with
what they were talking about. "You have a vanity plate that
says what?"

"I-M-A-P-A-K-N," Leroy chortled. "I'm a packin'."

"If you paid any attention at all you'd have already noticed
it," Lucille snapped. "Now stop all this nonsense and get down
to business."

Leroy took the hint. "Things are just getting started, Jolene,"
he said, dropping back into his serious voice. "HazMat's inside

and the bomb dogs are on the way. This is a serious situation we've got here. Don't know what all we're dealing with."

We're not dealing with your first string criminals, that's for sure. Then again, past experience told me they hadn't sent the first string HazMat team either. I couldn't bring myself to ask about the gung-ho guy who'd shown up at Mother's house a few months back with unfettered enthusiasm, an instruction booklet, lit cigarette, gasoline and Tyvek suit. He'd managed not to blow himself up that day, but he was clearly in line for a Darwin Award at some point. "Think there's another bomb?"

His eyes kind of popped open a little wider, signaling me that he hadn't exactly thought of that possibility. "Can't say about any of that, Jolene. Everything's still under investigation. Can't say a word to anybody about anything. We're securing the area now. May even have to shut the whole town down. This is serious."

"Yes, very serious, I got that part. Where's Jerry?"

"He's busy. You can't be bothering him right now. He wouldn't talk to you anyway. He's the one that put out the gag order. We can't say nothing to nobody. Even you."

One would think that sort of specific directive would not be necessary, but one would be wrong. The don't-tell-Jolene-anything order kind of hurt my feelings. "Okay then, where's the press hanging out?"

He frowned for a second then the light bulb came on and he nodded. "Oh, yeah, I guess you could do that, say you're with the press and all. They're over at the Dairy Queen, just outside the roadblock. You really ought to put on your press badge though."

You betcha.

The Bowman City DQ was packed. Clusters of locals outnumbered the reporter types by about twenty to one. There was one local news van with a live feed setup waiting for something interesting to happen, but the crew did not appear to be on pins and needles. In fact, if the wristwatch checking was any indication, they were ready to move on to a livelier locale. There is only so much of an adrenaline rush to be had from flying livestock pellets, although I couldn't help but wonder how this would play out in CNN's "situation room."

These days, this sort of thing could be twisted up with all kinds of supposition and conjecture, and within seconds an entire segment of the US population would be on pins and needles. *"Breaking News! A feed store in north central Texas has exploded. Response teams have been called and the area is being evacuated. We do not yet know the motive for the bombing or if there are other bombs in the area. There has been no official link to Muslim Terrorists at this time. The national threat level has not been changed. Repeat, the threat level remains at yellow. If a terror threat is determined, we will be the first to let you know. To repeat, the feed store bombing has not been linked to any known terrorist cells. We have a live feed now from local channel—"*

"Jolene!" Lucille whacked me on the arm. "What are you daydreaming about?"

Nothing. Absolutely nothing. "Just grateful that the place isn't crawling with reporters."

"Well, I'm not. I need to talk to a decent writer who will say what needs said about this park business and give it the attention it deserves."

Yes, I got the implication and it wasn't going to get me to write a story for her. I pulled the Buick into the DQ lot and stared a little more. Now that I was in the midst of it all, I couldn't exactly remember why it was imperative for me to rush right over. And how much trouble was there anyway? It didn't look all that intense to me. Aside from the nosy gossip types, most of the crowd looked bored.

"There's Tiger," Lucille whispered, facing me and cocking her head toward the windshield obviously and repeatedly. "Bobcat's next to him. That's Lily on the left, twittering around, and Iris is behind them all, slunk over to the side like black alley cat. And I suppose you can see for yourself where Bony Butt is."

I really couldn't. What I saw were two old hippie-looking guys, each near sixty, with gray ponytails and goatees. Lily's long reddish-blonde hair was woven into two neat braids that hung over her shoulders. She wore what used to be called a peasant blouse with a broomstick skirt and earthy sandals. Iris, however, was not exactly as I'd expected from Mother's description, although I couldn't really define what that might have been. She did look to be in her forties and she most assuredly had black hair—short and spiky like Halle Berry in that James Bond movie. She was tall, maybe five-foot-eight, thin and gorgeous, with light blue eyes that seemed to cut through the crowd even from here. She did not look brainwashed or on drugs. She wore a black tee-shirt with jeans, looking more commando than Cat Woman. Mother had gotten one thing right though, she did not look the least bit friendly.

A sharp jab in the side from my mother's elbow broke my stare.

"There she is. That's Bony Butt, if you can believe it."

I followed Lucille's head bobbing and finger pointing until I finally caught a glimpse of Ethel, standing just behind Bobcat. Her formerly gray hair was indeed dyed a color suspiciously close to Frivolous Fawn, not that I would say so aloud, that being one of Mother's most recent choices. The compact helmet hairdo was a little more relaxed than I remembered, and it did look like she was wearing jeans and some kind of tailored jacket. I was kind of impressed. Ethel had taken herself from the 1950s to maybe the mid-eighties, and it was a definite improvement.

The Great Horned Toad Messiah, on the other hand, was an old hippie. Tiger stood ramrod straight, arms crossed, eyes closed. A standing meditation maybe? His sidekick Bobcat held a similar pose—sans the serenity part. Of course, it would be darned hard for anyone to be Zen if you had Bony Butt buzzing you like a wasp.

"Look over there," Lucille said, craning her neck this way and that. "That's Gilbert Moore. The one I was telling you about that was out behind the house when the pole truck was there."

I followed her pointing painted nail to a very tall and big man leaning against the DQ's brick wall not too far from the toad crowd. He wore dark sunglasses, a tan tee shirt tucked in to his jeans and work boots. With a toothpick twirling in his mouth and thick arms crossed over his chest, he gave off a cocky vibe. Arrogant asshole would be my bet. And while that was generally just a cover for insecurity, my patience in dealing with such types was severely lacking. His size was intimidating, no question about that, but there was something else about him that made me uneasy. Something I just couldn't put my finger on. "Was the equipment out behind the house his then?"

"Well, I believe some of it was, yes, although he wouldn't admit to anything that I could tell, just kept talking down to me like I didn't know my head from a hole in the ground," Lucille said, scowling. "I left him message, but he wouldn't ever call me back. He even hung up on me once without saying a word, like I wouldn't notice the phone clicking off in my ear. I ought to go over there and tell him what I think about him and his ways."

That wasn't necessarily a bad plan, but confronting an over-grown asshole at the Dairy Queen wasn't necessarily a good one either. Then again, he didn't scare me, and I had some questions of my own, such as what he was doing here. "I'll go talk to him."

Mother jabbed me again and pointed at Bobcat and Bony Butt, who now appeared to be clutching each other and/or holding hands. "Would you just look at that? It's just sickening. I'm going over there right now and tell them to get themselves a room and stop their lustful groping out here in public. Nobody ought to have to bear witness to such things."

From what I could tell, Bobcat's part in the bodily contact was more related to self-defense and damage control than lust. But, these things amuse Lucille, so I let her focus on Ethel's love life while I turned my attention back to the tough big guy and what he was doing here. Only I couldn't find him. Iris stood a few feet from where he'd been, but Gilbert Moore was gone.

The rattle of a diesel engine and tires crunching on gravel caught my attention, and I looked out my window just in time to see a white crew cab pickup speed away from the Dairy Queen with the missing big man behind the wheel. For once, I would have no trouble identifying a getaway vehicle. Gilbert Moore's truck was a flatbed dually with two big poles that started at the back and came together in an A-frame over the cab. Fitted in beneath and around the poles were all kinds of equipment, racks, reels and toolboxes. It was definitely a work truck, and from the gas bottles chained up behind the cab, I'd say he was a welder. He'd probably built the back part himself and never bothered finishing it out with paint because the bare metal was covered in rust. Other distinguishing features included a row of yellow running lights just above the windshield and a gash in the passenger door. I had no idea why it mattered, but I knew I could pick out Gilbert Moore's truck from a mile away, coming or going.

Back at Toad Hall, Iris had rejoined the inner circle. Bony Butt was still latched on to Bobcat's arm and Lily was now holding Tiger's. What a happy loving group. "So, are they watching over their own crime scene, or waiting to create another one?" I wondered aloud.

"There's no proof that they did anything," she said, eyeing me as she formulated her response. "They're probably just here because they're concerned about the chickens."

"The chickens!" I said with inauthentic enthusiasm. "You know, I bet you're right. Let's go ask them about the poor little chickens."

Before I could kill the car and unlock the doors, Mother had grabbed my arm and was pointing—nay, stabbing—a long nail at the windshield. "Look! She's here!"

Oh, I knew where this was going. *Please, God, not Kimberlee Fletcher.*

Either because she wasn't much of a reporter, or in spite of it, Kimberlee had somehow made the mere mention of my name by the media a slur. Double ditto for my mother, who, on our last encounter, had rather crudely let little Kimberlee know what she thought of her. I didn't want a repeat. Or something worse.

"Look!" Lucille shrieked again. "She's here. Candace Carlton is here!"

Huh? I blinked a few times, trying to bring my mind into focus. My eyes had been wide open, but I had just been staring through the crowd. "Kimberlee?"

"No, no, no. The little snot's probably around somewhere, but who cares. Channel 3's Candace Carlton is here," Lucille breathily exclaimed yet again. "And she's coming this way. With a microphone!" She patted her hair and rubbed her lips together. "I just wish I had time to freshen my makeup."

Now, let's be clear on a few things. When convenient, my mother is routinely incapacitated by arthritis, bursitis, diverticulitis and any other "itis" that she can dream up. Also when convenient, she is as nimble as a fourteen-year-old gymnast. Thus, she was out of the car and sprinting toward Candace Carlton's microphone before I could say "shit."

Funny what thoughts go through your mind in times such as these. The one taunting me this time was in the voice of my 20-year-old daughter, scolding me for cursing. She is above such things, you see, and considers me both of lowly character and deficient vocabulary for resorting to such epithets. She uses highbrow words bigger than that too, in normal conversation even. She could not be my natural child. And if there was any genetic link between her and the 73-year-old lunatic running across the parking lot toward the TV cameras, I couldn't identify it.

I thumped my head against the steering wheel and slumped down in my seat, trying to disappear. It wouldn't work, of course. Never did. But what was I going to do, run out there and drag her back to the car while the cameras were rolling? Or just let her go say whatever came to mind so she could get herself on the news? Again, no good options.

Tap. Tap. Tap.

I jerked up in my seat and snapped my head toward the window. I must have gasped, screamed, cursed, or perhaps all three, because Kimberlee Fletcher jumped back from the car as if I'd slapped her.

I slowly lowered the window and eyed the young *Redwater Falls Times* reporter. She was wearing jeans and a tight tee shirt, and her blond hair was hanging ponytail-like out the back of a tan ball cap. Yes, she was chewing gum too.

"What do you want, Kimberlee?"

"Your mother is over there, giving Candy an exclusive. I want one from you."

If I hadn't just about jumped out of my skin when she rapped on the window, I might have laughed. Unfortunately, being scared makes me bitchy. "You are truly insane."

Kimberlee snickered and smacked her gum. "That's what everybody says about you." *Smack, smack.* "Crazy things happen when you show up in town."

"Oh, right. I keep forgetting. Nothing weird ever happens until I arrive. How do you ever find anything to write about when I'm not here?"

Kimberlee snickered and popped her gum then nodded to the motley group of endangered species standing in the shade of the Dairy Queen. "They came down from Colorado, just like you. Word is they're out of Boulder, which makes sense because from what I hear it's the hippie capital of the world next to California and maybe Oregon. Are they neighbors of yours?"

"I live nowhere near Boulder, Kimmy, and they are my neighbors about like the people who live in Plano are yours."

The knitting of her brow told me she was working very hard to connect those dots. Lovely, just lovely. "Question, Kimmy. Have you ever been over 50 miles from your home here?"

Her pointy little jaw dropped open in question then started working as her brain found something to relate to. "I have been to all kinds of places on church trips." She took a breath and scowled. "Where I've been or haven't is none of your business. I'm the one asking the questions here."

"I'll take that as a no."

"I go to Dallas and Oklahoma City all the time. Just because you live in Denver doesn't make you special. You aren't nearly as smart as your mother thinks you are either, and you sure don't know anything about anything that goes on around here."

There was a phrase in there that threw up all kinds of red flags. No, not the part about me not knowing anything, we all know that's true. It was the part about my mother thinking I'm smart, which we all know is not true. Before I could ask where she got her faulty information, Mother Dearest bounced back into the car and slammed the door. Her interview had apparently not gone well.

"That Carlton hussy is more interested in prissing for the camera than she is in getting a good story. I tried to tell her about the park and the idiots who are trying to ruin my life, and all she wanted to do was show off her bosoms and talk about those stupid chickens. I've had enough of this, Jolene. Get me out of here."

"Oh, but I was just about to buy Kimberlee here a big glass of iced tea and continue our chat. She was just telling me about all the nice things you said about me." I watched in amusement as pure panic flashed across Lucille's face. "Besides, I want to talk to her some more about all the crazy things going on around here. I've got an idea for a fresh story angle I want to share with her. Want to join us?"

"No," Lucille and Kimberlee barked in unison. The resounding answer came from both Lucille and Kimberlee, interestingly, but neither was getting off that easy. And, God help me, I really did want to talk to Kimberlee. "Fine, Mother, you stay in the car. I'll crack the windows, but I'm locking the doors and taking the keys. You'll be fine in the shade. Oh, and if you decide you want to come in, better beep the horn as the security alarm goes off if the doors are opened from the inside."

Funny thing, but both Kimberlee and Lucille were marching toward the DQ before I could even grab my billfold.

"I don't know what you're up to," Kimberlee hissed, "but I'm going to write about it."

"Slow news year?"

"Not at all," she said, with a toss of her ponytail and an obvious smirk. "I've gotten two promotions because of the articles I've written about you and your mother. Those bring in tons of letters and sell lots of papers. You're great for my career."

That stopped me in my tracks. "Career? Sweetcakes, you don't actually have a career. What you have is Uncle Fletch's clout keeping you in a job no matter how much ludicrous crap you dream up and call news."

Kimberlee gasped and sputtered and almost let her bubble gum fall out of her mouth. She never actually articulated a "how dare you" but she tried real hard.

"I'll tell you another thing," Lucille said, pointing a finger, an acceptable one this time, at Kimberlee. "My Jolene's going to get to the bottom of all these shenanigans around here and you better stay out of her way. She's a real reporter and investigates things like they should be. We won't be taking any guff from the likes of you!"

And with that, Her Highness spun on her heel, tipped up her nose and marched regally inside the Dairy Queen.

I started to follow then stopped in the shade of the overhang outside and turned back to Kimberlee. "You know, it's too bad you're so intent on printing crap. There's really a pretty good story here. If you actually did some research and learned to look beyond the obvious, you might make a decent reporter some day."

"What do you mean?"

"Any idiot can report what happened. It's the 'why' that will get you a great story." I nodded to the toadies. "We know why they say they're here, but is there more? And what about that really tall guy in the dark glasses that was standing off to the side of them? Why is he here?"

She frowned for a minute. "You mean Gilbert Moore?" I nodded and her eyes began to sparkle with either journalistic zeal or gossip-mongering, the line between the two being fuzzy at best. "What do you know that I don't?"

I hated to admit it, but the little twit's chances of success as a reporter were far better than mine had ever been. You see, even though I can't seem to avoid it in Texas, I hate having drama in my own life, and I surely don't want to experience it vicariously through anyone else's. Kimmy, on the other hand, lives for such things, making her inherently nosey and therefore naturally hard-wired to succeed at the job.

"I don't know anything particular," I said, not envying her "gift" one bit. "But the fact that Gilbert was here at all is worth considering. So, what do you know about him?"

Her eyes twinkled. "I've heard a lot of juicy stories. I think most of them are even true."

I sighed. "Would any of them be something besides gossip that might be remotely pertinent to what's going on now?"

She sighed too. "Probably not."

"Okay, more specifically, do you know anything about the work he does?"

"Well, yeah, it's mostly oil field stuff. He works for Uncle Fletch sometimes, and I heard something about a deal with Barnett Shale out of Dallas, whoever that is."

I made good mental notes of that revelation, just in case. "Would that be for oil well drilling?"

"Why do you ask that?" Kimmy glared at me again, my question snapping her antennas back up. "You're working on a story and trying to pump me for information, aren't you?"

"A byline is the last thing on my mind, Kimmy. I'm just trying to find out anything that will help my mother." I motioned toward the building. "Let's go stand in the shade for a few minutes. I have some things I want to talk to you about."

Kimmy reluctantly followed me and as I leaned up against the red brick wall, I waved to my mother inside, who had popped her head up like a prairie dog to see what I was doing.

"So, we've got a 'Save the Horny Toads' rally gone bad at the courthouse yesterday, a feed store bombing to free baby chicks today, and a bunch of out-of-state activists on the scene at both. All supposedly because somebody's putting an RV park in the middle of nowhere at the edge of Kickapoo, Texas. And then, of course, there was that heavy equipment that was working night and day out at the Little Ranch a few weeks back. Gilbert Moore was there and then here he is again today. These are all things to check into."

Kimmy frowned and start smacking again. "I don't see why you think all of these things could be related."

"Well, some are obvious, others less so. If I were here in a professional capacity, which I am not, I wouldn't ignore any of it. I'd be checking and cross checking every angle I could. You never know where you'll find that one piece of evidence or even person that ties everything together."

"I know that," Kimmy snapped. "The first thing I did was check out those animal rights people. Other than what's on their website, there's not much to be found. They won't talk when you try to interview them and the only quotes I got were stock lines about how we have to treat animals like people and that we have to quit destroying the planet. None of them would give me a real name."

"Makes you wonder, doesn't it?" As she nodded in agreement, I added, "They sure got here quick too. Did anybody even mention horny toads before they got here? Has anybody even seen a horny toad around here in the last twenty years? There are many, many angles to this, Kimmy."

She chewed on that for a few seconds along with her gum. "You could be right. I hadn't thought of it that way."

"Well, now you have, so get to it. I'll do the same. Call me and we'll compare notes. Maybe between the two of us, we can find out what's really going on."

She smacked thoughtfully a few more times then said, "Why are you doing this? You hate me."

"You've written a lot of crap, Kimmy, no question about that. If you put your energy into writing about things that actually matter, and getting the real truth about them, I think you could be a decent journalist."

"Meaning I'm not now?"

"You know the answer to that, and I'm not going to lie to make you feel better. The truth is I have more experience than you do in life and otherwise. I'm also a better writer than you will ever be." She puffed up at that as I knew she would. "But," I said, pausing for emphasis, "I have never been and never will be the reporter you already are."

She leaned away from the wall and stood a little straighter, but still said nothing and didn't even make a smack.

"You've got talent and you've got the right personality. Now use them in a good way. Get in there and dig for some answers."

"You really mean that or are you just trying to get me to find things out for you?"

"Both. You *can* find out things that I can't. There's a good story here and you could use it to move yourself from gossip columnist to investigative reporter. Besides, I'd rather have you helping me than looking for some kind of salacious angle from which to create a story about me."

Bewilderment flickered across her face.

"It means scandalous, sensational."

She nodded and began smacking away. "Okay. Thanks. I think."

We exchanged phone numbers, just in case either one of us decided to follow through on the deal.

"Oh, and Kimmy, here's another professional tip, lose the gum."

In the car headed back to Kickapoo, Lucille was quiet for several miles, which was more than fine with me. I needed the time to think, and the thing in the forefront of my mind was that I needed to get back and walk the property behind the house. I also wanted to go talk to the owner of the land. Why he wasn't the focus of Lucille's activities seemed odd. She'd made the comment that he'd gotten in over his head, but what did that mean?

"When we get back, I'm going out behind the house and walk the property. Probably should talk to Bob Little first though, instead of trespassing."

"There's no need in that. You're not trespassing. You go on and look around. I wanted to do that too, but it didn't seem safe to go out there by myself. Merline wouldn't go with me because she was afraid she'd snag her spangles on the mesquite thorns, and Agnes wouldn't set foot back there because she was just sure we'd all come back covered from head to toe in chiggers."

Glad she'd mentioned that. "You have spray, right?"

"I still have some of the old kind, the stuff that actually worked before they watered it all down. You can't buy the good stuff anymore."

No, you couldn't. And if you've never had chigger bites, well, take a stroll through the Texas weeds with bare legs. You'll be a fast believer in bathing in DEET, DDT or something equally toxic before you do it again. And by the way, hairspray, alcohol, nail polish or any other home remedy you've been told about does not make them either die or crawl out of the hole they've dug in your skin. But go ahead and give it a shot. The sting is a good distraction.

"After I take a look around out back," I said. "I'm going to drive up and talk to Bob Little. Do you want to go with me?"

"He's probably not even home," Lucille said, fiddling with her purse. "Besides, I told you he's as much in the dark about all this as I am. He's just getting bullied, that's all. I don't think you need to be bothering him about it all. He's had a hard enough time with everything as it is."

It was beyond odd that she didn't want me to talk to Bob Little—the one person who knew what was going on and why.

"I know you had to talk to him about what was going on back there. What did he say about it? Is it drilling or what?"

Lucille frowned. "Like I told you, he got into something he ought not have, and he signed some papers that he thought were just for an inspection and appraisal of the property. But somehow, whatever he signed allowed them to come in and do all kinds of things. All I know is that it's real bad and he's real sorry he didn't shoot them the first time they drove up the driveway. He was trying to do a good thing and it just turned out real bad."

"I'd like to see the agreement he signed if he'd be willing. If he really wants out of this, maybe I can help. It would also help me know better how to deal with your situation." I nodded to her purse. "Call him."

Lucille begrudgingly took out her phone and dialed. "See, I told you, he's not at home."

"Try his mobile phone, assuming he has one."

"Everybody on the planet has one, Jolene." She dialed again and waited then flipped her phone closed. "He's not answering there either," she said, relief in her tone and her face. "I suppose he's out somewhere. Probably turned his phone off too, tired of people bothering him."

"You know, I haven't been up to his place since I was a kid. I'd really like to see the view again. I think I'll just drive up there anyway. Maybe he'll be back by then."

"No," Lucille said, entirely too quickly. "We can't do that." She stuffed her phone back in her purse, shoveling around like she needed to make room for it, which she did not. "He locks the gate, what with all the snoopers we've had around. We wouldn't even be able to get in."

My own phone rang and I knew immediately that it was Jerry. About time, too.

"Hi," I said, anticipation, invitation and promise of consummation all rolled up into one word. It took about two seconds for my hot plans to go up in smoke. Three more seconds and the winds were blowing toward decidedly pissed. From what I could tell, I wouldn't be seeing Jerry at all tonight, much less doing anything else. Some police chief was in town and he had to deal with him about something, it was very important, blah

blah blah. If he managed to get free, he'd do something or other later, blah blah blah. I'd quit listening because not only had my plans for a romantic evening gone down in flames, I got the feeling he was lying to me. "Fine, Jerry." Okay, I know it wasn't the mature reaction, but it was the one I had. "Whatever."

"Jolene, I'm sorry. I really am. I'll make it up to you."

I wanted to believe him. I really did. But I'd played the fool before with my lying ex-husband as well as the jerk I fell in love with after him, and I'd vowed never to do it again. It wasn't Jerry's fault. He'd never ever treated me the way those other two men had, but the triggers were obviously still there. It was that old feeling again, the one that started with a stab in the gut then a sharp rip all the way up to my heart. Gutted like a fish was the best way I could describe it. I'd felt that about ten times a day with the last guy I'd fallen for. I'd never felt it with Jerry before. Never. But I felt it now. "Jerry, I have to be straight with you. You know what I've been through. I've had two men who lied to me repeatedly and told me that I was wrong for having the feelings I had that told me they were lying." Yes, it was a little hard to follow, but he was getting the point. "I'm having that feeling now."

Silence. Looong silence.

Oh, this was so not good. *Zing.* Gutted again. "It's fine, Jerry," I said, hearing the hurt tinged with anger in my own voice and not knowing how to hide it. "I'll just talk to you later."

"Jolene, honey, listen." He paused then said softly, "I'm not like him, Jo. You have to believe that. I do have to meet with this guy tonight and I really can't tell you any more than that. Your instincts are good, and I'd explain if I could, but I can't yet. Trust me. Please."

Oh, how I wanted to. I really wanted to. "I have to talk about this with you later." Emotion knotted in my throat, making it really hard to talk. "I have to go. Bye." As I clicked off the phone, I thought I heard him say, "I love you." Well, I'd heard that before too.

Mother fished around in her purse and pulled out a package of tissues and handed me one. "I don't' know what all that was about, but Jerry Don is not a liar. I'm just sure you're wrong about whatever you're thinking."

She was always sure I was wrong about something, maybe everything, but in this case, I really hoped she was right. I wiped my nose. "I just know what I feel."

"That's just old garbage that should have been long burned and buried, but you know how you are, you hang on to things long past the time they should have been let go of." Lucille handed me another tissue. "Now, let's go to the cemetery."

Huh? What had she said? "The cemetery?"

"Well, yes, I haven't been there in a while and I don't suppose you have either."

"I really don't think a trip to the cemetery is going to make me feel better."

She shrugged. "It might."

"Only if you dig a hole beside Dad and leave me in it."

"See there, you've got your smart mouth back, you must be feeling better already."

No, I wasn't. It had been a long time since I'd had that particular feeling—the fish gutting one. But any time it cropped up, it meant, without exception, that someone who held my heart in his hands was lying to me or doing something that would somehow cause me pain. Even when I let the guy convince me I was wrong about what I was feeling, it always, and I mean always, turned out that I wasn't. I might not have gotten the details exactly right, but the feeling was never wrong. At least Jerry hadn't tried to tell me that what I was feeling was wrong. In fact, he'd told me I was right. And he'd asked me trust him. Of course, I'd heard those words before too. "Dammit," I said, belatedly realizing I'd said it aloud.

"You're making too much out of it and you very well know it. Now, snap out of it, we need to go get flowers." Lucille opened her purse and dug around inside, searching for something. "I had a coupon for that hobby store that you always insist we go to, the one that has those great big flowers you like."

Yes, cemetery flower shopping is a passion of mine. "I assume you'll want to go get a cherry-limeade first," I said, knowing that the cemetery ritual required it.

"And a hamburger and onion rings. You know how your dad loved onion rings."

Lucille had developed this little routine right after my dad died to distract me and wear me down until we were at the cemetery before I knew what was going on. I was on to her now, but it apparently still worked. And, in my current mental state I couldn't think of a reason not to go, although I was really sure there was one.

The food and flower gathering stops took longer than usual since Lucille couldn't make up her mind about anything, including the size of her drink (she finally went with large since it fit best in the cup holder). She eventually found her coupon, and after extensive deliberations, we came out of the store with enough flowers to cover a float in the Rose Parade.

After arriving at the cemetery, I set the sacks by the marker, pulled out a handful of big flowers and started the de-tagging process.

Mother bent over the brass vase and started removing the faded spring flowers from the Styrofoam cone. "Jerry Don's not like that dumb Danny or that other one that I told you was a mistake from the very beginning. I knew it the minute I laid eyes on him, but you wouldn't listen to me." She shook her head and tossed the old flowers aside. "Even when he pulled that first dumb stunt, I tried to tell you again, but you just wouldn't see it. It was real clear to me what you'd gotten tangled up with."

"I know, Mother, I know." She was right, no point in denying it or trying to explain it. "Everybody saw who he really was but me."

"You better pay attention to what I'm telling you this time. It'll save you some grief." She stood and dusted her hands. "Now, you fix up the new ones."

I did as I was told and knelt down by the vase, keeping an eye out for fire ants. I started with the tall orange gladiolus stems and white calla lilies.

"Jerry Don is a good man," Mother said, gathering up the old flowers and putting them in a sack. "He and I have our disagreements, but they're mostly because he just doesn't understand about certain things. Not his fault, really, and I generally don't hold it against him." She shook her head and clucked her tongue. "But for goodness sakes, Jolene, he's the county sheriff, not God. He can't just reschedule crimes and such so he can go on a date with you."

I knew that, sort of. "It wasn't a crime or a case; it was some police chief that was in town for some reason or other that he had to deal with. That's all he'd say about it."

"But you don't believe him."

I filled in around the tall stems with white daisy clusters and stuck in some silver sparkly stick things that Lucille had insisted on. "I know he wasn't telling me the truth about it. I could feel it."

"Well, I think you're jumping to conclusions. Things can look one way when they're really something else entirely."

"Yeah, believing that is what got me in trouble before."

"That was different. You knew good and well that you couldn't trust either one of them as far as you could throw them, they showed you that over and over again, but you just ignored it. Jerry hasn't ever done any of that, now has he?"

I made a final adjustment to my floral creation and stood. "No."

Lucille patted the top of the arrangement then turned to walk to the car. "Glad we got that done."

I grabbed the remaining sacks and trash and followed her.

Once we were on the road, she said, "We all have our reasons for doing what we do, Jolene. Somebody else might think we're crazy, or even mean." She dabbed a tissue on her nose, sniffling just a little. "But if they knew all the facts, well, they'd realize they might've done the same thing if they'd been in the same spot. You remember that."

"I will." As I turned onto the highway back to Kickapoo, I realized the sun was setting fast right along with my opportunity for daylight reconnaissance of the mesquite patch. I also remembered what I should have been doing instead of spending half the day on the cemetery ritual. "It's going to be dark before long and I'd really like to meet with Bob Little before it gets any later. Why don't you try calling him again?"

"No point in that. Even if he is home, it'll be too late by the time we get there. Bobby goes to bed early. It would be best if waited until in the morning."

Why did I get the feeling that had been the plan all along?

The sun had just dipped out of sight when we pulled up to Mother's house. However, there was still plenty of light to see the Bowman County Sheriff's white Expedition sitting in front of the house.

My eyes filled with tears yet again, only this time I wasn't sad. I pulled the Buick into the garage then hurried out to meet Jerry, who was also coming toward me.

"I told you I'd come," he said, pulling me to him. "I can't stay, but I wanted to see you."

He explained about the police chief who was there because of some top secret something and getting something or other arranged. He couldn't tell me much about it, but said he would later and everything would be okay.

Truth is, I didn't really care what he had to do, what mattered to me was that he'd driven all the way over from Bowman City because he wanted to see me. That mattered a lot. I mattered to him.

Jerry didn't know how much longer it was going to take, but said he'd call later. "Jolene," he said, kissing me deeply one more time. "Trust me."

God help me, I did.

As Jerry drove away, I caught a glimpse of a curtain swaying. It was no great surprise that my mother had been watching the whole scene. Lucille is and always will be Lucille. However, there had been some odd—perhaps even borderline compassionate—behavior on her part at the cemetery. To begin with, she'd gone easy on me, giving me only a brief version of "how could you be that stupid" and really limiting her use of "I told you so." In addition, I am pretty sure she also gave me some actual usable motherly advice, which is just plain weird.

As I turned and walked toward the house, I realized that I was feeling good about things with Jerry. I trusted him.

On the other hand, regardless of whatever bonding moment might have occurred with my mother, trusting *her* was still completely out of the question.

Chapter Five

I awoke to the sound of gunfire.

It took a few seconds to figure that out, of course, but only a few, as gunfire tops the list of things likely to occur when I am in the general proximity of my mother.

It still startled me. Okay, it terrified me. I did not grow up with this sort of thing. Really. The woman has not been a geriatric road warrior all her life, only since she hit about seventy, which coincided rather closely with the sudden death of my father. Neither of us took it very well, but I'm pretty sure Lucille lost her freaking mind. The current situation—specifics unknown but definitely involving bullets—would tend to support that theory.

It is important to note that I assimilated this jumble of thoughts rather quickly— and while racing through the house to the front porch to see firsthand the full extent of the crisis. I stumbled into the living room and flattened myself against the wall by the front door, police-style, then stuck my nose around the doorframe and peeked out.

There, at the edge of the porch, in all her glory and bathrobe, was my mother and her Little Lady. No, her "Little Lady" is not a cocker spaniel. It is a laser-sighted 9 mm Glock, which at the moment was rapidly blowing holes into the side of a white four-door compact sedan.

Between shots, I heard a high-pitched shriek that sounded something like "stop" or "don't shoot" or some other phrase that my mother was sure to ignore.

Since the shooting was decidedly a one-way affair, I stepped into the doorway to get a better view and tentatively grabbed the latch of the glass storm door. In an oversized tee shirt and not much else, I didn't feel particularly motivated to wrestle her for the gun, and telling her to stop was a waste of good air. As

I mulled over other impractical options such as buying a stun gun and simply going back to bed until she got bored, I noticed an odd sound. Silence. Reverberating Silence. The gunfire had stopped. My ears, however, were ringing like a church bell.

Mother turned toward me, dropped out an empty clip from the pistol and said, loudly, "I've got three full clips in my top left dresser drawer, the one with my underwear. You run get them, Jolene. And hurry up about it," she yelled. "He might get away."

I had serious doubts about that—not about what was in the underwear drawer—but the getting away part. Before I could ask any questions or voice my, um, concerns, a squeaky "don't shoot" chirped from behind the bullet-riddled car.

"I'm unarmed," the voice continued. "Please don't shoot me. I'll come out with my hands up."

Yeah, that'd be great. With his hands up. "Mother, who's behind that car and what have you done to him?"

"That's Demon Seed," Lucille said venomously. "And he hasn't got a scratch on him. Yet."

"Who?"

"He's nothing but a lying little weasel. He's the one trying to take my property and ruin my life. Now, go get me those clips or get out of my way."

"Take your house?"

"Steal my house is more like it, the lying little twerp. The clips, Jolene, hurry up."

"You know, you've pretty much destroyed his car," which best I could tell was a Hyundai. "Let's call that good for the day."

"I'm making a statement here," Lucille groused, "and I haven't even shot out all the tires yet. The fool won't be thinking he can walk all over me when he's afoot!"

If you can come up with a reasonable response to that, well, you're way ahead of me. The best I could do was to try to distract her. "You know, we haven't been shopping together in ages. Why don't we get dressed and run into town to the mall. Don't you need a new purse?" Yes, it was truly a desperate moment.

TURKEY RANCH ROAD RAGE

"I have a new purse, thank you very much, and the mall is not open yet anyway, and you don't give a hoot about shopping with or without me." Lucille Jackson puffed out her chest and pointed a long acrylic nail to the front of the yard, where a sidewalk would traditionally be, if indeed Kickapoo had such things. "You look right there. I put up my signs just as plain as day. He chose to ignore them so he got just what he asked for. I have rights."

She was right about one thing. A garden of yellow and white squares had apparently cropped up in the yard when I wasn't looking. "Just because you put up 'no trespassing' signs, doesn't mean—"

"Those signs mean just what they say 'Trespassers will be shot'. Plain and simple." She nodded her head for emphasis, the piled high hair not daring to wiggle. "Five of them. And I know he can read because he tried to get me to sign a contract to hand him over my life for little of nothing, the dirty rotten scumbag. He was just asking for it."

Choosing to ignore her logic for as long as possible, I did a quick count of the signs and came up with six, not five. One was obviously handmade as it was larger and floppier than the others. Poster board was my guess. No, I did not ask what it said. "How about you give me the Little Lady and I'll go out and talk to the man hiding behind the car?"

"That'd be a good idea," came a squeaky voice. "My name is Damon Saide and I'm here on behalf of the Parks for Progress group. I just came by to explain some things to your mother about my offer. I meant no harm. Can we talk about this?"

He was awfully darned accommodating, considering he'd been pinned behind his car by flying bullets for ten minutes. Not to mention the fact that the car was probably totaled, Lucille having focused on the front half of the vehicle.

"Meant no harm my hind foot," Lucille said, trying to push around me so she could go get more bullets. "Get out of my way, Jolene, that stupid boy's trying to steal your inheritance."

Ah, my inheritance. That was certainly going to get my attention. First of all, I have no doubts whatsoever that my mother will outlive me by at least twenty years. I'm absolutely certain of it, in fact. Secondly, a house such as my mother's in the thriving metropolis of Kickapoo, Texas, is worth less than your average Suburban—without the full leather package. So, my inheritance wasn't a real big issue. But, trying to take advantage of my mother was. "Who are you and who sent you? And don't bother saying Parks for Progress again. I want names. Of people."

A bit of reddish hair and then some squinty eyes peaked out from behind the front quarter panel. "I represent a confidential client. I'm not at liberty to divulge names at this time, but I assure you, this is a serious offer and the money is available."

"Really? Well, it seems my mother has a nine-millimeter handgun representing her and she's real serious about it too. How do you figure that's going to work out for your confidential client? Or you, for that matter?"

"I told you I needed those clips," Lucille said, pulling the slide back on the gun and letting it spring forward. "He needs shot. I bet if I shot off his toes one by one he'd start talking."

"There's no call for violence," Demon Seed squeaked. "We were trying to be accommodating—"

The wail of a distant siren cut him off.

"You hear that, Jolene, that's the sheriff. You've yammered so long I lost my chance to shoot the lying rat." She sounded really disappointed. "I sure wish I'd thought about shooting off his toes earlier. We'd have been long done before now."

"Well, there's always next time," I added helpfully.

The siren grew closer, and, knowing how these things went, I figured I ought to be wearing pants when the cavalry arrived. I smiled at my mother and said, "I'll just go slip on some jeans."

"A bra too, Jolene. It'll probably be Leroy that shows up and God knows he doesn't need a reason to stare at your chest."

I feared she was right on both counts, not that I was going to praise her for it. One sane comment does not erase a dozen bullet holes in a Hyundai. Still, boobs swinging free and loose beneath a tee shirt would get me more of Leroy's attention than I could stand, so off I scurried to correct the problem.

It took me less than a minute and a half to get myself properly attired in shorts, tee shirt and required undergarments. When I stepped out on the porch, however, I saw not Leroy, but his father, Deputy Fritz Harper—Mother's boyfriend.

Although, from the way she was shaking her finger at him and screeching at the top of her lungs, I didn't think they were real sweet on each other at the moment.

Off to the side and slightly behind Fritz stood a skinny little man, not much taller than I am, with pale skin and reddish blond hair. He was nodding and trying to look very earnest. I'm not one to let others' opinions influence me—especially not my mother's—but there was something about him that just didn't hit me right. Funny, too, he did remind me of a weasel.

I made my way toward the group. Fritz noticed me first and began waving me over, frantically. He, like many before him, assumed I have some influence with my mother. The man should know better. He does know better, which just meant he was really desperate. I could certainly relate to that.

"So," I said, stepping toward Fritz, "what's the charge?" Attempted murder was my first guess, but I went with door number two. "Assault with a deadly weapon?"

Fritz shook his head. "Nah, can't really see that."

"Discharging a firearm in the city limits?" This was my mother's sweetheart, after all.

Again the negative. "If Miz Jennings across the street wants to press charges for disturbing the peace, I'd have to do that, but she don't. She only called in because she was worried about Lucille. Said there was a suspicious looking character lurking around the house and it looked like he was trying to get inside."

I suppose he had been attempting to knock on the door, but I hadn't actually witnessed anything before the gunfire started.

"That's exactly right. He was sneaking around my house, trying to break in," Lucille said firmly and with a straight face. "The little weasel scared me half to death. I thought he was some ugly rapist on the loose."

Said weasel shifted about from foot to foot, but didn't act the least bit offended, or concerned about Lucille's accusations, or more accurately, fabrications.

I glanced at Fritz. "So what are you going to do?"

"We'll figure out what charges ought to be filed once we get back to the station."

"Fine," I said, with not a hint of cheer. I'd known it would come to this. It always comes to this. "Give me a minute to brush my teeth and grab my purse—"

"Oh, no, Jolene, you don't have to go," Fritz said. "I'll take Mister Saide here on over by myself. Probably all we can really do is charge him with trespassing, but we'll haul him in to sort things out. I'll take your statements before we go."

Huh? *He's* the one going to jail? The guy who was dodging bullets behind his now-ruined car is the one in trouble? While I grappled with my rapidly deteriorating mental state, it somehow occurred to me that it was not time for me to be out of bed, much less dealing with law enforcement officers, or bullets, or my mother. "What time is it any way?"

"Seven thirty-five," Damon Saide said helpfully. "I've tried to catch her at home later in the day and she's rarely here. I thought this would be my best opportunity to talk with her." He smiled amicably, with not a hint that he'd just been hiding behind his car in fear for his life and was now headed to jail. "I brought a new contract for her to look at. I am sure she'll be pleased with the new terms."

"Quit talking about me like I'm not standing right here, hearing every word you say, you little twerp," Lucille snapped. "And I'll be pleased when you get yourself off my property. Don't you set foot out here again either or I can't be responsible for what might happen to you."

I didn't see that she was shouldering any responsibility for anything now, but maybe I just wasn't seeing the whole picture. Come to think of it, I didn't want to see any more of the picture at all. "I'm going back to my room, climb back into bed and hope this was all just a really bad dream."

"Oh, no, Jolene, you can't do that. You need to get your shower right now and get dressed. We've got to be at the rally by nine."

Chapter Six

No, there had been no previous warning about "the rally" and no, I didn't know what the rally was even for, although an anti-park demonstration was a fairly good guess.

Lucille hadn't done much explaining either, only order-giving. I'll spare you the "are you going to wear 'that'," and the "put on some makeup" scenes, but the battle lines were clearly drawn. I wore the shorts and tee shirt anyway. Again she insisted we take her car. She also insisted that I drive so she could concentrate on "other things." Probably what hell she could inflict on me next and the series of lies she could tell about it. Not that I was jaded or cynical at this point.

She was still deep in thought as I pulled her Buick off the highway onto Turkey Ranch Road and drove a couple miles down the blacktop.

The sides of the right-of-way had been recently mowed and the smell of fresh cut grass filtered in through the air conditioner. I could see a group of vehicles ahead and drove toward them. About thirty people and two news van trucks with cameras rolling were clustered at the entrance to the Little Ranch. Rock pillars supporting a big iron archway with "Little Ranch" welded into the top of the frame made a photogenic backdrop.

"We're late, Jolene, and you know how I hate to be late," Lucille said in a frantic, maybe even panicked, huff. "I just cannot stand to be late, and if we're not fifteen minutes early, we are late!"

The obligatory "it's your fault" was plainly inferred and did not need to be stated aloud. My stomach didn't knot up with childhood angst as I have matured past all that, but I did help myself to two Tums from Mother's bottle in the seat just to be on the safe side.

The green digital numbers on the dash glowed eight-fifty. "We aren't late, Mother, we're actually about ten minutes early."

"Well, obviously we're not early enough! We should have been here by eight thirty at the latest. Oh, my Lord!" Lucille gasped and pointed through the gate and up the hill.

The topography in these parts is relatively flat to really flat, but in this one place, there happened to be a plateau-like spot that jutted up above the surrounding prairie. Naturally, the house was built on it. There were even real trees up there around the house and it had the only view, so to speak, for miles. It was a picturesque setting even from here, except for all the police cars with flashing lights.

"What on earth is going on here?" Lucille said, still not sure what she had been late for.

The Buick was still rolling to a stop as she vaulted out and raced into the middle of the crowd.

I found a place to park without blocking the road then made my way back to where my mother had jumped out. It didn't take but a few seconds—and the guiding light of a TV camera—to locate Lucille Jackson. She was in the middle of an interview with a local news personality. I'm not sure the guy behind the mike understood what was happening to him, but I sure did. My mother was appearing to be a cooperative witness when, in fact, she was actually grilling the reporter for what he knew.

It wasn't pretty and I'm sorry that I had to bear witness to it, but I did find out what was going on.

Bob Little was missing.

Apparently one of the out of town activists had gone up to talk to him earlier this morning to explain about the rally, ask permission, get his side of the story, that sort of thing, and Little Bob was nowhere to be found. There were, however, definite signs of foul play. Exactly what signs, no one knew, but they were indeed definite, and foul, or so went the rumor.

Dismissing the reporter, Mother pulled a purple umbrella from her infamous purse and popped it open for some purple shade. She then dug out her glittery gold glasses case and pulled out oversized shades, which were darned close to the color of the umbrella as well as the big purple hoops clipped to her earlobes. Properly outfitted and color-coordinated, she made her way through the growing crowd, trawling for more information. I kept a discreet distance behind her, wishing for my own shade-on-a-stick, purple or otherwise, since it was already hot enough to bake biscuits.

After a half hour or so, Mother gave up her crusade and headed back toward the car, something I'd wanted to do from the beginning.

I fished in my pocket for the keys and when I looked up, a flash of reflective light on the road from the house caught my eye. "What's that?"

Mother spun around and surveyed the long driveway. "Why, it looks like a car!"

While I mentally berated myself for my keen vision and big mouth, Mother high-tailed it back through the crowd to the iron gate and planted herself front and center on the right side so she'd be next to the driver's window as the car came through. I reluctantly followed.

As the vehicle got closer, there was no doubt it was the sheriff's vehicle and Jerry was behind the wheel. We exchanged glances, but there was no opportunity for much else as media people swarmed the truck.

Butting aside seasoned news reporters, Lucille grabbed on to the truck's door. "Now, Jerry Don Parker, I need to have a word with you. I want to know just exactly what's going on around here. What makes you think something's happened to Bob?" Lucille leaned closer to the car window. "And who's that in there with you? Is that a witness in there with you? Is she the one that saw the foul play? "

Lights flashed and reporters shoved microphones toward the open sheriff's car, the swarm trying to nudge Lucille aside. Mother didn't budge and Jerry didn't respond to any of their questions immediately. The gritty glare he sent in my direction, however, spoke volumes as he has been down this road with Lucille before. When he still said nothing, I figured I should get a look at his passenger and foul play witness for future reference. About a year ago I would have assumed that none of this was my concern and I would have kept my nose out of it. I am much wiser now.

Engaging my journalistic objectivity, I jostled myself away from a pushy cameraman who was filming a reporter giving the short version. I finally heard what she was saying, "Local businessman and rancher Robert John Little is believed to be missing. The Little Ranch is the site of a proposed private camping park that has drawn protests from some local residents. The Bowman County sheriff's office has been at the home investigating." The well-dressed woman turned around and shoved the microphone toward the vehicle where Jerry sat. "Can you tell us what you found, Sheriff?"

I leaned around Mother to get a better look at Jerry.

I blinked, frowned and then looked again.

My eyes nearly popped out of my head.

A barely-out-of-her-teens girl with auburn hair peeked out from beneath a floppy straw hat. She was clearly trying to avoid the cameras, but I still saw her put her finger to her lips in a universal signal to keep my mouth shut.

I am very certain that I did not keep my mouth shut. In fact, I'm pretty sure it was flopping open and shut like a carp sucking reeds. She didn't need to worry about me saying anything though. I couldn't. In fact, I could barely gasp.

Jerry Don Parker mumbled something to the reporters that amounted to "no comment," then promptly sped away.

With *my daughter* in the passenger seat.

Chapter
Seven

"**N**ow, Jolene, don't you be getting all upset," Lucille said, racing along behind me. "Remember what I told you yesterday at the cemetery, about people doing things and needing to hear their explanations before you go jumping to conclusions. You remember that?"

Oh, I remembered. I'd also just had a refresher in what it feels like to be gutted like a fish too. I was remembering that really well at the moment and I didn't like it. "I suggest you start explaining," I said, hurrying toward the car. She didn't respond immediately, but I knew she was still right behind me. "You'd better start talking, and fast."

"Now, Jolene," Lucille hollered, sprinting along quite deftly behind me. "It's not what you're thinking."

"You have no idea what I'm thinking," I said, pulling the car keys out of my pocket as I marched toward the car.

"Well, with that imagination of yours, and your insecurities and such, well, I suppose you might be thinking there's something untoward going on with Sarah and Jerry Don, which of course there isn't, it is strictly business."

I shot her a glare and kept walking. "And exactly what business would that be and how would you know about it?"

"Well, I guess I don't exactly know."

Oh, she knew. My hands were shaking, but I pointed the clicker at the Buick then opened the car door and hopped in, starting the car in one smooth motion. I gripped the steering wheel with both hands, not only to still the shaking but to keep from doing bodily harm to the lying deceitful woman climbing into the car next to me.

Mother had managed to decompress her umbrella during the sprint and she closed the door and buckled up in record time. She was huffing and puffing a little, probably more out of fear than physical exertion. She was also probably using it to get a little sympathy in hopes it would buy her some time to make up more lies. It wouldn't.

There was really only one thing to do, go after them. I knew if I headed south on Turkey Ranch Road, I'd hit the main highway, but I also knew there was a short cut to the county seat and jail. "What's the quickest way to Bowman City from here?"

Lucille fidgeted in her seat, and from the corner of my eye I thought I could see beads of sweat on her face. It was not from the heat or the hurrying to the car either. I had no idea what the woman had done, or why she needed Sarah here to help her do it, but I would. Oh, but I would. "Which way?" I repeated.

"Well, you can take this on out to the cutoff. It runs into the main highway." She reached up and fiddled with her hair. "I suppose a drive to Bowman City is probably just as good a thing to do as any other, although we were just there yesterday."

If my eyes could have indeed nailed her to the wall, they would have, or at least to the Buick's plush velour seat. "Since my daughter is with the Bowman County Sheriff and that's where his office is, it seems like that would be the place to go. So either you don't want me to go there or you know something I don't. Let's hear it," I said through gritted teeth. Now."

"Well, you don't have to be so hateful about it. Just look at you, you've gotten yourself worked up into such a state, why you're acting like you did back in high school when you got so jealous over that Rhonda girl." She shook her head and tsk-tsked. "Like I said, I'm sure there's a very good explanation for why Sarah was in the truck with Jerry Don."

I was quite sure there wasn't. But my concern was far different than she implied.

There's no point pretending that some fearful thoughts hadn't shot through my brain. My daughter was beautiful, intelligent, charming and young, and I had plenty of experience with men who couldn't be trusted around such things, my ex-husband's adulterous cavorting with a twenty-something twit being a fine and appropriate example. It had shaken my self confidence for a while, but eventually I realized that Danny, like water, had simply been seeking his own level. I'd sworn I'd never get myself entangled with another immature, self-absorbed, emotionally unavailable man. But, clearly having not learned my lesson, I immediately did. It was a brutal ride; an emotional roller coaster with highs like I could have never imagined and lows that nearly buried me. The man pushed every fear button I had then slammed me for feeling insecure about it. Yes, I needed professional help for a couple of months, but I managed to re-grow a spine and got out of the relationship. I avoided dating for a long time after that, fumbled through a few dates here and there, and pretty much decided to give up on the whole idea of having a mate. Then, of course, my mother became insane, and one thing led to another and I found myself re-smitten with Jerry Don Parker. Now the question became, did I really trust him.

During my indulgent trip down memory lane, Lucille had been babbling nonstop. Luckily, I've mastered the technique of half-listening to her, which worked out pretty well since less than half of what she says has a point to it and the rest is lies, I don't really miss much.

Her tale about Sarah coming down from Boulder with some of her ecology class friends for a "field trip" was fairly believable—unless you knew that Lucille had instigated the whole thing and that there was no actual ecology class, at least not one I'd paid for. The fact that she was in town "under cover" was right up there with plausible since being Lucille's granddaughter—or my daughter—she was guaranteed guilt by association if she played that straight. So, yes, being an out-of-state enviro-nut gave her a clean slate—sort of. Why that was important was anything but clear, however. And exactly none of it explained one damn thing about why she was leaving a crime scene with the sheriff.

Realizing my hands had gone numb from gripping the steering wheel so tightly, I stretched out my fingers to relieve any sliver of tension I could. It didn't help that much. "I'm going to ask you one more time. Why is Sarah here and where is she?" She didn't answer or try to change the subject so I picked up my phone. "Fine. I probably should call Jerry anyway and let him know—"

"No!" Lucille shrieked.

I put the phone back down. "That's right. It would be a little awkward, now wouldn't it?"

Lucille squirmed in her seat. "Yes, well, it might be best if we didn't alert him to Sarah's true identity just yet."

"And why might that be?" I asked, knowing full well she wouldn't answer. "You of all people should know this is not some spy movie, this is reality; people get shot." My arm started twitching its own reminder. "Dammit, that's my daughter you're using to play your games. You might not care that you've put her in danger, but I sure do." Yes, I said it on purpose. I wanted her to feel bad and guilty. "Now you tell me what's going on."

"How dare you! I would never put my granddaughter in danger, and I can't believe you'd suggest such a thing. Sarah's just fine." She tipped her nose up even higher. "Besides, she's a grown woman and she doesn't need you checking up on her."

"Oh, really?" I picked up the phone again. "You are unbelievable."

"All right, Jolene," she said, grumbling. "I suppose if you're going to be pushy about it, we might run by the motel and see if she's there. I don't expect she is, but we could go there if you just have to go checking up on her like she's a three-year-old."

Trying to stir up an argument to distract me wasn't going to work this time. "So, where is this motel we might just run by?"

She huffed and pouted. "It's out off the expressway."

That cleared up nothing. Several US highways converge in Redwater Falls, and besides that, I am not up on the local jargon of what "the expressway" actually means. "How about you tell me which highway and the name of the motel; those seem like things that would be real helpful about now.""

"You don't have to be so snippy."

I turned and glared, not even blinking. "It is beyond my comprehension that you have the nerve to sit there and say these things to me after what all you've done, it really is."

She clamped her lips shut, wiggled her jaw around for a few seconds then finally said, "It's the New Falls Motel out near the falls. You can take the Seymour Highway into town. You know how to do that, don't you?"

No, I really didn't. As ridiculous as it may sound, I can navigate Denver with my eyes closed, but I still get lost in Redwater Falls, Texas. In my defense, there's little rhyme or reason to the layout of the town that I've ever identified. Of course, it is also possible that I might have a mental block or ten about the place. "You just tell me where to turn and maybe I'll let you live."

"Now there is just no call to talk to me like that."

I turned toward her very slowly and stared into her lying eyes.

"Well, all right, for goodness sakes, you don't have to give me the evil eye. Just make a U turn and head back to the highway. Take a right when you get there and go all the way into town until you get to the new highway."

I took a deep breath and let it out very slowly then put the car in gear and swung around as directed. Once we were on the main road to town, I felt myself calm down just a little. After a few more miles I felt in enough control to ask some additional pertinent questions. "Here is the way this is going to go. I am going to ask a simple question and you are going to give me a simple answer. Yes?"

She nodded, but the muscle in her jaw pulsed with tension.

"When did Sarah get here?"

"Sunday."

"Hmmm." That was interesting. Jerry had called on Monday because he'd arrested Lucille for shooting the county maintenance truck. There had been people outside his window with picket signs about stopping the park and saving the lizards. A coincidence or a one-two punch for attracting attention? "Lucky for you the county was mowing the grass that morning."

She pinched her lips together, her nostrils flaring at the restraint it was taking not to speak.

"It was clever, I'll give you that," I said, throwing out a little bait. "You and the other two Musketeers had yourselves a private event out on Turkey Ranch Road Monday morning and made sure you got arrested so you could be martyrs for the rally at the courthouse that afternoon. Pretty creative. Have anything to say about that?"

Lucille crossed her arms again, huffed and puffed and turned her face toward the window. "I didn't hear a question."

Ah, technicalities. "Okay, just out of curiosity, what were you going to do if there hadn't been a truck to shoot?"

She snapped her head around, eyed me for a few seconds, and then unclamped her lips. "Well, Miz Smarty Pants, if you must know, having the county out there mowing the grass was just fate. It wouldn't have mattered one whit if there hadn't been a truck there. We were going to paint our car windows with 'Save Our Homes' and 'Stop the Park' and such in real big red letters. They make red shoe polish now, you know, not just white and black, although we did plan to outline in white too so the letters would show up real good. We were going to park our cars in a line across the highway so someone would call the cops, and then, of course, the news people would show up and take pictures of our cars with the writing on the windows. It was a good plan. It was just easier to shoot the truck."

"Well, of course, anyone could see that."

She nodded in agreement then eyed me. "I don't care what you think, it worked out fine."

Indeed it had. She'd accomplished her goal of getting arrested without all of the effort of window painting. With the SPASI trio hauled off to jail there was a good—and media friendly—reason to rally at the courthouse. But wasn't that a bit extreme, even for my mother? How much of this had the AAC people orchestrated? Was it a combined effort? "Where was Sarah when you were blowing holes in a radiator?"

"She wasn't with us, if that's what you're asking. I didn't want her getting arrested. That wouldn't have helped anything. She did come to the jail later though to comfort me."

That wasn't what I was asking since I already knew there were only the three senior citizens arrested. "Fine, don't answer the question. Sarah will tell me."

A flash of panic swept across her face and she began to fidget in the seat. "Now, there's no need in upsetting Sarah with any of this."

Noticing semi-familiar territory, I figured I needed a little guidance from my reluctant navigator. "Don't I need to turn left at the next light?"

"Well, I suppose you can if you want to."

"Yes or no?"

"Yes," she grumbled.

I moved into the far left lane of the one-way street, made the turn and then merged onto the expressway. "You can string this out for a little while more if you want to, but I'll be getting some straight answers very soon from Jerry and Sarah, and then we'll just see how this all works out for you."

I would like to say that my vague threats had her shaking in her seat ready to confess everything. I can't, but I'd like to. In fact, I wondered if she'd even heard me since she had twisted herself halfway around in the seat to stare out the passenger side window. Apparently the view of the Hilton Hotel building was captivating. "You want me to pull in?"

She snapped back around. "I know what the place looks like and so do you. Besides, it's easier if you go on up to the second exit and come back on the service road on the other side," she volunteered, suddenly becoming helpful and chatty. "The third exit up is the one that takes you to the falls, but you know that. I suppose you know that they have the pumps all working now. They've added more bushes and flowers and such up around the falls and the walkways too. Oh, and more lights. The lights show it all up so nice at night, but it's still real pretty in the daytime. After all that unfortunate business there last time, it would be good for you to go see it looking nice and serene now that it's all fixed up."

By fixed up she meant that the fire truck hoses were no longer needed to make the falls and that there were hopefully no more bodies I sighed and turned at the appropriate light, made my way west over the interstate and began looking for the motel. This area of town is a virtual forest of motels, gas and restaurant signs, and, quite frankly, it just feels creepy. I drove past four big chain hotels and/or motels, two gas stations and a Waffle House. Desperation would be the only thing that would entice me to stop at any of them. Seeing the sign for the New Falls Motel, and then glimpsing the building itself, I was pretty sure that even desperation wouldn't lure me in.

The closer we got, the more I started wondering exactly what I was going to say to and do with my newly-delinquent daughter. This was new territory for me. Even in her teen years, Sarah had never caused me any trouble to speak of. She just wasn't like that. Or hadn't been. Now that Lucille was involved, there was no telling what I was dealing with. "If this little adventure of yours causes her problems at school, you're going to be the one paying for her to retake the classes she blew because she was down here getting into trouble with you."

"She's not in trouble, Jolene," Lucille said, straightening herself up in the seat. "Besides, it's spring break."

"Last month."

"Well, you may be right, we talked about several options." Lucille laced her fingers together and worked her palms from side to side. "It's still not a problem though because there's the extra credit for community service that she'll get for working on this for the community and the horny toads and such."

"Oh, for godsake, she's not in junior high. Besides, the girl makes straight A's. At least she did until she went AWOL and missed classes this week."

"I told you, it's all taken care of," Lucille hissed. "Besides, Sarah's not a girl anymore and she can decide what she can manage and still get her grades."

"Why, you're absolutely right, and I'm sure you'll feel exactly the same way when you're the one paying her tuition."

Lucille scowled. "She's a very capable young woman and you're making a big deal over nothing. I'm telling you, there's no problem at school. And besides, she leaves tomorrow anyway."

"Well that's not soon enough," I snapped, wondering about that revelation and how it had factored in to their whole plan, whatever that might have been. "What time?"

"You can't change her ticket, if that's what you're thinking. It's one of those online bid tickets and it can't be changed. I ordered it from Agnes' computer. We got her an 'e-ticket.' Just the niftiest thing. Really no ticket at all and we had the best time bidding for it. One hundred and forty-nine dollars round trip. Isn't that something? Got her a shuttle ride too so she could just hop off the plane and be up here from Dallas in no time."

Of all the thoughts racing through my brain at the moment, the one that thundered the loudest was that my mother—who I didn't think knew a computer from a toaster—had gotten a better deal online than I had. *And* she'd arranged a shuttle and hotel room and who knew what else. This from a woman who says she doesn't know how to put gas in her own car. It was truly mind-boggling. So much so that we were in front of the motel before I realized it.

The first thing that alerted me to our arrival was the sparkling waterfall on the sign. The second was the flashing blue and red lights from the police cruisers in the parking lot. My heart lodged firmly in my throat. I wanted to believe that whatever was going on had nothing to do with Sarah, but I knew better.

The fact that Lucille was clutching the dash and pressing her nose against the windshield was a pretty good confirmation as well. Still, a shred of logic managed to keep pure panic at bay. Sarah had been with Jerry a half hour ago, and it was unlikely that he would have dropped her off, and then seconds later a herd of cops showed up. Possible, but not likely. I whipped into the lot and pulled up to the closest police cruiser. An officer was at my window before I had fully stopped.

"The parking lot is closed, ma'am."

"Sheriff Parker of Bowman County is a friend of mine," I said, hearing a hint of panic in my own voice. "He was supposed to be heading this way with my daughter, who has a room here. Did they get here? Do you know where they went? I need to know that she's okay."

"This is Redwater Falls jurisdiction, ma'am. Sheriff Parker wouldn't be here. You'll need to move along," he said, acknowledging the first dozen words I'd said and ignoring the rest.

Beside me, Lucille pointed, her finger shaking, the acrylic nail clattering against the windshield. "Oh, my Lord, that's the room! They're going in there!"

The officer leaned closer to the window and narrowed his eyes. "What did you say?"

Lucille snapped around, pointing and gasping. "I rented that room! That's room one twelve. That's where the trouble is, isn't it? I see the door open. Oh, my Lord. You tell me what's going on, right now!"

The officer paused for a second, looked us over again, scowling, and then straightened to stand beside the car. "Stay put," he said gruffly, punching the radio clipped to his collar.

He turned away as he spoke, but I heard enough snippets to figure out that he was asking what he should do.

I was wondering the same thing. There were no happy reasons that the police department had six cruisers in the parking lot of the motel with the door to my daughter's room open. "Mother, call Jerry. Now."

When the officer turned back, I leaned out the window and said, "My daughter was with Sheriff Parker and they should have been here about fifteen or twenty minutes ago, maybe less. My mother's trying to call him right now, but I need to know that my daughter is all right. Please."

The officer glanced at his watch. "We've been on this call about forty minutes and the parking lot's been closed." He took out a pad and pen. "What does your daughter look like?"

"She's about five-eight, medium brown hair—"

"She looks just like Jolene there," Lucille said, interrupting and pointing to me. "Only younger. And taller. Have you seen her? Was she here?" She didn't give the officer time to answer, just kept babbling. "Jerry's not answering his phone and we need to talk to somebody about this. What about that nice young detective friend of yours?" she said to me then directed her commentary back to the officer. "He's a real cute blond-headed boy. Richard, wasn't it?"

"Rick. Detective Rick Rankin," I said.

"Has he been here?" Lucille asked, panic beginning to seep into her voice as well. "Can we talk to him? We really need to talk to him. Richard will know what to do about all this. Do you know how to get in touch with him?"

Asking for Rick apparently caught the officer off guard because he glared at me for several long seconds then leaned around and looked at Lucille the same way. Then, his narrow annoyed eyes widened in awe, but not admiration. Surprise would be a nice description. "Well, I'll be damned," he said, quite unprofessionally. He recovered enough to tip his hat to Mother, "Miz Jackson." And then to me, with a highly in appropriate snicker, "Just get in from Colorado?"

Rather than explore the obvious—that my mother and I were well known throughout the law enforcement community—I focused on the important. "What is going on here and how does it involve my daughter?"

The officer just stood there, shaking his head. "Rick's gonna be real sorry he missed this. He took over as chief in Tyler a couple of months ago. We'll have to call and tell him the game's over. Man, wish I could remember who had this week in the pool. I lost out back in March, but we had bets down through June. I think Cutter has this week, no, maybe he lost out last week."

"Young man," Lucille bellowed. "I do not know what you're rambling on about but you had better be telling me what's happened here right now or you'll wish you had."

"Ditto," I said, only I understood exactly what the rambling had been about. The Redwater Falls police officers had placed bets on when I, and apparently my mother, would show up again, specifically at the scene of a crime. Made me wonder a lot of things, but the only thing worth wondering aloud was whether it could be any kind of crime scene or just one involving a homicide. "Officer," I said as calmly as possible. "Exactly what kind of crime are you investigating in my daughter's room?"

No sooner had the words left my mouth than a white Suburban with an official seal on the door pulled into the lot to answer my question.

The county medical examiner had just arrived.

Chapter Eight

Being questioned by, and providing statements to, law enforcement officials is tedious business, particularly when you don't have a clue what is or has been going on. Lucille, on the other hand, knew plenty but was being deliberately obtuse as usual. This skill does come in handy for wearing down the interrogator, however, so by the time they started quizzing me, they weren't even sure why they wanted to or what was even worth asking. Lucille has that effect on people. Even professionals.

We did eventually get confirmation that Sarah was all right and still in the company of Sheriff Parker. That lifted a great weight from my shoulders, but there were a few knots left in my stomach. After talking to the police officers, I had little in the way of facts to work with, but the questions they asked me had sent up fields of red flags. They'd asked about drugs, medications, plastic tubing, glass jars and a metal detector. I kept asking them if they were sure they had the right room, even though Lucille had specifically pointed it out. And what in the hell did all that stuff have to do with anything, especially my daughter? Nothing good that I could think of, and it seemed like a pretty good reason to panic.

"Jolene," Lucille said, interrupting my launch sequence to hysteria. "Officer Pete says we can leave now."

I shook my head a bit and ran my fingers through my hair, reconnecting to reality, such as it was. "Did you hear what he said?"

"Yes, Jolene, I did. Now, let's go."

"Drugs, Mother. Tubing and jars and other strange things. In Sarah's room."

"Yes, Jolene, I heard him and I heard you. But we're done here. We need to leave."

I guess I was still standing there kind of stunned, but when I heard her say "do you want me to drive?" I snapped right out of it. "Fine. Let's go. But you will be talking."

When we got back into the Buick, Lucille handed me her cell phone. "It's all ready to go. Just punch the talk button and it'll dial Jerry Don's number again. Maybe he'll answer this time. We need to find out what's really going on."

Yes, we certainly did. "Starting with where my daughter is and has been seems a pretty high priority."

"Well, at least we know she's safe because she's with Jerry Don." She said the right words, but there was no mistaking the worry in her voice. She waved at the phone in my hand. "Hurry up. Call him."

I dialed the phone as directed even though I knew it wasn't likely that Jerry could talk to me at the moment. However, as the ringing clicked over to voicemail, I was glad I'd called because just hearing his recorded voice made me feel a little better. "Jerry, it's Jolene. Mother and I are at the New Falls Motel. I think there's been—"

Lucille snatched the phone out of my hands. "You call back real soon, Jerry Don."

I glared once again at my mother. "Nice, Mother, real nice."

"No need in getting all mushy. It's my phone number that comes up."

"What did you do that for?"

"There's no point in leaving some long message. The only thing we care about is that Sarah is okay, and we'll find that out when he calls back."

I started the car and pulled out of the parking lot, heading back to Kickapoo. "Yes, we will, and then he's going to know all about your charade. What he does with you because of it, is yours to worry about."

Lucille huffed and picked up the phone, put it back in her purse then dug out a tube of lipstick. She flipped open the visor mirror and expertly painted her lips with an ample coat of a purplish pink. After blotting with a tissue, she said, "I do not know what everybody sees in that actress who has the big lips, like they're something special, sexy even. And those tattoos, she's got. Well, why in the world would anybody want to do that to themselves? Women especially. You can kind of overlook it in men because they really don't have any better sense, but I just really thought women were smarter than to do that."

No, I did not respond. Even when she isn't trying to distract me from her lies and schemes, these kinds of conversations with Lucille are painful. Actually, all kinds of conversations with Lucille are painful.

"I don't know what it is with women and tattoos these days. Even young girls are sneaking off and getting them. Agnes' granddaughter Jennifer, you remember her mother Darlene, she was a few years younger than you in school. Well, anyway, the girl had a big ol' butterfly needled into her ankle. I thought Agnes was just going to die. And did you know that when Agnes said something to her about it, Darlene said she'd let her do it, and worse still, Darlene and her daughter had gotten holes punched in their navels at the same time. Darlene! At her age, doing something like that. Can you imagine?"

Actually, I could. Getting your belly button pierced after a divorce was a pretty darned common way of reminding yourself you weren't dead. I wouldn't be enlightening the Queen of Judgment about why I understood, however. "It is just pitiful what this world has come to," I said in the best Lucille imitation I could muster. "Pitiful."

She eyed me suspiciously, wondering if I was being sarcastic, which I was. "I am probably the only woman around who hasn't pierced her ears for the sake of beauty," she said, jiggling her long dangly clip-ons. "But I suppose if people want to mutilate their bodies, that's their business. Just like the man back there in the motel room. My Lord, from the way they were talking he must have been decorated up like one of those natives in the National Geographic."

I snapped my head around toward my mother. "What?"

"The National Geogra—"

"Mother…"

"Well, I was feeling a little overheated and confused after talking to Officer Pete, so while he was interrogating you I went to look for a shady place to sit down. There was hardly any place at all that wasn't just out in the blazing sun, and there was no good place to sit at all, so I kept moving around until I finally got up under the porch, which is actually the sidewalk for the second floor. It was shade though, so I just leaned up against the side of the building and rested a bit, fanning myself as best I could. I'd hardly gotten my breath when some old grouchy woman came out shooed me off. I tried to explain that I was just resting, trying to avoid a heat stroke while I waited for you. I tried to move to suit her, but she sure didn't seem to want me anywhere near that open door."

I sighed. "Just tell me what you heard."

"There was a dead man in the room. They were guessing at how he might have died, but they couldn't tell right off."

I took in this information with a sense of surreal detachment. The medical examiner's arrival on the scene had indicated a corpse, but somehow the implications of all that hadn't really sunk in. That seemed to be one of the coping strategies I'd acquired for dealing with things around here. I just took in the facts, no matter how incredulous, ludicrous or unbelievable they might be, and dealt with what I had to in the moment. So, in the current moment, rather than speculate on why Sarah's room was the crime scene, I speculated on the cause of death of the man in the room. Having a heart attack while breaking and entering seemed kind of a stretch as did just happening to overdose on drugs while busy committing a crime, which seemed the angle the police were pursing according to what they had quizzed me about. "So, what about the drugs and jars and tubing? Did you hear anything about that?"

"Lots of prescription bottles," Lucille said. "I heard that much." She clasped her hands in her lap and actually looked a little worried. "And I heard them talking about him being real skinny. Said he'd probably looked dead before he died. He had a pony tail and tattoos all over."

As Lucille herself had pointed out, tattoos were common these days, however, ponytails were not, except with old hippie guys, some bikers and mullet holdouts. Combine those details with being skinny and dead, and it kind of pointed to a crackhead or a meth addict. "Did you hear anything else?"

She shook her head. "No, but I think it might have been Tiger."

"Tiger?" Now that she mentioned it, skinny guys with tattoos and ponytails also generally described the two guys of AAC. But what would a sixty-ish possible cult leader and probable chicken feed bomber be doing in Sarah's room—with bottles of prescription medications? Frankly, a random break-in would be easier to believe—and deal with. I smelled a rat. Several of them even. "So, Mother, if it was really Tiger, why would *your* protest partner be in the room *you* rented for your granddaughter? With drugs and jars and tubing?"

Lucille's eyes darted to me then back to the landscape. She sensed a trap, but she was nowhere near ready to chew off her leg to get out of it, i.e. telling the truth. "Well, I don't know that I could rightly say. And I don't know for certain it was him, I was just speculating. I don't know what all is going on here anymore than you do. I was just trying to help by getting all the information that I could, and now here you are making me feel like I'm on trial or something."

You know, she's good. Somehow her scheming and lying had just become my fault, and she was being wrongfully picked on when she had just been doing her best to help. Amazing. It also was dawning on me that Lucille was not nearly as upset about this as one would expect a concerned and appropriately guilt-ridden grandmother to be. "In case you hadn't noticed, Mother, a man was apparently murdered in your granddaughter's motel room while, at the same time, coincidentally, she was being hauled away from a different crime scene by the sheriff. Since neither of those situations could have occurred without your efforts and machinations, it seems to me you ought to be feeling a little remorse about now."

Her jaw dropped open in indignation.

I held up my hand. "Do not bother telling me how awful I'm being to you and how none of this is your fault. In fact, unless you're ready to confess, do not say anything at all right now."

I needed time to think. Obviously, Lucille was lying. I believed that she had rented the room, maybe even for Sarah at first, but for whatever reason Tiger had been staying there. Which meant, Sarah hadn't. And that brought up a whole new line of questions, such as where *had* she been staying and why. Still, if Jerry had indeed taken Sarah to the motel, he would know about the dead guy. Therefore, the next obvious law enforcement thing to do would be to take her for official questioning on that incident, which meant that he would have gone to the nearby police station in Redwater. I had to keep reminding myself that Jerry didn't know Sarah was my daughter and wouldn't be doing anything that wasn't by the book. But if that were true, what official business had prompted him to take her to the motel in the first place? It was just one more thing that didn't make sense. I slowed down, waited for a break in traffic and made a U-turn. "I'm headed to the police station. You have about five minutes to convince me why I shouldn't haul you in to tell your stories to somebody there."

"Well, it wouldn't do a darned bit of good, Miz Smarty Pants, because there is nothing to tell."

"There's plenty to tell, not the least of which is why a room rented by you, supposedly for your granddaughter, has a dead man in it. And if she wasn't staying in it, where was she and why the intrigue? If, by some miracle you answered those questions, we could move on to why Sarah was at the Little Ranch this morning."

"Well, now there's no call to get all snippy about it. It's all very easy to explain." She cut her eyes to me but kept talking, fast. "I did rent the room, as I believe I said, but I just let Sarah handle things how she thought best. I specifically told her not to tell me in case I was questioned about anything since it was none of anybody's business what she did or didn't do."

She meant me, of course. "So what was Tiger doing there?"

"I suppose Sarah felt sorry for him. I think the others may be staying close by."

So, why, I wondered, did she bring me here? No sooner had my brain asked the question than I had my answer. Because she knew Sarah wouldn't be here and it would satisfy me and she could keep her secrets, whatever they were, secret. "Okay, now that you've given me a grand non-answer about all that, why don't you try your hand at why Sarah was at Bob Little's place?"

"See, see how you're being, that's why I can't tell you things. You just go berserk and have one of your fits and turn on me like a skunk with rabies."

I gripped the steering wheel with both hands and growled, "Out with it."

She huffed and twisted her mouth this way and that then said, "Oh, all right, it was just a quick visit, that's all. Merline and Agnes were going to talk to Bob before the protest and Sarah went along with them. Bob really took to Sarah; they just hit it off first thing so it seemed like a good idea for her to go up there too, him being at his wits end over all the trouble. Those park people had him to the point he was afraid not to sell. We just needed to know if anything had changed before the rally. If things had gone like they were supposed to, Sarah would have been long gone before we got there, especially since you made us late."

Right. Not taking that bait. "So, the three of them went up to talk to Bob Little but he wasn't there. Something was wrong at the house—the proverbial signs of foul play—so they called the sheriff. Is that it?"

"Well, I guess so, Jolene. Nobody called and gave me the details. You heard the same things I did standing outside the gate there, but, yes, I'd suppose that was what happened."

"And yet no one but my daughter came down the hill with the sheriff. I find that odd, don't you? Were Merline and Agnes still up there? Have they called to tell you anything?"

"I have not talked to either one of them." She studied her fingernails. "I am sure they'll call when they can."

"Okay, Mother, here's what we're going to do. I'm heading to the police station to see if Jerry's truck is there. Even if it isn't, I'm dropping you off to go inside and see if Sarah is there. He could have left her with a detective."

"Seems like a waste of time to me, but I suppose we can do that if you insist."

"I do."

It took less than ten minutes to drive to the police department, circle the place three times and determine that Jerry wasn't there and neither was a decent parking place. I stopped in a loading zone while Lucille ran inside to ask about Sarah.

"Well," she said, climbing back in the car. "That was certainly pointless. I waited and waited at the front desk while they called everybody under the sun, including the janitor, to finally decide that Sarah wasn't there. Then," she hissed, "they had the nerve to tell me to go to Bowman County if I had business with the sheriff. That's what our tax dollars pay for." She shook her head and clucked her tongue. "Protect and serve, my hind foot."

"You told them your name, didn't you?"

"Well, yes, they made me." Her mouth dropped open and she sucked in an indignant breath. "You don't think they were lying to me because of their stupid game, do you?"

Harassing her, yes, lying no. I shook my head. "No, and you should probably be grateful they didn't hold you for questioning, considering. But, they do have a point. I bet there's somebody in Bowman City who'll tell us where the sheriff is, and if Sarah is with him."

Lucille thought about that for a moment. She was still keeping up a good front, but she'd lost some of her confidence that all was right with the world and that her orchestrated charade was still intact. "I suppose I could call Fritz, if you want me to, and ask him."

I'd already thought of that myself, and I was a little surprised at her volunteering to call. Even so, I figured a personal visit had a better chance of success. "Nah, let's surprise them."

"If any of those Harpers know anything, I'll get it out of them," Lucille said confidently. "They know better than to try to lie to me."

I took a left and headed toward the new overpass that would connect us to the old Bowman City highway. After we were headed out of town, I set the cruise and said, "Now then, why don't you tell me the rest of the story. Actually, just start from the very beginning. The very beginning. How did you find out there was a park being built in the first place?"

Lucille reached down for her purse again, unzipped it and fiddled around for a few seconds then pulled out a pink tissue. She opened her palm and I realized she'd nabbed the tube of lipstick again. She flipped open the mirror and drew on another layer of color she didn't need. She dabbed the tissue then rolled her lips together again. "There was a story in the paper. I guess that was how I first found out about it, although Demon Seed showed up about the same time, so I'm not really sure. That was all bad enough, but what really stirred things up was those hippies showing up."

"Tiger and Company."

"Yes," she said, settling back in her seat. "I got a little curious. I mean, they just sort of appeared out of the blue, the bunch of them loaded up in two vans with camper trailers, which was kind of odd since that was the very thing we were trying to stop. Of course, having one at the rally was kind of handy." She paused briefly to breathe, or maybe remind herself what she didn't want to tell. "Anyway, they were saying they were here to stop the park, which was certainly what I wanted to do, as did anybody with a lick of sense, so I talked to them. They took to me right off, but there was just something fishy about the whole deal. So I took it upon myself to see what they were up to. They had Colorado license plates on their vans and said they were from Boulder. Well, with Sarah living in the very same place and all, I called and had her do some checking up on them."

Keep in mind that from where I live, I can be where Sarah lives in Boulder almost as quickly as I can be in downtown Denver. And, let's not forget that I am a reporter of sorts. Not that it mattered, of course. She wouldn't have called me if I was on the same block until it was absolutely the last possible option or she was in jail. And even then, she hadn't called me. Jerry had. "Oh, I understand, Mother. Why on earth would you call a professional journalist who does research for a living when you can have a busy college student without a clue handle it? Makes perfect sense to me."

"See there. That hateful attitude is exactly why I didn't ask you to do anything and why I don't tell you things. The entire park would have been built before you quit telling me why I didn't need to know what I wanted to know, and I darned well knew I wanted to know it. Besides that, you'd have probably scared them off before they did me any good at all."

Ah, they might smell fishy, but they were potential worker bees and she wasn't going to take any chances of me messing up her plans with little details like facts. The bullet-induced scar in my shoulder began to twitch again. So did the muscle between my eye and cheekbone. "Do continue."

"Well," she said, oblivious to anything outside her own head, "it turns out that AAC just has a post office box up in Colorado. They have a phone number, but you can only leave a message. They don't answer the phone. Ever. Even the phones they used to call back show up blocked, cell phones too, and they won't give you their numbers. Got real snooty about it with me. Said it was for safety." She harrumphed and crossed her arms. "I didn't think it was very safe for me not being able to get hold of them if we were going to work together. Know-it-alls, all of them. And it doesn't seem to me any of it was very safe for Tiger either, now was it?"

"Apparently not."

I hadn't actually tried to contact any environmental subversives lately, but you wouldn't really expect them to be listed in the phone book or have an office on Main Street. Then again, you never know. These are strange times. "Okay, A-A-C. Your buddy group is called Ack?"

"Now that's just ridiculous. Who in the world would call their group Ack? It's said exactly like it looks, A-A-C. All Animals Count."

Nothing my mother was involved in of late was exactly as it looked. And while I'd originally thought Lucille might have been set up by the AAC, I now wasn't so sure who was using whom. Mother Shrewdness is not dumb, and we have established her talents at manipulation and even blackmail, although she is prickly about such things being pointed out. "So, Sarah didn't find out anything else about them?"

Lucille shook her head. "No, just that they champion causes for animals and somehow they'd heard about the horny toads and the campers, and wanted to be involved."

"I see," I said, although I didn't. I couldn't cite statistics on it, but I had to wonder how many horny toads were even left in the state since the ants from Hell arrived and began their unhindered carnage. I'd guess that the lizards had a way better chance at dodging travel trailers than fire ant swarms. "Okay, clear something up for me here. Is this a private park or one that will be owned by the city or county or other government group?"

Lucille shook her head, looking genuinely confused. "I really don't know, Jolene, I really don't. It seems like they make it sound one way or the other, depending on what they're trying to get away with. I thought the city of Kickapoo was involved somehow for a while, but now I just don't know. None of it makes good sense."

"Neither does Sarah coming down here if she'd already found out all she could in Boulder."

Lucille fiddled with her seat belt then inspected her nails again. "Mostly, we just wanted to visit. It had been way too long since we'd spent any time together at all."

"Uh huh. Which is why you put her in a motel in Redwater Falls. Togetherness. And why she wasn't really staying there and you pretend you don't know where she was staying. More togetherness and visiting opportunities."

"Well, now, that was just what we needed to do under the circumstances. You make it out like there was some big conspiracy plan."

"Because there was. There is. And the sooner you fess up about it the better because this room you so generously provided to her—or somebody—is now a crime scene, remember?"

She frowned for a minute, opened her mouth to defend herself then began to nod enthusiastically. "Well, you know, that's exactly right. I have just had enough of all this myself. And you are right. It was a conspiracy. A conspiracy to steal my house!" She metaphorically jumped up on her high horse, leaping over all the details she didn't want to address. Technically, she just sat up straighter in the seat and wagged her finger. "Did you know what that little weasel Damon Saide said to me when he showed up on my doorstep?"

I presumed she meant the first time, not the time she shot at him. But it could have been both times, or every time, for all I knew.

"The lying little turd told me he was stealing my house for the good of the community and it was my civic duty to let him. Said he could get my house one way or another anyway. You just wouldn't believe the things he was saying, trying to scare me into giving in, treating me like I was senile." Lucille had worked herself up into a good little fit of indignant outrage.

"Thought he could run roughshod right over me and then have me tell him thank you for it." Lucille looked like she could bite the heads off rats and never blink. "Well, I guess he found out otherwise."

To say the least.

She had deftly avoided my question, of course, and I was neither shocked nor dismayed nor even peeved at this point. What I was, however, was seeing things with a different light. Imminent Domain. Thanks to a whole bunch of new—and not well-publicized—laws, it was now easier than ever for the government to take away the rights of private citizens. Actually, they'd already taken plenty, just not many people had noticed. I sure didn't want to be the one to tell her, but these days, pretty much any government entity could indeed take property for whatever reason it deemed to be for the good of the community, even for private development. People were fighting it all around the country, but most folks were oblivious to the issue.

Actually, people were happily oblivious to a lot of significant issues. As long as they could refinance their mortgages, put gas in their cars and keep American Idol coming in on the TV they really didn't care to know the truth about a lot of things, such as UFOs, weather manipulation, injected RFID chips, three spontaneously collapsing buildings in New York City and two more wars for profit. Willful ignorance is the biggest conspiracy of all. But I digress. "Did you ever tell me who this Saide guy worked for? Was it the city?"

"I don't know who put the little twerp up to his dirty work and I do not care. He's an idiot and I threw his stupid little card right back in his stupid little face. He's got to be in cahoots with somebody. He's sure not smart enough to think very big on his own." Lucille glared out the window, tapping her foot as flat land and mesquite trees whizzed past. "For all I know, the little weasel just wanted to steal my house first and then resell it to the park people so he could make himself a big fat profit. Houses like mine are going for big money these days, what with all the Redwater people trying to get into the Kickapoo School District."

I suppose now would be the appropriate time to point out that the "rush" to the land of superior educational opportunities in Kickapoo simply meant that by moving the family to the small town ten or fifteen miles away, their kid could actually get issued a jersey on a football team. In big city Redwater high schools, there were no average white guy slots. It was nothing new. The same thing had been going on when I was a teenager. To be fair, though, there were at least twice as many kids in the latest graduating class than there had been in mine twenty-five years ago. Still, it had not created a wild upward spiral in housing prices. Reality aside, we still had a guy who wanted my mother's house, and was willing to threaten her and dodge bullets to get it. We also had a missing ranch owner who'd apparently been threatened too and was selling his land because of it.

I'd done a few articles on legitimate park development projects and conservation easement purchases several years ago and had a fair knowledge of the major groups funding such things. I didn't know how the new imminent domain rules had changed that process, but middlemen had been used to purchase property for government purposes. If the park project were a city deal, they'd get what they wanted. But why not just take it rather than send a go-between to try to buy it? Getting shot by Lucille was one good reason.

"Something about this has bothered me from the beginning," I said. "Actually a lot of things have. For one, what makes this couple thousand acres of mesquites and old salts flats more special than those on the other side of the highway, or on the other side of that? That one spot isn't the only place where you can stand in hundred-and-twenty-degree heat and watch mesquite thorns grow."

"Your hateful attitude about your home place is just uncalled for. I didn't rear you like that, and it just makes me spitting mad to hear you condemning things around here. I don't see why it's so hard for you to believe that people are just dying to turn my life upside down to suit their own purposes. I suppose you just don't give a hoot if my life gets ruined."

Melodramatics aside, I did understand her distress, and shared it even. But it didn't get me any closer to the why of it all. I'd admit that there were plenty of RV pads plopped in the middle of nowhere with nothing to do except park, plug in, sleep and dump the waste tank. Every space was filled on a lot of them, too, so what did I know? "You are absolutely right, Mother. It's a perfectly wonderful place for an RV Park—flat, easy highway access, and the bluff where the Little house is located adds historic and visual interest. That part is unique and that must be the draw."

"Well, it may very well be, but it doesn't mean I have to go along with it. I do not have to agree to anything I don't want to."

A strange—or maybe not so strange—thought finally made its way to the foreground. I've been around enough to know that cutting a good ol' boy deal at taxpayer expense was not a new thing. Maybe that's all that was going on here. If so, wouldn't Bob Little have to be in on it? None of it explained why they had to have Mother's house too though. Maybe the park was a cover for something and they didn't want Lucille watching what they were doing. Not that great motivation-wise, but a possibility. This was Texas after all. And somebody was out there with equipment and a drill rig for some reason. "I saw the pump jacks were going again behind the fence. Maybe this whole thing really is about oil."

"Those oil wells have never quit pumping since we've lived here," Lucille said. "They're not big producers, just real steady."

"Lucky for Bob Little, I guess. But if that's true, why sell the land for a park and have to give up your steady producers? Does he retain mineral rights? Will the pumps keep pumping with the park there? Why drill for more if you're selling?"

"Well, I don't know about any of that, Jolene. I don't meddle in other people's business. But I do know that Bobby isn't hurting for money. He still has some part in that plastic company over on the north side of Redwater that he started about the time you were born. Some big outfit from Pennsylvania's been trying to buy him out though."

"Hmmm," I said. "Does he still work at it?"

"No, he hired good people to do that long ago. He goes in every now and then, and he studies the books, but he doesn't have to do anything." Lucille turned and stared out the window. "Not like when he started it. He was there day and night then."

"That's never good on a family."

"Didn't have one," she said absently. "His wife had just died."

"Oh."

After a few seconds she turned back around and shook her finger at me. "You just don't know what all he's been through. They tricked him like they tried to trick me, only worse. He won't talk about it much, thinks he's protecting me, but that's what's going on."

She'd apparently moved back to the drama at the ranch but I was still visiting the plastic factory. I remembered hearing something about a parts company back when. Twenty-five years ago there weren't many big factory type places around and a bunch of the guys and a few girls went to work there right out of high school, assembly line work, as best I could recall. It was good money, twice what they could make anywhere else. "I sure never knew that Bob Little owned that big plastics factory. The main building was blue metal as I recall, kind of northwest of Redwater, right? What was the name of that place?"

"Oh, it's one of those funny foreign words that the college kids use funny symbols for on their tee shirts." Lucille's brow wrinkled as she thought on it. "Kind of like Ortega, you know, like that Mexican man who used to work for Jimmie Sue's dad back when he had that track for training race horses."

"Neither the race horses, Jimmie Sue nor the worker to whose name she was slandering had any relevance to the actual topic of interest so I ignored the attempted rabbit trail. "You mean Omega."

"Yes, that was it. See it did sound like Ortega. Just an 'm' instead of the 'rt.' Omega Plastics. That's what it was called."

I knew it hadn't been called Little Plastic Parts Company. That, I would have remembered. "You know, I find it very interesting that Rancher Bob, our missing in action owner of the would-be park land, is also a manufacturing mogul. Between the oil and cows and plastic parts, the guy's got to be loaded with money. Maybe somebody kidnapped him or killed him for it. Wouldn't be the first time that sort of thing happened."

"That's ridiculous." She snatched her purse and settled it in her lap." It's just about that stupid park, that's all."

"It's also about a dead man, the missing man and my daughter's circumstantial ties to both."

"Well, don't you go jumping to any conclusions." She clutched her purse tightly and fiddled with the handles, twisting the straps this way and that. "You don't know nearly as much as you think you do."

And that, I feared, was the most truthful thing she'd said all day.

Chapter Nine

B y the time we finally reached Bowman City, I had ferreted out a boatload of pointless trivia and one possibly important fact. Namely that Tiger, along with his ever-present sidekick and supporting female flower team, had nearly gotten into a fistfight with Saide at the courthouse rally. I couldn't imagine the little guy that had hidden behind the Korean import doing much physical sparring, but Lucille had assured me he was "red as a beet" and shaking his "gnarly little fist" at Tiger, who, she pointed out, could have broken that "spindly little white neck of his like a chicken bone" if he'd had a mind to. He'd apparently planned to do exactly that until somehow things started exploding and paint started flying.

I made a mental sigh. I couldn't even replay Lucille's tales without them being one long string of run-on thoughts. Anyway, if nothing else, it was probably worth knowing that Tiger's "hippie goons" looked ready to "peench" the weasel's little head off. Pushing aside the vernacular and imagery from Mother's theatrical ruminations, I took a good look at the town square in front of us.

The courtyard of the Bowman County building was trampled down in large round spots, like inept aliens had missed the cornfield and settled on the courthouse lawn instead. Spatters of fluorescent green and pink paint dotted the crushed grass and three black sooty spots lined the sidewalk. Not major league damage, but more than just a minor irritation too. As we walked to the door, I couldn't help but wonder how much reclamation work had to be done to get it back to even this condition.

Inside the hallowed courthouse halls we didn't exactly find a "field of dreams" either. In fact, we racked up two strikes right off the bat without even trying. The "no Jerry" was an obvious and didn't count. But since we needed inside information from pliable sources, the "no Leroy" and "no Fritz" most assuredly did. The fact that there was another Harper on duty did not up batting average even a little. It did, however, upset my stomach.

The first thing you noticed about Larry Harper was the wad of tobacco hanging down from his lip. Yes, *down* from beneath his *upper* lip. The black-brown blob that perched atop his front teeth caused his upper lip to puff out until it almost touched his nose. It was not pretty. He also had a more traditional wad in his left cheek, which made him look like a lopsided pocket gopher. I couldn't begin to guess how much nicotine was coursing through his veins. The best we could hope for was that it was enough for him to connect the dots in his inherently deficient and seriously addicted brain.

Lucille had different concerns. "Don't you even think about spitting in front of me, Lawrence Harper," she said, skipping past the usual introductory pleasantries to avoid as much grossness as possible. "I've told your father just what I think about that nasty business of yours. If he'd been the one to walk in here instead of me, well, I think you know just what that would mean."

Apparently Larry did because he shoved his little Styrofoam spit cup under the desk and swallowed. The pained grimace on his face indicated this was not a preferred activity.

"And what are you doing here anyway?" Lucille continued. "You got yourself fired again didn't you? How hard can it be to shove a little stick in a tank and write down how much oil it shows? What'd you get caught at this time?" She pointed a manicured nail. "You were sleeping on the job again, weren't you?"

The flurry of questions continued unanswered, but the probable scenario was that Larry had gotten fired from his gauging job on the justifiable grounds of stupidity, and his father—mother's current beau—had gotten him back on at the sheriff's department. It was not a win-win scenario for anyone, except maybe the oil company.

Larry turned his back to us and stuck his pudgy—and still oil-stained—fingers into his mouth, presumably to remove the contraband. When he turned back it wasn't actually much of an improvement, but his cheek and lip were less unnaturally puffy. "You gonna tell my daddy about this?" he asked Lucille.

"Depends," Mother Shrewdness said. "Where is your father?"

"Oh, he and Leroy are out on a call. Nothing exciting, just a fender bender."

"What about Sheriff Parker? Where is he?"

"He's—"Larry Harper began to twitch and wiggle like he had bugs crawling on him, which he probably did. "He's not here."

"Well, I darn well know he's not here, Lawrence. Everybody knows there's been a murder out at a motel and he's taken a witness in for questioning to help out the Redwater Po-lice."

Larry frowned a bit while he puzzled with that information, fearing he was expected to comment about it in some way, which, of course, he was.

Now, I do realize that it appears that I was just standing around doing nothing while my mother was taking the lead in the interrogation, and that is indeed an accurate assessment. Mother Experience seemed to have a far better plan for handling Larry Harper than I did and I saw no good reason to interfere. Technically, one might call her technique blackmail. I didn't much care what anybody called it as long as it helped me find my daughter. And Jerry.

"Now, Lawrence, I very well know Jerry Don has been back over this way and I know you know where he went after he did because he said he would call in and let the office know where he was going when he decided what he was going to do. Now, you better hurry up and tell us just exactly where we can find him so neither one of us gets into trouble."

The words had come fast and furious, and the supposed point was in there somewhere if you could keep up, which Larry couldn't. "I think I'm gonna get in trouble no matter what I do," Larry said with accidental understanding.

"Where is Sheriff Parker?" Lucille asked again, only straight to the point.

"It's confidential."

Lucille nodded. "I can keep things confidential too, Lawrence. Or I can tell what I know to people who aren't gonna like it and let the chips fall where they may, and those are mighty big chips. Did you ever get that last landlord you had the run-in with paid back?"

Larry moaned, the exact circumstances of his rock-and-a-hard-place situation finally sinking in. "So if I don't tell you where the sheriff went, you'll tell Daddy about the chew. That's it, ain't it? I know it is, and then I'll be out of the house and fired all in one kick in the teeth, and it's none of his goddamned business what I do anyway." He scowled at Lucille. "Yours either."

Lucille slapped her long-nailed hand to her chest theatrically. "Why Larry Harper I don't know what on earth you're talking about. I never said any such thing about one having anything to do with the other." She paused and gave him a look that said exactly the opposite. "But my memory does come and go." She leaned over the counter toward him. "Now where is Jerry Don?"

Larry growled and muttered to himself for longer than you'd think a person could. He boldly grabbed his spit cup from beneath the counter and used it. When he finally looked back at us, he was grinning—maliciously. "She's real pretty, you know."

My stomach turned a quick and unhappy flip, and it wasn't due to the brown speckled teeth he was flashing at me.

"She can't be more than twenty-two or three," he said, looking right at me. "I saw her when she was here for the horny toad rally." He whistled appreciatively. "You ain't bad, Jolene, but that girl's got it going on. Can't blame Jerry for taking off with her."

Before I could even think about what to say or do, Lucille's hand shot out and grabbed Larry by the collar of his uniform. There might have been a little throat and jowl caught in her clutches as well. "You tell me where they are, Larry Harper, or you're gonna be picking those rotten teeth of yours up off the floor."

I was shocked at Lucille's physical attack, but Larry was awe-stricken. Eyes wide and chins jiggling, he didn't know what to do.

Lucille let go and jabbed a nail at his nose. "Speak, boy."

Larry blinked his buggy eyes and swallowed hard. "He took her to his old place."

"His rent house down the street?" Mother asked.

Larry shook his head. "No, his old house." He glanced at me again and laughed. "He took the girl out to stay with the dyke."

"Shit."

Chapter
Ten

"**O**ne word," Lucille said, pointing the car's air conditioning vents toward her face. "You said one word the whole entire time we were in there and what was it? 'Shit.' That's what it was. Shit." She shook her head and tsk-tsked hard enough to spit her bridgework into the next county. "I taught you better than that, Jolene. I just don't know what's gotten in to you."

This from the woman who'd just blackmailed and assaulted a deputy. "Kind of makes you wonder where I learned such filthy language, doesn't it?" I waited for her obligatory scowl and huff then said, "You know, I have about five thousand questions for you and my daughter. Want to start talking?"

Of course she didn't. But I already had a clue and it explained a lot. I knew this morning that something was far from official with Jerry having Sarah in the car like that. He knew exactly who Sarah was, and because of that he had taken her to Amy's. And there was only one good reason I could think of for him to do that and it was protection; he was hiding her out where she'd be safe. I did not want to think about safe from what, so I just imprinted my brain with the fact that she was okay now. Before I could remember what was not okay and had to be dealt with, a catchy little tune began playing from inside Mother's purse.

It took me a few seconds to figure out that Lucille's phone was playing an old Marty Robbins song. "Out in the West Texas town of El Paso, I fell in love with a Mexican girl..." She seemed not to hear it at all.

"Phone's ringing," I said helpfully.

"Oh, I'm sure it's nothing important. They can just leave a message. I'll check on it later."

I wasn't buying that for even a second. Thankfully, we were parked safely in front of the courthouse and not speeding down the road at 98 miles per hour, so I snatched her purse away and went for the phone.

"Now, you stop that!" Lucille shrieked, barely missing getting a hand on the purse. "That's my private phone. You have no business—"

I found it on the first try and flipped open the cover. "Hello?"

"Who is this?" an older woman's voice screeched. "I know I dialed the right number so you tell me, oh, it's *you*," she added without taking a breath. "Where's your hussy mother? Put her on the phone. Right now."

I took a wild guess on my caller's identity. "Well, Ethel Fossy, so very good of you to call to chat."

"You shut your nasty mouth and get your mother on the phone. Bobcat wants to talk to her right now."

I slapped Lucille's hands away. "Mother's busy. I'm available though."

It sounded like she'd covered the phone and was talking to someone, presumably Bobcat. A man's voice came on the line. "I want to talk to you. You and your mother meet me at the Bowman City Dairy Queen in an hour."

"I'll be there in ten minutes," I said, annoyed with everyone and everything.

"Twenty. And park at the back by the elm tree."

I was in no mood to be ordered around, although having the chance to get some answers from him sounded pretty good. "I'll be inside having a chicken basket and ice tea. You find me."

Click.

I turned to my mother. "That was Bobcat. Want to guess what he wants?"

"You said it was Ethel."

"Bobcat took the phone. He wants to meet with us."

Lucille's annoyance at Ethel—and me—melted into bewilderment. "Us? He doesn't even know you. Do you think he knows about Tiger?" She twisted on her purse straps again, playing with them like worry beads. "I don't know why he'd want to talk to me about any of that, it's not like I had anything to do with anything, although I did rent the room, but that doesn't make any difference about anything. Do you think that's it? No, no that couldn't be it." Mother's concern was very real whether her voiced reasons were or not. "If he doesn't know about Tiger, why would he want to talk to me?"

She was definitely confused, concerned and worried, probably with good reasons that I couldn't begin guess at. "Maybe he wants to have a strategy session."

"Well, I sure doubt that," she said, her anxiety shifting to indignation. "They never cared what I had to say about anything before, well, that one time they did, but that can't be it. Besides, Bobcat never much cared about anything one way or another unless Tiger told him he should. It was odd, but I guess you'd say they were pretty close so it seems like he'd have to know about Tiger being dead and all, wouldn't he?"

"You'd sure think so."

"Well, if he doesn't, I'm sure not going to be the one to tell him," Lucille said with conviction. "Those two were buddies back in the war, and I don't think either one of them is right in the head."

Great. Now she tells me. Being in Vietnam together didn't seem pertinent except from a brotherhood loyalty standpoint, and of course their potential mutual mental instability. But if you overlooked the buddy aspect, you had to allow for the option that Bobcat had killed Tiger so he could be the new messiah. It wasn't a really good option and seemed pretty farfetched and ludicrous solution comes out on top fairly often around here. Hard to speculate about much since there was obviously a lot we didn't know about either of them.

We also didn't know whether the Dairy Queen in Bowman City had the same special soft ice as the one in Kickapoo. Yes, it was an odd thought to have at that moment, but my brain was overheating and needed a distraction. At least we could answer the ice question in just a few minutes. "Let's get a glass of tea and a bite to eat when we get there. We'll talk about what we're going to say."

"I have no idea why he even wants to see us, Jolene, so I surely don't know what I'd need to say about it."

"I don't either, but we for sure won't be talking about Tiger being dead or what we saw or heard in regard to it. What I want to know is why they really came here, not that I think he'd actually tell me."

"He won't. He'll rant and rave about all kinds of things that don't make a bit of sense, but you ask him something normal and he clams right up. Half our meetings were spent with him telling the wildest tales you ever did hear, and getting all mad about the government and cover-ups and secrets such. If you believed half of what he said you'd never want to set foot outside your door. He's a weird one. They all are."

Couldn't really argue with her about that, but weird or not, I wanted somebody to give me some answers about something.

The one and only bright spot in the entire situation was that I at least had some answers about Sarah, well, just her location and that she wasn't in danger. That I no longer had to chase her down to confirm that was an added relief because I had no idea what I was going to say to her when I did. As far as I knew, she hadn't broken any laws. She also wasn't a kid anymore. She was twenty years old, and in spite of what I might like, she didn't have to tell me her every move. "At least we know Sarah is okay since she's with Amy."

"Yes, that is a relief," she said through lips being painted with a fresh coat of color. At some point, the family matriarch had stopped wringing her hands and had taken up preening in the visor mirror. "I think just a touch of sparkle above the cheekbone would be nice. We could be outside and the natural light would bounce up well from that, really highlighting my eyes."

"Here's a highlight for you, Mother, if I thought I could take you to Amy's and keep you out of trouble as well, I would do it in a heartbeat. Unfortunately, that creates more complications at the moment than I want to deal with."

"Well, you won't be dumping me off like a bag of dirty laundry, I'll tell you that," she said, snapping the mirror cover closed and flipping up the visor. Lucille shoved her emergency makeup kit back in her purse and finished off her lips with her tissue routine. "You may not give a hoot about me and want to get rid of me any chance you get but, hateful as you are, you're still my daughter, and I won't allow you to meet up with those hippies by yourself."

I ran my fingers through my hair, pressing hard against my skull. "The only reason you're going is because I have no other choice. So forget whatever ideas you had stewing in your head about causing trouble between Bobcat and Ethel."

She sucked in her breath in outrage.

"Save it. He could be dangerous and I don't want you at risk."

"Don't you be worrying about me, Missy. I can take care of myself, and I can sure enough handle the likes of those two."

"I'm sure you can, but don't. I'll do the talking." I watched her to see if there was any flicker of a chance that she was actually going to do what I asked. There wasn't. And then a shiver of knowing shuddered through me. "Oh, my god, you've got your gun, don't you?"

She clutched her purse tightly. "I have a permit."

Chapter Eleven

T he Bowman City Dairy Queen was a newer cousin to the Kickapoo establishment, meaning it was remodeled in the eighties with basic brown booths rather than seventies orange and olive green. The gold-ish colored tile with scalloped brown edges on the floor dated it like expired milk, but it had the glorious saving grace of employing not a single soul who could possibly know me. And, presumably it had chicken baskets.

While Mother availed herself of the facilities, I gave my order to the anonymous woman in the red apron behind the counter. My thoughts flew in a variety of directions, but mostly on what it might be that I needed to know from Bobcat—or what he thought he needed from me. And the whys of it all.

"Hussy."

I did flinch, but I didn't turn around. There was no need. I knew who it was. I flipped the top on my cell phone clipped at my waist to check the time. "Twenty minutes, Ethel. I still have twenty minutes before I have to deal with you or your new boyfriend-messiah-dude."

She sputtered your basic righteous indignation rhetoric then lowered her voice and growled, "He's out back by the tree now. Move it."

"And I'm in here ordering chicken baskets and ice tea." I put the change in my wallet and turned around. I gasped, jumping back as if I'd been bitten. I'm not sure, but I think I must have said, "Oh, my God," "Holy shit!" "What the hell" or perhaps something significantly worse, because Ethel went pale. And when the blood made its way back up to her head, she came uncorked.

She began screeching about taking the Lord's name in vain, which clearly I had not. She transitioned quickly into a fire and brimstone rant on my heathen ways and how God was going to send me to Hell for them all. She didn't stop there, but I only half heard her because quite frankly I was awestruck.

I'd seen Ethel at a distance outside this very place earlier yesterday and noticed she was wearing jeans and looked a little different than when we'd had our little run-ins in the past, but it was nothing compared to the "different" I saw before me now. Gone were the polyester pants and long-sleeved flowered shirt with a collar that tied in a big bow. Bony Butt was now sporting a tight-fitting tank top and hip huggers.

Yes, I said tank top and hip huggers.

And makeup. She had more makeup painted on her face than a celebrity drag queen. I hoped her friends were serious about that exorcism thing because Ethel had indeed been possessed. Before I could think of anything at all to say, Mother came sashaying up to the counter, glaring big condescending holes through Ethel.

"And you had the nerve to call *me* a slut," Lucille said, loud enough that a collective gasp rippled through the restaurant. "Surely to God you didn't paint your eyelids turquoise on purpose. And quite frankly, Ethel, it ought to still be against your religion to be showing off all that old wrinkled skin of yours. Good Lord, what are you thinking?'"

While Ethel sputtered and gasped, sucking in air for another internal combustion, I turned and stepped between them. I handed Mother the order ticket then walked directly out the door to find the elm tree out back. It seemed the least unpleasant of my options at the moment.

As it turned out I didn't need the tree for a marker. The pony-tailed cigarette-smoking old guy pacing beside a van was pretty hard to miss. I took it slow as I walked to the back of the parking lot. I really hadn't seen things going quite like this, but with Mother occupied elsewhere, I had one less thing to worry about. And what Bobcat wanted from me was enough of a worry. I walked up near where he'd stopped by the van. "Mr. Bobcat, I presume," I said because I couldn't think of anything else.

"Mr. Bobcat? Did you really say that? Jesus Christ."

"Aw, you don't have to call me that, Jolene will do."

He flicked his cigarette butt on the ground. "Ethel said you were a smartass."

"I really doubt that Ethel Fossy said the word ass."

"You'd be surprised," he muttered. "But that's all beside the goddamned point."

The unmistakable sound of tires spinning in gravel interrupted our scintillating conversation.

I jerked around to see a cloud of dust and Mother's Buick speeding away. "What the—"

"Well, shit," Bobcat muttered.

"What's going on? What is she doing? Is that Ethel with her?"

Something jabbed me in the side as Bobcat grabbed my arm. Realization and fear froze me like a statue, but I did manage to glance down enough to see that there was indeed a pistol wedged against my ribcage.

"Get in," Bobcat said, pushing me toward the van's sliding passenger side door and shoving me inside.

The van's cargo area had two bucket seats identical to the ones in the front. I stumbled over the first and fell headfirst into the second as he closed the door.

Raising my head, I saw the other door handle. If I could just reach it I might be able to open the door enough to fall out the other side. Before I could try it, however, Bobcat scooped his arm under me, twirled me around and sat me in the seat, right side up. "You don't want to do that. There are easier ways to kill yourself."

"Good to know," I muttered.

A woman with long reddish-blond braids sat behind the wheel. Lily. Her reflection in the rear view mirror just showed a blank expression, not anxious or on edge like you'd expect a getaway driver to be. Her eyes did look puffy and red though, like she'd either been crying or maybe was on drugs. She put the van in gear and started pulling forward. "Oh, no," she slammed on the brakes and looked in the rear view mirror at me. "I bet you didn't get to eat, we hardly gave you any time inside at all," she said, with a mellow airy voice. "We'll just go get your food and you can take it with you, yes, that's what we'll do." She started again, drove a few more feet then hit the brakes again, hard.

My brain and internal organs lurched with the jerky movements of the van, sending my senses spinning. Motion sickness hits me fast and hard, and another round of that I'd be taking the gun and shooting myself.

"You didn't order any meat did you?" Lily asked with both suspicion and condemnation. "I just can't condone that sort of thing—"

"Jesus Christ, Lily, just drive," Bobcat said, getting surlier by the second.

Lily hit the gas and lurched forward. "We have to be sure she has food, no one should have to go hungry," she said, as if I was a gerbil she'd just picked up at the pet store. As she pulled the van into the drive-through lane, she added, "You really should put the gun away."

Bobcat laid the gun in his lap, but kept his grip. "It's Texas, nobody cares."

"I care," Lily said, rolling down the windows down and pointing to me so the lady behind the counter would connect the dots.

Any other time I would've had to produce a receipt, driver's license and birth certificate to pick up at the drive-through window that which had been paid for at the inside counter. But not today. Before I could wink, blink, or send hand signals, the clerk had grabbed a sack off the counter and cheerfully tossed it to my kidnapper. She then handed Lily the white Styrofoam cups one at a time, which she in turn handed back to Bobcat, one at a time so he could keep one hand on the gun. "Ya'll have a nice day" drifted out as the DQ lady slammed the little glass window.

Bobcat had put the first cup in the holder on the door and held the second out toward me. "Have a drink."

Sure, why not. No need to be dead and thirsty. I took the cup, and may have even taken a sip, I don't really know, you do funny things when a gun is pointed at you. And it can sometimes help the nausea. The drink, not the gun.

Lily opened the sack and peered inside. "These don't look like salads," she said, suspicion morphing into angst. "You didn't order chicken, did you?"

Of course it was chicken, the grownup versions of the ones she'd freed from the feed store. However, since she looked genuinely distressed and disturbed at the fact that there might be cooked animal parts in the sack, I tried to smooth things over. I'm ever the people pleaser—even at gunpoint, maybe especially at gunpoint. "No, no, its tofu, southern fried tofu. It's new on the menu. Comes with organic gravy and whole grain toast. And an onion ring. Onions are nature's wonder food, you know."

"Yes, of course I know that," she snapped, "but fried foods are *so* unhealthy."

So are bullets. "You know, you're absolutely right," I said, still trying the agreeable and pleasant tactic, and hoping for a chance to flee without getting shot. "I'm not that hungry anyway so I'll just take these unhealthy things over to that trash can by the front door and throw them away. Somebody has to make a stand. It won't take but a second."

"Stay put." Bobcat leaned forward and grabbed the sack from the van's console then said to Lily, "Forget about the goddamned food and drive."

Lily did. And not in a smooth easy fashion either. The gas/brake grasshopper crap was getting old fast. I was apparently in the middle of some kind of power struggle between these two, and the one who seemed to be losing was me.

Out on the highway, the ride smoothed out and Bobcat pulled out a rectangular white box and set it in his lap then held out the sack to me. "Eat. I'm not going to kill you."

"Again, good to know." I set my tea in the door's cup holder and took the sack. "If that's the case though, you might want to rethink the kidnapping at gunpoint drill. It's really confusing."

Bobcat opened his box and the smell of hot fried chicken wafted through the van. I took out my own box and did the same just to have something to do with my hands. Or maybe I thought I could spear him with a French fry or blind him with gravy, I don't know.

Lily coughed and grabbed a bottle of spring water, presumably to keep from gagging at the odor and/or idea of grease-laden animal flesh being consumed by lesser, unenlightened beings in the backseat. I had no problem with that label for myself, however, it did bring up a bit of a conundrum for Carnivore Bob since he had to have been a part of the feed store fiasco to free the chicks. Curious, that. It was on the tip of my tongue to ask him about it and my hand put a French fry in my mouth to stop me. It could not possibly be in my best interests to point out that he was not who he wanted people to think he was. Not while being hauled at gunpoint away from the only speck of civilization there was within miles.

Bobcat stuck the pistol in the seat pocket in front of him. "Went into autopilot. It happens sometimes." He shrugged. "Saw Lucille coming and had to do something. Didn't want to deal with her today."

I couldn't fault him for that. I'd considered taking a bullet myself for the same reason. "So you nab me and Ethel gets my mother?"

Bobcat eyed his four strips of breaded and fried contraband along with a pile of French fries, a little tub of white gravy and big slice of greasy Texas Toast. "I love this shit." He opened his gravy and sighed then grabbed and dipped and stuffed, talking as he chewed. "Ethel was just supposed to keep her busy inside while you and me talked outside. That's all. I don't know why they left or what the hell they're doing." He grabbed another chicken strip, dipped the end in the gravy and shoved the whole thing in his mouth. "They won't kill each other."

Obviously, he did not know Lucille very well, or have a clue as to how far off the deep end Ethel Fossy was actually dangling these days. No point in explaining that, however. And, since I figured he'd get around to what he wanted with me, I could jump in now and find out what I wanted to know about him. "Okay, let's cut to the chase. You didn't come here because of the horny toads, did you?"

Bobcat stuffed in another bite of country-fried bliss. "Haven't seen a single one of the little bastards."

"Stop it! Lily twisted the cap back on her water bottle and banged it down into the cup holder. "You may not care about the lizards, but I do! Every day acres and acres of native habitat are either plowed over by humans or overrun by invasive species, which is a double irony because it's the most invasive of all species—the humans—that have arrogantly and thoughtlessly spread scourges across this beautiful land."

She delivered this passionate speech while speeding through a panoramic backdrop of scrub mesquites—an invasive scourge if there ever was one—and a mirror image of the land she was apparently hell bent on "saving."

"But all is not lost," she continued. There are still people like Tiger and me out there who do care about the planet, and we do make a difference. We just have to stand up for what we believe. It's not just about the horny toads, it's about everything. This is serious. People are dying over what's happening here and nobody even cares." Lily paused and blinked for a moment, her eyes looking a little misty in the van's rear view mirror. "Somebody has to do something about what's going on here."

In that moment, Lily sounded like a real activist, which I'd already dismissed as even a possibility. I might have to reconsider. At least for Lily. I wasn't sure what Bobcat was. I also still didn't know what they wanted with me except maybe to sell me a "Save the Planet" bumper sticker or something.

"Yeah, yeah," Bobcat muttered. "I know why we're here and I'll do my part. I'm just saying there's a lot of bullshit out there too." He scowled and pinched up a wad of fries. "Hell yes, we gotta stop spewing toxic shit into the air and dumping glowing turds in the water so we don't poison ourselves." He stuffed in the fries and kept talking. "But it ain't gonna keep those ice caps from melting and freezing. Global warming, my ass. That freeze-thaw shit was going on long before the goddamned gods were chanting 'Let us make man in our own image' over a goddamned Petri dish."

Repetitive and disturbing expletives aside, he had a point, and he wasn't the first one to make it. It wasn't the current politically correct point of view, but it did have some solid scientific evidence on its side. Unfortunately, people eagerly ignore facts when said facts make them uncomfortable. And acknowledging that cooling and warming cycles have happened before and they're going to happen again—no matter how many hybrid cars we build—is darned uncomfortable for most folks. That doesn't mean it's okay to pollute or that we shouldn't develop more efficient energy sources. It does, however, mean that we need to at least pay equal attention to the messages that the flash frozen and perfectly preserved wooly mammoths left us. "Then again," I said, deciding to find out how closely he and Ethel's views of the world lined up. "I've heard that Jesus is coming soon so it all could be a moot point."

"Yeah, well, if he is, he's coming in a spaceship and he ain't alone." Bobcat snorted and sucked down a big swig of tea. "Dumbasses don't even realize it's the same goddamned thing. And all that shit they think matters, doesn't. If the goddamned aliens that put us in this ant farm do decide to save some of our sorry asses, they'll take who they want for their own reasons. It won't make a shit that Ethel never heard a piano played in church or that some old crows never cut their hair or wore pants. And unless there's a strip search before Scotty beams them up, I can't figure how special underwear is gonna make a shit on who's getting' saved and who ain't."

I found it seriously disturbing that I knew exactly what he was talking about, and worse, I'd said basically the same things myself, although perhaps with fewer vulgarities.

"Stop it! Stop it right now," Lily said, pounding her hands on the steering wheel. "That has nothing to do with anything. This is about right here, right now, and you shut up about all that crazy crap."

Bobcat grabbed his last chicken strip and waved it at her dismissively. "I told you I'd do what you wanted, but goddamn, once this shit's all over, then what are you gonna have to obsess about? Ethel ain't the only one living in a jail of her own making."

"Shut up!" Lily slammed on the brakes, throwing Bobcat and me against the front seats. "You don't tell me what to do anymore."

As she hit the gas and started driving again, I realized we were not too terribly far from Kickapoo.

Lily glared at Bobcat in the rear view mirror as she drove then adjusted it so she could see me better. After a few minutes, she seemed to get herself under control. After a few more, she said, "What do you know about Bob Little and your mother?"

I hadn't seen that line of questioning coming, and I sure had no answers. "I…I don't know anything."

Lily's composure shattered. "You've got to know!" Her nose flared with every breath. "You swore to me, Bobcat!"

Bobcat crumpled up his empty chicken basket box then grabbed the sack from the floor and stuffed his trash in it. "Goddammit, Lily, take another pill or something," Bobcat said. "I'll handle this."

I saw him eyeing the meal I'd barely touched so I handed it to him. I figured the more bread and gravy he ate, the less he'd want to do. It sure worked that way for me.

He grinned and he settled the box in his lap. "I love this shit."

"In the late sixties," Lily said, her voice quivering, "early seventies, what do you remember?"

She meant me, of course, and this was a test I knew I would never pass. "The Monkees, Barbie dolls and ponies." I knew this was not what they wanted to hear, but I didn't have anything better. "I was a kid."

The box lunch in Bobcat's hand shook and crinkled under his grip. His eyes narrowed and the side of his mouth twitched. "What about the goddamn war? You telling me you don't remember anything about *that*?"

So much for the gravy and grease lethargy plan. "Well, yes, of course, but they're little kid memories. I was, what, eight?"

And then, like a color slide slipping into the tray of an old projector, I saw an overstocked shop filled with black leather jackets, psychedelic PEACE tee shirts and strange paraphernalia inside glass cases. Sweet-smelling incense mingled with the leather and there were belts everywhere. It was the only place in Redwater you could get POW bracelets. Lucille hadn't wanted to, but I'd begged, and once she got there… The next slide in the mental tray blazed onto the screen and I could see my mother in the store, wistfully fondling a fringed leather motorcycle jacket and telling me she used to have one along with matching leather pants. When we got home she showed me a 1950s era photo of her and Dad, sitting on a Harley in matching full leather outfits.

Dad held the handlebars, his boots planted wide to balance the bike, a cigarette dangling from his lips. Mother sported a trendy leather cap set on her head at a jaunty angle with a stylish scarf tossed over her shoulder. Her arms were wrapped around his waist with a sultry come hither look plastered on her face. And I only now remembered it. "I really do not know the woman who says she is my mother."

Lily muttered something that seemed in agreement with my assessment. I couldn't make out any of the words, but the tone told me none were complimentary.

While I'd taken my side trip down memory lane, Bobcat had apparently escaped his own mental flashbacks and now seemed okay, relatively speaking. "What do you know about that land behind your mother's house?"

"You mean the land they want to build the park on?"

Lily slammed her water bottle into the console's cup holder. "You can't be this dense."

Oh, yes I can and I am. "Look, I'm not trying to be secretive or cagey or anything else. I simply have no idea what you're asking me or what you really want to know. That land was just a place for me to get dumped off a horse and have to walk home from."

"You better jog your memory," Bobcat said between bites of my half-eaten lunch. "It's pretty goddamned important."

Lily glanced in the mirror then kept looking at me, far longer than seemed prudent for the driver of a vehicle speeding down the highway at 70 miles per hour. "Your dad died about three years ago, right?"

If changing topics to keep me disoriented was her goal, she was succeeding admirably. "Yes, he died the day before Thanksgiving, three years ago."

Bobcat scooped up the last of my fries. "Heard Lucille didn't take it too well."

That would be one way to put it.

My dad had dropped dead of a heart attack early that morning, and by the time I arrived that afternoon, Lucille was pretty much a zombie. As an only child, that left all the decision making, arranging, scheduling and general business of things entirely to me. I eventually found out that her condition was not just a normal state of shock. Before I got there, some idiot doctor had loaded her up with the latest "FDA-approved" designer anxiety drug to help her deal with the shock and grief of her husband dying in front of her.

What neither the doctor nor the drug rep/pusher knew, presumably, was that the maker of the pills—a best-left-unnamed-because-I-don't-want-to-die pharmaceutical giant—had conveniently overlooked a few pertinent details about how the drug actually worked in order to get it on the market. Specifically, third party testing showed that the drug made rats chew off their own feet and/or hurl themselves into walls. It also made my mother semi-comatose. At first. Then, as she "adjusted to the medication," paranoia set in, followed by panic attacks, severe ones, and she became afraid to leave the house. She thought she was having heart attacks, thus prompting the brilliant doctor to up the dosage of the offending drug and then added heart, diuretic and sleeping pills to counteract the side effects, presumably. It nearly killed her, and it took me a year of coaxing, convincing and threats to get her off all that crap. "She had a hard time, yes."

"It's going to get harder," Lily said. "A lot harder."

Bobcat wadded up the second box and stowed the trash. "Who owns the mineral rights to the Little Ranch?"

I had a very bad feeling about that question. I went with the obvious, knowing full well it wasn't. "Bob Little?"

"Besides him."

The van jerked to a stop. Somehow, we were now in Kickapoo, parked beside my mother's house, facing the Little property. I was pretty sure this was my hint at the answer and there was a part of me that wasn't even surprised. "Why would my mother own mineral rights on Bob Little's property?"

Bobcat shook his head and flipped his ponytail back over his shoulder. "Goddamn, you really don't know shit."

Lily screeched and clutched the steering wheel, looking like she wanted to bang her head against it. I could relate.

"If you'd just asked," I said, my voice rising in pitch and volume, "I could have told you that in the parking lot at the Dairy Queen and saved all the pointless drama!"

"Oh, hell." Bobcat picked up his phone and dialed. "Buttercup, when you're finished, you and Lucille come on over to the Dairy Queen in Kickapoo. Well, good. Yes a half an hour will be fine." After he'd hung up from leaving the message, he glared at me and growled, "I don't want to hear any shit about Ethel."

At least we agreed on that. "Okay, I don't get it. If you wanted me staring out behind my mother's house, why didn't you just meet me here to begin with?"

"I figured it would be easier to separate you and Lucille if Ethel was there and she wasn't likely to get invited over for tea by your mother." He shrugged. "Beside, you were already headed to Bowman City."

I had been, of course, but how did he know that? Rather than ask, I unclipped my phone from my jeans and dialed my mother. He didn't try to stop me. But she didn't answer either so I also left a message that included the words "call me" at least three times. Since it seemed like Lucille and I were both about to be released from captivity, I relaxed a little, but I was more confused than ever.

Bobcat pointed across to a row of tall mesquite trees. "Bob Little had a string of wells that came in big in the fifties. He hit 'em hard for about ten years. There's one over there."

I knew the area he was talking about. At one time you could see some of the pump jacks and tanks from the house. "I'd planned to walk the property last night but it didn't work out. I have no idea what's there, I haven't stepped foot on the place in twenty-five years."

As we sat there, the van still running, I glanced to the mirror at Lily. She was staring straight ahead again, a digital camera in her hands, taking pictures. While Lily snapped away, I tried to remember what I could about anything to do with oil, Bob Little, the property or my deceitful mother. There were some fuzzy areas in my memory banks that seemed like they might be important if only I could drag them out into the light. But I couldn't.

"He had some other stuff going on in the Seventies," Bobcat said. "Remember anything about that? A bunch of trucks, dozers, lights at night, anything like that?"

"Look," I said, trying to sound as sincere as I was. "I don't know much of anything about anything. It's news to me that my mother is in any way connected to the Little Ranch at all. As for what might have happened in the seventies, well, my focus was elsewhere. I can tell you what dress I wore to what banquet, I can describe my black velvet platform shoes in exquisite detail and I can tell you my favorite kind of hot rollers and why, but they could have plowed up that whole ranch during that time and I wouldn't have even noticed."

Bobcat shook his head. "Nobody has their head that far up their ass."

"Clearly you have never been a teenage girl nor had to live with one."

Bobcat scowled. "You have to remember something besides just bullshit."

"Well, I don't," I said, waving my hands in frustration. "Clearly you know what you want me to remember, so just tell me and I'll see what I can come up with."

"If I tell you then it ain't remembering, now is it?" He stared out the window for several long minutes then shook his head again and said, "You'd be wise to keep your daughter stashed wherever she is."

Prickles raced up my spine. They knew about Sarah. "Why? Is she in danger? She doesn't know anything either."

"Just keep her off the streets for a while." He waved a hand to Lily to drive on. "Wouldn't hurt you to do the same. Lucille too."

"You think somebody's after us? Is it the same people who killed Tiger?"

Lily sucked in her breath and slammed on the brakes. "What do you know about that? Tell me!"

"Lily, just drive. She doesn't know anything you don't."

After a few long seconds of staring at nothing, Lily turned the van around and pulled out onto the street.

Bobcat stared out the window as we headed to the Kickapoo DQ.

After a few seconds of silence, I said, "Would you tell me why you think we're in danger?"

"I already did."

"Any chance you'd explain that and save me some grief?"

"Nope."

Chapter
Twelve

As we rolled into the hometown Dairy Queen parking lot, Bobcat said, "Looks like your mother beat us here." I followed his gaze to Lucille's Buick. "Looks like it. I guess if you want to chat you know how to find me."

Bobcat leaned over me and opened the van's door then motioned me out. "Yeah, we know."

I barely had my feet on the gravel when the van took off, Bobcat slamming the door as they fled. When I turned toward the DQ door, I knew why they were in such a hurry to escape. Ethel Fossy had darted out the front door and was racing after the van, arms waving. My mother was on Ethel's heels, speed walking with as much dignity and grace as one can across a gravel parking lot in front of a semi-fast food restaurant next to a busy US highway in gold glittered shoes.

"Ethel, you idiot," Lucille yelled. "You get back here. Quit chasing after that man like some dog in heat."

Ethel stopped in her tracks and spun around. "How dare you! I'm not—" She crimped her lips together and glared at Lucille. After a last longing glance in the direction the van had fled, Ethel let out a heavy sigh then obediently marched back into the Dairy Queen.

What was going on here? What had I just witnessed? My mother was directing Ethel like the best of beauty queen coaches. Wait a minute! Then it hit me. Ethel was no longer wearing a tank top or hip huggers. She was wearing nice slacks and a tailored blazer, and not one hint of blue eye shadow, although her cheeks were tastefully blushed and her lashes looked thickened and lengthened.

Apparently, while I'd been touring the county with Bobcat and Lily, my mother had whisked her long-time nemesis and avowed mortal enemy away from the Bowman City DQ for a brainwashing and a makeover. Was that really Ethel? And my mother? I'd seen it with my own eyes and even I didn't believe it.

Lucille shoved my shoulder, pushing me along behind Ethel. "Quit standing there with your mouth open catching flies. I've had to reorder my chicken basket and it's probably getting cold. Come on."

I didn't wait for her to grab my arm and drag me inside, but I didn't necessarily go willingly either. I had some questions for my mother, not the least of which was why she'd run off and left me at the DQ to be kidnapped.

I did not get to ask those questions, however, because I couldn't get a word in edgewise. I was also trapped on the inside of the booth against the window and therefore had to endure a conversation that no one should have to. Completely oblivious to my presence, Lucille and Ethel enthusiastically debated the pros and cons of chemical peels, Botox and facelifts, old and new trends in lingerie, and having younger men for lovers, for which they both agreed condoms were a real good idea.

I'm not kidding. I sincerely wish I were. But I am not.

It seemed like it took six hours for my mother to eat her food—and catch Ethel up on the new world order. In reality, my torture lasted only about twenty minutes, but it was twenty minutes of pure hell, and I'd have rather been back in the van with a gun pointed at me. Yes, really. The stress of the day was taking its toll, and as soon as Ethel's personal trainer put the last French fry into her mouth, I gave her a full body nudge. "All done. Let's go."

Ethel jumped a little, either startled because she'd forgotten I was there or that I could and would speak.

Lucille glared and scowled and huffed and all the typical things my mother does when she is seriously annoyed with me.

I didn't care. Somewhere in the last few seconds I'd gone from fairly oblivious to seriously annoyed myself. I hurriedly stacked the trash on the red plastic tray, grabbed my cup and nudged her again. "Let me out. I've had all the fun I can stand." She didn't move immediately and that just added fuel to the fire that had already been lit. "I've got to go, Mother, really I do. Right now. Move."

Ethel sucked in an indignant breath. "Are you going to let her talk to you like that?"

Lucille turned and glared at me again. However, she was between the proverbial rock and a hard place. If she snapped back at me as she so dearly wanted to do, she'd save face with Ethel and might win the battle. But my last straw had clearly snapped and that made me a loose cannon, which gave her zero chance of winning the war. She gritted her teeth, slid to the end of the booth and stood. She huffed and sputtered, still wanting very badly to give me a what-for. But since all eyes were already on us, she was more concerned with avoiding the equivalent of an international incident at the Dairy Queen.

I had no such concerns. I might have been in some level of shock for the last twenty minutes, but I was remembering clearly now, and what I remembered was that Ethel Fossy had not only verbally abused us in public every chance she got, she'd started vicious rumors, sent threatening hate mail and was consistently and vocally self-righteous and judgmental. Just because Mary Kay Yoda had given her a few tips on makeup, hair and clothing, it didn't change the fact that her protégé from the dark side would still happily burn me at the stake given the opportunity.

I slid out of the booth, grabbed the tray of trash and looked down at Bony Butt. "Well, Ethel, this whole extreme makeover thing you've got going is pretty impressive, I'll give you that. But there's still that old saying about leopards and spots and such. Then again, a Bobcat may trump leopards and spots, and you could have really turned over a new leaf, or at least nailed an old hippie."

Lucille groaned. "Oh, my Lord, Jolene."

Ethel's face turned so red that the expertly applied blush and highlights completely disappeared. "What do you mean by that?"

"I'm not casting stones. Hooking up with Bobcat has clearly done you a world of good. Makes you feel alive again, doesn't it?"

"Oh, my Lord," Lucille repeated, darting her eyes around the room to quantify witnesses.

"And finding yourself a godly man too," I continued. "Why, I'd say he uses the word 'god' at least twice in every sentence."

Mother grabbed me by the arm and dragged me to the door. "Why do you say these things?"

It was a rhetorical question; she had no intention of me answering. I fully intended to, of course, but Ethel raced up beside us and cut off whatever clever remark might have fallen out of my mouth.

"Are you going to let her get away with that?" Ethel said, her voice elevated with indignation and outrage. "If she was my daughter, she wouldn't be getting away with that."

Lucille grabbed the red tray out of my hands and set it on top of the trash can and shoved me toward the door. "Don't pay her any mind, Ethel. She's still real tired from her trip, jet lag and all that."

"I just never dreamed this was what you had to put up with."

"Well, Ethel," I said, "there just wasn't time to do it your way. If I had to say it behind your back and then wait for it to make the rounds on the gossip mill, well, it could take days or at least an hour."

"What an awful thing to say! I do not gossip!" Ethel gaped and worked her jaw up and down. "You're right, Lucille, after all you've done for her and she still doesn't care at all about other people's feelings. It *is* just like a knife to the heart."

I shoved open the door and walked out.

Mother scurried out of the restaurant behind me, huffing and clucking as she followed me to the car. She clicked open the locks, opened the passenger door and flung herself inside. After I was seated, she tossed me the keys and said, "There's no reason for you to be snippy. These situations are delicate and I just said what I had to in order to get Ethel to open up to me." She gripped the handles of her purse and huffed. "You obviously do not understand a single thing about psychology or finesse in communication."

"Obviously." I stuck the key in the ignition and started the engine. "But I apparently excel at heart knifing." I laughed, not because it was all that funny, but because it was funny enough to give me a way to release some tension other than yelling or crying. I laughed again.

"I don't see what's so funny."

"Of course you don't. You've had a grand time today. Your morning started out perfectly with a cup of coffee and a shooting."

She sucked in an indignant breath then muttered, "He had it coming."

"For most folks, that would have been a full day of fun in and of itself, but no, you were only getting started." I ignored her scowl. "After a stimulating experience at the Little Ranch, Grannie Columbo was off to outsmart the cops at the motel room with the dead guy."

"You can't be blaming me for all that."

I raised a hand to stop her. "And just because the town's morality watchdog has rediscovered life in the immoral fast line doesn't mean you have to conduct a fashion intervention to support it."

She gave me a look that said she hadn't exactly thought of it that way then muttered something under her breath that included "hateful" and "pitiful."

"I, on the other hand," I said, raising my voice appropriately for drama, "was dragged along for the ride of shock and fear, none of which would have been necessary had you told me the truth from the beginning. My icing on the day's cake was being kidnapped at gunpoint by two psychos after you abandoned me in the parking lot of the Dairy Queen. But not to worry, I'm fine."

"Oh, good grief, Jolene, I can very well see that you're just fine," she snapped, jumping back on the defensive and sweeping away any pesky twinge of guilt that might have occurred. "You're certainly cranky and hateful, but you're fine. As for Bobcat, he's got a foul mouth, but he's harmless."

"No, he's a jumpy guy with posttraumatic stress disorder and a gun."

She waved a dismissive hand. "Well, I knew you wanted to talk to him alone and see what you could find out behind my back anyway, not that he knows anything."

I looked at her for a few long moments, thinking that she hadn't always been this way. However, that was only true to a point. Lucille had always been Lucille—she'd just kept it under wraps and within the socially acceptable boundaries. Now, she had no such restrictions and she was doing exactly what she wanted to do and didn't care what anybody thought about it. In theory, I admired that attitude. In practice, it left a lot to be desired for me.

Lucille dug around in her purse and huffed. "Well, I have just had enough of all this. I believe it's time we went home."

"Finally, we agree on something."

Mother Compassion scowled at me as she held up her phone and hit a speed dial number. "Agnes, where are you? . . .Okay, well, good. Would you go to the Dairy Queen and get Ethel and take her home? . . . Yes, that Ethel. . . . Well, it's a very long story and I don't have time to explain, but she darn well looks better than she did. I have done my Christian service for the next year, maybe five, I'll tell you that for sure. . . . Well, I know you aren't going to like it, Agnes. I surely didn't like it either, but I'm in a bind and I need your help. . . . Yes, I'll tell you all about it later. I'm with Jolene right now and she's having one of her snits so I can't talk. . . . Yes, okay, I know I owe you. Bye."

I did not say one word, not one, just put the car in drive and drove. We'd barely made it out of the DQ lot when we met a sheriff's vehicle. It passed us then whipped around, lit up the blue flashing lights and headed after us.

Even though I knew better, my automatic reaction was to look down at the Buick's speedometer. For the record, I was going twelve miles per hour. I pulled over to the shoulder and the car pulled up behind us, without the lights.

"What's wrong?" Lucille said. "What'd you do?"

Before I could respond at all, Sheriff Jerry Don Parker was opening my door.

"Well, it's about darned time," Lucille said, snapping back around in her seat. "I've got some questions and I want some answers."

"Miz Jackson," Jerry said, nodding to Lucille over my shoulder. Then, he looked back at me. "I'd like to talk to you alone."

The way he made that sound made me real sure that I would like it too.

"I don't suppose you could take your hands off her long enough to tell me what's going on around here," Lucille snarled.

"We've got dead people, and missing people, and crazy people, and I'd like some answers."

"We'll just be a minute or two," he said, ignoring her demands and slamming the door.

And there, in the span of a very few seconds, my whole outlook on life had changed. The cavalry—i.e. Jerry—had arrived and freed the little peptides in my brain that had been pinned down by enemy fire. The tension that had me ready to snap melted into a glorious rush of endorphins and every cell in my body felt it.

Jerry led me back to the Expedition and opened the passenger door, blocking us from most of the viewing public passing along on the highway, but most especially from my mother. "We have got to find a way to do better than this," he said, wrapping his arms around me. "But, I'll take what I can get."

Yes, well, ditto. I'll spare you the private details, but it was just about as good as you could get standing beside a sheriff's vehicle on the side of the road in Kickapoo, Texas, in broad daylight with your mother watching. And no, it wasn't nearly enough.

He broke away just a bit and looked down at me. "Hmm, I figured the first thing you'd do was quiz me about this morning."

It took a few seconds for his words to penetrate the rather pleasant haze in my head. "What?"

Jerry brushed a windswept curl away from my face and smiled. "Sarah's okay. I took her to Amy's."

My eyes widened as he confirmed what I'd suspected. "I was sure you knew who she was."

"Kind of hard to miss."

"I was shocked, seeing her in Texas, and with you."

He smiled. "And a little jealous."

"Just a little," I agreed. I pushed back from him. "Does she know what's going on?"

"No, I really think she was just indulging Lucille."

"Well, she wasn't really staying in that motel room where the dead guy was. I figured that much out."

Jerry nodded. "Yes, I know. She was at the Hilton." Before I could voice any further questions, he said, "One of them better come clean about all this very soon or I'm going to get involved where I said I wouldn't."

No matter how I tried to prevent it, Jerry seemed to get dragged into my family messes. Now, however, it wasn't only my mother causing trouble, it was my daughter too. "I'm sorry, Jerry, I really am."

He ran his fingers over my cheek and behind my neck, making light butterfly circles with his fingertips. "I'm just glad you're here."

Every tingling fiber of my being screamed in agreement. I didn't care where I was or how it came about, all that mattered was that we were together and it felt really, really good. However, before I drifted completely out into the stratosphere of desire, I had to tell him what had happened today or at least a fast forward version of it. "I just spent the last few hours with Bobcat and Lily in a van, and not by choice, driving around the countryside for reasons still unknown, although clearly related to the property behind my mother's house. Those people have issues. In a semi-related but probably irrelevant incident, my mother gave Ethel a makeover." When he raised a questioning eyebrow, I added, "It's a long story and I know you don't have the time right now, but I do need to talk to you about some things soon. In fact," I said, running my hands over his chest and tugging on his shirt, urging him closer, "there are a lot of things we need to deal with. Very soon. And not on the side of the road."

He leaned in for what I thought was one last hug, but before I knew it his hands were under my hips, pulling me against him and sliding me up onto the edge of the seat. "I want you," he whispered, gently tugging my legs apart and pressing forward. "It's been so long."

"Oh, God." I wrapped my arms around him and ran my hands down his back, pulling him closer. "You feel so good."

He groaned in response then pressed light kisses against my face. He nibbled at my ear then moved to my neck, kissing and gently nipping in a way that he knew made me absolutely crazy. Every touch of his mouth sent hot quivers through me.

"Oh, God," I groaned again, moving, tugging, trying to get closer, my whole being begging him for more.

His hands still under my hips, he lifted me to fit fully against him. The connection was instant and electric. His scent filled my nostrils, sending me even higher, and I could taste him. With my breasts pressed tight against his chest and my hands on his back, I could feel every part of him as if there were no clothes between us.

His breath hot in my ear, he held me there, caressing me, pressing hard against me, our bodies pulsing in rhythm, seeming to blend together. With a groan, he moved his mouth to mine. As we kissed, hot waves erupted from where our hips joined. Tingling warmth shot up my spine and rippled through me, finally bursting into that incredible peak moment of pure feeling.

Panting as if I'd just run a marathon, I floated down from the sensation, Jerry still holding me, his breathing becoming steady and soft.

The reality of what had just happened fully hit me. I'd never have believed such a thing to be possible, especially without any skin-to-skin contact. But it did, at least for me. Between gasps, I think I tried to say "how did you do that?" and "what about you?" but he kept pressing tiny kisses to my face and whispering really sweet things such as "just enjoy it" so I did.

After my breathing slowed to a reasonable pace, Jerry pulled away a little and looked down at me, smiling. I have to say, he seemed pretty pleased with himself. I was pretty pleased too, of course. Reality was also beginning to seep back in, and it occurred to me to wonder if anyone passing by could have seen inside the car. I preferred to believe they couldn't, but even if they had, it probably would have just looked like two people hugging. But it had been so much more.

"I just want to keep touching you," he said, stroking my cheek. "You have no idea what you do to me."

"I think it's pretty clear what you just did to me."

He grinned. "You just keep thinking about that until I get back later."

I wasn't likely to ever forget *that*. I'd be telling that story when I was 83.

He stepped back and adjusted his clothing then slid me out of the seat onto the ground in front of him. He kept hold of me, which was a good thing since my legs were like Jell-O and I would have crumpled to the ground if he hadn't.

"I wish I could stay," he said, his voice rumbling through me with real regret. "But I have some things that have to be dealt with today. I don't know how it will go, but if at all possible, I want to take you to a nice dinner tonight. I don't want to talk business the whole time either."

Agreed. And frankly, the nice dinner was optional in my book. A Dr Pepper and a package of crackers from a hotel vending machine would work for me. Actually, just the hotel worked for me, but I refrained from saying so since one might think I would be at least semi-satisfied for a few minutes. I wasn't, of course. With Jerry, I just wanted more. "Any guess on time?"

He shook his head, gave me another quick kiss and said, "No, but I hope no more than a couple of hours."

My legs were plenty wobbly, but I managed to make it back to the car with some measure of decorum. I am certain, however, that the look on my face telegraphed exactly what I'd been up to. I smiled as Jerry walked away.

Oh, things were definitely looking up now. And nobody, especially not my mother, was going to ruin it. Not tonight. I took a deep breath and tried to put on a straight face as I climbed back into the car with Lucille.

She didn't ask any questions, which was odd, but I was grateful for the reprieve. As we drove on to her house, which took all of three minutes, I felt myself deflating like a tire with bullet hole in it and I had no desire to ask my mother any questions about anything. To tell the truth, the only thing I really wanted to think about was having Jerry Don Parker all to myself in a few hours—and what all went with that. I pulled into the garage, parked the car and went inside.

After a visit to the bathroom, I nabbed a bottle of Lucille's spring water, chugged half of it then stretched myself out on the couch. I put a pillow beneath my head and covered myself with a soft and cozy velour blanket. There was nothing at all that I had to do and I was going to do exactly that until Jerry arrived. It felt so good to just stretch out and relax and not have to think about anything except my fantasies.

My mother, on the other hand, was not in need of relaxation at all. Apparently energized by the day's events, she was zipping around the house like a crazed bee. She was making me tired just watching her. As my mind wandered, she checked her message machine, changed clothes, re-glazed her hair and re-painted her face. My chicken-fried brain started catching up with what was going on about the time she stopped in front of me with her purse over her arm and mischief sparkling in her eyes.

"Now, Jolene, be sure and lock the door when you leave," she said, a little breathless. "You have your key? I'm going over to Agnes' house for a minute, but I plan to meet Fritz later on. At any rate, I'm probably going to be late so don't wait up." She was halfway out the door when she poked her head back in and said, "Ethel looked good, didn't she? I did a good job with her and in such a short time too." Rapid-fire comments kept coming and I was only catching every other one. "Oh, and I forgive you for all your hatefulness. Are you spending the night here or at Jerry Don's?"

What? Me? Hateful? And what about Jerry Don? Where was I sleeping? What kind of question was that for a mother to ask her daughter? I guess I looked shocked, which of course I was, because she didn't wait for me to answer.

"Oh, good grief, Jolene, grow up, you're not seventeen anymore. You don't have to be sneaking around like you did in high school. Just leave me a note on where you'll be and when you'll be back so I won't worry. Sex is just a normal part of life and there's no sense in getting all prudish about it. I thought maybe you'd learned something from my talk with Ethel this afternoon." She tsk-tsked and shook her head as she grabbed the door handle. "I swear, you'd think by now you'd know to pay attention when I talk. Why, you were half the reason I was even taking the time to talk about such things, what with you and Jerry getting friendly again and all."

What the hell? The door slammed behind her before I could either sputter with outrage or perhaps throw something. Who was that woman? She could not possibly be my mother. And what was with all the "sex is normal" talk? She'd had an entirely different view of these matters when I was a teenager, I assure you. Anytime I even thought about stepping a foot out the door

I got the lecture on…. Wait a minute. Where was *she* going? And why? She wasn't allowed out alone, was she? Wasn't I supposed to be watching her for some reason?

The synapses in my brain that weren't percolating on grease and gravy were tied up daydreaming about Jerry Don Parker. The remaining active brain cells were abandoning their posts in record numbers. After a few seconds, I couldn't remember why letting Lucille run off unattended and uncensored was a bad thing. Or why I should care.

I jerked awake, instantly alert.

And terrified.

Why? What was going on? I blinked, but I couldn't see anything in the darkened living room. I could feel something though. Someone?

There were no lights. I'd left a light on, hadn't I?

What woke me? Why was I scared? What time was it?

A creak of the floor.

Oh, God, someone was in here.

I froze in place on the couch. I didn't breathe. Couldn't breathe.

Thump. Something fell on the kitchen floor.

Pure panic flooded me and I shot upright.

Meaty hands grabbed my head and shoved me back down. Sweaty palms covered my eyes. Steel fingers grabbed my legs.

I jerked and twisted, punched and kicked. I grabbed thick hairy arms and dug my fingers into them.

The hairy grip loosened. "Goddammit!" He caught my arms and bent them back over my head.

I screamed and kicked.

Someone caught my feet and slammed them down on the couch.

I twisted and jerked.

Duct tape. I heard the unmistakable sound of duct tape ripping.

I saw a shadowy figure coming toward me. He slapped the tape over my mouth. Then another piece over my eyes.

I couldn't see.

I couldn't move.

I couldn't breathe.

I tried to move, kick and punch, but I couldn't do anything. *I am going to die. And there's not a thing I can do about it.*

More ripping duct tape.

I screamed behind the tape, the noise coming out of my nose. My panicked lungs wanted to gulp in air from my mouth, but couldn't. I moved my jaw, trying to loosen the tape, but it only made my panic worse. I was suffocating. I was going to die.

I twisted. I jerked.

"Stop it, bitch," a gruff male voice yelled.

"Shut up," a second man hissed.

More tape ripping.

My ankles slammed together. Tape strapped them tight. Someone sat on them. Heavy pressure. Then to my wrists. Crushed and taped.

I couldn't breathe, I couldn't see and I couldn't move the lower half of my body. In seconds, I wouldn't be able to move my top half. Adrenaline shooting through me, I took everything I had and slammed myself upward.

Bam!

"Goddammit," the hairy man howled again.

Splintering pain shot through my head and shards of light burst behind my blindfolded eyes. My head had connected with something—someone. I slumped back, thousands of dull needles stabbing my brain, the world swirling around me even though I couldn't see it.

Sweat popped out from every pore and my stomach lurched up into my throat. I was going to throw up. A wave of darkness swept over me. I was slipping into oblivion. Nausea again. *Oh, God, what was happening?*

There was no time for an answer because I was jerked off the couch by one of them and slung over his thick shoulder. The stench of stale cigarette smoke and ripe onions seared my nose, and my duct-taped mouth gagged for all it was worth. My world was spinning and diving, and I tried to focus on anything to try to stop it. My tied hands flopped against his back, which felt spongy and damp beneath his shirt. My cheek rubbed against a rough strap, probably denim, so I figured he was wearing overalls.

Mother's garage door grumbled and growled as it opened, and a car engine revved up somewhere outside. Yes, a car, not a truck, or at least not a big one or diesel variety. I caught a whiff of gasoline and choking thick exhaust. Older. Ten years or more. Maybe. Geez, in truth it could be a brand new Mercedes for all I knew, but the thoughts kept my mind distracted from hysteria.

The car pulled into the garage and the big man carried me toward it. I heard footsteps and then a car door creaked open. He flopped me off his shoulder and tossed me in the seat. My nose buried into a smelly semi-plush cushion. Had to be a car. With rotted velour seats and god-knows-what imbedded in them.

The door at my feet closed and two other doors creaked open. The seat jiggled beside my head as one of the men sat down. It wasn't the overalls guy because I couldn't smell him. He turned me over on my side and put my head on what had to be his leg. I felt him lean over me, rustling with something in the floorboard. A ringing clang told me it was something metal, heavy thick metal, banging up against another similar metal object. More jiggling, another clank of metal and an audible hiss.

His hand grabbed the back of my head and something covered my nose.

Oh, God. It was some kind of gas. And I was not laughing.

Chapter Thirteen

T he first thing I noticed when I started coming around was the pounding behind my eyes. The second was the throbbing that shot out from there in every direction. The third thing I realized was that I couldn't be dead because dead people didn't have headaches. Indeed dead people didn't have bodies at all and therefore no heads to ache, and from the way mine was thumping I was fairly sure it was still right where I'd left it. I might still be alive, but there was no guarantee I would stay that way.

I did a quick physical inventory. In addition to my exploding head, my body ached in more places than I could count, much of it due to being slung around and trussed up with tape, which I still was. I also realized that I wasn't in the car. Not the right smell or feel or sound. The place was quiet except for the hum of a machine with a fan, maybe a window air conditioning unit, running off to my right. I was probably in a house on a couch, but I was definitely not back at Mother's. The rough and scratchy material of the sofa stunk of age and cigarette smoke. *Oh, God, I was going to throw up.*

Highly unpleasant noises gurgled up into my throat, and this time, there was no stopping it. I swung my tied hands to the side, feeling for the edge of the couch. I had to get off my back and somehow rip the tape off my mouth before the contents of my stomach came up and choked me to death. Clutching the couch, I tried to swing my ankles to the floor. As I did, my whole body rolled instead and my hands slammed against the floor, snapping my wrists back in unison. I slumped against the couch as razor-sharp pains spiked up both arms. Another flush of intense nausea roiled through me, and at that moment I sincerely wished they'd just shot me. My death wish was followed immediately by gut-wrenching contractions, the no-stopping-it-now-you're-gonna-puke spasms.

Just as the inevitable lurched up, an arm reached under my belly and jerked me up off the floor while another hand ripped the tape off my mouth.

The man tossed me back to the floor and I went about the business of emptying my stomach.

Although I was fairly preoccupied, I was still coherent enough to hear the men cursing. Several voices, all jumbled, and apparently none pleased with the unhappy turn of events, which was a shame since I was having such a great time myself.

When I finished, someone, yanked me to my feet, which I now realized were bare and standing on what felt like old shag carpeting. The man wiped a rag over my face and then down my shirt, huffing and snorting his distaste for the task. He then grabbed me around the waist and carried me across the room, presumably away from the mess. He set me down and, still woozy and trussed, I couldn't keep my balance and started to fall. He caught me again and I heard more grumbling. I felt hands on my ankles then a jerk. Tape and skin ripped away from my legs. I screamed. And cursed. After a string of pain-induced comments, I managed to ask, "What in the hell do you want with me?"

Silence.

I sensed that someone was still standing close to me, and since I didn't smell onions and cigarettes, I knew it wasn't the big guy who'd hauled me out of Mother's house. It was probably the smaller guy who gassed me, or maybe a third guy to whom I hadn't been properly introduced.

Since no one had said a word, I assumed that was a good thing. If they intended to kill me, they wouldn't care what they said or if I saw their faces. Buoyed with this new rationalization, I began to create scenarios that ultimately ended in my rapid release in the alive-and-well state. This, of course, led to the conclusion that I should share these thoughts. I do strange things when I'm terrified. "It seems to me that maybe things haven't gone exactly according to plan for you gentlemen."

They darn well hadn't for me. "My guess is that you've gotten yourselves into something you didn't really intend to."

Still, no words, but I could sense a building tension in the room. I chose to interpret it as agreement with my assessment. "Well, these things happen. Mistakes are made," I said, trying to sound very agreeable, understanding and accommodating. "There is an easy way out of it though."

I waited for a response, but there was none, and it is really hard carrying on a conversation with yourself when you can't see who is in the room—or even what kind of room it is. I envisioned a crappy little house at the edge of town with some dumb guys who've screwed up and don't know how to get out of it. "Tell you what, guys," I said, sounding pretty calm if I do say so myself. "Let's all just hop back in the car and drive around for a while. You don't have to go very far, just make it seem like it. I have no idea where I am and don't care." I was on a roll now. "You can just drop me off somewhere. I haven't seen any of you or anything for that matter. Other than tying me up and making me sick, you've been perfect gentlemen. Just put me out near a convenience store or some place with a phone and we'll forget any of this ever happened. Okay?"

Shuffling, mumbling, whispering and rustling sounds told me they might actually be thinking about it.

"If we stop this right now, we're all safe. However, if I turn up missing, people will look for me, one thing will lead to another and you'll be in for the long haul."

More foot shuffling and throat clearing. Hopefully they were also doing a few affirmative nods and hand signals, ones that directed somebody to do something that got me out of the mess alive. To further them along in that direction, I said, "Here's an idea—"

Someone grabbed me by the arm and dragged me across the room. I stumbled along behind him, wishing I could see where I was going. The shag carpet turned to a hard surface, maybe linoleum that felt gritty beneath my feet. Probably the kitchen.

I heard a door open and felt a whoosh of fresh air. I stumbled outside just as a car engine cranked up. I was put back in the car, and even though I was seated upright this time, it seemed to smell even worse than before. I suppose they noticed it too, because I heard coughing and windows rolling down. Then I heard the clank of cylinders and the happy hiss.

An arm wrapped around my shoulders and gripped my head as another hand forced the cup over my nose.

Aw, geez, not again...

Chapter
Fourteen

"**J**olene!"

I heard the voice and knew it was my mother's, but I couldn't respond to it.

"What have you been doing in here? You smell like vomit. Have you been drinking? Are you drunk? I leave the house for five minutes and look what I come back to. You did this once when you were a kid. You thought I didn't know about it, but I did. You didn't pull one over on me like you thought you did. You were sick as a dog then too. And now here you are, a grown woman. Why, I cannot believe it. Now, you get up off that couch and get yourself into the bathroom and get cleaned up. This is just pitiful."

With a concerted effort, I raised my hands to my head, threaded my fingers through my hair, and pulled. "Ow!" Yes, this was real. Of course, it could be just a dream and I was only imagining that I pulled my hair. I groaned and pulled again, trying to drag myself back into assured reality. Nah, it really hurt. My eyes felt glued shut but I managed to crack the lids apart slightly. Wiping the hair away from my face, I saw the fuzzy image of my mother standing above me.

"Oh, my Lord!" Lucille shrieked. "What on earth happened to your face!"

I tried not to move too fast and slid my hands to my cheeks, then upward. My forehead stung like sunburn. So did the skin around my mouth. And my lips, I realized, were raw and swollen. And it was sticky.

"Half your eyebrows are gone!"

"The wonders of duct tape," I muttered, making the connection without really understanding why. Part of my brain was working, but it was not firing on all cylinders. How did I get back here? What happened after the last gassing? How'd I remember that? What time is it? Then, somehow the jumper cables connected to my brain, the engine turned over and I just knew. "Call Jerry. Tell him I was kidnapped."

"What!"

Autopilot was kicking in. "Lock all the doors. Get your gun."

"What!" Her voice escalated into a shriek.

Lucille was exactly one more "what" away from serious panic. I couldn't blame her. I wasn't sure I believed what had happened and I'd been there for it. I took a deep breath and pushed myself upright, gingerly opening my eyes as wide as I could and trying to blink the room into focus. No focus. God, I had a hangover and I hadn't even been drinking. "Gas. Must have been the gas. " I had to get some kind of control over the nausea so I could think. "I need Benadryl and water."

Mother stood there for a few seconds, just staring, then scurried off and brought it back to me. I took a whole tablet instead of my usual half. I needed help, badly. It would take a good twenty minutes to kick in and we had to get moving now.

"What happened to you, Jolene?" she said, twisting her hands.

Another flood of remembering. "Some men took me from this very couch sometime after you left. I don't know why. They stuck a mask over my face and gassed me. I don't remember much after that. I saw things though. Strange things. But my eyes were taped closed so I couldn't have." I shook my head. That made no sense. "They took me to a house somewhere, said not a single word to me, then gassed me again and brought me back here. At least that's all I remember. Oh, and I threw up."

"Why, that's, that's…"

"Hard to believe. Yeah, for me too." I rubbed my temples and tilted my head slowly to the side to test for vertigo. The room swayed a little but didn't go into full tilt and whirl. I took that as a good sign. Still, I would be lucky to be able to walk across the room, much less anything else. "What time is it?"

"Around midnight. Fritz just left. Oh, my Lord, Jolene, why on earth would somebody kidnap you? Are you hurt?"

My personal inventory had turned up general muscle soreness but apparently no broken bones. My wrists were definitely sore and being taped up had really pissed me off, and I was sure I was bruised, but there was nothing really serious that I could tell. "Nothing serious. As to why, I don't know. The only thing I could figure is that they made a mistake." Then, like a hairspray can to the head, it hit me. I'd been in Mother's house on Mother's couch. *Oh, my God! They'd meant to get Lucille.* "We have to get out of here!"

The urge to jump and run was great, but the resulting falling on my face would hamper our exit so I took it slow and eased myself up. I also tried to keep my voice calm and direct. "Is the car in the garage?"

"Yes," Lucille said, frozen in place and not looking so very good herself. "I just put it in."

"Good."

I pushed myself fully upright and stared straight ahead, trying to get my balance. Whatever they had knocked me out with had not done my system any good. I am highly sensitive to drugs of any variety, including the antihistamine I'd just ingested. Without any nausea to fight, a whole tablet would put me out like a light for at least six hours. Tonight, however, there was plenty to fight and getting sleepy was the least of my worries.

Other than oxygen, nitrogen and helium, the only other gas in a cylinder that I could come up with was nitrous oxide. Laughing gas—like at the dental office—although I didn't remember anything being the least bit funny. Rounding out my knowledge of NO2 was a newspaper article—actually, I'd only read the headline and the lead—about some idiot falling out a window after recreationally gassing himself at a party. Lost all muscle control and sense of balance and just toppled out. The floor swayed beneath me, confirming that I could encounter a similar fate, but I managed to stay upright. The antihistamine combo might not have been such a great plan after all. "We have to get out of here, Mother, and I can't drive." Hell, I couldn't even walk. "You'll have to drive us to town. We'll head to the police station in Redwater because it is closer than Bowman City and the road has fewer stretches of open highway."

Lucille just stood there, staring.

"Mother? Did you hear me?"

Lucille nodded ever so slightly. "To the station."

"Do not go bonkers on me, Lucille. You have to do this. Go into your room and get your gun."

"My gun," she murmured.

Oh, boy. "Your clips are all loaded, right?" I waited for her to nod then repeated what she needed to do. "Go get your gun and all your clips. Bring them in here."

"In here."

"Yes. We need to leave so you have to hurry."

She nodded again but didn't move.

"The gun, Mother. Now!"

She jumped then stared at me for a second with wide eyes. After a few blinks and a shake of her head, she ran.

While Mother scurried to collect the artillery, I did a more thorough personal damage assessment. I could see again, pretty clearly, which was nice, although I doubted I wanted to venture too close to any mirrors. Standing was going reasonably well and I hadn't thrown up. Both good points. My mouth tasted horrible and was as dry as cotton so I took a shaky step toward the kitchen, intending to get a drink, then froze. What if they were still in the house, waiting to get Lucille as they'd intended? God, why hadn't I thought of that first? "Mother!"

She came running into the room, a gun case in one hand and a bulging blue Wal-Mart sack in the other. "What is it?"

"We've got to get out of here. Right now. They might still be in here somewhere."

Lucille's eyes widened a notch more then began to narrow into a glare. She still looked petrified, but there was a burning ember of mad mixed in, and that was a good sign. "Get my purse, Jolene. It's right there on the dining room table in front of you. Keys are in the car. I'll be right there."

I stumbled to the table and grabbed the purse. "I can't drive, Mother."

"Well, I most certainly can," she said, back to her old self. "You just get yourself in the car. I'm right behind you."

Using the walls and furniture as makeshift crutches, I ricocheted my way to the garage. Within seconds, we were in the car and headed toward Redwater Falls.

As we pulled out of the drive, I made a quick survey of the neighborhood. A few porch lights, two cars in driveways—and one parked in the street a half block in front of us. Not necessarily anything to worry about. I kept my eye on it anyway. As our headlights glared through the car, I caught a glimpse of what looked like a head above the headrest. Someone was sitting behind the wheel. "Let's go," I said, not telling her what I'd seen.

As we passed the dark sedan, its engine revved and the headlights flashed on. The lights went off and on a couple of times and then it lurched forward after us.

Lucille sucked in her breath. "Well, shit!"

"Go, Mother. Just watch in front of you," I coached. "It's probably nothing."

She kept glancing at the rear view mirror anyway. "Nothing, my hind foot! Now, that just makes me mad. Like he was just sitting there waiting on us to leave."

"Yeah, that's what bad guys do. We've all seen the same movies. Now go!"

"Well, I'll not have it! Following me like that after I left my very own house. Why, the very nerve."

Mother's paralyzing fear had vaporized and in its place was a serious case of rage—one might call it road rage on a technicality, but that's really kind of limiting for Lucille.

The tailing car rushed up on us, then immediately backed off about ten car lengths—maybe because Lucille punched the gas and sprayed them with half-inch chunks of gravel. Muttering and cursing, Mother proceeded to take the next turn on two wheels. More gravel flew and the Buick fishtailed.

My stomach did the same. I prayed for the Benadryl to kick in, but every punch of the gas pedal and yank of the steering wheel pushed me closer to another unhappy upheaval. Consumed with fighting the nausea, I couldn't do much looking over my shoulder at the car behind us or worry about how fast—or insanely—Lucille was driving. Both were potentially fatal, but when motion sickness has its hooks in me, I don't much care about anything else and feel like dying anyway. This would be one of those mixed blessing things.

When we hit the pavement, Lucille punched up into passing gear. And kept it there.

I'd rolled my window down to help stave off the nausea, but the wind noise made the speed even more terrifying. That bugs the size of pigeons were smacking against the windshield like hail was a little disconcerting as well.

"Damn grasshoppers." Lucille gripped the steering wheel with both hands and leaned forward, her nose just above her clenched fingers, squinting to see through the darkness and bug splatters. "Good thing I know the roads."

Yes, a good thing, that. I chanced a glance in her direction and had an unfortunate thought, considering the current circumstances. "Did you ever have that last cataract surgery?"

She wiggled her butt in the seat and leaned a half-inch closer to the windshield. "I can see just fine out of my good eye, now shut your mouth so I can concentrate on driving."

Crap. I'd just survived being kidnapped, gassed twice and manhandled by a smelly ape and now I was going to die in car crash? Seemed kind of anticlimactic.

Since there was only one way to Redwater Falls from Kickapoo and we were on it, there were no shortcuts and no options until we hit the edge of town, which was about ten miles away. The car behind us was keeping up with us and maybe even getting closer. It was hard for me to tell since even a quick glance sent me reeling.

"Oh, my Lord," Lucille shrieked. "He's flashing his headlights at us like we don't know he's back there. "Did you call the police?"

"I'm trying. If I look down to dial the phone…" I said, doing just that. A wave of nausea hit.

"Well, I sure wish you'd try harder because that car is just getting closer." She stomped her foot on the accelerator—hard—but the car didn't respond. "This damn Buick won't go over ninety-seven."

Yes, that meant that's how fast we were going. Ninety-seven miles per hour in the dark on a two-lane road with a half-blind geriatric at the wheel and a windshield covered with bug guts. What could go wrong?

"Now, he's waving something out the window! Oh, my Lord," she screeched, bobbing her head up and down between looking forward and looking in the mirror. "He's gonna shoot!" She unclutched one hand from the steering wheel and wagged it at the floorboard. "Get my gun out of my purse and hand it to me. Hurry up!"

I don't usually agree with my mother on much of anything, especially regarding firearms. Maybe it was pure fear, revenge for the kidnapping or a motion sickness death wish, whatever the case, we were on the same page tonight. I kept my eyes focused on the road straight ahead and felt around beneath my legs for her purse then pulled it up into my lap. I fished around inside and found the soft case, fumbled with the zipper and pulled out the gun. "Is it loaded?"

"Of course it's loaded, Jolene, what good is a gun if it's not loaded? Now, hand it to me."

"You can't shoot, you're driving. You can't do both."

"Well then, you reach over here and hold the wheel."

"That seems like a really bad plan going a hundred miles an hour, not that anything we're doing here is a good one." I lifted the gun and held it out in front of me, trying to get it level enough with my line of vision to see what I was dealing with. "You just pay attention to the road."

Lucille sucked in her breath. You're not going to try to shoot it are you?"

"If I have to. I've done it before." At the handgun handling and safety class Jerry wishes he'd never taken me to. "Are you sure you saw a gun?"

"I'll tell you what, I'll just stop this car. You can hunt around for the number nine on your phone while I shoot them all myself right here and now!" She let off the accelerator. "Yes, ma'am, that's exactly what I'll do."

"Do not stop this car!"

She jumped and the car lurched forward. "All right! Quit yelling at me!"

"Just keep driving." I clutched the door and tried to balance with the movement. "I'll try to get them to back off."

Lucille growled and clutched the wheel tighter, possibly realizing that I had a point. Possibly. "Well, you be careful with it." She paused for added emphasis. "Be real careful."

Now, do not think that her concern was for my safety. Oh, no, indeed. You see, her concern was for the gun. That pistol is like a daughter to her. Actually, no, much better than that. She loves the gun and has great admiration and respect for it, not that any of my childhood neuroses were cropping up at this particular inopportune moment. As I held the gun in my hand, something about it felt different. Or maybe I just didn't really remember. Or care. Until now. "Does this damn thing have a clip in it?"

"I already told you it's loaded. I always keep a full clip in it at the house. It comes in handy as you well know."

Indeed I did know that. A lot of people knew that.

"It's on safety, of course. I always have the safety on. You know about the safety, right?"

"I took the damn class, Mother. I know about the safety."

"Well, you most certainly do not know about the safety because they're all a little different. This one is real easy to find with your thumb there on the left side. Flip it forward."

I fumbled around until I thought I had the safety released. Doing it all by feel was harder than you'd think. "Is there one in the chamber?"

"Now why would you ask a dumb thing like that? I thought you took a class, Jolene. Didn't they teach you anything at all? Oh, for Pete's sake just take it off safety, chamber a round and shoot. Like in the movies."

Nothing was ever like in the movies. "This doesn't feel right," I said, trying to find a comfortable hold. The handgrip's different. Rubbery and fatter."

"That's the laser sight. Don't you know anything?"

"Apparently not."

"Oh, that's right. The laser's new. It's a new gun too, but you wouldn't know the difference about that. This one is a Kimber Ultra-Elite. The name kind of bothered me at first, what with that little twerp Kimberlee always coming to mind over it. Then I decided to just call her Miss Ellie and that just works out fine."

"Oh, for godsakes."

Lucille wiggled her fingers on the steering wheel and glanced at the rear view mirror. "Well, I enjoy my guns. Now, get it pointed out the window and get on with it. This one works the same way as my Little Lady, except for the laser. The old sight had a switch, remember. Well, this is better. Just squeeze the handgrip. You'll see a red dot. Or, you could just shoot the thing. You supposedly had a class."

Oh, if only we had time for me to supposedly and properly respond to that little comment. I squeezed the handle and a red dot of light danced across the dash of the car. Okay. I had the safety off and could work the sight. Now all I had to do was chamber a round and shoot. I did not want to do it.

"Did you chamber the first round, Jolene, because I didn't hear it. It's a real distinctive sound and I didn't hear it. I don't have time to explain every little thing to you so why don't you just hand it over here to me and I'll take care of it."

Oh, how I'd like to unleash my scathing wit on Mother Control Freak about now. "Just chill, I'm getting it!"

"Well, you better hurry up. They're getting closer," she said, eyeing the mirror. "I'd go for the radiator."

"Yes, Mother, I realize you have a thing for radiators."

"Don't be getting smart with me, Missy, I hit what I shoot at," she snapped.

I took a deep breath and told myself I had no choice. The vehicle was maybe four car lengths behind us, and any Driver's Ed student knows that's not safe. Not safe at all when you're going ninety-seven miles per hour. I took a deep breath and stared straight ahead to keep what little balance I'd found. My hands were shaking, but I held the gun in front of me with my left hand and pulled the slide back with the right. *Snap.* "Fine. Done."

"Well, it is about time. I knew I hadn't heard you do that, I just knew it. Now lean out there and shoot 'em!"

I did not want to do this. Still shaking, I slid around in the seat and worked my knees up under me and leaned my left arm on the door. I snaked the gun out the window, using my left hand and leaned out so I could see. However, going backwards made the world spin in the wrong direction and the hurricane force winds whipped my hair around, stinging my eyes. This did not seem like a good plan on any level.

"Hurry up! Shoot!"

I held as steady as I could, keeping close to the car so they couldn't see what I was doing or shoot at me easily if they were so inclined. Besides, I didn't want to kill anybody, I only wanted to keep whoever it was from following us, warn them off. It had seemed the only choice we had a minute ago. "I don't think we should do this."

"Shoot!"

"They haven't really done anything wrong."

"Shoot! Now!"

I aimed the pistol toward the car and looked for the squiggly red dot. With the hair in my eyes I couldn't see much of anything except headlights blinding me. They apparently could see the red laser beam, however, because they started backing off in a hurry.

"Shoot!" Lucille screeched again. She let off the gas and hit the brakes, which was sort of not the point of a getaway, but adrenaline was screaming just as loud as she was. "Shoot it! Hurry!"

So I did.

Twice.

And then I leaned the whole top half of my body out the window and shot again, this time with two hands on the grip. Rapid fire. "I'm empty," I said, ducking back inside.

She punched the accelerator and we were off again. "Looks like you at least got a headlight, she said, glancing in the rear view mirror. "But they're still coming. Hurry up and reload."

"I'm doing the best I can here, Mother, now where's the damn clip release?" She told me—in excruciating detail—adding further tedious instructions on how to release one clip and slide in a new one. "I'm not a monkey doing brain surgery. I know how to change a damn clip for godsake. You just get us to the police station."

"I know what to do, Jolene, now would you let me drive."

"Absolutely, Mother Dear. I wouldn't dare presume you don't know what you're doing and that I needed to tell you how to do every little thing as if you're a three-year-old."

"Yes, well, that's why you ought not do it." She leaned closer to the steering wheel. "I'm glad you're feeling better, Jolene, really I am, but would you kindly shut up so I can watch the road. You're distracting me. And it's dark."

Meaning, she couldn't see for shit.

I managed a glance in the side mirror. "Looks like they've stopped chasing us. You can slow down some now." And significantly reduce our chances of a one-car fatality. "I'll let you know if I see lights again."

"Well, maybe you did hit the radiator after all," she said, begrudgingly. "Even a blind hog finds an acorn every now and then." She let off the accelerator. By the time we were down to 75 it seemed like we were crawling. "They could still be driving without their lights, so you pay attention. I'll speed up again if I have to, don't you worry about that."

Nope, that was not one of the blind hog's worries. I had plenty of others, however.

After a few minutes, I saw a cluster of lights and what looked like a tall tower sticking up out of the middle of it up ahead on the right. "Is that an oil well going in over there?"

Lucille glanced over but did a good job of keeping her eyes and the car on the road. It seemed like she'd slowed down a little more too. "Yes, I believe it is."

"Is that what you saw behind your house?"

"Sort of. I don't think it was that big though. There was other equipment around, but I don't know about those boxes and things, I really couldn't see all of it."

As we went flying by the road that led out to the rig, I noticed a truck pulling away from the group and heading toward us. It had a row of yellow lights across the cab and a pole sticking up behind. "That's Gilbert Moore coming out of there."

"Well, what's he doing out here in the middle of the night?"

"That's a rig. Maybe it's his or maybe he was just out there fixing something on it. Guess he works all hours."

"Well, I don't trust him and now here he is again. I wish I'd cornered him at the Dairy Queen when I had the chance. If we weren't running for our lives, I'd drive right over there right now and pin him in where he'd have to face me. He'd be giving me some straight answers, that's what he'd be doing."

I watched the lights on the truck from the side mirror. He was almost out to the road."

"You keep an eye out and see where he goes. If he follows us, you just shoot him too."

"Sounds perfectly reasonable to me." It really did. "I'll go for the radiator."

She glanced over at me, unsure of whether she should expound on the fact that I'd learned something from her or chastise me for being a smartass. Yes, we know which it was, but thankfully she kept silent for once.

I didn't realize I'd been holding my breath until I saw Gilbert Moore's truck turn the other way and a gush of air burst from my lips. "He's not following us."

"Hmmph. That's too bad. I had plans for him."

Chapter
Fifteen

Lucille pulled up to the Redwater Falls Police Station in less than five minutes. We even arrived without anyone tailing us or a fatal high speed car crash. Mother parked near the door in a "no parking" area and we hurried inside.

There were a couple of things that convinced the officer at the front desk that we needed help. One was, of course, the very obvious use of duct tape on my face. That in itself, he noted, wasn't particularly unusual, or even indicative of a crime, but it did get his attention and was a good backup for the story we told.

What got us the instant royal treatment, however, was the simple stating of our names. In fact, his rather dour face erupted in glee, or perhaps appreciation. The good sergeant, it seemed, had been the lucky winner of the station's one-would-think-illegal betting pool on when Mother and I would be involved in another crime or something to that effect. While this certainly was not a pleasant discovery, the thousand dollars in prize money had definitely bought us some good will with Sergeant Jackpot.

He promptly made us comfortable in an interrogation room with an assortment of drinks while he went about tending our car as well as locating Jerry and a Redwater detective to deal with us. He was very nice in a "come see my prize-winning catch" sort of way. To his credit, he didn't laugh in front of us.

Mother had explained to the sergeant about the awful stress she'd been through and insisted on an immediate trip to the ladies room to freshen up. While Lucille was gone primping, I guzzled two bottles of water to try to re-hydrate myself and flush out the toxins in my system. When she got back I was definitely ready for my turn at "freshening up."

Unfortunately, the second I walked in the restroom door, I saw myself in a mirror. I screamed, horrified then smacked my hand over my mouth to stop myself, which was a really dumb thing to do since my lips looked like two slices of over-ripe plums and felt like they'd been peeled. And that was the least of my problems.

Now, I'm not one of those women who is obsessed with her looks. I do make an effort with my hair and I wear a basic amount of makeup, mostly mascara and a concealer for my perpetual dark circles. I am generally neat, clean, presentable, and sometimes even cute. The person in the mirror was none of those things. Not one. And on top of it all, she looked like somebody had smacked her in the face with a baseball bat. Twice. Of course it had to be a bat with tweezers because I was missing about half of each eyebrow. There was not much epi left in the dermis of my forehead or mouth area either, and my hair was both matted down and sticking up. I truly wanted to cry.

Instead, I slunk into the stall and tended to business, then slunk back out and reassessed my options. I couldn't re-grow skin or eyebrows in the next ten minutes but I could wash my face and maybe my hair. And the smell had to be dealt with, so there was also some laundry about to be done in the sink. What the slimy pink hand soap would do to my clothes was not nearly as worrisome as what it was going to do to my hair. The wall dryer would work just swell for my hair and shirt, however, so there was some hope.

Feeling a little better—I always feel better when I have a plan—I grabbed a stack of paper towels, stripped off my shirt and started methodically soaping, rinsing and drying.

It took a while, but I was able to scrub a lot of the adhesive off my face—or at least the skin that had adhesive stuck to it. Luckily I had more eyebrows left than I'd first thought. The sticky stuff had gooed them up in little clumps, and except for a big hole in the middle on the left brow; I was in pretty good shape. The extended scrubbing also made my whole face pretty red so the stripes weren't so obvious anymore. I had "brushed" my teeth and mouth with a wet and soapy paper towel, which was just as horrible as it sounds, but after much rinsing, my mouth felt reasonably clean. I wet and fluffed my hair back into fair shape and was wringing out my shirt when Sergeant Jackpot burst through the bathroom door.

"What are you doing!"

Incredulous, furious and hysterical would all be words I'd use to describe the uniformed maniac who stood in the doorway of the ladies room, waving his arms and bellowing at me. Of course it could have just been my own hysteria creeping in since I was holding my shirt in my hands and had on nothing but a bra above my shorts.

"What have you done!" he yelled, pointing at the wet shirt I was clutching. "You weren't supposed to do that!"

"What, wash my shirt?"

"Yes! No! You can't wash anything. You're evidence. I can't believe you did this! Do you have any idea how much trouble I'm in now because of you? I should have just locked you in a cell. You! I knew better. I knew! But nooooo, I had to be nice." He said this last word with a sarcastic singsong effect. "You've really done it now."

"*I've* done it!" Yes, I yelled right back. "I'm the one who was kidnapped, drugged and chased across town by lunatics. If you wanted me to stay looking like something the cat dragged up, you should have said so instead of strutting around patting yourself on the back for the money you made off me. And maybe, if instead of running off to gossip about who was in the interrogation room, you had actually done your job, we wouldn't have this problem."

"What!" It was more of a booming bellow than an actual word. "Why, you little..."

Oh, I'd hit that nail on the head. "Hey! How was I supposed to know I couldn't wash my face? Am I a mind reader too? You want to make bets on that? If you do, you might not like the odds. Because I'm betting you're in bigger trouble than I am right now."

A crowd had gathered behind the apoplectic sergeant, who'd been holding the door open, and I felt a little naked, to say the least. At about this same time, Jackpot realized he wasn't exactly presenting a professional image to the impromptu audience.

As more uniforms appeared in my line of vision, I decided a graceful retreat might be the better course of action for both of us. "Look, Sergeant, I didn't wash my shirt and hair to ruin your life. Frankly, all I cared about was trying to not stink."

No, it wasn't a good suck-up, but it was as good as it was going to get. Chuckles rippled through the crowd packing the hallway at the edge of the door, breaking some of the tension, but Jackpot couldn't let it go. He continued to paw and snort and repeat himself.

"I cannot believe this," he said again. "You should have known. There are sixteen different cop shows on every hour of every day. Everybody knows you have to collect evidence. You have to have evidence. Any idiot knows that. The criminals sure know it. I can't believe you did this!"

I'd given him a graceful out and he'd rejected it. Fine. We could do things his way. As I geared up for a "get out of here or" kind of threat, I noticed a familiar face working his way through the crowd. I relaxed a little, actually a lot. My knight in shining armor had arrived. I mouthed "I'm sorry," but Sheriff Parker just shook his head. It didn't bother me, this head shaking. I've gotten used to it. Find it kind of cute even. Now scowling with head shaking, that's a different thing. But this was the slow, side-to-side disbelief thing. He was probably more worried than mad. I lifted the corners of my mouth in a fake little smile.

Jerry put a hand on Sergeant Loser's shoulder. "It's done. Let me handle it."

"Handle what?" Jackpot said, still glaring directly at me. "There's nothing left to handle. She has once again single hand-edly made the entire Redwater Falls Police Department look like a bunch of fools."

Wow, I was more powerful than I'd imagined. But he didn't really mean the whole department, he meant himself, although that didn't make much sense either. Basically, I'd embarrassed him by walking out of the interrogation room without permission, nothing more. Well, besides accusing him of being incompetent at his job. "My mother helped."

"Let me talk to her alone," Jerry said, "and find out exactly what happened. This might not even be your problem."

"Huh?" Jackpot took another look at Jerry and belatedly figured out whose hand was gripping his shoulder. Possibilities and hope began to spring forth and ease the wrinkles and red blotches from his face. "Thank God you're here, Sheriff," he said, it dawning on him that perhaps there were boundary issues that could be exploited. "You make it so she's not my problem, and I'll be the happiest man in this county. Make it so she never sets foot in the city limits of Redwater Falls again and I'll have a statue carved in your honor. Why I'd—" He stopped himself, realizing he was groveling. Then very authoritatively and for the benefit of the crowd, he said, "You let me know when this is handled, Sheriff." Cutting his eyes to me, he whispered to Jerry, "I don't know how you do it. She can't be that good in bed."

"I heard that!" He practically ran out of the restroom, but I stomped toward the door with not a single care that I wasn't wearing a shirt. I was going to rip out his ugly little tongue and stuff it up his nose. "Did you hear that?" I said indignantly to Jerry, although I knew very well he had. A good portion of the crowd had heard it too, and many were eyeing me accordingly, trying to decide for themselves. Idiots. "Yes, I am, you want details, what?"

Jerry pushed the crowd back and stepped inside, closing the door behind him. "Jolene, Jolene, Jolene…"

"You can chew me out in just a minute, Jerry, I have some unfinished business down the hall."

He caught my arm as I tried to make good on my threat. "Jolene, Jolene, Jolene…"

"Oh, save it."

Now, I have been scolded by Jerry before, and I do not like it, not one little bit. I liked it even less when there was a significant chance that I deserved it, which I did not. Still, I felt obligated to attempt a defense. "That man who just insulted me is an ass. Did you know he won a betting pool about me? Did you know this stupid department *had* a betting pool about me? Did you know that? And then I walk in the door and he hears my name and…" I stopped and looked at Jerry again and I did not like what I was seeing. "Oh, my God! If you—"

"They wouldn't let me actually place a bet." His lips twitched up a little at the corners. "Said it would be like insider trading."

My mouth fell open in absolute outrage, but before I could even sputter, he had wrapped his arms around me and sealed my lips with his own for a quick kiss. He leaned back and ran his thumb between my brows and along my cheek, trying to smooth away the frown. "I'd heard about the pool through the grapevine, but I didn't feel the need to dignify it with any kind of comment. Enough said?"

"Yes." I laid my face against his chest and held on to him. "It's been a really long day, Jerry."

He held me and rubbed my back for a few moments then said, "I've heard the condensed version of what happened to you tonight. Let's get you dressed and we'll go through it chapter and verse."

I leaned back and looked up at him. "I didn't know, Jerry, really I didn't. It did not occur to me that somebody wanted to pick over me like they do a corpse. I just felt gross and dirty and I wanted to clean up. I didn't know it was going to be a major crime to wash my shirt." I'm not a fan of crime shows, but I'd seen enough bits and pieces to know that spending the night with the forensics people would have been pleasant. "Would you want somebody putting plastic bags on your hands and cleaning your fingernails like a corpse? That's what they do, isn't it?"

He stroked his hand through my damp hair and brushed his fingers across my cheek. "It's okay. It will mean we won't have physical evidence from you to connect you to where you were taken, but there are still things we can do. We should probably get blood work to see if they can determine what you were drugged with."

"What's the point? It was nitrous oxide." I saw his raised eyebrow so I explained. "No, I'm not positive, but it seemed right. There was a bit of a high but I went out quick and I felt horrible afterward. But there were two cylinders clanging together, not just one, so I don't know how that works."

"If it was nox, that's good."

"Why?"

"They mixed it with oxygen. Knew what they were doing. Otherwise, you'd probably have frostbite or be paralyzed or dead."

"Great. I was kidnapped by knowledgeable druggies. I'm so fortunate." It could have been worse, that was for certain, but it had been damn bad enough and I was shaken. A traitorous tear leaked out of one eye. "I really didn't mean to screw this up, Jerry, really I didn't."

"It's okay." He kissed me again. "Now, put your shirt back on."

Yes, I'd forgotten I'd been standing in front of the world in my bra. "I have to dry it first." My voice sounded kind of pitiful even to me. I pushed away, shuffled over to the wall-mounted hand dryer and punched the button. Hot air burst from the nozzle and I held my shirt beneath it, wiggling and jiggling it for maximum heat coverage. "You go on. I'll be out in a few minutes."

"That's not going to dry anytime soon. My undershirt wouldn't cover up much so I'll go find you something."

As he turned toward the door, it opened and a plastic-covered white shirt came flying in. Jerry bent down and picked up a hanger with a man's dress shirt, fresh from the laundry. "Peace offering, I do believe."

"They just didn't want to see what I'd do if they handed me an orange jumpsuit, that's all. Probably because somebody has a bet on when that will happen too."

He shook his head. "It's going to be okay, Jolene. And really, you're doing better than I'd expected. After what I heard, I was prepared for you to be hysterical."

"Hysterical? Me? Nah, I was just standing half-naked in the police station bathroom screaming at a cop while half the police station watched. I am calm, collected and in complete control." I ripped the plastic off the shirt and started unbuttoning a heavily starched size 18 1/2 Big and Tall. Once I got it on and buttoned, I was not sure I'd improved the situation all that much. I looked more like a five-year-old playing dress-up. So, I rolled up the sleeves and unbuttoned the bottom four buttons, tying the ends in front, low across my hips. "Truth is, if I let myself think about what really happened, I'd be a wreck. Hysterical is just one mental replay away."

"You're going to have to talk about it, Jolene, when we get back in the room. Are you ready for that?"

"No, but I'll do it anyway. I'll even try not to yell and will be appropriately traumatized for the interview, because I am traumatized. It was not a fun experience tonight, Jerry, believe me, and in case you didn't know by now I use a lot of denial, anger and sarcasm to deal with these horrific situations I seem to find myself in here in the great state of Texas." Yes, my voice was escalating. "So just because I'm not bawling my eyes out right this second doesn't mean I'm not upset. Because I can be really upset and you might not even know it. I hide it real well sometimes," I said, my voice quivering just a little. I was hiding nothing and we both knew it. "I really do."

"I will certainly have to remember that," he said, trying to chuckle and make it sound sincere. The incident had shaken him and he was worried. He wasn't showing it, not even a little, but I knew. He was trying to help me get through the interview before the emotion of it all overwhelmed me. "You'll be talking to Lieutenant Daniel Perez. He's a good guy. Probably won't have a crush on you like Rick did since he's got kids your age, but you never know." He attempted a little fake laugh to lighten the mood, but since it didn't seem to be working, he shrugged. "He does his job well."

Actually, it had worked a little—the topical distraction, not the fake laugh—as I was willing to think of anything besides recent events. "Rick had a crush on me? Really?"

He frowned. "I was speculating."

It was darned flattering to be sure that Detective Rick Rankin, AKA Surfer Dude, had lusted after me. I'd suspected it myself, had even teased Rick about it, but it was nice hearing Jerry acknowledge it. Couldn't hurt for him to think that someone else found me attractive, particularly a hot young guy. "He moved to Tyler, right? East of Dallas? Gosh, what was he twenty-two, twenty-three?"

"Actually, Jolene, he's thirty-two and recently engaged."

"Really?" I'd always liked Rick and it was kind of nice to know he'd found somebody. He always seemed lonely to me. "Have you met her? Is she nice? Smart? Pretty?"

"Yes to all," Jerry said. "Now, come on, let's get this over with."

No sooner had the words left his mouth than my mother walked by carrying a cup of coffee, another bottle of water and a can of Dr Pepper. She didn't even bat an eye at my shirt. "At least you smell better."

It was a pretty fair compliment in Lucille-ese, so I considerately carried the Dr Pepper for her as we marched back to the interrogation room. I chugged down half the can before we got there for courage. I was not looking forward to the inquisition no matter how cavalier I pretended to be.

Mother put the bottle of water on the table, then sat herself down, took a dainty sip of coffee and said, "I should draw in your eyebrow before we talk to the detective. That looks pitiful."

"That's very thoughtful, Mother, but the Dr Pepper and the ego boost are good enough for now." I plopped myself down in the chair beside her and took another long swig. "Besides, I kind of like it. Sets off the big red stripe where my lips used to be."

Lucille tsk-tsked me as only she can do. "I have foundation that would cover that up."

I scowled some more.

Jerry sat down next to me, leaned back and crossed his arms. "Try to behave."

About one more directive from either of them and it was going to get ugly. Really ugly.

The door opened and a short olive-skinned man carrying a manila file folder, clipboard, yellow legal pad and pocket-sized recorder marched in. "Well, ladies," he said, unceremoniously dumping his cargo on the table. "I'd be lying if I said I hadn't heard about you two. Probably couldn't find two people in the building who haven't."

"Lies," Lucille said, setting her coffee cup on the table so she could bang her fist for emphasis. "All lies, I tell you. The entire Redwater Police Department is just a bunch of gossiping, betting-pool cheaters that make up wicked lies about innocent citizens to suit their tawdry imaginations. My daughter Jolene hasn't done a thing wrong. Ever."

Oh, if only I had that statement in writing. She didn't mean a word of it, of course, and the glaringly obvious omission of her own culpability was comforting to no one.

"And," she continued, "there's certainly no cause to be picking on a frail senior citizen who can barely get herself over to the senior center to take her meals. It's an outrage, I tell you!"

Yes, an outrage indeed. I tried to keep a blank face while Jerry did the sighing for both of us, and gave a weak shrug in the detective's direction. There really wasn't much you could say anyway.

Lieutenant Daniel Perez was about five-five, with silver-streaked black hair and a gold-rimmed front tooth. His gray suit was rumpled and his tie askew. He looked almost as tired as I felt.

"My information about you came from police reports, Miz Jackson," he said to Lucille. "I think it's fair to say that you and your daughter have been involved in a number of our cases for one reason or another. But that's not why we're here now, is it?"

I glanced at my mother, who was tapping her fingers on the table, looking around the room, appearing to have not heard one word he'd said.

Perez took a seat at the end of the table. "You should know, however, that we have reports of a car matching the one you drove up in racing down Seymour Highway at speeds nearing one hundred miles per hour."

"Well, that's why we're here, for pity's sake," Lucille said, an obvious "duh" in her tone. "And if it weren't for the fact that my Buick is rigged with a governor, we'd have been here a lot sooner."

"Gunfire was also reported."

"Then I guess you know also," Lucille said, not skipping a beat, "that it's just a thousand wonders we're not dead. Are you going to find out who was trying to kill us or just keep making it out like we did something wrong?"

We hadn't even gotten started and this had already gone bad. I rubbed my eyes and tried to hold my head up. "We were running for our lives tonight, detective. You know that. As for the other, uh, situations we wound up in, well, there were extenuating circumstances."

"Oh, Jolene, you don't have to make excuses for us to this man," Mother said, more than a little irate. "We have simply been victims of circumstance. We were just doing our best to take control of the unfortunate situations we found ourselves in and not be victims, just like tonight. Why, who knows how many gangs of murderers would be running loose if not for us doing what we had to." She pointed an infamous nail at Perez. "You people should be grateful to us instead of criticizing."

Perez looked at Lucille in sincere disbelief. After a few seconds, he realized—as we all have—that there are times when there is just nothing to be said and you just have to move along. He punched the button on the recorder, said some memorized legal spiel and ended with, "Tell me what happened tonight."

Figuring I'd better spit out as much as I could before Mother threw another rock at the hornet's nest—and had it captured on tape—I said, "We'd just gotten back from grabbing a bite at the Dairy Queen. Mother went over to a friend's house and I stayed there, waiting on a call from..."

"Me," Jerry said. "She was waiting on a call from me. We were planning to have dinner, but I got tied up and couldn't make it."

That was a detail I needed to piece into the whole picture later. "Anyway," I said, back to the point. "The short version is that I was at my mother's house, asleep on the couch, when for reasons I can't imagine, some lunatics broke in, tied me up, gassed me, hauled me off to some dumpy house where they said not one word, just watched as I threw up, gassed me again and left me back at my mother's on the couch, considerably worse for the wear. There was no apparent point to the whole fiasco at least as far as I know at this point."

I didn't volunteer that my mother was most likely the intended target because it was likely to add a good two hours to our time in the room. I'd just tell Jerry and let him figure out what to do with my assumption. "Once again, I was minding my own business, not bothering anyone, and somebody very literally dragged me out of the house and into the middle of whatever kind of mess this whole thing is."

Lucille banged her fist on the table. "Some hoodlums kidnapped my Jolene from my very own home and just about killed her and I want to know what you're going to do about it."

Perez tapped his pen on the paper of his clipboard. "Well, ma'am, I'm going to ask official questions and write official answers on this report. We'll have an official tape of everything else you've said if we need it."

Lucille eyed the little machine as if it were a rattlesnake, which was probably a good thing. Maybe it would keep her quiet. Unfortunately, Perez reached over and clicked it off.

"As you might guess, Miz Jackson, there's not much we can do now that any physical evidence we might have collected is headed to the sewer." Perez tapped a little more on the paper then pointed the pen at Jerry. "This incident actually occurred in Kickapoo so this is technically your jurisdiction, Sheriff, not mine. And frankly, writing up this report is more effort than I feel inclined to make right now just for drill."

Jerry just nodded. "I know what you're thinking, Lieutenant, but let's get the details down in case we need to file it officially. If we stumble onto the house where Jolene was taken, your crime scene unit's going to get the call anyway. And this will just make a cleaner case."

Perez eyed me. "Your conflict of interest issues aren't my problem, Sheriff."

"Actually," Jerry said, "the conflict of interest potential is significant on several fronts." He nodded toward Lucille. "One of my deputies is dating Miz Jackson."

Perez looked at Jerry with your basic "you've got to be kidding" look and shook his head. "It's still not my problem. You have the resources to handle this, and I don't see a good reason why we should get involved, and there are two very good ones why we shouldn't."

Yes, he meant me and my mother, what else would he mean? I really missed Rick.

Jerry just smiled a little. "As far as technicalities go, Lieutenant, you have two women, one obviously injured, who showed up at your station because they believed they were running for their lives. Gunfire was reported in Redwater jurisdiction. You have to write it up."

Perez grumbled and muttered. He knew what he had to do; he just hadn't accepted his mission yet. "I have choices, Sheriff."

"I know you do," Jerry said. "But I think you'll eventually find that this incident is related to the homicide at the New Falls Motel this morning."

The detective raised an eyebrow. "What do you know about that?"

Jerry nodded. "It's in the report."

"You see," Lucille added helpfully, "Jerry had this nice girl with him and when he took her back to her motel room, not that there was anything untoward with all that, but when he did, well, it seems there was already someone in it. Dead. Can you believe that? Well, I suppose you can since your people were there taking pictures of it all." She shook her head and tsk-tsked, her theatrics in full swing. "I do not know what this world is coming to. And do you know we found out your very own police department had a tawdry little game going on about Jolene and me? A betting pool they called it. Did you know about that? Isn't that illegal? I sure think it must be. Why the whole thing just makes me wonder why we pay taxes at all, this sort of thing happening right under our noses."

Deflect and redirect. Lucille is a master.

Perez glared at Lucille then at me as if he were waiting for something. I just shrugged so he turned his squinting eyes back on Lucille. "Exactly what do you know about the incident at the motel this morning, Miz Jackson, specifically about the girl?"

Lucille scanned the room, studying her options. "I saw her this morning, in the truck with Jerry Don," she said, trying to find out what they knew and didn't. "She's real pretty, if that's what you mean."

Perez sighed heavily, an acquired habit when Lucille is present. He looked again at me and at Jerry, that time with sympathy or maybe pity. "We know she's your granddaughter, Miz Jackson," Perez said, cutting to the chase. "Why is she here and how is she involved with the death this morning?"

Lucille's mouth dropped open and her eyes flashed. She clickety-clacked her nails on the table, not at all amused that her charade had been found out. "Sarah had nothing to do with anything, so don't you be dragging her into this. Why a respectable citizen can't rent a room without some hoodlum showing up dead in it is beyond me. What do you say about that, that's what I want to know?" She huffed and puffed and lifted her chin, but when Perez just kept glaring at her, she added. "I suppose you very well know too that Jerry Don took her out to his ex-wife's house so she'd be safe, although I don't know why we have to worry about hiding out all the time in our family. What is this world coming to?"

I propped my elbows on the table and dropped my forehead into my palms. This was going to be a long and tedious process.

"Actually, Jolene," Jerry said, jumping in when Lucille took another breath. "I had to make some arrangements for Sarah last night, trying to get her back to Denver as soon as possible, which is why I stood you up for dinner. It wound up taking a lot longer than it should have. I tried to call and tell you, but you didn't answer. I left a message. I figured you were asleep."

I raised my head slowly and looked at him. "Oh, I was asleep alright."

"Jolene…"

"You could've called back, Jerry." Fears, tears and anger formed a big ball in my throat. "Or come over when you got finished." Oh, the doubts and insecurities, fueled by fear, sleep deprivation and a couple of near-death experiences pushed me right over the edge. "I was kidnapped, Jerry. They taped me up like a bag of trash and gassed me. Twice. I somehow manage to live through that only to get to stare death in the face again from my half-blind mother driving a hundred miles an hour in the dark with a lunatic chasing us. And you didn't even check on me!"

Lucille slammed her hand on the table. "I most certainly am not blind, Missy! Half or otherwise. I got you here alive, didn't I? Didn't I? If that lunatic had caught us it would have been your fault, not mine. If you'd let me have the gun I would have got him stopped on the first try. And you very well know that my car only goes ninety-seven."

"Jolene…"

Lieutenant Daniel Perez pulled off his glasses, tossed them on the table and rubbed his eyes. "Let's start over. And this time, could I get the version that doesn't sound like Mister Magoo starring in *The Dukes of Hazard*."

"I'll explain later, okay?" Jerry said, squeezing my leg under the table.

No, it really wasn't okay. Nothing was okay. I was close to cracking and Jerry knew it. He squeezed one more time then lifted his arm and slipped it around my shoulders, pulling me over toward him. I scooted my chair closer to him and relaxed a little.

Jerry started telling Perez the basics of why I was in Texas in the first place. Mother and I jumped in when necessary, and by the time we were through explaining about the RV park, the weasel Saide, the quartet from AAC, SPASI and, of course, my daughter the undercover mole, Lieutenant Daniel Perez's was just sort of staring, shaking his head from side-to-side. I feared we hadn't cleared things up for him as he'd hoped.

After a few heavy sighs and an exasperated ruffling of his hair, he said, "Jerry, I've known you for what, seven, eight years? I've always found you to be a good man, a fine officer and strictly by the book." He glanced at me then back at the sheriff. "What the hell's happened to you?"

Lucille jumped up from her chair, slapped her hand on the table yet again and leaned forward to waggle a long purple nail at the detective. "Don't you be badmouthing Jerry Don or blaming my Jolene for anything. Why, Jerry Don Parker's the finest law officer in the entire county, maybe even the whole state. He hasn't done one thing wrong and neither have we. He always does the right thing, which is why we're all here right now, doing the right thing and all. Why, he's even had to arrest me twice, bless his heart. Locked me right up in the jailhouse like a common criminal, even though he just hated doing it. He had to, of course, because I'd broken the law. I had to do what I had to do, of course, and he did what he had to do, and you better be apologizing to him right this min—" She snapped around toward Jerry, realization widening her eyes. "Oh, my Lord. You knew it was Sarah all along, not just right now, didn't you? You knew on Monday at the courthouse, and this morning at Bob's place. Why…why…you…."

"Little slow on the uptake there, Mother," I muttered then realized she wasn't the only one riding the short bus. "Wait a minute!" The courthouse? Sarah had come in on Sunday so it seems like I knew she was supposed to be at the rally, but… No, surely not. "She was at the rally, but surely not… My mouth fell open and I glared at my mother. "You put your own grand-daughter in a cage!"

"She wasn't really naked, Jolene, if that's what you're thinking. It was a body suit. Agnes got it, painted it all up and made the foam horns and tail and such. It was real cute."

I looked between my mother and Jerry. "I expect this sort of thing from her, but not you. This isn't like you, Jerry."

"No, it isn't and I am very sorry I got myself into it. I knew exactly why Sarah was in town and I should have told you. Big mistake." He turned to stare directly at Lucille. "Won't happen again. Ever."

Lucille's eyes darted from Jerry to me, back to Jerry, and then, in a flash she flipped her switch from "butter him up" to "rip him to shreds." "Now that is just plain dishonest, Mister. You let me go on thinking you didn't know anything at all about Sarah when you very well knew she was my granddaughter. Just let me go on having to act like we didn't know each other to keep up appearances. Why, the very nerve. I know your mamma taught you better than to lie to your elders. Why, leading us all on like that is just a plain outrage. It's a crime!"

"Lucille," Jerry said, although he'd never called her by her first name that I could remember. "Did you actually hear what you just said?"

Her eyes darted this way and that, indicating that it was perhaps sinking in. "I know what I said. And I meant it." More eye darting and a little scowling. "You better just be truthful with my Jolene, that's all I've got to say. You go lying to her and you'll have to answer to me. I won't have it, I tell you. She deserves better."

It wasn't a great effort, but considering the time of day, the circumstances and the exhaustion I knew I felt, I'd give her a B+ on it. She hadn't exactly saved face but she never admitted anything either. Admit nothing, deny everything and counterattack. It's an art form with her. She just wears you down so that you'd rather hit yourself in the head with a hammer than ask her another question and then have to listen to whatever lies she makes up.

"I can't take any more of this." I looked at Jerry. "I'm mad at you, but I don't have the energy to get the full list on why and I do not want to deal with it right now. I will, but not now."

"It's not as bad as you think," he said. "It's going to be okay, Jo, it really is."

He did not say "trust me," which was smart on his part because I would have probably come completely unhinged. "I want a bath."

Perez looked at Jerry with what could only be called pity. "I'll send somebody out to the Jackson house, but they can't go back there until we have our people go through it."

Meaning they didn't want to deal with us anymore tonight. "Sounds good to me. I'll be at the Hilton. Mother can go with me. Separate rooms. Hers needs a padlock."

"Actually..." Jerry nodded to Lucille. "Deputy Harper is waiting outside for you."

"Well, you can just forget that," Lucille snapped. "I'm not going anywhere with that tobacco spitting fool Larry Harper. If that boy had a brain he'd have it out playing with it. And I'm not going with Leroy either, even if he does take good pictures. I'm not going anywhere with either one of them and that is final."

"Fritz is waiting in the car," Jerry said, much more calmly than I would have. "He's offered to take you back to his house until we have the situation under control. It's up to you, of course. I believe there's a free semi-private cell here."

Lucille's eyes narrowed in fury then lit up like big hazel sparklers. "Fritz is out there waiting? For me? Now, isn't that just the sweetest thing you ever heard of? He's just so thoughtful and he is just crazy about me." She fairly purred. "And if Fritz thinks it's best that I go with him then I suppose I'd better, him being a deputy and all. He just takes such good care of me."

Sheriff Parker didn't roll his eyes, but he sure looked like he wanted to. "He's parked right outside the front door where you came in. He's in your car. His personal car, a dark blue Chevy sedan, was hit by something from another car a few hours ago when he was driving from Kickapoo to Redwater. He drove the car on in, but the headlight is out. It could have other damage as well so he'd prefer not to drive it until he checks that out."

Oh, God. "Fritz?" I croaked.

Jerry nodded.

Oh, this was just dandy. Our hundred-mile-an-hour race for our lives down a dark two-lane road with a half-blind geriatric behind the wheel was not to escape a deranged killer, but to elude mother's deputy sheriff boyfriend. Oh, how I wished he were kidding. "We were running from Fritz, really?"

"He wasn't hurt." Jerry shot me a sideways glance. "We were all lucky on that one."

Yeah, damned lucky. I turned toward my mother. "You'd just been out with the man not five minutes before and he'd been driving that very same car," I said, my voice escalating in pitch and decibel level. "Didn't it ring a bell?"

Lucille squirmed in her seat, but Jerry answered for her. "Fritz said he generally sees Lucille safely inside, but Jolene was there, so he just walked her to the door. Since it was so late, he parked down the street to wait until she turned off all the lights, just to be sure everything was okay."

"Oh," Lucille sighed, putting a hand to her chest. "Wasn't that sweet of him?"

Oh, this was far from sweet. "So when we came screeching past him like the Hounds of Hell were on our tail, he rightly assumed that something was wrong and followed." I groaned and rubbed my hands across my forehead for another countless time. "We could have killed him."

"I doubt that. It's a thousand wonders you even hit a headlight," Lucille said, completely ignoring the real issue. "Obviously she's not much of a shot or she'd have at least hit the radiator, and with a laser sight even," she said as if I weren't even in the room. "Of course, I was outrunning him so it really wasn't that big of a deal. Jolene gets scared though." Lucille batted her eyelids and sighed dreamily. "But wasn't that just the sweetest thing? Fritz kept right up with us, even with Jolene shooting at him. He's just crazy about me."

I sputtered and stuttered, but Jerry gave me a "don't bother" look. Oh, I was going to bother. "Mother—"

"Fritz is just glad you're all right, Miz Jackson," Jerry said, interrupting what could have been a long and lovely rebuttal. Then to the detective, "I think we've done about all we can do here." And had all any of us could take. "I'll walk Lucille out to the car then I'll take Jolene over to the hotel."

Daniel Perez nodded, grabbed his glasses and papers, and stood. His gaze went from me to my mother and back to me. He held up his hand with his index finger and thumb about a half inch apart. "I came this close to winning that pot. If you two had just waited three more days, I would've had myself a nice down payment on a new Harley, been out on paid leave and some other poor slob would be in my shoes right now wishing he wasn't." He paused for what he seemed to think was dramatic effect. After his dreams rode off into the sunset, he nodded to Jerry. "Wouldn't trade places with you, Sheriff, for all the tea in China."

Yes, I gave him a dirty look, but I kept my mouth shut. Because, unfortunately, he had a point.

Chapter Sixteen

It was somewhere between three and four in the morning, I think, when I flopped onto the bed in the hotel room. Jerry had gotten me a toothbrush, toothpaste and other essentials when we checked in—and I'd already availed myself of them—and I was not long for the conscious world.

"You know," he said, sitting on the edge of the bed and pulling off his boots. "We can't keep counting on your mother to get into trouble so we can see each other."

"There are other ways?" It didn't have my usual sarcastic inflection because I really was tired, but he smiled anyway.

He pulled off his shirt and undershirt and tossed them aside. "Clayton was nice, but not nearly long enough."

Okay, I might have neglected to mention that Jerry and I had snuck away for a weekend last month and met in Clayton, New Mexico, which is about halfway. And no, we did not go there to see the dinosaur tracks or have our pictures made with the plaster dinosaurs that alert you to the ancient nature of the area. It was better than not seeing each other at all, but it had really just made us realize that our long distance romance wasn't going to cut it for much longer.

When he'd finished undressing, he stretched out beside me and pulled me to him. "You've been awfully cavalier about everything that happened. Are you sure you're okay?"

I snuggled my face against his shoulder. "I have never been so scared in my entire life. It was worse than facing a gun and being shot, Jerry, and I've been shot."

He stroked my hair. "I know."

Hot tears welled up in my eyes. "They tied me up. I couldn't do anything. Nothing."

He kissed the top of my head and hugged me closer.

I was a single sob away from breaking down completely, but the more I thought over the events, the more my mind began to shift my emotions into anger. "They could have done anything they wanted to me, Jerry. Rape, torture, murder, all of the above and there was not one damn thing I could do about it. Not one. I couldn't even spit in their faces. They didn't rape me, I know that for sure, but I just bet the stinky one copped a feel or two, the slimy bastard. He slung me around like I was a sack of..." I felt myself shaking. "And you know what pisses me off the most? I think they were after my mother. My mother, for godsakes. What they did to me *would* have killed her!"

He hugged me again and rubbed his hands up over me as if trying to warm me up or maybe build a cocoon around me. "It's okay now. You're safe."

"Well, they're not. When I find the sorry bastards who did this, I'm going to kill them. You need to know that, Jerry. They are dead men. Dead. And I don't need the gun you bought me to get the job done. That would be entirely too easy."

He pressed tiny kisses to the top of my head again. "The police will find them, Jo. You're okay now."

I heard him, I really did, but I wasn't okay. And as much as I love Jerry holding me, I had to get up. My whole body felt like a live wire, popping and hissing inside. I squeezed his arm then lifted it off me and hopped out of bed. I'd ping-ponged again up from the depths of oblivion and the surge of energy had to be dealt with somehow. Since I didn't know what else to do, I scurried to the bathroom and got a drink. Unfortunately, there was a mirror in the bathroom, and more unfortunate yet, I looked into it. And began to cry.

I don't know when Jerry came up behind me, or when I turned into him and just sobbed. I just know it happened, and I kept crying. For a long time. Somehow during the release, my brain kept working, and when I could finally breathe normally again, the first words out of my mouth were "Damon Saide."

Jerry stepped away, grabbed a washcloth, ran warm water on it then handed it to me.

I took the warm cloth and rubbed it over my face. It did feel good, even on the raw places. "I have to find him."

"Let's get some sleep," he said, wrapping an arm around my shoulders and guiding me back to bed.

I tossed the washcloth aside and went with him. I settled back into the bed, but my mind wouldn't stop. "Do you know where he is?"

Jerry said nothing for long seconds then sighed. "He left the station about noon."

"What about his car?"

"Most of the bullets hit the door. He drove it away."

"He did this. You know he did."

"We'll find him, Jo."

"This is just crazy, Jerry. Crazy."

I could feel myself fading fast, yet a barrage of random thoughts flooded my mind. Most were fleeting and forgotten as fast as they appeared, but one just hung there, lingering, for no apparent reason. None of this was really about a park. Or the horny toads. "Jerry, what do you gain by turning a pasture with old oil wells on it into an RV park?"

He nudged me over, facing away from him then pulled me back against him, his breath breezing rhythmically against my neck. "About fifteen dollars a day per camper."

"Hardly seems worth killing someone over, or even a felony kidnapping, now does it?"

"Could be more money than you'd think. But then people do stupid things for really stupid reasons."

God knows it's the reason behind a substantial number of activities in these parts, but this time, it just seemed too convenient. "How did Tiger die anyway?"

"He had enough drugs in his system to kill him."

"So maybe it wasn't murder."

"He had cancer so there are several possibilities," he mumbled, kissing me again. "Go to sleep, Jo."

He hugged me a little tighter and his breathing became rhythmic, melting away my tension and fear and taking all my "what if" questions with them. In that moment I felt so safe and so loved—just like I wanted it to be for us, all the time. I snuggled against him and sighed. "This is so nice. I wish it could be like this forever."

"Be careful what you wish for," he mumbled.

I didn't know for sure what he meant by that—or maybe I did and just didn't want to spoil my lovely romantic fantasy by injecting reality into it. I knew exactly what "forever" meant with Jerry Don Parker, and it did not include moving away from his children to be with me in Colorado. That left me with the unpleasant possibility that Hell might indeed freeze over and I would stupidly find myself living in it. I shuddered at the thought, and a pained groan slipped from my lips.

His breath was steady and even, and I thought he'd fallen asleep until he said, "It won't be like this all the time when you're here, Jo. It won't."

I wondered who he was trying to convince, me or himself.

Chapter Seventeen

Morning came entirely too soon. The bedside clock's big red numbers said it was eight-fifty. Jerry must have just left—probably what woke me up. Oh, how really easy it would be to go back to sleep and continue my coma for about five more hours. I could do it too, in a second and a half. Except something wouldn't let me. My subconscious had been working all night—about four hours or so—and was fairly screaming at me that I needed to do something. I pushed myself up to a sitting position to make the transition to the real world a little less painful, and I noticed several loose sheets from a note pad on the little table beside the bed. I grabbed them and begged my eyes to focus long enough to read them.

They were from Jerry, but they didn't make a great deal of sense. "Went to get clothes. Be back soon." Meaning, one must assume, that Jerry was gone and would be back at some point.

That he'd gone to get clothes made sense since he hadn't brought a bag to this impromptu sleepover. But neither had I and I sure needed something better to wear than yesterday's kidnapping costume. That thought stirred up highly unpleasant memories, which I promptly stuffed away and thought about a more agreeable subject—food. And I was indeed hungry. My stomach grumbled loudly in support. I couldn't remember the last time I'd eaten. Now there was a second good reason to drag myself out of bed and into the shower—a trip to the hotel restaurant.

Funny thing about me and showers, I get many of my great insights standing naked under running water. No, you don't need a visual; it's just the way it is. And, true to form, the message came to me as I gazed—with eyes closed, of course—upward toward the heavens. Jerry had made some pretty heady implications last night and the possibilities for interpretation were both scary and really scary. Oddly, I couldn't decide what it was that I hoped he had meant. "For godsakes, Jolene," I said out loud and to no one but myself. "You're not seventeen. Stop it."

I might not be a teenager, but sometimes it sure felt like it. Still, the reality of the situation was that Jerry hadn't really said anything of substance, nothing had changed, and I needed to get my mind off of what might be and deal with what was. The short list I'd come up with included murder, mayhem and why my mother owned mineral rights on Bob Little's property, if indeed she actually did.

It made no obvious sense, of course. But that meant nothing. Lucille was involved and therefore logic was not. And in order to cut down on the lies she could tell, I needed to gather as many facts as I could before I tried to corner her for answers. Mineral rights were generally recorded in property ownership records, and there should at least be a date on when she got the mineral rights and how much of a share she actually had. That meant I needed county records from the county courthouse.

I knew from unrelated experience that there were plenty of counties that had put their property ownership records online. I didn't know about Texas, but, my typical disparaging comments aside, I doubted that the Lone Star state was any farther behind than its neighbors. That meant they'd probably started the process, but it was a county-by-county crapshoot.

If Bowman County ownership data was available online, knowing the section, township and range for Kickapoo might help me narrow the search. Then again, it occurred to me that Texas was, by its own admission a whole other country, and as such, was fairly guaranteed to have foreign ways. Indeed, now that I thought about it, I recalled some obscure something about Spanish land grants and hybrid mapping that was sure to turn a simple search into a typical Kickapoo SNAFU (look it up). Whatever the case, I was starting with what I knew and hoped that something would be relevant or at least lead me in that direction.

Longitude and latitude was a piece of cake, thanks to satellite imaging. *Ha! That would be kind of cool. I could look up my mother's house from space. And while I was at it, I could scope out the*

Little Ranch and see what made it so appealing for an RV park. Why hadn't I thought of it before?

As I rinsed the hotel conditioner from my hair, my thoughts hopped to what Jerry had said about Tiger dying of an overdose. That didn't automatically mean murder, but it didn't automatically exclude it either. He could have accidentally killed himself, and suicide was an obvious option. But why come to Texas to die and not go out with some sort of theatrics? He'd blown up the feed store, sort of, and the exploding paint cans at the rally had been a pretty decent show, so why would a dedicated protester die alone without making some kind of major point out of it?

He wouldn't. That meant it was either murder or it was unintentional. Or, he could have made a suicidal point, framing someone for his death and we just didn't know about it yet.

I really wanted more information to narrow my field of choices. I doubted Perez would even take my call at this point or tell me anything even if he did. The only other source I could think of that would know more details was the medical examiner Yes, obvious, but I felt a little squeamish about it. I didn't know of any law that said citizens couldn't call and ask a few questions, but it sure seemed that Jerry would not be pleased to hear about my inquiring mind. Still, a dead man had been found in a motel room that was supposedly rented to my daughter. I had rights. No, actually I didn't, and that approach was not going to get me anywhere with either Jerry or the medical examiner.

Let's be clear. I am not good at deceit. The straightforward approach is the only one that works for me, only it wasn't going to work this time. This time, I needed a good cover story, which is just a fancy way of saying a big fat lie. You'd think a good reporter would be good at such things, but as I may have mentioned a time or two, I am not a good reporter, investigative or otherwise. I write stories; I do not infiltrate and probe.

I snapped the big white towel from the rack on the wall, wrapped it around me and headed for the desk. The phone book was in the drawer, and after a little searching, I found the number I was looking for. After a couple of mental and oral dress rehearsals, I dialed.

After only one transfer, I hit pay dirt with a young man named Travis. "Hey, Travis, this is Barbie down at the *Times and Record News*," I said, doing a pretty decent Kimberlee-esque airhead impression despite my unfortunate choice of a fake name. "Kimberlee asked me to call and get the final cause of death on that man who was found in the motel room yesterday. I'd really appreciate it if you could look that up real quick for me."

"You're the third person who's called about that this morning."

Third? Oh, crap. "Kimberlee called already? Because if she did I'm really going to be in trouble. I'm new and—"

"No one from the paper called."

"Well, that's a relief," I said, although it really wasn't since now I wanted to know who else was calling about this. "A lot of people are interested in this I guess."

"I'll tell you exactly what I told the others. We still don't have all the labs back, and I can't give you anything official until it's official."

I hadn't counted on that. Actually, I guess I hadn't counted on anything. I'd just gotten a wild idea and acted on it. That was one of my finest character traits, seeing what needed done and just doing it. It was also a fairly significant flaw in that I didn't necessarily apply long range thinking to the process and wound up in situations just like this one where I had to then improvise. "How long do you figure he would have lived, with the cancer and all, if he hadn't overdosed?"

"I never said he overdosed. Or that he didn't. He could have died two months ago or lived another two, depending on what he needed to do. We leave when we're ready."

Huh? A philosopher? At the morgue? "Unless someone helps us along."

"It can work either way. Read Richard Bach's *Illusions*. Things aren't always the way they seem."

The non-Barbie Jolene was having a hard time keeping her mouth shut. I wanted to tell him that I'd read the damn book. Many times. And, I too recommended it to people who I thought needed to expand their closed little minds, so I knew what he was doing. One part of me wanted to let him know that

I knew way more than he did about these topics, and the other part wanted to find out just how far down the rabbit hole the county medical examiner's esoteric knowledge went. Neither was going to happen so I decided to put my little ego aside and do a little backhanded fishing. This is, of course, yet another skill I have not mastered. "I've known a lot of people who died of lung cancer. Tough to go through and tough to watch. It really sucks."

"Death isn't good or bad, it is simply a transition from one state of awareness to another. How it occurs can be affected by freewill and choice, ours as well as that of others. Either way, if you leave without getting the lessons you came here for, you repeat them." He paused for a few long seconds then said, "Hepatocellular carcinoma, Barbara. Primary liver cancer. Look it up." *Click.*

"It was Barbie," I muttered, hanging up the phone.

That had been a bizarre conversation on all levels. I jotted down what he'd said on the hotel-provided notepad and I absently added "look it up." Something about the way he'd said that had sort of stopped me in my tracks. He'd also hung up on me, which would typically really tick me off, but it didn't. He told me what kind of cancer Tiger had, and to look it up. There was something there, I just knew it. Something he suspected but couldn't say for sure. No doubt people around here thought him to be exceptionally weird.

I continued talking to myself all the way to the closet. I wasn't looking forward to wearing yesterday's clothes, but I didn't have much choice. As I slid back the mirrored closet door, I realized I actually had no choices at all. The only things of mine in the closet were my sandals. Jerry had apparently taken everything else—and I do mean everything. My bra, semi-stained shorts, sink-washed shirt and even the borrowed white, big and tall were gone.

Now, I could jump to conclusions and assume that he took my clothes to purposely keep me trapped in the hotel room naked, which was a distinct possibility. Or, I could assume that he kindly and thoughtfully took my clothes to have them cleaned. Or both.

At the moment, the why of it didn't much matter. The fact was that I had nothing to wear. And since I couldn't walk down the hall naked or in a bath towel, I called the front desk to see about the possibilities of having a robe sent up. Amazingly, within minutes, a robe was on its way to my door. It would have to do for now, and if my laundry didn't make a timely return, I'd have to figure out how to get something delivered from the mall somehow.

Within ten minutes, I was swaddled in a thick white terry cloth robe and my little toes were tucked into my sandals. I had a package of peanut butter crackers from the vending machine in one hand and a glass of water in the other. Yes, water. After last night's gassing, just the thought of a sickly sweet Dr Pepper made my stomach roll. I wolfed down a few crackers on the elevator then washed them down as I searched for the hotel's business center. The gold wall plates with the arrows helped considerably.

The room was fairly large—and thankfully unoccupied—with a worktable, a fax machine and a desk with a newer looking computer. A laminated sheet that said "Internet Use Instructions and Agreement" was taped to the desk, advising me that, basically, if I touched the keyboard I agreed to everything on it. Computer use was free, but printouts, copies and faxes required a credit card. I hadn't brought one of those with me, so the hotel pen and note pad were just going to have to do. I did have a couple of dollars just in case. I also had a long list of topics to research and decided that starting with the simplest seemed wise.

From the beginning, the whole park thing had seemed ridiculous. It wasn't public land, yet there was an implied link with the city of Redwater Falls as well as Kickapoo. I'd start with the official city websites then move on to AAC, Damon Saide, hepato-whatever cancer, then find Kickapoo on GoogleEarth and eventually check the online records at Bowman County. I also needed at least do a quick search on Gilbert Moore, Commissioner Fletcher and Barnett Shale. I wanted time to research everything thoroughly, but I didn't have it. I'd spend two hours and stop, get some real food.

The City of Redwater website was easy to find but there was nothing at all about the park on it. Nothing. A search for Parks for Progress came up with something in New Jersey and it wasn't even a good match. I did, however, get a hit on AAC immediately. Nice website, official-looking. Someone had done a decent job, in a template sort of way. It got less impressive when you started following up the "events" that AAC had supposedly engineered. Either they never happened at all or they were actually pulled off by a different group, and AAC had simply stolen the photos and stories from other websites. And, of course, there were no faces or names on the AAC site to incriminate anyone. And no, I didn't get very far on the owner of the domain name either. Registered to a reseller.

For the kind of group it was, AAC could be considered legit even if the success stories were bogus or stolen. But it made me wonder if the people in town saying they were with AAC really were. And furthermore, there wasn't even a blip in the national news archives about any of this. Contrary to what my mother and a deceitful sheriff would have liked me to believe, this was very much a local story. It was at least an eight on the Kickapoo absurdity scale, but it was not national news.

Damon Saide didn't register on any of the people finders or search engines. An alternative spelling picked up a quote that said, "the bitch must die," which was kind of creepy, but thankfully not relevant. I figured the name was bogus anyway. Just like Tiger and Bobcat and the flower girls that hung around with them. I ran out of tails to chase, and wound up with more questions than when I started.

I couldn't spend a lot of time on any of it, so I hurriedly put in Gilbert Moore and drilling. I got a Yellow Pages listing, but nothing more. Then, I remembered Barnett Shale, which was easy to remember since it was such an odd name. I hit the search button.

"What the hell," I muttered, looking at the top search listings. Barnett Shale wasn't a who, it was a what, a very big what. It was a natural gas field in North Central Texas. I read quickly and made notes on location, depths and the whys and wherefores of it all. Like many activities in the petroleum industry, what had been previously unprofitable was now wildly lucrative. That didn't automatically mean that oil and or gas was being harvested behind Mother's house, but it didn't mean they weren't either. From what I could tell, Kickapoo would be on the far northwest edge of the known field, which made it iffy, but not impossible. I started to click another link to try to figure out how iffy, but realized that I could get lost in researching that and get nothing else done. For now, all I needed was an overview, and I definitely had that. So, I refocused back on the park with new eyes.

There were a few local news stories on the park, the protest, county truck vandalism and the feed store incident, but even the local media had lost interest and column inches without any meat behind the hype. There was nothing significant about the Barnett Shale play, as they called it, just a general mention. There were, however, letters to the editor from my mother. I only found two, which was two too many. She had made exaggerated accusations and vague threats with a lot of rambling and very little detail. Why the newspaper had published such nonsense was beyond me. Quite a few readers wrote in with the same concerns and—I'm only guessing here—that Kimberlee had to spend some time in the Bridal and Fashion department, or maybe the obits, as penance for letting the drivel get printed in not only the editorials, but for referencing it her "news" stories. You had to give her credit though, Mother did give entertaining quotes.

The computer's clock told me I'd burned about forty minutes, which was great, considering what I'd found, but the hard stuff was still ahead.

I don't like to visit medical sites—physically or in cyberspace—because I am suspicious of the medical community in general. There are a lot of reasons for it, which would take a couple of days to relate, but mostly it's because they approach things from the wrong angle—an unnatural one. They'll either drug it or cut it, and that's if you survive their toxic tests. Seriously, it wasn't the cancer that killed my favorite aunt. It was the biopsy they did "just to be sure" she had it. Apparently the fact that she'd been a smoker and lived with one for forty years, had a mass the size of a grapefruit in her chest and was coughing up lung tissue just wasn't convincing enough. Nope, a biopsy was essential as was apparently the collapsed lung and other resulting complications that killed her. I really wish I were making that up, I really do.

Now, don't get me wrong, I'm grateful to have good and important medical care available and a lot of lives are saved by some really dedicated people. But in every day doctoring, it seems that either people pick a pill off a TV ad that they think will magically fix their lives or some drug rep pitches the latest "approved" pill for the same reason. Big Pharma knows Americans want quick fixes and they've dreamed up a pill for just about everything, creating conditions and disorders as needed to help everybody feel better about the scam. There are exceptions to this, of course, but there are no exceptions to the fact that the unhindered power of the pharmaceutical companies in this country scares the living crap out of me.

Stopping myself from riding that train of thought any longer and wasting any more time on things I had no control over, I went directly to the American Cancer Society site. Hepatocellular carcinoma popped right up, and I found out in a hurry that primary adult liver cancer is rare, but that the hepatocellular variety accounted for 75% of the rarities. Smoking and drinking were big contributors, as was Hepatitis B and C. Tiger was a good contender in all three categories, although at a distance he hadn't looked yellow that I could recall. Also on the list of risk factors were heredity, aflatoxins, arsenic in drinking water and chemical exposure, specifically vinyl chloride from plastics manufacturing and thorium dioxide from x-ray testing. The conditions and symptoms sounded horrible, and killing himself to stop the pain of it all was a highly credible option. However, none of it explained why he'd chosen to spend the last days of his life in Redwater Falls, Texas. I had money left from my vending machine purchases so I fed a dollar bill into the printer/copier and printed out the info.

My next stop on the web was GoogleEarth, which was thankfully already available on the hotel's computer, and in no time I was zooming in on Kickapoo, Texas. As the satellite homed in on mother's address, a wide expanse of mottled white with splotches of green around the perimeter flashed on the screen.

When the image stopped on Lucille's house, I immediately scrolled east to see what I'd just gotten a glimpse of.

"What the hell," I muttered yet again as the area came into focus. Several huge areas of whitish dirt splayed across the screen. Red dirt that was pockmarked with small areas of sparse vegetation filled in around the bare white stuff. "Is that what drilling and oil wells do or are they mining something?" I muttered to myself.

Moving back to the west, the aerial view showed a meandering strip of mesquite brush, which you could see from Lucille's kitchen window. It concealed her view from all but the tops of the pump jacks when they bobbed up. The relatively small area between the oil well and the storage tanks that I remembered, the salt flats, had somehow morphed into sprawling white areas of nothing, with multi-colored mounds of dirt dotted and patches of mesquites. There were several other huge bare areas as well that I didn't remember at all. I sure wished I had an aerial view from the sixties when I used to play back there. I wonder if it looked the same then. I made myself a note to look up where I could get historical aerials. I put another dollar in the machine and printed, zooming in and out to get the best possible views. The image pixilated and blurred when I got very close in, but I did what I could.

I never made it to the virtual courthouse, if indeed Bowman County had one, because I'd started to feel shaky. I wasn't sure if it was from lack of food, lack of sleep or the very real feeling that what I had just found in my view from space was bad.

I managed to get back to the room and order food, but I couldn't stop thinking about what I'd found. Technically speaking, it really wasn't much of anything. I'd learned a few things about cancer and chemicals that might or might not be relevant to anything, and I'd educated myself about Barnett Shale. Damon Saide, Gilbert Moore and AAC were pretty much a bust, but the satellite imagery I'd stumbled on was anything but. And I couldn't stop thinking about it.

I laid out the aerial photos on the table and tried to think of all the possible reasons the land looked as it did. One possibility was a toxic waste dump, but I had no basis for it. It all could be perfectly normal. The ground may have simply been cleared for campsites. That they would have scenic views of the pump jacks and storage tanks could be the whole idea. People paid good money to go experience ranch life by shoveling manure and castrating calves, so it wasn't a stretch that they'd pay to pretend they had their own real live oil well out the front door of the travel trailer. The gift shop would be filled with souvenir pump jacks and mini bottles of crude. Black gold. Texas Tea. It was one of those ideas that sounded so stupid it just might work.

But again, why the strong-arm tactics for Mother? Why kidnap me? Why not say these things up front and get community support? Why not mitigate the horny toad issue with protected habit and viewing areas for tourists? "Good questions, Jolene. Really good questions."

I just had no good answers.

A call to room service got a veggie omelet headed my way, and gave me a few minutes to think. I sat in the room's wingback chair and propped my feet on the ottoman, sipping on a cup of hot Earl Grey tea that I'd made in the room's coffee pot. My beloved staple of liquid tar still held no appeal whatsoever and I wondered if I'd ever be able to drink it again. Or maybe it was just the overall bad feeling I had that was making me ill. I sipped a little more tea then let my mind wander where it wanted to.

Apparently it wandered to sleep because the next thing I knew I was jerking and jumping awake, with some semi-awareness of a knock on the door. It took a couple more seconds of re-orientation and another knock to figure out that there really was someone at the door. The re-engaging brain cells screamed "food" so I hurried over, flipped back the security latches, and swung the door open wide for delivery of my breakfast.

Jerry, not room service, stood in the doorway, holding his room key as if he'd just swiped it in the reader. At his feet were a pile of shopping sacks. He put the card in his pocket, picked up the sacks and eyed my robe. "I didn't expect you to be up yet."

"Me either," I said, closing the door behind him. "I like your shirt and jeans."

"Didn't want to take the time to go home," he said, tossing the sacks on the bed. "Where'd you get the robe?"

"Room service." Another knock. "More room service. Food this time." I smiled. "I could get used to this."

Jerry went to the door and got the tray for me then carried it over and set it on the table in the corner. "If you want to just make a snack of that I'll take you out somewhere."

I am generally always ready to go out to eat, but I had Jerry alone with no one to bother us and I liked that a lot. "How about we share it and just spend some time here?"

"Perfect."

I divided the food and set us each a plate on the table with the glass of orange juice between us. Apparently he was as hungry as I was because we both inhaled the food without saying a word.

Jerry drank half the juice then handed me the glass. "Now, aren't you going to ask me what's in the sacks?"

"Well, I was kind of hoping it was something I could wear since you took everything I had."

He reached over and ran a finger along the collar of my robe. "And I was hoping," he said, his voice dipping into a low rumble, "that you'd still be in bed how and where I left you."

That electrical connection shot through me once again. I sucked in my breath and shivered all at the same time. "And I can be."

His fingers ran under my robe and slid it off my shoulders. "I want you."

And so it was.

After *that*, a nap was the natural course of action.

When I did awaken, it was with visions of white splotches as seen from space. Still snuggled tight against Jerry, his arms wrapped around me and his breath steady and soft in my ear, I didn't want to move. Ever. But I also knew what I had found earlier was important. And a trip to the bathroom was in order anyway, so I gently scooted out of bed.

When I returned, Jerry was sitting up in bed looking through my papers. "You've been quite busy this morning."

I put on my new robe and climbed back in bed beside him. "Just went downstairs to the business center." I propped up some pillows and settled myself where I could show him things easily. "I really just went down to see if I could find out about mineral rights on the Little property and figured I needed some kind of way to locate the parcel so I went to GoogleEarth. When I did, however, this is what I saw. Never made it to the county records."

"Hmmm," he said, letting out a long and labored sigh. "We have several law enforcement departments working on these cases, competent people, specifically trained in criminal investigations. And yet, you somehow think you can find out things that nobody else can."

"Maybe I can. Maybe I have."

He sighed again.

"Now stop that. That was your 'Jolene thinks she's discovered something but really hasn't and I have to listen to it' sigh."

He raised an eyebrow. "You got all that out of a sigh?"

"And my intuition."

"More like past experience and guilt." He reached over and pulled me to him. "You know, I'm a pretty self-confident guy and there aren't a lot of things that get to me. But even I have limits, and taking jokes from every uniformed yahoo in the two-county region is a little tough on the ego sometimes."

He hadn't actually said "because of you" but he didn't have to. Even if you didn't count the fiascos of my previous two misadventures here, the fact that the Redwater Falls Police Department had a betting pool on when I'd show up at a felony this time was a little over the top in anybody's book. Add to that my own stupidity of last night. I hadn't deliberately gotten myself kidnapped, of course. But I had indeed shot at a deputy during a high-speed chase, and that couldn't sound good no matter how you put it, even though it was an honest mistake. Let's not forget the bathroom confrontation with Sergeant Big Mouth in front of every officer in the building either. "Fine. You might have a point. And if you don't want to see what I've got, that's fine too."

"I didn't say that." He gave me a quick kiss then pointed to the top paper. "Hepatocellular carcinoma?"

"Primary adult liver cancer. That's what Tiger had." I saw him cut his eyes toward me so I just confessed without him asking. "I called the medical examiner's office, okay? I didn't get much else, except that it sounded like he should have already been dead months ago."

"It's rare," Jerry said, continuing to scan the pages I had printed. "Can be caused by chemical exposure, specifically vinyl chloride, thorium dioxide and arsenic, as well as aflatoxins in foods, whatever those are."

He read a bit more then added, "Interesting, yes, but how is it relevant?"

"I don't know that it is. Obviously Tiger knew he was dying, and it may have just been a coincidence that this is where it happened, assuming it was accidental."

Jerry nodded. "But if it was suicide, why come to Redwater Falls for it?"

"Exactly. Is there anything in the case that points to him trying to frame someone for murder?"

Jerry shook his head. "Not that I know of." He shuffled to the next page and saw the first aerial photo. "What's this?"

"I have several. A zoomed out satellite overview of Mother's house and the Little Ranch with other views closer in." I showed him where the house was located in proximity to the bare areas. I also told about the possible explanations I could come up with. "I even wondered if it was some kind of mining operation, but what are they mining, dirt?"

"Maybe they really are just clearing camper pads," he said.

"Maybe, although it sure looks like some of those may be mounds, not flat spots. It's hard to tell."

"Yes, it is," he agreed. Jerry went through all the photos again. "I really don't know what to make of this."

"Me either. But as a side note, Bobcat told me that my mother owns mineral rights on the Little Ranch, which is why I went downstairs to get on the internet. I wanted to know if it was true."

He looked at me in disbelief. "Really?"

I shrugged. "I thought that I might be able to confirm that online, or find out how much and when, but I never got that far. I needed to eat. Do you think it could be true?"

"Bowman County records aren't online yet so you wouldn't have gotten far anyway. They are in process though. Just need funding." He shuffled back through the papers a couple more times. "I've got to admit this is worth looking into." He motioned to the pile of sacks. "See if there's anything in here that fits. It looks like you have created work for me to do."

The first sack I opened had a whole array of black lacey things, including several packages of black silk thigh highs. "Oh, now this looks like fun."

He grinned. "And it will be. But better check the other bags for something more practical to wear unless you want to just stay here and wait for me."

"Going now to get dressed." I grabbed all the sacks and headed back to the bathroom. As I set them inside, I turned back and said, "Jerry, thank you. For everything."

"You're worth it."

I knew he wasn't talking about just money either, although it looked like he's spent plenty. He was talking about our long distance relationship and the trouble with my mother and the ribbing he had to take from his peers. It was a big deal and I wanted to tell him I appreciated it, but I really couldn't face the reality of it all myself at the moment. And, there really was more information I'd found out that he needed to know about. "I won't be long, but look at the Barnett Shale paper too. Got that tip from Kimberlee Fletcher, if you can believe that. They could be drilling for gas out there. I told you about the drill rig Mother saw, right?"

"Gas wells might make sense. Barnett Shale though is closer to Dallas. I suppose there might be an extension up this way. Typically, front men come into a potential area before word gets out and buy the properties and mineral rights for little of nothing, which is what Saide appeared to be trying to do."

That part certainly fit, but it was only one part. "I suppose the park could have been a backhanded way to get the land if his first try didn't work, but it still seems a stretch."

"Maybe, but greed is a powerful motivator." Jerry shook his head. "I've seen a lot of things since I took this job that I would have never believed before. If a person gets fixated on something or someone, they can justify anything—theft, murder, kidnapping, arson, you name it."

That I could understand, on so many levels. "So what do we really know?"

He shook his head. "We have a dead guy with a rare liver cancer. You were kidnapped. Bob Little is missing, which we have no leads on, and then there appears to be fresh dirt work behind your mother's house. Is it from drilling? Or burying a body? Both?" He sighed. "I'll get someone out to the site to investigate as soon as possible."

"Those satellite photos aren't live though, Jerry, so if there are any burial plots showing up, they aren't recent ones. There's no sign of equipment or trucks in the photos either. We need the live version where we can get daily images from the last few months or at least today. Can you get that sort of thing?"

In answer, he pulled out his phone and dialed.

I figured he was calling Perez, so I got busy.

I indulged myself with an inventory of the black lacey things, which I absolutely loved. But that little adventure would have to wait. I could hear bits of conversation and knew we would be heading out promptly, so I went with the best of the basics from what he'd brought me. The black lace bra and matching accessories were duplicated in beige so I went that direction to go with the cream colored top I'd chosen. Basic jeans completed the ensemble. I had my purse, and therefore all three items of makeup, so I lined my lower eyelids, thickened my lashes, concealed my dark circles and used my mother's eyebrow pencil to draw in the missing piece. So, for a variety of reasons, I felt pretty darned good when I walked out.

"Oh, honey," Jerry said appreciatively, looking me over as he pulled on his last boot and stood. "You look just like you did back in high school."

Now that was true love, blind and delusional. Still, I appreciated him saying it, and he actually looked like he halfway meant it. "And that is one of the many reasons I love you."

Chapter Eighteen

erry had given me quite a few clothing options to pick from, but I'd chosen a cream-colored peasant-type top with a lace-up front. It was fairly low cut with a wide band at the bottom that tied at my hips, giving it a blousy but fitted look. I loved it. I admit I would have never bought the jeans he had—they were way too low cut in the front—but they actually fit perfectly and the fact that I had hardly eaten any food in days helped considerably. It also helped that the shirt picked up where the jeans left off and no skin was exposed. The outfit was indeed very much like what I'd worn in high school—when I wasn't wearing stylish dresses or coordinated polyester pant-suits. Yes, most of the time I looked like I was going to a board meeting not a high school classroom. I've gotten over it.

In spite of Jerry's obvious appreciation, I still had the uneasy feeling that I looked like a pathetic forty-something geezer-in-denial. But Jerry was thrilled and that was absolutely all that mattered. A couple of appreciative looks in the hotel lobby bolstered my confidence as well—but since they didn't know me I was compelled to look back after we'd passed them to be sure they weren't laughing. Thankfully, they hadn't been.

As we made our way to the sheriff's car, I assumed we would be heading to either Kickapoo or the courthouse. In spite of my exceptional intuitive and psychic abilities, my assuming skills apparently sucked since we went directly to the city morgue. As we parked and walked into the side entrance, I couldn't help but wonder if Philosopher Travis would still be there and if so, if he'd recognize my voice. Odds were heavily weighted toward "yes." That could complicate things a bit, but I would at least be in a better position (i.e. not masquerading as an airhead) to deal with his pithy comments. I knew stuff too. He wasn't the only thinker in town.

The morgue didn't shock me as it had the first time I'd been there, but the house of the recently dead is still creepy. Jerry signed us in and we headed down a long sterile hallway. A young Asian man in a long white lab coat waited for us beside a set of stainless steel double doors. The guy on the phone hadn't had even a hint of an Asian accent, or Texan for that matter, so I relaxed a little. If I got lucky, I might avoid Travis completely, and in doing so also avoid the need for any unpleasant explanations.

"Hello, Sheriff," the young man said.

"Hi, Travis."

Oh, crap. I don't think I said it out loud, but the young man turned toward me as if I had.

Jerry seemed not to notice the fact that Mr. Medical Examiner dude was staring at me like I was under a microscope or my unease over it. "This is Jolene Jackson," he said.

He nodded in my direction and I nodded in his. I kept my mouth shut for obvious reasons. I don't know why he did. The whole thing was disconcerting. The things he said, the way he looked at me, well, it just felt weird. And then there was his general physical appearance. I don't know what I'd expected Travis-from-the-morgue to look like, but the Asian Mario Lopez leading us down the hallways definitely wasn't it.

"I have nothing more than I did this morning, Sheriff. Although I did get another call regarding the case." He glanced in my direction, although there was no reason why since I hadn't said one word and there was no way he could know it had been me. "A woman from the newspaper."

Apparently he was psychic too because he continued to stare at me as if he did know. Or I could have just been feeling extremely guilty. Lucille did a stunning job in instilling that. So, figuring confession was the best plan at this point, I said, "That was me. And I apologize for the misrepresentation. I do write for a paper, however. In Denver."

"I know." Then, he said something I would have never guessed would flow from the lips of anyone living in Redwater Falls, Texas, "We are where we want to be though, aren't we, Jolene?"

Now why would he say that? Oh, I knew very well what the phrase meant. God knows my best friend Tanya said it to me enough times when I was unhappily married to Danny, adding that *"If you wanted it to be different, it would be."* It had really pissed me off until I finally realized she was right and got myself a divorce. Still, I'd argue that the morgue in Redwater Falls, Texas, was not where I wanted to be. Ever. The only reason I was in town was because I'd been forced to come tend to my mother. All right fine, nobody dragged me onto the plane and strapped me in. I made the choice. I knew all that. I say such things every day myself. And quite frankly I prefer it when I am the one pointing these things out to other people. "Yes, we all have free will and choice," I said, and probably not all that Zen-like either. "So then it follows that Tiger was where he wanted to be, dead in Redwater in a cheesy motel."

"Of course." He turned and held a door open for us. "And now he's here. Let's go see him."

This guy was starting to seriously annoy me. I walked through the door first, and as Jerry came through behind me I thought I heard Morgue-man suggest that dinner and a movie would be a superior bonding activity to the one we were currently experiencing. You think? Really?

We followed Travis down the hallway, each in our own thoughts. I don't know how he knew, but he was right. Jerry and I hadn't been to a movie together since high school. And the more I thought about it, we hadn't really even been on a date since we'd reconnected, unless you counted our recent rendez-vous in New Mexico, which I guess you had to, sort of. Still, it was weird. What *did* we have between us? We'd been apart for twenty-five years then became instantly in love the second we saw each other again and were both free? Yes, I would have to say so. Actually, we never really fell out of love, I guess. But even so, where did that leave us? With way too many hurdles to jump over to be together full time, that's where. It also left us on our date at the morgue, which I had no chance of forgetting since we were walking into the cold storage room.

When we finally got around to unrolling the pertinent locker drawer, running from the room, vomiting and blacking out were all viable options. I didn't go to medical school for a reason. Back when I was young and impressionable, Lucille had informed me that women had three choices—nurse, secretary and teacher. Even if I had bought into her theory, which obviously I had not, my list went down to two in a hurry since I couldn't even dissect a frog in high school biology class, for godsakes. And here we were with something way bigger than a frog, and he'd already been dissected, not that there's been much to work with. Even with the sheet up to his chin, he looked like a concentration camp victim, the mere photos of which had scarred me for life. I turned away from Tiger's body.

Behind me, Jerry and Travis chatted about various details, mostly, I think, about Tiger's tattoos. I busied myself with studying the tags on the drawers, trying to decode their cataloging method. I wasn't doing that well at it, however, because even though I wasn't looking at the body, I could still see it. I could have gone my whole life and been perfectly happy without seeing that. I do not know how people make careers out of this stuff, I truly do not.

"Jolene, take a look at this," Jerry said, his words registering in my head a few seconds after the sound had hit my ears. "He's almost completely covered in body art."

Mother had told me about the tattoos, but I hadn't known the extent of them. I was about to though. I didn't want to, but I knew Jerry wouldn't have asked if he didn't think I needed to see it for some reason. I took a breath and turned around. They'd pulled the sheet away and Tiger was indeed pretty much solid ink from his neck to as far south as I wanted to see. His legs were decorated too, but I didn't dwell anywhere long.

"I ordered a set of photos for you, Sheriff," Travis said. "They are probably ready. I'll only be a few moments."

Travis left us standing beside Tiger's body, Jerry concentrating on the tattoos, and me trying to think of absolutely anything except the corpse in front of me. "Have you talked to Amy today?" I asked, my thoughts jumping around like a ping pong ball. "I've tried to call Sarah several times and she's not answering her phone. You think she's okay?"

"She's fine, Jolene," Jerry said, still analyzing. "That's one thing you don't have to worry about."

Maybe not, but I still did.

"Look at this," he said, pointing to an eagle, globe and anchor. "He was a Marine."

I made myself look. "Okay."

"What else do you see?"

I saw a lot of things. There were so many figures and words it was hard to focus on just one. Tiger's body had a wolf head in the center of his chest, not a tiger as one might expect. He had an eagle on one pectoral muscle and a buffalo on the other. The words "Freedom" and "Truth" and "Justice" floated between them. Wide bands of interlocking antlers encircled each bicep, and he had a couple of pattern things here and there. His forearms were almost solid in overlaid images, your basic serpents, roses, and naked women jumping out from the mix. His remaining chest was as decorated as his arms, and the designs continued around to his back. He had a red heart with "Mom" on the top of his right shoulder and a blue waterfall with "Death" on his left. "What do you think that stands for?"

Jerry leaned closer and looked at the shoulder. "Maybe symbolic for something he lived through in the war."

"Or maybe he just wishes he could throw his mom over the waterfall and she'd die. That's where I'd go with it." Jerry gave me a sideways glance so I made a second effort. "Okay, fine. He's obviously into causes, save the whales and all that, so maybe it's symbolic. Water is life. Without it, there's death. Nothing can replace water. Idyllic waterfall, symbolic of purity, etcetera, etcetera."

Jerry turned to look at me, but actually stared right through me for several long seconds. He was still staring when Travis came back in with the photos.

"Here you go, Sheriff."

Jerry blinked himself back to reality and took the envelope. "What kind of cancer did he have?"

"As I told her this morning, hepatocellular carcinoma, stage four."

"Primary adult liver cancer," Jerry added.

"You looked it up," Travis said, glancing at me. I nodded and he continued. "Then you know it is the most common form of primary liver cancer. But it's rare for liver to be the primary, it's usually secondary. Most liver cancers start somewhere else, such as the lung, colon or pancreas, and then metastasize to the liver. His didn't. But if you do have a primary liver cancer, and he did, he had the most common type. Stage four indicates that it's spread and is inoperable. Understand?"

Actually, I did. And the research I'd done had helped as well. I even halfway had an idea of what might be going on, but I wanted him to confirm my hunches. Educated and experienced professionals are good for that sort of thing. "What usually causes it?"

"You want me to tell you what you already know," he said simply.

Okay, granted I am as transparent and easy to read as a neon sign behind glass, but this was something more. He was just plain weird and my threshold for such things is pretty darned high. "Yes, tell me what I know. That would be dandy. You could also throw in a few things I don't just for grins."

Travis stared at me for an annoyingly long moment. He clearly had no sense of humor whatsoever. "There are a lot of factors that increase the risk. The obvious are hepatitis B and C, and cirrhosis from alcohol use, which applies in this case. Heredity and smoking are typical contributors as well, but chemical exposure can be a significant factor."

Jerry and I both looked at each other.

"What about aflatoxins?" I asked.

"Food fungus," Travis said. "Not that likely. Arsenic and vinyl chloride exposures are more probable, and the effects of both acute and/or chronic exposures are exacerbated by alcohol abuse."

Jerry said, "Will lab results confirm that?"

"No," Travis said. "Documented exposures, including industrial and military, could indicate a link."

"But that's not your concern," I said. "You just need to determine cause of death and rule out homicide."

Travis nodded.

"Toxic chemical exposure," Jerry said, thinking aloud. "Carcinogens. How?"

"He had to inhale, ingest or absorb them through his skin, or maybe all three," I added, glancing to Jerry then to Travis, who nodded again. "Could the exposure have been a long time ago, or would it have to be fairly recent?"

"Either," Travis said. "Each of us is different. How, when or even if we develop a disease is related to many factors, not the least of which is the need to address an underlying emotional or spiritual issue. Many people need illness to redefine their focus, to reorder priorities, to journey inward and discover self."

"Whatever the case, anybody who dedicates that much money, time and pain to body decorating has serious issues." As Travis nodded in agreement, another thought occurred to me. "You know with all your insights and abilities, Travis, it's just a shame you can't talk to his spirit and ask him these questions."

"They don't talk until they're ready," he said simply.

Jerry didn't bat an eye at this exchange, which I found quite intriguing. We hadn't had a lot of time to devote to other worldly topics and this sure opened the door for that conversation, eventually. After a few moments, Jerry asked how long Tiger could have continued to live, considering his condition if he hadn't overdosed.

"He was in significant pain. Will and purpose had likely been his life blood for some time," Travis said, confirming what he'd told me this morning. "There's nothing more I can help you with, Sheriff. You know the way out."

It wasn't a question. We were being dismissed. Yet, Jackie Chan Chopra probably had some dual meaning he was implying as well, but it made no sense to me. Jerry nodded to Travis and thanked him. I gave him a happy little wave and marched along beside Sheriff Parker out of the building.

As we stepped outside, I said, "Has he ever told you what alien race left him here and when they're coming back for him?"

Jerry chuckled and clicked open the doors of the Expedition. "He has three Ph Ds."

"Big deal. What he needs is a sense of humor and a life. And for godsake, why would anybody need three Ph Ds? And why would anybody who had them come here?" I caught Jerry's raised eyebrow. "It's a reasonable question."

"I believe he said something about being needed here, balancing energies or some such thing." Jerry gave me a half grin. "Also said he enjoys challenging people to open their minds."

"And he annoys those who already have just to amuse himself."

Jerry climbed into the car. "Perhaps."

I followed suit and as we pulled away from the morgue, my thoughts shifted to more important topics. "The cancer matters. Tiger may have killed himself accidentally or on purpose, or somebody else may have helped him out, but his illness matters."

"It's possible," Jerry agreed. "The man knew he was dying and he was in a lot of pain. That part matters."

"And he deliberately drove to Redwater Falls to spend his last days on earth trying to stop a camping park and/or save horny toads?"

"Why not? He wore his dedication to such things all over his body."

"That might be true for him, but his entourage was a mixed bag. Bobcat didn't care about the lizards, but Lily sure did. She was pretty melodramatic, but I don't think she was faking it. She really seemed genuinely ill when she realized that pieces of chicken were about to be eaten." When I saw Jerry's quizzical look, I added, "It's a long story and not important. The main thing is that they were both very interested in the land directly behind my mother's house. Not the whole park area, just that land."

"I'm guessing they were interested in the oil and gas activity, right?" When I nodded, he added, "That could be a link with the Barnett Shale and Gilbert Moore. And if Lucille does own mineral rights on Bob Little's place then she becomes very significant."

"Maybe Saide was trying to buy her property so he could get her to sign away mineral rights at the same time without realizing it, get them for basically nothing."

"Definitely a possibility." Jerry thumped his fingers on the steering wheel. "But if she knew she had mineral rights and they were drilling back there, wouldn't she have to be informed about it, and wouldn't she have benefitted from it?"

"You'd think so."

"Describe the man who was trying to buy your mother's place," Jerry said. "I wasn't there when Fritz brought him in."

"Damon Saide really does kind of look like a weasel—an albino weasel with reddish blonde hair. Skinny guy, about my height, freckles, beady eyes. Thick hair on the back of his hands, not so much on his head."

"He was at the courthouse rally on Monday."

"That's right!" I said, another memory falling into place. "Mother said she saw him arguing with Tiger, like they were going to get into a fistfight."

"Yes, it didn't come to that, and I lost track of them when the explosions started."

"He doesn't seem real smart to me, Jerry. When Mother was trying to kill him, he just hid behind the car and then acted like nothing was wrong when she stopped shooting. He was entirely too accommodating and understanding. If he's the brains behind the park scheme then he's a really good actor."

Jerry straightened himself in the seat and started the car. "Do you know how to get in touch with him? Does Lucille?"

"No. Mother said she threw his card away, but I don't know if she really did or not."

"Right. That would be my guess too." Jerry grabbed his phone from the case at his waist and called Fritz. After a typical merry-go-round of nonsense with Lucille, she eventually admitted to having kept Saide's card for evidence, and finally gave Jerry the phone number. When he hung up, he turned to me and said, "I probably shouldn't tell you this, but the forensic work is finished at your mother's house. She can go home anytime."

And thus, so could I. "But you're not telling her?"

"I think she's better off staying with Fritz for a couple of days. Makes it a lot easier on all concerned."

One would hope.

Jerry dialed the number Lucille had given him, listened for about fifteen seconds and hung up. "Message machine. I wish we still had Saide in custody."

"Yeah, too bad that charge of failing to provide my mother with a moving target didn't stick."

Jerry ignored my clever remark, which was probably just as well. The claim of self-defense even seemed almost reasonable at the moment. Geez, what had made me start thinking these crazy things were all perfectly normal?

Jerry dialed again. "A white compact with bullet holes in it is pretty easy to spot though." He made several calls, including one to his office and one to Perez.

When he'd finished putting out an alert for the car and the weasel, I said, "Now, about Sarah... Mother said she was supposed to leave today. At least I think that's what she said. Do you know anything about that?"

Jerry caught up with my abrupt shift in topics. "I understood that she was heading to Dallas yesterday to try to change her ticket. She should already be back in Denver."

"There is no changing that kind of a ticket, Jerry. Either you're on the flight you picked or you pay for another ticket, and I highly doubt that occurred." I grabbed my phone and tried her dorm room. Not surprisingly, there was no answer. I tried her cell phone. After about six rings it went to voicemail. I tried again and she picked up.

"Mom! What's up?" She was out of breath and a little nervous-sounding. "Everything okay down there?"

"Well, relatively speaking, I guess. Have you made it back yet?"

"No, still traveling," she said, still a bit shaky on the tone and breathing. "But I should be there before long."

I listened astutely for any background noise that might tell me where she actually was. I've honestly never been a snoopy mother, but facts are facts and Little Miss Sarah had been hanging out with the wrong crowd lately, namely her grandmother. I had plenty of questions for her and pinning her down on her whereabouts wasn't going to help me get other more important answers. "You know Tiger is dead, right?"

"Who?" Oh, she tried to sound oblivious, but it was half-hearted at best.

"You know, the man who was staying in your room at the motel. You know, the room your grandmother rented for you at the New Falls Motel."

"Oh." Pause. "Well, I really don't know anything about any of that."

The obvious follow-up question was "why not?" But why bother? I already knew she hadn't been staying there. She'd been at the Hilton. We'd get to that later. What we did know was that Lucille had rented the room, either directly or indirectly, for Tiger and Company—we just didn't know why. And Lucille Junior obviously wasn't going to tell me. She wasn't going to answer my next question either but I was going to ask it anyway. "Now, tell me again why you were in Kickapoo."

"I just wanted to visit, and Gram needed support with all the trouble she was having. She has Merline and Agnes, of course, but we're her only family and we all live seven hundred miles away. I was able to get away so I did. She really appreciated it," Sarah said, running every sentence together as fast as she could, having had a good week of training at such things from the master.

"You know, I actually stayed across the highway from the motel where the dead guy was found. I was at the Hilton last night. What a coincidence, huh?"

There was a long silence punctuated by a few heavy breaths into the phone. "Oh, wow, look at the time. Sorry, Mom, but I have to go. I'm going to be late. Love you. Bye."

Much like her father, it was what she *hadn't* said that was telling. Dodging any direct response to fact statements was crucial since when caught, it could be said that no direct lies had been told. That paternal genetic defect, along with her grandmother's obvious ones, had combined to create a latent tendency for stupidity that apparently struck at age 20. I tossed the phone into the seat. "My daughter is neither in Boulder nor headed in that direction. She's right here. She didn't leave, Jerry, I know she didn't."

"She was supposed to change the ticket," he muttered.

"She probably said she'd try to. There is a distinct difference."

He kind of growled, reality dawning on him. "I should have known better."

The man was making an obvious inference to the girl's lineage and not just her grandmother or her father either. He was wrong, of course. Insanity skips a generation. I was not in charge of either my daughter or my mother's behavior, and yet, I felt responsible, guilty even, like I should apologize to Jerry for both of them. My scarred little psyche is a nest of such ten-headed snakes which prompt me to suck up self-help books faster than Dr. Phil can say "How's that working out for you?" But back to the point, which was now my lying daughter—a not so refreshing change of pace from my lying mother. And you wonder why I need therapy.

He frowned. "You really think she'd do that? Not get on the plane?"

I just shook my head. The man knew the truth. He was just in denial. I know the place well, spend a lot time there myself. "I repeat. She is Lucille Jackson's granddaughter."

Jerry turned toward me, an air of seriousness dropping over him. "Jo, there's something I have to tell you. I should have already told you—"

"Hey, I'm getting a call. Maybe she's calling back to confess." I grabbed the phone and a tingle of fear shot through me as I looked at the number. "Caller ID blocked." I showed the screen to Jerry and he nodded for me to answer. "Hello."

"Miz Jackson, this is Damon Saide."

The little weasel's voice was easy to confirm. And, just hearing it conjured up a vision of the little twerp. "Well, Mr. Saide, what can I do for you?"

"You seem to be reasonable and I was hoping we could talk about the proposal I have for your mother's property."

He sounded awfully eager and I wondered exactly how he'd gotten my phone number. It made me wary, to say the least, although I certainly wanted to meet with him. I doubted Jerry would be quite as enthusiastic. "Hold on a minute."

I pushed the mute button and gave Jerry the details.

He gritted his teeth and his nostrils flared, but after a few long seconds he nodded okay. "Give us an hour."

I unmuted the phone. "Mr. Saide, I'm in Redwater right now—"

"Great. There's a Settler's Restaurant on the north end of town by the new expressway, Fourteenth Street, I believe. I'll buy you a late lunch. I'll be there in thirty minutes."

Shit. I wanted more time but I also didn't want to miss the chance to get the weasel in front of me. "Lunch won't be necessary, but that will be fine. Give me a number where I can call you back in case something happens and I can't make it after all."

"Well, my phone doesn't work very well down here sometimes. If you aren't there, I'll call you. Looking forward to meeting with you." *Click.*

And with that, he hung up. I looked at Jerry. "Settler's in thirty minutes."

Jerry said nothing, just glanced at his watch and picked up his own phone. Predictably, he called Perez. Only he couldn't reach Perez. From the sound of things, the personnel options they offered Jerry for surreptitiously presiding over my meeting with the weasel were not options at all. That meant it was just me and the weasel, with Jerry close by.

"We'd better hurry," Jerry said, turning to get us headed in the right direction. "We'll have to park somewhere else and walk over to the restaurant separately. I'll go first and get settled at a table. You sit as close as you can."

"At least you're not wearing a uniform to scare him off."

"Don't count on him not noticing me," Jerry said. "Just because he plays dumb, doesn't mean he is."

He had a point. Still, we'd be in a public place. How scary could it be?

Chapter Nineteen

Apparently it would be very scary, according to the dissertation I got from Sheriff Parker on the drive over. Jerry's coaching me on what to do, what not to do and what could happen if I screwed up, combined with the large glass of *strong* iced tea I'd just chugged down, had me about to jump out of my skin. That Jerry was seated at one booth across and down from me, watching me, did not reduce my nervousness.

My original take on Damon Saide was that he was too wimpy to be a killer. Jerry had nixed that delusion with entirely too many colorful examples of timid-looking homicidal maniacs, and now that the beady-eyed guy was heading toward my table, I was convinced that he had planted fields of bodies across the country just after they signed the appropriate property transfer papers. I bet he hated puppies and kittens too.

Let me start over. You know how some people just creep you out? Damon Saide was the poster boy for creepy. Nothing you could really put your finger on, just a weird vibe. His looks weren't abnormal, he wasn't even really ugly. He didn't drool or chew his fingers that I could tell, but there was just something about him that made me want to be far, far away.

"Good afternoon, Mr. Saide," I said politely, although I did not offer my hand or stand up. I pegged him to have a limp grasp and I was already squeamish enough. "Please have a seat."

He slid into the booth across from me. "Well, Jolene, I'm certainly glad to have this chance to talk to you alone. I've had quite the time with your mother. Apparently she misinterpreted my proposal and I've been unable to sit down with her and explain the actual details."

Mother didn't have any official papers from Damon Saide, other than a business card, since she'd thrown them all in his face when she kicked him out of her house, or something like that. "I'd like to see your original written proposal, Mr. Saide. It was upsetting to her and I'd like to understand why."

Mr. Weasel fiddled with a cheap black briefcase in the booth beside him and popped open the latches. I couldn't see what was in there, but after a few seconds he pulled out a file folder and set it on the table. "A simple purchase offer, really. The offer is generous. Fifty thousand." He slid out the tax assessor's form and tapped his finger on the figure. "As you can see, the county has it listed at only thirty-eight thousand two hundred. We're willing to offer more to compensate for the inconvenience."

"It doesn't matter what the county has a house valued at. It would bring fifty thousand on the open market without even trying, so your offer isn't 'generous' by any stretch."

"That may have been true a few years ago, but property values across the country have dropped dramatically, as you must certainly be aware."

The property value fluctuations were dramatic in some parts of the country, yes, but this area had never inflated so I doubted there'd been a drop at all. "Why is it again that you need my mother's property when you've got two thousand acres of nothing behind it to plant concrete pads on?"

"Well," he said, clearing his throat, "As I explained to your mother—"

The waitress stopped at our booth with a glass of water for Damon Saide and her order pad ready. "Tea," he said. "Unsweet."

"I'm fine for now," I said to the waitress, keeping my attention on Saide. "You were saying that my mother's property was essential because…"

"Yes, of course. The property would give us westerly access as well as additional housing for staff or a secondary headquarters."

Even if we agreed to believe the park was legit, it didn't make sense to buy a residential property for any of the reasons he cited. And why hers and not one of the others down the street? And what about the Little house? Was that not part of the deal too? "Let me see the contract and maybe I can help." I did not say help with what.

"We hoped the situation would be a win-win for both of us," he continued, ignoring my request. "Your mother is getting on in years, and it would be easier for her to sell to us than on the open market. She could get an apartment and not be bothered with any potential traffic from the park."

I didn't say a word, but my look seemed to adequately relay my "save the bullshit" message.

The waitress returned with the weasel's tea and he immediately grabbed some little pink packets and started pouring them in.

I took a sip of my own tea and watched him stir the white powder into his drink, thinking that he was as fake as the crap he was using for sugar. I didn't like him or what he was up to. I also had a very personal bone to pick with him about his knowledge of duct tape and gas, but that would have to wait. "I'm not even going to pretend that I believe access plays any role in what you're up to. So, Mr. Saide, what is it that's really motivating you?"

His eyes blinked reptilian-like and he shifted in his seat a little, but overall he was still acting as cool and collected as he had hunkered down behind his car with bullets flying. "As I said earlier, the property would give us an alternative access route for emergency and staff only, and the residence would serve as park offices or staff housing. We could move much quicker with structures already in place. We hoped to have the facilities ready for the annual bicycle race this summer. That's why it's so important to get the properties under contract as soon as possible."

He was good at his game, I'd give him that. And in another time or place, his proposals and rationalizations would have been plausible, believable even. There had been a similar situation in Colorado a few years back where his arguments would have made perfect sense because of geographic access and the limited land available. But not here. You could go miles in any direction and find the same type land with willing and eager sellers. Before I could ask him about that, however, he said, "As I told your mother, we'll be fair. If she doesn't want to take our initial offer, we'll hire an appraiser to come out and take a look at the property. We'll agree to pay whatever he determines the fair market value of the house to be."

"So," I said, trying to conceal my fury at his attempted scam. "If the appraisal comes back at sixty thousand, you'll pay that, no questions asked?" He nodded eagerly, thinking he was reeling me in. "And if your appraiser comes back with a figure of twenty-eight thousand then that will be the amount paid as well, correct?"

He shifted in his seat again. "Well, yes, but certainly that's an extreme difference and we don't anticipate that low of a figure. We use only registered and licensed appraisers so it would be a true fair market valuation. Of course, she could just take our original offer and not worry about it."

And I could just reach across the table and rip his black heart out through his throat too. Instead, I gritted my teeth and nodded my head, pretending I was carefully considering his offer. I couldn't help but wonder how many people, particularly older folks, had been taken by such tactics. How many people had literally given their houses away because some little weasel scared them into it? "So, do you have a contract with those terms in it that I can present to my mother?"

He fiddled around in the briefcase beside him in the booth. "Well, not specifically as we could never come to terms on which option she preferred. I'll draw up the papers for the set sales price or the appraisal option, whichever she chooses." He smiled, trying to look understanding and chummy. "We want this to work out, Miz Jackson, but we do need an answer quickly. This offer will not be good indefinitely."

"And why would that be?"

"We need to move quickly." He eyed me suspiciously. "The area needs the facilities. We'd hoped to have part of it open in time for the bicycle race this summer."

"Yes, you said that already. The bicycle race. And the tourists coming to see the falls. Just essential to have an RV park out near Kickapoo for all that." I smiled, and it was about as sincere as you'd think it was. "You still didn't answer my question. What are you going to do if my mother won't sell to you and you are forced to withdraw your non-indefinite offer?"

"We do have other options," he said, condescension dripping from his lips.

Yeah, like murder and kidnapping. "Who do you work for, Mr. Saide?"

He plucked a business card from his brief case and slid it to me. "Parks for Progress. It's a private investment group."

I took the card and studied it. Very basic and nothing I didn't already know. The private investment group admission was a new revelation however. "So, who would some of these private investors be? Who do you answer to directly?"

He still kept smiling. "That's confidential, of course."

Here we were, two gladiators smiling at each other with fake little smiles, volleying veiled accusations and withholding information, just waiting for a chance to lunge in for the kill. I hate these kinds of cat and mouse games. "Of course, confidential. All supposedly public projects by private groups with private interests are kept confidential. No need for the public to be bothered with the pesky details of who's doing what and why."

Damon Saide's congenial smile slipped to rodent-like sneer. "This is a project that is in the best interests of the community, Miz Jackson," he said dropping all pretenses. "You might mention to your mother that we have new laws in this country that allow property to be taken for the greater good. We can get the acquisition taken care of however we need to. If we want the property, we'll get it."

"Bullshit."

His little beady eyes bugged open as if he'd never heard the word before or he was just in shock that I would dare question him.

"If you could use that tactic, Saide, you already would have. And while we're at it," I said, taking a sip of tea and watching him closely. "I find it very interesting that a man eaten up with cancer chose to spend his last day on this planet with a fist in your face on the courthouse lawn, ostensibly because of lizards."

Saide's eyes narrowed to little slits. "What are you trying to say?"

"I know this park is a cover." I waited a few seconds to help him assume that I knew for what. "I know why you killed Tiger and I know why you didn't kill me last night when you had the chance."

His pale freckled skin bloomed bright red. He might have a poker face otherwise, but he couldn't stop the rosy flush. "I have no idea what you're talking about."

Oh, but he did. "Did you really think you could gas her then force her to sign sale papers and no one would notice?" I paused again, watching his face, his eyelids blinking rapidly, a thin sheen of sweat glistening across his brow. "What you did to me would have killed her, which was probably your intent. Then there's the problem with Bob Little. He wouldn't sign your papers either so I'm figuring he's dead too, just no body yet."

The weasel's freckled face ripened until he looked like a cherry tomato with brown heat spots. "Your accusations are ridiculous."

I stayed as calm as I could and scooted to the edge of the booth, ready to stand. "Guys like you don't do well in prison, you know."

His hand shot out and grabbed my arm. "You don't know what you're getting into," he hissed, his hot sweaty fingers digging into the flesh just above my wrist. "This isn't a game."

I swallowed down a wave of sickening bile. I was already half leaning over the table so I dug my fingers under his index finger and bent it backward off my arm.

He squealed and released me.

"I don't play games," I said, my voice and body both shaking.

He clutched his finger with his other hand, his eyes watering and his nostrils flaring.

I held out the arm he'd just grabbed as if it were infected. "Now, if you'll excuse me, I've got to run to the police station and get more prints taken."

His stared for a few seconds then his lips curled into a sneer. "You have nothing."

Jerry had walked up to the booth and was standing just behind weasel, although he hadn't yet noticed that.

"I have your finger prints on my skin. Just like I did last night."

He scowled and shoved the file folders back into his brief-case. He jerked himself up out of the booth and spun to his left, directly into Jerry. The briefcase he'd tucked under his right arm popped free and fell open on the floor.

I jumped out of the booth and lunged, but Damon Saide beat me to it. He snapped up the briefcase and tucked it under his arm like a football. Jerry grabbed at him, but Saide spun and darted to the side, shoving me forward into Jerry who was following. My head rammed into Jerry's legs, knocking him backward. He grabbed me by the back of the shirt, but I still fell to the floor, and he fell with me. Untangling himself, he jumped up and ran after the weasel.

As I got to my feet, I realized that every neck in the place was twisting around to see what was going on. Once Jerry made it out the front door, that left me as the center of attention. "He's a sheriff," I said, gasping and holding onto the back of the booth to steady myself, my heart pounding in my throat and ears. They all just stared at me like I was a going to rob them or something. "Seriously, he's a sheriff and he'll catch the bad guy. Everything is okay." I fumbled in my pocket, pulled out a ten and laid it on the table and scurried out of the restaurant.

I only made it a few steps out of the front door when Jerry zoomed up in the SUV. "Get in," he yelled. I did and he screeched out of the lot as I shut the door. He was also making a call to the Redwater Police to send out the troops all at the same time. After he hung up, he said, "The only thing I can figure is that he must have parked by the front door and left it running with a door opener in his pocket. He was pulling away as I ran out. I'm still going up a few blocks to see if I see the car."

The bullet-ridden white import would be easy enough to spot, but we both knew we wouldn't. The weasel was long gone. "What do you think he'll do next?"

Jerry pulled up to the next red light and stopped, looking south on the one-way street with a light on every corner. "He probably turned here, but then where?" The light turned green and we followed his thoughts down the street, slowing and glancing up and down each street as we passed. After about five blocks, he turned left and headed back toward downtown. "If he was behind the kidnapping then he still has unfinished business with your mother. He'll go after her."

I'd had similar thoughts myself, but hearing him say it made it entirely too real.

"It's a good thing she went with Fritz," Jerry said, before I could speak. He looked over at me, pointedly. "Still, underestimating Saide would be a serious mistake."

I shivered at the truth of his words. "I wonder who he's really working for."

"I'll talk to Perez while you're getting prints lifted from your arm and see if he's found out anything on that."

"Hey, I was only kidding about that fingerprint thing, using it to worry the weasel."

"Well, you're right. New technology. They can try a couple of things." He read my unspoken question accurately. "Yes, even in Redwater."

Well, I hadn't seen that one coming. I had no idea what process the fingerprints-off-skin thing actually involved, but I knew for certain I didn't want to participate in it. "Seriously, Jerry, what's the point? Even if they did get prints off my arm there's nothing to match with."

"It's true we didn't charge him with a crime when Fritz brought him from your mother's house so there aren't any prints from that. And, by the way, we both know who should have been arrested and booked in that incident." He paused unnecessarily for emphases. "At the least we should get a match from DMV. I want to know who this guy is and now we have a chance at that."

"I suppose."

"Good job in getting him to do that, by the way."

You'd think I'd be pleased at the compliment even though it hadn't been a planned effort, only a snappy comeback after the fact. Whatever the case, I feared my moment of cleverness was about to earn me yet another experience I could do without.

Chapter Twenty

T rue to his word, Mr. Sheriff busied himself with official business while I lay like a corpse for two forensics experts to painstakingly powder, photograph, wrap and peel my arm with some kind of special Polaroid film-like stuff. It was not a speedy process and by the time I realized this was going to take three days past forever, I couldn't get away. The sound of their muttering indicated it was not especially fulfilling for them either, but the arm hair comments and speculation about my soaping and lotioning habits were just uncalled for. Apparently most of their customers were not adept as I at snappy comebacks—or any kind of comebacks for that matter—since every time I said something to defend myself they just about jumped out of their own skins. While it was amusing the first two or three times, it didn't help speed things along so I finally just played dead. They seemed a lot happier with that.

Since I had nothing better to do, I tried to remember exactly what, if anything, Saide had revealed. He hadn't said anything I didn't know, but when his briefcase fell open, I had seen an aerial photo, similar to the one I'd printed. His copy had circles and Xs on it and a bunch of odd numbers. Marking the oil wells? Or development sites? Or something else? It probably meant nothing. Aerial photos were easy to get and it made good sense to have a view from above if you were laying out a park. As much as I wanted it to be, it probably wasn't a clue to anything. Feeling the last air of enthusiasm trickle out of that balloon, I sighed, which caused the forensics people to jump and suck in their collective breath. "Are you almost finished?" I asked. One guy gave me a quick nod and I was just sure they wanted this over with as much as I did.

As soon as the crime lab people freed me, I made a beeline to Jerry and Perez. Not exactly a beeline, perhaps, as Perez wasn't in his office as I'd expected. In fact, he and Jerry were back in the interrogation room, and when I walked in, they had the aerial photos I'd printed spread out on the table. They were seated facing each other, each holding a photo, studying it.

Jerry motioned me to the table for a closer look. "This is Olive Street. Here's your mother's house. It borders the ranch here. There's another strip with three houses in the next block that border the ranch too. In reality, there are over two miles of properties that are adjacent to the Little Ranch."

"Damon Saide's aerial had marks on it," I said. "Circles and Xs and numbers. Did you see that, Jerry, when the briefcase fell open?"

"Yes, but I didn't see it well enough to identify a point of reference."

"Is it possible," I said, "that some of the numbers could have been GPS points." GPS, or Global Positioning System, allows people holding special machines to download 'You Are Here' coordinates from the stars, or at least the satellites. Accuracy and price are intimately connected, but a decent consumer model can generally get within a three-foot radius of the intended mark. "I'm sure there were points right behind Mother's house. What could that mean?"

Jerry set the photo aside and unfolded what looked like a county tax map and spread it on the table. "That's the big question," Jerry said, running his finger across a series of squares. "Your mother's house is on this center lot with a vacant one on each side. The houses in the next block are on similar sized lots, but all have houses built on them. They all look like they were platted at the same time and each has a separate parcel number."

I looked at the map, trying to put it into perspective with views from the ground and the air. It was harder than it sounds.

He pointed to a large tract of land that was obviously the Little Ranch, however, there were four medium-sized squares between the ranch and Mother's house. "However, if you'll look here, these four forty-acre parcels aren't part of the Little Ranch, although they look like they should be," he said, tapping the map. "These parcels are out of the corner nearest your mother's place."

I squinted and leaned back as far as I could, but the letters wouldn't come into focus. It was only when Jerry pulled the glasses from his face that I realized he'd been wearing them. "I don't really need them either," he said, handing them to me. "But they do help."

You know, I wouldn't go back and be seventeen again for anything, but being over forty kind of sucks sometimes. I put on the glasses and studied the county ownership map. From what I could tell, Bob Little owned a huge chunk of land beginning at the edge of Kickapoo and continuing to the east and north all the way to Turkey Ranch Road on the east, the main highway on the north and another road to the south. The only exception was the four parcels on the western edge that bordered Kickapoo. It was very clear that a large strip of land had been carved out of the Little Ranch, and that particular tract was behind my mother's house. Then I saw the name on the four parcels. I turned to Jerry. "Why is her name there?"

"Because she's the owner of record."

"What?"

"One hundred and sixty acres," Perez said, thumbing through a folder, obviously looking for something in particular. "Her house is in the city limits of Kickapoo. The land behind it isn't. She's owned it for forty years or so."

"Is that so..." I muttered

Perez shuffled through more papers. "Do you remember her every saying anything about that land?"

"Just that if I touched the white crusty stuff over there, I'd die."

"Salt flats," Jerry said.

Perez nodded. "So you weren't supposed to go over there?"

"No, it was okay. I rode horses over there."

"But when you went over there as a kid, you believed that land was Bob Little's?"

"Absolutely." But what did I believe now? I tried to recall her recent references to that land. General concepts wouldn't do. "I can't remember her exact words about it lately, but whatever she said still led me to believe that Bob Little owned that land. She also mentioned the oil wells and implied they were his too." Something tickled the back of my memory, some odd comments that she'd made that I'd wanted to remember. "She said Bobby had gotten in over his head with it all. I wish I could remember more."

Jerry said, "I'd sure like to know why it needed to be a secret that she owned the land or the oil wells."

"I do remember that she recently said those wells were low producers, but real steady. I remember thinking that it was odd that Bob would want to give up his steady producers for a park." I shook my head at the effort to make sense of the senseless. "But if Lucille was the one getting the real steady royalties, she wouldn't want Bob selling her gravy train either, would she? But then he wasn't. He was only selling his land. Or maybe that was what Saide was really after, the oil wells, and they were on her land. God, it's confusing."

Jerry looked at me and frowned. "It really doesn't make good sense."

Perez pulled out another file with more papers. "I did some research on the oil wells on the Little property when the park story first came out in the newspaper and your mother wrote in protesting." Finding the paper he was looking for, he said, "In Texas, the oil and gas industry is regulated by the Railroad Commission. They have production records online back to 1993. There hasn't been anything produced under the Little name since at least then. I didn't know about your mother's involvement, of course, so I didn't look for that. I started checking on her after Jerry called this morning. Didn't get much though."

"Those pump jacks are still moving, no question about that," I said. "Maybe the production records are under a company name we don't recognize."

"Could be. Or a series of them." Perez gathered his papers and shoved them back into the folder. "Lease records are at the courthouse." Walking to the door, he said, "Jerry, you know what I'm going to say."

"Yeah, Dan, I do." Jerry stood and gathered the papers we'd brought. "Come on, Jolene. We have a lot of ground to cover."

"Well, I don't know what he was going to say." I followed Jerry to the door where Perez stood. "What was he going to say?"

"Basically the same thing he said before, that this has nothing to do with any case he's working, but he'd let me know what he gets back on Saide. He'd also say that if he were me, he'd go talk to your mother and make a visit to the courthouse, and if by chance it winds up pertaining to his case to let him know." Jerry glanced at Perez. "Is that about right?"

"Yep."

Oh, there was plenty more, but giving a dissertation on it didn't seem prudent at the moment. "But you de-fingerprinted me."

"As a favor to him," Perez said, nodding toward Jerry.

"Well, I want to file assault charges." I glanced between the men, trying to see if that was something that could be done or not. "I was assaulted in the restaurant. You have his fingerprints already and that's who I want to file a complaint on."

Perez sighed. "It's already done. You told the story when you got here and we wrote it down. You signed. Remember?"

"Well, yes, but I thought that was just a release so you could torture me."

We did both," Perez said. "We're efficient every now and then, and it helps that we have a drawer full of forms already filled out with your name on them. Saves time."

I looked over at Jerry. "He's kidding, right? Tell me he's kidding."

"He's doing everything he can," Jerry said as Perez walked out of the room. "Now, what we need to do is go talk to your mother and then do a little research at the courthouse."

"You know, Jerry, the morgue guy was right. Just once, couldn't we try dinner and a movie?"

Chapter Twenty-One

We arrived at Fritz Harper's house around seven without fanfare. They'd been warned we were coming so we at least avoided a scene at the door. That did not, however, ensure a simple question and answer episode with my mother. Nothing can do that. Nothing.

We migrated to the kitchen and seated ourselves around Fritz's table, apparently so Lucille could hop up and down to pretend to be the perfect hostess and conveniently delay our questioning. Jerry quizzed Lucille about the land behind her house, the oil wells, who owned what, etc. Mother had offered him water, tea, coffee and tour of Fritz's real nice home, but had not once addressed any of his questions directly. She phrased most of her comments with "Bobby said" or just played dumb about knowing anything.

I took a sip of iced tea that Mother had graciously—and stallingly—made. "You know, Mother, I must say this performance is just not up to your standards. You're usually better prepared, have better tales to tell."

"I do not tell tales," Lucille said, scowling. "I've said all I'm going to say about any of it. There's nothing more to say and I won't. Period. Tales my hind foot."

Jerry looked at me then at Lucille. "I can't imagine what you're trying to hide, but we'll find out eventually. I'd think you know that by now."

Lucille just huffed and scowled and clamped her lips shut.

The woman had a secret, no doubt about that, and it must be a doozy. And of all the things to have a secret about, owning 160 acres with oil wells out behind the house would not have been on any list I could have dreamed up. Neither would Bobcat's assertion about Lucille owning mineral rights on Bob Little's ranch. I stood up and sort of smiled at Jerry. "I'd say a trip to

PAULA BOYD

the Bowman County Courthouse records room would be our
first order of business in the morning. No telling what we'll find
there."

"I could pull a few strings and get in tonight," he said, still
staring at Lucille. "There is definitely information there that we
need and the sooner we get some answers, the better."

Mother turned rather pale beneath her pancake makeup
and painted on blush. "Well, now, I don't think there's anything
you need at that courthouse, and who'd want to go digging
through old dusty records anyway. Those old records are in
such a jumble, why it's just a waste of time. No point to it at all."

"There's a point," Jerry said tersely. "And you know exactly
what it is."

Lucille tapped her nails on the table and thought about how
much—make that little—she could get away with telling. No, I
didn't read her mind. We all know how she operates.

I sat back down. "Out with it, Mother. We'll find out sooner
or later."

"Oh, alright then." She scowled. "You very well know
we bought those lots years ago and had the house moved in.
They're city lots and I am not happy about that as you well
know."

"Guess you could move the house back a couple hundred
feet and be out of the city limits if it bothers you so much, you
owning the hundred and sixty acres and all."

"That would be silly." She squirmed in her seat and tapped
her nails some more. "As for the other, well, it's not a crime to
own land and it sure isn't anybody's business. Besides, I may
own land in Alaska or Hi-wah-ya too for all you know."

"Right. Speaking of what all I don't know, just why, when
and how did you acquire the acreage and why didn't you ever
tell me about it?"

Lucille hopped up from the table and made a dash for the
kitchen sink. "Because it just didn't matter," she said, turning
on the faucet to rinse out a glass. "I just don't see how any of
this has anything to do with anything!"

"Miz Jackson," Jerry said, and not sweetly either, as he
scooted his chair back away from the table. "I've reached my
limit."

He never got to say another word, however, because Lucille spun around from the sink and slapped a dish towel at the table. "Fine! If you must know I got that land from Mr. Little years ago." She twisted the dishcloth in her hands and paced. "Bobby and I have been friends for a lot of years. He was just trying to protect my interests and I was trying to protect his. Nothing to make a federal case out of. Something from a long time ago that's none of your business. I never paid any attention to the land, just let him handle things. It's nothing anybody needs to be sticking their noses into, I'll tell you that for sure, and it just seems that's always what you two are trying to do, stick your noses in my business. I'll have you know that I made it a point to let you two do what you were going to do when you were back in school whether I thought you ought to be doing it or not, and I didn't meddle, no I did not, because I know that people need their privacy. And private things are just that. Private. This is none of your business and it doesn't have anything to do with anything so you just leave it alone."

She had said nothing, and yet sometime during her rant, I'd had a revelation and my jaw had apparently flopped open. I noticed this when I sucked in a breath and uttered, "Oh, my God."

Lucille smacked her hand on the table again. "Well, now, just what does that mean, Missy?"

"You and Bob Little?"

"What?" she snapped, the implication dawning on her as she spoke. "You better not be meaning what I'm thinking you're meaning. You just get your dirty little mind out of the gutter. We were just old friends and that's all there is to it. I just don't see why you'd think anything else at all, stir something up when there's no reason for it at all."

As she tried to convince me there was nothing I needed to be concerned about, I became absolutely certain there was. My childhood memories as they related to Bob Little were few and far between. I remembered him stopping by the house a couple of times. I also remembered driving up to his house once, but I didn't go inside with her. She was upset at the time, but I don't remember why. Lucille had been upset more often than not when I was little, so it wasn't anything out of the ordinary. The trip up to the plateau was the only reason I even remembered it at all. It had been like driving up a mountain, relatively speaking, which in this part of Texas that was a pretty big deal.

A landslide of thoughts and suppositions crashed to the forefront and I could not stop myself. "So help me, if you tell me that I'm yours and Bob Little's love child, I am just sure I'll implode, or explode, or some other ode. Whatever the case, it will not be pretty!" Yes, my voice escalated just a tad. "Is that what this is about?"

Lucille scowled, but did not, as one would expect, leap to deny my accusation. She straightened herself upright and crossed her arms, standing beside the table with her nose in the air, probably hoping a decent lie would find its way to her tongue. Clearly there was a well-marked path to follow so the odds were in her favor. "How dare you say such a thing to me," she said, standing her ground.

"I'll take that as a yes."

She flung her arms to the side and snapped the dishtowel again. "You most certainly will not!" Her hands fisted and she looked like she was trying to tear the towel to bits. "I cannot believe you're doing this to me, I just cannot. Why, the very nerve." And then she said the one thing that was guaranteed to always, always make things worse." After all I've done for you."

"That's it," I said, smacking my own hand on the table before I realized what I'd done. "I've heard you say that my entire life and I've had enough of it. Mother's are supposed to do things for their children; it's called being a parent. And since I've been on my own since the age of seventeen, I'm not that enthusiastic about polishing your martyr's crown. So, frankly, I don't ever want to hear about how much you've done for me ever again. Because if I do, I'm going to start listing what you've done *to* me and I won't stop for about six weeks. Got it?"

The daggers shooting out from between the narrowed slits of her eyelids said she had. She was sucking in a breath to return fire when I sensed Jerry behind me. He must have been glaring at Lucille because she pressed her lips together in thin hard lines and marched back to the sink.

"Jo," Jerry said, putting a hand on my shoulder. "That's not going to get us anywhere."

"It most certainly will not," Lucille snapped, spinning around to face the table again. And I'll tell you one thing, Miss Hateful Know-it-all, you don't know half as much you think you do, you surely do not. And 'love child,' just what is that supposed to mean?" She glared and gritted her teeth. "I just cannot believe you would say such a thing to me. Why, the very nerve. I tried to shelter you from all that nasty business and just look what it got me, you turning on me like a rabid skunk. You might as well have just ripped my heart out and stomped on it, right here on the kitchen floor."

Her eyes looked a little wet, but I wasn't buying that charade. If she had actual tears it was because she was so mad she could spit. And, like the horny toads, was preparing to do so—out her eyes. I didn't voice any of these thoughts, of course, just leaned back in the chair, crossed my arms and did my own thinking and fuming.

"Well, that's just always the way of it, I suppose," she said, sniffing just a bit to try to elicit some pity. "It's just exactly like I've always said, the ones you love the most do you the dirtiest."

That was not the first time I'd heard that particular phrase either, of course. But I sure didn't have to hear any more. And if I stayed, she was going to hear some particular phrases from me. I patted Jerry's hand, which was still on my shoulder, then stood. "Do what you will with her; I'll be in the car."

As the storm door hissed closed slowly behind me, I noticed a shadow off to my right on the porch. Fritz sat in a wooden rocker with a bowl of something in his lap. I hadn't even realized he'd exiled himself from his own house. Smart man.

He tapped the bowl. "Sunflower seeds?"

"No, thank you though."

"My Uncle Walter told me that sunflower seeds were the secret to a happy marriage. Kept a bowl of them out all the time. Whenever he felt the need, he'd get himself a handful. You think about it, you're either working the salt off the shell, cracking it and getting the seed out or spitting out the hull. You can't do a lot of talking when you're busy working the seeds. Cuts way down on the chances that you'll say something wrong and find yourself in more trouble. Odds are you don't know what you did wrong anyway, and if you just keeping working the seeds, it'll all blow over on its own."

"From the size of that bowl, I'd say you do plenty of seed working."

He cackled at that one. "I don't mind. She's worth it."

The man was clearly out of his head and/or delusionally in love. Hard to imagine, but that sure did seem like the case. No sane man would put up with her otherwise.

"She don't mean no harm, you know," he said, the rocker creaking beneath him. "She just has funny ways about things sometimes."

Yes, and her funny ways included lying, scheming, interfering with an official investigation and destruction of public and private property to name a very few. She was a real catch. "Yes, well, I may have a slightly different view of things."

"She thinks you hung the moon, you know."

No, I did not know. In fact, my take on that would be that I was the last one capable of moon hanging. In her opinion, I wasn't even capable of writing about moon hanging. "Well, then I guess we're in the dark phase now because I apparently just stomped her heart all across the kitchen floor."

"Aw, I do that at least twice a week." He chuckled and rubbed his chin. "She don't really mean it. That's just her way."

It certainly was, and I'd had more than enough of her passive aggressive theatrics to last me five lifetimes. "Do you know what she's up to?" This time. "She's hiding something."

"Nah, but it ain't ever as bad as she seems to think it is."

In my experience it was always far worse—and bizarre— than anything I could imagine. "I think she's pushed Jerry too far this time."

Fritz shrugged then reached down beside him and picked up a glass of ice tea. "Don't you worry, she'll come around. That mother of yours is a fine woman and she'll set things to rights and everything will all work out just fine."

Yes, and the pigs were perched in the mesquites ready for takeoff.

Fritz's little love bubble of delusion would burst soon enough without my help so I muttered an "I hope so," waved and hurried to the car.

I didn't have the keys to the Expedition so I had to leave the door open for air. I could, however, lean the seat back, and did. I tried a little deep breathing and focusing on nothingness, but my lying mother's words kept popping back into my head.

Love child? She hadn't denied my accusations either, which most likely meant they were true. That, however, was a reality that I couldn't really wrap my brain around just yet. I kept working at it, however, and by the time Jerry opened the door and got in, I had worked through the denial stage and was ready to join anger on the dance floor. "Dare I ask if you learned anything of importance?"

"She said she hadn't heard from Sarah." He buckled up and started the car. "It was the one thing she said that I actually believed."

That didn't make me feel better about anything. I raised the seat up and closed the door. "Do you think Sarah's okay?"

He sighed and nodded. "Yes, I do."

"I could fix that for her. She and her grandmother are both scheming liars. I do not know how it is that I am related to either of them." I leaned back against the headrest. "Do you know how hard it is to find out your life is a lie? That your dad really wasn't your father?"

"You don't know that for a fact, Jolene. But if it is true, don't be so quick to judge." He pulled away from Fritz's house and drove slowly down the dirt road toward the highway. Taking my hand, he said, "People do a lot of things because of love. If you and I had lived in the same town after high school, I can't say for sure what I'd have done, married or not. Can you?"

Oh, now why did he have to go and say that? I'd like to think I'd have taken the high road and stayed far, far away from him, but how realistic was that? With Jerry Don Parker readily available to me, I think we all know what I'd have done. But would I have stayed married to Danny while I did it? No, I couldn't have. Then again, the fact that I'd stayed married to Danny longer than twenty minutes, or hell, that I'd even gone ahead with the ceremony after him not showing up on time because he'd lost the wedding band—Freudian slip is an understatement—does not point to someone capable of making good decisions. And let's not forget my even better decision of running away from Jerry in the first place or there would have been no Danny. "You're right, Jerry. I've done a lot of things I wish I hadn't. I had reasons, of course. I even thought they were good reasons at the time. But they weren't. They were stupid. Plain stupid."

He squeezed my hand again, knowing exactly what I meant. "Let's don't go there, okay? We're here now. That's what counts." He moved his hand back to the steering wheel and pressed his palm against it as if to push away the thoughts of what could have been if we hadn't been foolish teenagers. We rode in silence for a long minute or two when he finally said, "Do you think she knows where Bob Little is?"

That thought hadn't even occurred to me, but once it had, the answer came instantly. "Yes." If Lucille and Bob were such "good friends," then why wasn't she worrying about him, begging Jerry to find him? Tiger was dead and it would be logical to fear the same fate for the man missing under mysterious circumstances. Yet Lucille hadn't even mentioned being concerned about him. "Oh, yeah, she knows."

We rode in silence for a few more miles until all the details came together in a nice neat package in my head. Okay, not all the details—we know how things work in my head—but certainly enough supposition to home in on the whereabouts of one Little Bob Little. "She knows exactly where he is, Jerry. And you know what? So do I."

He glanced over at me with his typical skepticism. "And where would that be?"

"The lake cabin. She's hiding him at her lake cabin."

Chapter Twenty-Two

"**H**mmm."

"That's it, 'hmmm'?" The more I thought about it, the more right it got. I stopped short of suggesting that we go get him, but it was implied. "He's there, Jerry, he's got to be."

Jerry Don Parker did not immediately slam on the brakes, whip the car around or otherwise head to the lake as one would expect. He did pick up the phone and started punching in numbers, however the words "we'll be at the courthouse in less than ten minutes" were what came out of his mouth instead of something pertaining to the supposed missing person and a SWAT team headed to the lake.

"I take it we aren't going to race to the cabin."

"No." He glanced over at me, then back at the road and kept driving. "If he is there, then he isn't missing and there's been no foul play. I can't arrest him for anything so I can't keep him in custody. He's probably sitting on the couch with a bag of chips and a beer, watching Survivor. I'd like to keep it that way until we get some other questions answered."

"Well, I'm ready to get to him right now and have him answer a few questions for me that my lying mother won't. I want answers, Jerry. Right now."

"We'll get to that. It just makes sense to get the facts first."

"Facts would be good," I agreed, thinking such things had been severely lacking up to this point. "My birth certificate is disqualified for obvious reasons, but facts could likely be had from a few polygraphs, DNA testing and perhaps a little water boarding."

"I was leaning more toward checking mineral rights ownership records."

"Oh."

Jerry's phone rang and he answered, but didn't say much. "I'll check it out," he said, ending the call. "That was Perez. Some lab results came back."

Maybe now we'd have some of those facts he wanted so badly, like the official cause of death for Tiger. "And?"

"Did you always have city water?"

Huh? That was an odd question. "As far as I know."

"Is there a well on your mother's property?"

I thought about it for a minute, visually scanning the lot. I knew what a wellhead looked like; I had one at home in Colorado. I didn't remember anything like that specifically, but I did remember something. "There was something out away from the house that Dad always kept covered. He had a big heavy piece of iron pipe with a cap welded on the top that he set over it to keep it from freezing. I couldn't lift it. Why?"

"Some lab results were faxed to the motel this afternoon."

"To the motel? Where Tiger was?"

"Yes. Apparently Tiger had collected some water and soil samples and sent them off to a lab for analysis. They faxed back the results to the motel as he'd requested."

"So is that what he had the glass jars for?"

"How'd you know about that?"

"Mother overheard the police talking when we were there."

Jerry just shook his head. "According to what Perez was told, there are primary chemicals and then there are secondary ones, which had broken down from the original. These are apparently called daughter products and can be more hazardous than the original."

Yes, I recognized the obvious gold mine of opportunity for laughs at my expense in that statement, but thankfully Jerry did not, or pretended not to anyway.

"Perez had a list. I recognized a few like benzene, and trichlor-something-terrible. Some of the levels were several hundred thousand parts per million."

"That can't be good," I muttered.

"It isn't."

How bad was the question. How it all tied together was another. Tiger had come to town to help stop the park, presumably to save horny toads. His room contained soil and water sampling equipment, and a lab had faxed him back sample results. Bad results, apparently. In addition, aerial photos showed what looked like recent dirt work and some kind of drilling on the land behind my mother's house. Why? As much as I hated thinking about it, I very well knew that plenty of illegal dumping and burying of toxic waste had been done around the country as well as the world, especially years ago. Why not here? Of course, here. Maybe especially here. A sick feeling settled in my stomach. "That could mean some kind of serious contamination, Jerry. If it's in the groundwater, there's no telling how bad it is or how many people have been affected—are still being affected."

"We can't automatically assume," he said, "that the samples came from the Little Ranch."

"They did."

"Maybe. But they also could have come from your mother's."

Well, he had a point there. "Remember, Mother was complaining about people out behind her house drilling and doing all kinds of things. We assumed that to be the Little Ranch, but we now know it's actually her property."

"Right," Jerry said, "and since that land is hers, why didn't she stop them from doing something if she didn't want it?"

"She just said that she let Bob take care of all that. But again, why?"

Jerry tapped his fingers on the steering wheel. "I know that some of the chemicals Perez listed are related to the oil industry," Jerry said. "So if the samples came from the Little property, or your mother's, they could be typical of a recent spill, which is not that uncommon. Even small spills could have high concentrations in one area, so until we know where he sampled we're just speculating."

"Chemicals breakdown at different rates and change composition depending on a lot of factors. Tiger knew what he was looking for and if we had those lab results, we would too."

Jerry raised an eyebrow. "College chemistry class kicking in?"

"Actually, my formal training in chemistry occurred in the seventh grade when Coach Eastman made us use beakers and Bunsen burners for something or other." The look on his face told me I hadn't cleared up anything at all. "I read a lot, Jerry," I said, shrugging. "Environmental stuff is big in Colorado."

"Well, then how are you on microbiology?"

"There's been some real success with using specialized microbes for bioremediation of petroleum products and other hazardous wastes. It's expensive but good for the environment. But I'm guessing you really want to know about toxicology." I grinned. "I've dabbled, but Doctor-Doctor-Doctor Travis would be able to look at those lab results and tell us immediately what Tiger suspected and if it could have had anything to do with his cancer."

He turned and looked at me as if I'd just recited the Preamble to the Constitution in Chinese.

"Oh, don't look at me like that. The information is there for anyone who wants to take the time to read it, which I generally don't. I just happen to have a knack for remembering the highlights as I skim through. "

"I had no idea, Jolene," he said, glancing over at me again to be sure who was sitting in the car seat beside him. "No idea."

"Well, geez, Jerry, how much time do we ever have to talk about normal topics of conversation? We don't even discuss the weather. We talk about my mother and the dramas and mayhem she's stirred up, and, most importantly, how to keep us all from getting killed because of it."

"And that, my dear, is going to change."

I wanted to believe him, I really did. I saw no hope of it, however. Not even a glimmer. I glanced over at him and smiled. "But for now…"

"Right. It doesn't much matter what the temperature is or what oil is trading at." He paused for a minute then said, "Or maybe it does. If the property is contaminated, the question becomes whether it's related to the oil and gas activities or something else."

"Either way, we need to know when it happened. Were they out there digging to bury more or trying to find out how bad whatever's already there is?"

"If we could just look for bare dirt where they'd dug the holes that would be easy," Jerry said. "But around here, there's not a lot of good vegetation to begin with."

I thought about that and tried to correlate it with what I'd read about the topic. "If it wasn't related to an onsite spill, whatever is there was probably buried.

"Steel drums," Jerry said, nodding.

"The contamination might not have shown up right away. Nothing much would have looked different for a while."

Jerry nodded, thumping his fingers on the steering wheel. "How corrosive the soil is would determine how long it would take before the barrel rusted and leaked—if they were sealed well initially. If they weren't, they could have contaminated the soils immediately."

"If they didn't leak for years," I said, playing out the possible scenarios, "the land would look normal on the surface. But when they did leak, depending on how deep they were buried, the contamination would soak through the ground and the vegetation would die."

"Right. Anything that got a root in it would die. Soil and water conditions would be factors as well though," he said. "If the leak went down and not up then it could still look normal on the surface and be contaminating water below."

"Or, it could be doing both, Jerry. That placed looked horrible in the aerial. And Tiger found contamination in water somewhere, we just don't know where. Nothing about this is good. And we're back to the same questions we started with 'who' and 'why'."

"As we've talked, different people are motivated by different things. Love, money and revenge come to mind." Jerry propped an elbow on the door by the window and tapped a finger against his chin. "The seven deadly sins are always available too, you know. But don't forget redemption and protection. And remember, people will defend imagined threats just as vehemently as they will real ones."

"True. Our brains don't know the difference between real and imagined experiences and we feel the emotion of it either way."

"It's why I can do certain things," he said, reaching over and gently running his fingers along the back of my neck, "and you'll have a reaction as if I've done something far more intense."

Heat flushed through me, confirming his statement. "I think that's a different thing," I croaked.

He grinned and pulled his hand back. "It's still your brain doing the work. You've learned that when I touch you on the back of the neck, more good feelings follow."

No question about that. "So, Dr. Pavlov, since you've rung the bell do we still have to go to the courthouse?"

"Yes, Jolene, we do."

"Well, then I would say that you have used your power unwisely and it will never work again." I rolled the window down and stuck my head out, letting the cool night air crash against my face and hopefully un-trigger my brain.

"It'll still work," he said, chuckling. "You'll just be anticipating it even more."

I did not find the situation amusing at all. "Someday I'm going to figure out how to do that to you and then we'll see how you like it."

He leaned over and tickled my neck again. "You already do," he said in that deep rumbling voice that makes shiver. "You just don't realize it."

I jerked my head back in and glared at him. "Well, that's even worse."

He laughed. "Yeah, it really is."

Chapter Twenty-Three

T he Bowman County Courthouse was a looming ancient structure, at least by western world standards. Built in 1882, the brick and stone building was constructed on the typical town square program and was still in pretty good shape. It had been remodeled a time or two through the years, the most recent being in the late seventies, or somewhere thereabouts, probably during the last big oil boom. The dark stained wood, yellow walls and old-style asbestos floor tiles still gave it that "old world charm."

The sheriff's offices were on the backside of the courthouse, so from the front you couldn't tell that anyone was in the building. Other than our Expedition and an old Chevy Cavalier— our overtime clerk, no doubt—the place looked deserted. It also looked and felt creepy, like a place you would never ever want to be after dark. But here I was anyway. I didn't bother asking Jerry if we really had to go in because I already knew the answer. And, we were only a few feet from the front door.

The entry was fairly well lit, which took down the creep factor slightly. That the doors were already unlocked as we walked in did not. Inside, a few fluorescent lights hummed overhead, but the hallway was still dimly lit. Jerry headed directly to the stairs in front of us. When we got to the lower level, he led us down a narrow hallway. Various markers perched out from the walls on each side like street signs. "License Plates," "Property Taxes," standard stuff. "We went in the door under "Records."

A tall counter ran the length of the room, which was maybe twelve or fifteen feet with a swinging door on the left. The small open area in front of the counter had a couple of chairs and fake plants. Behind the counter, a couple of desks were set out in the open with panels forming cubicles behind and to the right. The left was mostly hidden from view, but it looked like it was stor-age of some kind. Probably the "records."

"Be right there, Sheriff," came a raspy female voice from a back cubicle.

In a few seconds, a thin, hard-looking woman in a low-cut silvery blouse and short black skirt came wobbling in on spiked heels. If she was going for a sexy strut, she missed by the prover-bial mile. I put her age somewhere near fifty, but it was hard to tell. A malodorous mix of sickeningly sweet perfume and stale cigarettes wafted over me. Even without the nasal evidence, the thick lines and coarse skin of her face said she'd been a heavy smoker for a very long time. Glassy eyes indicated that alco-hol, drugs or both were probably involved as well. Whatever her vices, none of them gave her a youthful glow. The cosmetic overkill didn't help either, and neither did her frizzy shoulder-length hair, which varied in color from a light mottled brown to shoe-polish black. The woman needed to get a professional dye job or give it up entirely. (Yes, it takes one to know one, but we are criticizing someone else at the moment and there is still much to be done.)

As I continued my assessment, she morphed from semi-sober off-duty records clerk into lust-crazed tramp on mission right before my very eyes. She put her hands on her breasts and thrust her chest forward, growling and panting. Thank God for the counter or she'd have been humping Jerry's leg like a scrag-gly poodle in heat.

Apparently she didn't see me lurking in the corner by the fake ficus tree, or maybe it just didn't matter. I couldn't help but wonder if this was the first time this nut job had done this.

She licked her lips and cooed, in a gravely sort of way, and ran her hands down over her waist and hips. "I'm glad you called. I knew you would, sooner or later." She lowered her lids into what she apparently thought was a seductive look. "Whatever you want, Sheriff, it's yours."

Oh, please. The only thing anyone could want from that was to throw up.

"What I want," Jerry said matter-of-factly, ignoring her overt and disgusting, display, "are the specific records I mentioned on the phone. Jolene and I would like to get finished with this as soon as possible."

"Jolene?" Cindy muttered, turning from lustful and languid to embarrassed and furious. "What!"

"Come on, honey," Jerry said, motioning me forward. "Cindy has the files pulled for us."

I stepped out from the corner, realizing that he'd just called me honey. And in an oh-so-subtle way put Cindy-slut in her place without a scene of any kind. Smooth. Really smooth and classy. I just loved that man.

Turning back to Cindy, he said, "Are those in the main room?"

Flaming tramp eyes were locked onto me and venom was sputtering from between her teeth. "Who are *you*?"

Sheriff Parker didn't miss a beat, just kept speaking as if Cindy were a sane and normal person, which clearly she was not. "Cindy, you remember Jolene Jackson, from high school. She's helping me tonight."

"Jolene," the tramp spat. "Jolene Jackson."

Why do people have to say it like that? *Jolene. Jolene Jackson.* With sputtering even. It's like my mere presence unleashes some primordial internal storm that requires a theatrical re-stating of my name before I even open my mouth. I just don't get it. And while I seemed to have struck an instant discord with her from twenty-five years ago, I didn't have the first clue about who she was.

I stepped up beside Jerry and gave her a fake little smile. "Hello."

Jerry put his arm around me affectionately and moved me in front of him, keeping his hand on my shoulder as he spoke to Cindy. Apparently this was something that Cindy did not like at all because flaming arrows were now shooting from her bloodshot eyeballs and spittle was foaming at the sides of her mouth.

"Is there a computer back there with access to the Internet?"

"The one on the desk," she growled. "Just like any other computer around here."

"We'll probably be about an hour," he said evenly, guiding me through the little swinging door.

With a vindictive huff, she added, "I don't care. I'm on time and a half." She flung herself around and clickety-clacked her spiked heels toward a back office, mumbling something that I am reasonably sure was not very nice at all.

Jerry chuckled and guided me down the office hallway toward the media rooms. I glanced at the various desks and divided cubbyholes lining two walls of the room. Ledgers, boxes, and folders were piled on a table behind where Jerry sat at the computer and little white boxes of microfilm and stacks of microfiche were scattered at various stations. The electronic age was being acknowledged, but all the records were apparently not in digital form just yet. However, Cindy had apparently written out explicit notes on what could be found where.

Jerry walked over to the computer in the center of the room, pulled out the chair and motioned me over. "If you'll get us an aerial view, I'll sort through what we have to work with over here." He then moved to the stacks of films and fiches. "By the way, that was Cynthia Ann Riley," he said, rummaging through the files. "Murphy now, although she's been divorced for a few years this last time. She was a grade behind us in school. And I'm smarter than that, Jolene, so don't even think about it."

Oh, I wasn't thinking about anything. I am not the jealous type and we all know it. "She sure thought it was her lucky day," I said smiling and waggling my eyebrows. "She wants you bad."

"You don't remember her, do you?"

"Not at all."

"She was in the band."

I ran down the band roster until something clicked, or actually smacked. "Oh, Cynthia. She played clarinet. I sort of remember her. Always smacking her lips and playing with her reeds."

"That's the one."

"Do I just inspire global hate or does she have a specific reason for her scorn?"

"I don't know, but envy and jealousy would be my guess. You excelled at everything and were pretty confident about it." Jerry coughed to cover a chuckle. "You could have been a little intimidating at times."

Me? I always felt intimidated. I never knew I'd been dishing it out. Yet another topic requiring further introspection. In the meantime, however, I'd found the site I needed and had zoomed down from space to the area around my mother's house. The clarity was exceptional. "Here it is. Now that I'm convinced it's a toxic waste dump, it looks even worse than it did this morning."

Jerry walked up behind me and leaned over my shoulder. "It definitely does not look good."

"That can't be all from normal production and salt and stuff, can it?"

"I'm sure some of it's normal. But that's a huge area, actually several huge areas. Not anything like I've ever seen before." He leaned closer. "It's hard to tell how much might be on your mother's property, but some of it certainly is."

"I can't believe that she'd condone deliberate contamination. She's a deceitful and borderline insane, but she wouldn't actively participate in that kind of thing, would she?"

"Probably not, but she's done plenty of things I wouldn't have guessed she would," he said, stepping away. "She's definitely hiding something."

He certainly had a point there, and I had the unpleasant feeling that we had only scratched the surface of what she'd been willing to do and was now willing to keep us from finding out about. "So where do we start?"

"I'll set you up over here to search property records. The county map shows ownership. Look for mineral rights or other assignments on each parcel. After that, we'll try to cross check names and numbers with Railroad Commission records."

"Okay," I said, hitting the print button. "I'll get a few views printed off so we can compare them with maps again. What are you going to do?"

"I have a hunch or two I want to check out. Shouldn't take long."

Records searches are tedious business and Jerry's estimate of an hour seemed highly optimistic. I hoped that was all the time we had to spend because otherwise it looked like we could be at it all night. I started searching through the ledgers, files and films as Jerry had directed. I had file numbers that were supposed to make things easier to find, but that upside down and backwards part of microfiche-ing is just confusing. I had finally worked out a system on how to find research and document the information on each parcel when Jerry interrupted.

"Jolene, you better come take a look at this for yourself."

I walked over to where he sat and looked at the screen. A familiar name jumped out at me. "Lucille Janette Aston." He was looking at marriage records. "Oh, my God," I said, seeing but not believing the official record. "She was married to Bob Little?"

"Right out of high school I would guess," Jerry said. "Cindy left instructions on how to access the vital records databases. We have birth, death, marriage and divorce records at our fingertips in one way or another. For all her faults, she's good at this part of her job."

I wasn't particularly enthusiastic about praising the tramp for much of anything, but said, "Yes, I'll give her that. She's doing her part to make these little skeletons just zoom out of my family closet at warp speed."

"The only thing this confirms is that your mother made a mistake as a teenager. Nothing more." When I started stuttering and sputtering, he added, "It doesn't mean she had an affair with him later."

"It doesn't mean she didn't."

"Step back from it for a minute and let's get some more facts. Go over to those old index file drawers over there and see if there are any divorce records filed here. Look up both names and get any corresponding file numbers."

"Fine. And you may as well find out how many more husbands she had before she married my father."

One part of my brain continued background stewing while the other did as directed and found the facts. As Jerry had suggested, the marriage had lasted less than a year. There were no children and there were no itemized property settlement documents although there were several pages of legalese that referenced a separate private settlement, which was not attached. Odds were pretty good that the 160-acre parcel of land was part of it. The city lots had been bought years later, no doubt because of their prime location next to the secret ranchland. I wondered if Dad ever even knew about it.

We learned that Lucille had not married anyone else before latching on to my father. Bob had married a woman named Glenda Hicks several years before. No record of divorce, however. I never remembered seeing him with a woman. Couldn't remember any kids. Then again, I was having enough trouble keeping up with the revelations of the moment much less what happened forty years ago.

In the last thirty-six hours, my head had collected a semi-truck load of details, not to mention a significant amount of nitrous oxide and duct tape, and the warning light was flashing on my overloaded circuits. Maybe more memories would work their way up through the fog tomorrow. Tonight, however, I was fading fast. I glanced down at my watch. It was after ten. Considering everything, it was a minor miracle I wasn't coma-tose. "I am just about to drop, Jerry. I don't think I can take much more tonight."

"Me either, Jolene." He pulled his phone from the case on his belt. "I'm going to call Fritz to make sure he doesn't let Lucille out of his sight. Technically, she's no guiltier than she was when we left her with him, but it sure seems like she will be."

"Now you sound like me," I said, trying to chuckle and failing.

"I know you're exhausted, but could you check one more thing while I make some calls? Then we can go."

I didn't want to, I promise you. "Sure."

Jerry stood up from where he'd been sitting at the computer. "See if there's a death record for Glenda Hicks Little. There are pull-down menus on the left side under the main topics."

I sat down and studied the website, found the correct category then followed the requisite links to a search engine. It took a couple of tries with variations on the name, but I had Glenda's death certificate on the screen faster than I would have ever guessed.

He clicked off the phone and shoved it back in its case. "Find it?"

"Yes. And now I know why I didn't remember her. She died the same year I was born. I never met her."

"What's the cause of death?"

"Complications of childbirth. Guess that explains why Bob Little has no children either. We didn't find where he remarried, right?"

"Right," Jerry said, staring intently at the screen.

"Something wrong?"

"I was just thinking."

"You think Glenda's death has something to do with what's going on now?" I turned and looked up at him. "You don't think Bob Little killed her and she's buried in one of those toxic waste pits, do you?"

He stood and shook his head. "You're tired. I wish I could tell you that a nice soft pillow was in your immediate future, but I can't."

"Why not?"

"Your mother is not at Fritz's house." He waved aside my sputtering commentary. "Don't bother. She apparently 'ran home to get a few things.' But he was just sure she'd be back any minute." He sighed. "The man knows better."

I groaned at the reality of what that meant, but my heart still went out to Fritz. He might be a "tough ol' coot" by reputation, but he was in way over his head with Lucille. "How long has she been gone?"

"She probably left the second after we did. And no, she's not answering her cell phone or her home phone either. Let's wrap this up and—" Jerry cocked his head to the side as if he'd heard something.

Chapter Twenty-Four

T he hairs on the back of my neck stood up like porcupine quills and a shiver jerked across my shoulders and down my back. "I heard something too."

Jerry looked toward the door. "Stay here. I'll go check it out."

Oh, no, he wasn't leaving me here alone. "Jerry…"

"Fine," he groaned, "but stay behind me."

A few hall lights were still on, just as they had been when we'd arrived. Nothing had changed, and yet everything felt different. We made our way quietly down the hall back toward the main records office. Something was not right. With every step, the ominous feeling became thicker and heavier. By the time we got to the tall counter, I could already imagine Cindy's ravaged body sprawled out, shot, stabbed or perhaps strangled. I knew it was coming, I just knew it.

As I looked over the counter toward the back offices, sure enough, there it was. *Oh, God.* On the floor by the office where we'd last seen her. Frizzy brown hair sprawled across the yellow asbestos floor tiles. One naked arm was outstretched above her head as if she'd been reaching for something and had just given up. "Oh, God, Jerry, I can't look."

As soon as the words left my mouth, I heard a shriek. And it wasn't mine.

The arm moved and so did the frizzy hair.

Another shriek. Mine that time.

"What the hell!" came a disturbed voice. A few seconds later, an unfortunately familiar head popped out from around the cubicle—Larry Harper.

"I'm on break, Jerry, swear to God," the probationary deputy said, obviously lacking both couth and clothing. "I was just leaving to get back down to the office. It's been real quiet.

Donnell's got things under control. Cindy thought she heard something so I came to check it out." He shrugged his fleshy shoulders. "One thing just led to another."

You know, I would have never believed it if I hadn't seen it with my very own eyes. I've heard stories about such things, but I truly did not believe they actually happened. I am sure that shock and disbelief were pasted on my face.

"This is what I have to deal with," Jerry muttered. "Or worse."

Cindy had somehow managed to semi-collect herself from the floor and hung her make-up smeared face out the door as well. She was obviously going for "see what you missed" look to Jerry, but nobody was envious. Nobody.

"Get dressed and get out of here," Jerry barked. "Both of you. I'll expect you both here in the morning at 8 am to finish up what I don't have time to deal with tonight."

"I'm not on shift then…" Larry started to protest, but the look on Jerry's face stopped him cold. "Okay, well, yeah. I'll be here. But just tell me now, am I fired?"

Jerry glared at him. "Eight o'clock, Larry. And you better hope I'm in a better mood than I am right now. Fired is the least of your worries." Then to Cindy—and it was not an amused look. "I'll lock the front door with my master key when we're done here. And don't even think about getting paid for this. I will deal with you in the morning as well. Now both of you, out."

He hadn't said it loudly, but they were zipping around like he was shooting bullets under their feet. A good trick considering they both looked drunk.

After they had stumbled out—and not well dressed I might add—I asked the obvious. "Are you going to fire them?"

He sighed. "If I told you they would be hard to replace with anything better, would you believe me?"

The old adage of good help being hard to find was a pathetic understatement these days. "Sadly, I would."

Click. A door closed somewhere down the hall where we had just been.

Jerry turned to me and gave me the universal "don't make a peep" signal. I didn't, although it sure felt like my heart had burst into a thundering rumba for all to hear. He motioned for me to follow him.

As we walked along the office wall, another door clicked closed. Jerry swung around the corner and burst through the employee access door into the hallway.

There was no way out on this end of the hallway except an alarmed emergency exit that was placarded to make sure even an idiot knew that bells, whistles and the National Guard would result if they pushed the bar on the door.

That left only the rooms where we had been and the restrooms as potential hiding places.

We headed to the restrooms. The entrance was a standard indented area with a water fountain in the center and a door on each side. Women on the left, men on the right.

Jerry motioned me back behind the wall on the men's side. I had a full view of the women's doorway and could see a light shining from beneath. Jerry flipped down the doorstop with his boot and kicked the door open in one quick move.

The door slammed back against the wall and stayed open.

He bent down and looked around the doorway, leading with his gun. He must have seen something because he was inside the room in a flash and I heard a stall door bang open.

"Stop! Oh, my Lord," came a familiar screech. "Don't shoot!"

"Jolene!" Jerry yelled.

I said nothing, just turned my back to the wall and banged my head back against it a couple of times. It did not make the nightmare go away or induce a coma so I just let myself slither down to the cool asbestos-covered floor. I didn't actually see what happened after I sat down and propped my forehead on my knees, but here's the gist of it.

Jerry probably holstered his pistol as he yelled at me again, "Get in here, Jolene."

"Just shoot her."

"Now, Jerry Don, I can explain everything," Lucille said, probably sashaying out of the stall with a long painted nail pointed at the sheriff. "I had just run home to get a few things and was on my way back when I needed to use the restroom. I was passing by the courthouse and saw the light on, and this being a public building and all." A pause, a screech. "Here, now, don't you be grabbing at me like that! Why, the very nerve." Another screech. "Now, Jerry Don Parker, you put those hand-cuffs away. I will tell your mother about this. Stop that! I haven't done a thing wrong. You can't do this!"

"I can and I am. You're going to jail right now, and you're not getting out—maybe ever," Jerry said, hauling her out of the bathroom.

Yes, of course, she whined pitifully at me as he pushed her into the hallway. I didn't even look up, but from my peripheral vision I could tell that she held her hands together in front of her.

Jerry stood beside me, waiting for me to get up. When I didn't, he put his hand down and wagged his fingers at me. I begrudgingly took his hand, hauled myself up off the floor and trudged along behind them toward the front door.

We were going to jail. Again. Oh joy.

It was a short trip around to the back of the courthouse to the Sheriff's Department, and of all the things to dread, it was the deputy on duty that sent my stomach churning. Just think-ing of him had beamed a horrible video clip onto my mental screen. Apparently, I'd blocked out a full conscious recording of the initial event when it had happened, but now a snapshot of fleshy Larry's goose-white skin covered with a patch of dark fur between his man boobs kept flashing in my head. I shuddered.

Thankfully, Larry Harper was neither naked nor conscious when we walked in. He was sound asleep in a chair behind the desk.

Jerry didn't growl, sigh or even grit his teeth, just nudged Lucille inside so he could slam the door. Hard.

Larry leaped to his feet and grabbed for his pants. "What? Huh?"

I guess he just never knew whether he had pants on or not, but knew it would be helpful to cover himself when he'd been caught and had to run. Or something like that.

"Get a cell ready for Miz Jackson," Jerry commanded.

Larry shook himself awake, his jowls quivering at the affront, and hitched up his pants. Finally figuring out what was going on, he snickered at Lucille. "Guess you ain't so high and mighty now."

Jerry's glare stopped him cold. "You'll be staying the rest of the night here to watch her, deputy. I'm calling your father in to cover your shift as well."

"Well, now, that's not necessary," Larry said, sensing bad things on all fronts. "You know, Pete comes on in a couple hours. I can handle—" Another glare from the sheriff and Larry grumbled "yes, sir" then scuttled off down the hall.

"We'll go to my office while your cell is being checked," Jerry said to Lucille. "But I am not spending all night asking questions that you refuse to answer. Either you give me a straight answer the first time I ask or you can sit in here until you're eighty-three."

Lucille had the good sense not to argue, and unlike all previous interviews with Her Highness, this one was short and sweet. No merry chase with distractions and denials and deliberately confusing statements. Nope. Not this time. This time, she simply refused to talk.

Jerry put up with that for about thirty seconds and then locked her up.

While Jerry was lining Larry out, yet again, I had a go at Mother Dearest through the bars. "This is a big one, huh?"

She stood there, arrogantly, nose tipped up, lips clamped shut.

"It is just amazing what's available these days. The county hasn't gotten their property tax files computerized yet, but they sure can access the state's vital statistics. Between the county and state, we had birth, death, marriage, divorce and property ownership records at our fingertips. Meaning, of course, that I know about your first marriage."

She sucked in her breath.

"And Bob's second marriage to Glenda Hicks, as well as her unfortunate demise shortly thereafter. Yep, it is just amazing what you can find out at the courthouse."

Her eyes widened and her composure wavered for a split second then she spun around and stomped to the corner and sat down on the bed. "Leroy let me watch TV last time I was in here. I don't see that it would hurt anything now. There's nothing on this time a night but infomercials, but it would be something to do. Prisoners ought to be allowed something to pass the time. You go tell that man to let me watch television."

I ignored her entertainment dilemma. "Did you hear any part of what I just said?"

"Yes, I believe I heard every word," she said, staring blankly at the wall, nose tipped upward. "And now that you've gone digging where you ought not have, I suppose you're relieved."

I grabbed the bars with both hands and strangled them as best I could. "We have got to get you on some kind of medication. That's all there is to it."

Lucille jumped up and lurched toward me, grabbing the bars beside my hands. "You can't do that. I just did what I thought was best. It doesn't make me bad or crazy. I did what I thought was best for you. Why couldn't you have just accepted that and let it be?"

I pushed away from the bars. "I can't take any more of this. I have no idea what you're talking about, but it seems that if I did, I wouldn't like it at all. I'm done." As I turned and walked, I heard Lucille suck in a couple of ragged breaths and choke back a sob. I met Jerry in the hallway. "She makes no sense. And now she's crying. I have no idea why. None."

He sighed and handed me his car keys. "I'll try talking to her one more time, but it won't take long. She can stay right where she is until morning. We can deal with her then."

"Good."

Chapter Twenty-Five

I sat in the Expedition with the windows down and seat fully reclined, listening to the crickets and feeling the thick Texas air on my skin. Nothing Lucille had said made sense. Nothing about anything made sense. But something about the way she'd looked at me in there, as if she'd been defeated somehow, had shaken me more than I wanted to admit. Whatever her secret was, it was devastating to her and it sure felt like it was going to be devastating to me too, if indeed I ever found out what it was. Was Bob Little really my biological father? Did she think I'd disown her if she admitted to an affair? Did she think I'd fall apart if I learned that she'd lied to me my whole life?

Maybe I would. At the moment, however, it was pretty easy to just be an observer and not feel much personal emotion at all. I know who raised me. Biology wouldn't change who my daddy was. Bertram Jackson had been and would always be my father regardless of what any DNA testing might say. And while I couldn't say I was thrilled about my mother's choices, I wasn't quite ready to crucify her for them either. Of course, I didn't really know anything for fact yet. It was all so surreal that it was easy to be detached. Easier still to just close my eyes and brain and escape into nothingness.

The next thing I knew I was sitting bolt upright, belatedly hearing the squeaky shriek that I had just emitted. In another microsecond I realized why I'd screamed. Jerry had opened the car door behind me on the passenger side.

And my mother was getting inside.

I sighed heavily, but said nothing, just raised my seat back up and waited for Jerry to start the car. He obviously had a good reason for this, which I would find out about sooner than I wanted to.

"We're all going to the lake cabin," he said simply. "There are some documents out there Lucille wants you to see and she'll explain everything then. Right, Lucille?"

"Yes, Jerry Don, that's right," she said, almost robotically. "I will do what I must."

We had a long, quiet and tedious ride for about eight minutes. Then, Lucille broke the silence. "You know, I spent my whole life trying to keep this very thing from happening."

I was tempted to ask exactly where that might be, but supposedly the answers were just around the corner, so to speak. The documents Jerry had mentioned were a new twist and definitely had me curious. But so did a lot of other things. One in particular kept nagging at me. If I was the result of an affair between Bob and Lucille, what about the child Glenda had died giving birth to? Did I have a half-sister or half-brother somewhere? Was that what she was going to show me?

The plot had thickened and I felt like I was swimming in quicksand. I massaged my temples, but it helped nothing. Was this somehow related to the park thing too? Was Tiger or Damon Saide my half brother? Was that why they were strong-arming Bob? Neither of them looked anything at all like me. Or Bob Little for that matter. Bob was a big man, tall and big. Damon Saide wasn't much taller than I was and Tiger was a muscled wiry type who was probably a couple of inches shy of six feet. I realize two green peas occasionally produce a white pea or pink flower or whatever the hell it is, but shouldn't the offspring bear some kind of similarity to at least one parent? Then again, I had no idea what that maternal side looked like. "Did you ever meet Bob's second wife?" I asked.

"Of course, I did," Lucille said tersely. "I suppose you want to know about her."

"Just curious."

"Oh, this just makes me so mad I could just spit," Lucille said, with fury and barely contained tears.

"That's a pretty strong reaction, even from the first wife," I said, glancing around briefly to gauge her reaction. "Were you jealous of Glenda or what?"

"Oh!" she shrieked. "This is the most pitiful moment in my whole entire life. I cannot believe you're saying that to me, I just cannot." Jerry turned as if to speak to her, but she cut him off. "Don't you start in on me again, Jerry Don Parker. I told you I'd tell her everything once we got to the cabin and I will. Then it will be done with and I don't ever want to hear any more of this ever again. I have always done what I thought was right and if you don't like it now, well, I guess that's just too bad."

I turned and looked at Jerry for some kind of explanation for her ranting.

He just reached over and squeezed my hand. "It's going to be okay."

As we pulled into the long driveway of the cabin, I noticed a new-looking carport off to the left about halfway between Mother's cabin and the next one. A mercury vapor light glowed on a pole beside it, illuminating a wide circle around and beneath the shelter. "Hey, look over there. That looks like an old sixty-six Mustang, just like I used to have." I was so tired I could hardly keep my eyes open, but seeing that had perked me up. "You remember, don't you, Jerry?"

"Yes, Jolene," Mother snapped, shifting in her seat and tapping her nails on the armrest. "Everyone remembers. Now, Jerry Don, you pull on up closer to the door."

Jerry did, slowly, but I couldn't help but keep looking over my shoulder at that car. My daddy had bought me one just like it when I was fourteen. Gosh, but I'd loved that car. Drove it to school cheerfully and illegally every single day from the time I got it. Almost killed a linebacker over it, in fact.

It was after a game one Friday night and we were all hanging out at the school. Joey Pettyjohn had been as full of himself as he was Wild Turkey, and had hopped up on the trunk of my most prized possession. By the time I got to him, he was rolling over to crawl up on the roof. As he turned, his coat zipper caught beneath his thigh and scraped two long stripes across the trunk, down to the metal. I came unglued.

Witness accounts vary, but the story goes that a petite little brown-haired cheerleader grabbed the 180-pound linebacker by his jacket and/or head and threw him off the car. As he jumped up and tried to assure her that it would "compound out," she shoved him down onto the gravel again and dared him to get up. Loudly. Joey got more votes for Football Queen that year than I did.

Never did get those scratches fixed though. And, I'd gotten older, times changed, and Dad eventually sold it to my cousin down in Houston. I hadn't even thought about it in years. "You think we could go look at it? Just for old time sake?"

Jerry rubbed his hand across his face and drove on closer to the cabin. "Maybe later. Two o'clock in the morning probably isn't the best time even if we didn't have other things to do such as hear your mother's confession and presumably Bob's as well."

"Fine then." I glanced back at her. "We're here so start talking."

She lifted her nose and turned toward the window. "I'd rather wait until we get inside."

"Right, because then we can all sit down and have a nice chat about what the crappie are biting on, why Bob's *not* really a missing person but *is* apparently a contributor to my gene pool and whether my dad knew about it. Then, if there's time, maybe we can all play a friendly game of Monopoly."

Lucille worked her mouth up and down like the aforementioned crappie. She chewed around on all the things she wanted to say back to me, but still did not actually spit out any words. Curious, that. She snorted and glared and gritted her teeth then finally turned toward Jerry. "Jerry Don, you take your flashlight and go down to the crappie house. Tiger gave me some papers to keep for him so nobody would get them. They're down there and we need to go get them."

I looked at Jerry and he looked at me. "What papers?" we said in unison.

"I don't know. He said it was best if I didn't look at them so I didn't. It was support for the cause, I suppose."

Jerry turned around in the seat and looked back at Lucille. "What about the documents you said would be out here? Where are those?"

"Yes, well, I said I have them and I do," Lucille snapped, still scowling. "They're in the crappie house too. They're all right there together."

"None of that silly safe deposit box stuff for us," I chirped. "We Jacksons use the crappie house."

Lucille glared at me again, but oddly did not direct "Missy" to shut her smart and/or hateful mouth. Instead, she lifted her nose and turned her head away from me and to Jerry. "Regarding Tiger's papers," she said coolly, "I didn't look at them because he asked me not to. I also knew that no one would think of looking there so they would be safe. Besides, Bob was here—"

"About that—"

"I did what I had to do," Lucille said, emotion cracking in her voice. "Bob trusted me and Tiger did too and I did what I thought was right. I have spent my whole life doing what I thought was right and now look at what's become of it."

I'd thought we were headed out here to clean the skeletons out of the family closet and reinvent my childhood memories so they resembled reality. But apparently, I was mistaken. Or either that was second or third on the list. At this point, I truly had no idea what to expect.

Jerry had eased up to the cabin, but was still a good thirty or forty feet away when Lucille opened her door. "Where's the flashlight? Just give it to me and I'll go get the papers," she said, hopping out.

"Absolutely not," Jerry barked, slamming on the brakes. "Get back in the car."

Lucille instantly obeyed, which seemed as shocking to her as it did to the rest of us. "Well, you wanted me out here. I just want this awful business over and done with."

He put the car in park and turned off the ignition. "I want you both to stay in the car until I get back." He opened the door and stepped out then leaned back in to look at Lucille. "Most especially you." He pulled a small flashlight from the side pocket. "Now, exactly where will I find these papers?"

"In a metal box inside the bench," Lucille said. "Just lift up the cushion and top. You can't miss it."

"Stay put," he reiterated, closing the door. He turned on his flashlight, which put out an intense beam for such a small unit, then headed down the hill to the lake.

We watched in silence, following Jerry by his light until he disappeared. After a few more long minutes of silence, Lucille said, "You know that old saying that blood is thicker than water?"

"Of course."

"Well, it's not true. Family is family. It doesn't matter about blood and I don't care what anybody says."

I guessed this was her way of telling me that Bertram was still my father even though his blood didn't flow in my veins. I knew that, of course, but as far as emotional intimacy with Lucille, this was new and unexplored territory. "Look, I know you had your reasons for doing what you did. It's easy to sit in judgment now, but I know from my own mistakes that if I could have done better I would have."

"I made my choices and I stand by them," she said defiantly.

I had no idea what rationalization and justification she'd concocted over the years, but it had to be really good to still inspire such vehemence. "You really wouldn't change a thing?"

"No, ma'am, I would not!" she snapped.

I shrugged. "Well, if Jerry had lived next door to me while I was married to Danny, I can't say for sure what I'd have done. I still think I'd have had some remorse over it."

"I did not cheat on your father!" Lucille snapped. "And I do not want to hear you saying that I did ever again!"

I leaned around the seat and stared at her. "Then why in the hell are we here and what is the big secret?"

"For such a smart girl you can be really stupid sometimes."

"I suppose I come by it honestly."

She glared harder. "I suppose you don't!"

A flicker of light flashed through the car as Jerry walked up the hill with the box.

"Jerry's back with your box of papers. Now you can start explaining your cryptic remarks so I know what the hell you're talking about because nothing you've said so far has made one bit of sense."

Before I'd finished my sentence, however, Lucille had leaped from the car and was scurrying toward the cabin door, key in hand.

I followed and Jerry turned that direction as well. He looked at me and I just shrugged.

Lucille grabbed the door handle with one hand and shoved her key in with the other.

Boom!

Chapter
Twenty-Six

T he cabin exploded, the concussion blowing out the doorway and windows.

Lucille flew back across the grass, landing in a heap about ten feet away. The door spun in the air, hurtling toward me. I dove to the ground as it slammed down between Mother and me.

Smoke boiled out from the cabin and debris rained down on us.

My ears roared and my whole body rolled. I dug my fingers into the grass, trying to still the earth as waves of dizziness swept through me.

Jerry jumped to his feet and ran toward Mother and knelt beside her, feeling her neck then checking her over. Then he ran to me.

"Jolene, are you okay?"

I nodded, hoping it was true.

"Your mother's been hurt."

I knew that. I'd seen her fly through the air and land in a heap. Yet hearing him say it, brought reality crashing in and pumped another fresh wave of fear and adrenalin through me. I pushed myself up on my hands and knees then Jerry helped me to stand.

"Go over there, but don't move her. Keep her airway open. I didn't see any major bleeding, but if you do, use pressure," he said, turning toward the car. "I'll call for help."

I nodded and staggered forward then dropped to the ground beside her.

Lucille lay on her left side, arm underneath and leg drawn up. Her right hand still clenched as if holding the key. She looked like a rag doll that had been run over by a bus, battered, limp and lifeless. Her always perfect hairdo was matted with debris and the stench of burnt hair stung my nose.

Something crashed inside the cabin and I snapped my gaze toward it. A few sparks shot up, but nothing blazed up immediately. I sure wished I could get Mother farther away. But even if Jerry hadn't told me not to move her, I wouldn't have considered it. From the way she laid on the ground, it was extremely likely that her shoulder, arm and hip had suffered damage to one degree or another. A concussion was probably a good guess as well.

These thoughts had flown by in literally milliseconds. And while my heart was racing and I didn't really know what to do, I was fairly clear headed, which was both a surprise and a relief. And then I thought I heard her moan.

"Mother?" I gently touched her face. "Can you hear me?"

Another moan and her lips moved. She muttered something, but I couldn't understand her.

"It's okay, Mother, I'm here. Just lie still. Help is coming."

As soon as the words left my mouth, Jerry was at my side.

"A helicopter is on the way," he said, laying out a tarp beside Lucille. "I told them to expect fractures and that she would need to be immobilized. Also a probable head injury. Did you find any significant bleeding?"

I shook my head. "No."

"Good," Jerry said. "Now, we're going to slide this tarp under her and then drag her away from the cabin just to be safe."

"You told me not to move her," I protested.

"That cabin could start blazing or something else could explode. I don't want either of you this close. I also don't want you out on the open."

He didn't explain and it was just as well since I did not want to think about who had planted the bomb in my mother's cabin or if they were still here, watching and waiting to do more.

Jerry gently lifted her top half and I slid the tarp under her as much as possible. We inched the tarp under her hip then slid it relatively easily under her legs. She moaned, loudly a few times, but never gained consciousness, which was a blessing for all of us.

"Hold that end and just keep her on the tarp. Let me do the pulling," he said, then quickly slid her away from the cabin to the back of the car.

After we stopped, I smoothed out the tarp and sat down beside her. We had been very careful to not alter her position any more than necessary so she still lay on her side.

Jerry bent down beside her and tipped her chin up. "Keep talking to her. Tell her it will be okay. I have to check the area." He must have sensed my panic because he reached down and squeezed my shoulder. "It's okay. I'll be back. I have to take the offensive or he'll flank us and we'll be targets. Understand?"

I nodded. And while I did understand, I did not want to think about it. I didn't want to think about Jerry going out after the shooter or that the shooter was probably working his way to a clear shot at us behind the car. I didn't want to, but I was. Lucille groaned and refocused me. "Mother? Can you hear me? It's Jolene? Mom?"

She moaned some more and moved her mouth a little as if she was trying to talk.

"Mother, it's Jolene. You're okay, just banged up pretty good. Can you tell me what hurts?"

"Jolene..." She moaned again. "It hurts."

"What hurts? Mother, can you tell me what hurts?"

"Everything. My leg. Oh, my leg."

I couldn't see anything obviously wrong with either leg, although I knew there certainly was. Since she was lying on her left side, most of the damage was likely there. I ran my hand lightly over her right leg. "Does it hurt here?" No response. I touched the left leg, just above the knee and she muttered and groaned. I touched again near her ankle and she screamed.

"Stop that!" she howled, her eyelids snapping open.

"Mother, it's Jolene, you've been hurt. You need to stay still."

"Oh, my Lord," she said, her eyes looking ahead but not really focused on anything. "My leg. It's on fire."

"How about your hip, does it hurt?"

"Everything hurts! Oh, my Lord, what have you done to me?"

Well, in a weird way it was comforting to hear her blame me. I knew it might just be adrenaline and/or a serious head injury talking, but dealing with Lucille's accusations made things seem sort of normal, and under the circumstances that was comforting. I knew it would be best to keep her talking and conscious, such as it was. Focusing on what was hurting and how bad wasn't going to help at the moment so I figured I could distract her by engaging in her favorite pastime—detailing my faults. "So, Mother, what is it that you think I did wrong?"

"Well, my Lord, Jolene, we don't have time for all that. I've got to be at the Dairy Queen by four. Merline and Agnes are waiting on me, and the special goes off at five."

"You've got plenty of time, Mother, don't worry about it or not."

She flung her left arm up and squinted as if looking at a wristwatch. "Oh, my Lord, would you just look at the time? I'm late. If I've told you once, I've told you a thousand times, if I'm not fifteen minutes early I'm late, late, late! Now let me up, I've got to go. Why are you keeping me down here?"

Well, the good news was that her right side looked in pretty good shape because she was waving her arm around and peddling with her leg to try to stand up. The left side was a different matter. I moved down toward her feet, caught her in mid-pedal and slipped off the right shoe.

"Don't you be taking my shoes," she screeched. "I need those. You can't have my shoes!"

Her left foot and ankle had already started to swell so something was wrong—broken ankle, foot, toes or all the above. Whatever the case, getting that shoe off now would probably help. I put my hand around her ankle and put some pressure on it before I tried tugging off the shoe. She didn't scream this time so I thought I could do it and not hurt her.

"What are you doing? Oooowwww!" she screeched as I slipped off her left shoe. "Why are you taking my shoes? Stop it. That hurts."

I kept saying things that I thought might be reassuring or calming, although I don't think she heard any of them. She kept babbling about getting to the DQ on time and how Merline would gloat if she was even ten seconds late and such. She did forget about her shoes though, which was good. I tried to convince her to stay as still as possible, but she ignored me. The pain, however, kept her in check to some degree. I kept my hand on her shoulder to keep her from trying to roll onto her back.

From the way she'd landed, the odds of her having a broken hip were extremely high if not guaranteed. And that would not be good. And I don't mean from the mere physical implications. A bullet wound was something to be flaunted. Even a broken shoulder had a barroom brawl kind of air about it. But a hip? That was not glamorous at all and would not play well in the local gossip mill at the DQ. Old people broke hips and she was definitely not old. She was going to be absolutely furious. That thought made me smile. Better furious than dead. "Just be still, Mother, you're going to be okay."

"Of course, I'm okay, and why wouldn't I be okay, and don't you be telling me what to do," she said in a flash of belligerence. It left as quickly as it has come and she was muttering and rocking her head from side to side. "I hurt."

"I know, but you're going to be just fine."

I continued to look her over closely to make sure I hadn't missed something that needed immediate attention. She didn't have major outward bleeding anywhere that I could see, but there had to be plenty of damage that I couldn't. "You've got a few bumps and scrapes to be dealt with, but you're okay." I repeated it to reassure myself as much as her. "It's going to be okay."

"Oh, it is not okay, not one little bit. But I did what I wanted to and I'm glad I did it," Lucille said, her face scrunched up in a mixture of pain and defiance. "You may not be, but I am."

"What?" Was she talking to me or just talking out of her head still? I certainly wasn't glad she'd just blown herself up and I didn't figure she was either. She was clearly on a different subject in another time and place. "It's okay," I repeated because I didn't know what else to say. "Everything is okay, Mother."

"That's right. I am your mother, Jolene, whether you like it or not," she said. "That's the way of it and don't you ever forget it."

"Never forget it," I agreed.

"I ought not have to go through this," she muttered.

"You're going to be okay, Mother."

She grimaced and sucked in a breath. "This just makes me so mad I could spit. I was supposed to be dead and gone," she said, obviously still talking out of her head.

"You're okay, Mother, help's on the way."

"There's no help for it now," she said. "It's all in the papers."

Two pickup trucks with flashing lights whipped into the drive. Volunteer fire fighters jumped from the trucks. One began tossing out flares along the road, the other ran toward us.

In the distance I heard the distinctive sound of a helicopter.

Time had both stood still and evaporated. On the one hand, it seemed like I had been watching my mother writhe in pain and talk out of her head for hours. On the other, it seemed like only a few minutes. Whatever the case, I was very glad that professional help was only seconds away.

When the first firefighter arrived, I gave him the condensed version of what had happened. I also explained why I had one hand on her good arm and the other on her undamaged leg. He nodded, gave her a quick look then put his hands next to mine and told me I could relax. I couldn't, of course, but I did move and let him take over. As the second guy arrived, I scooted back out of the way. They kept talking to her and to me, emphasizing that she had to stay as immobile as possible until the medical crew arrived. She wouldn't respond to their statements or questions, just kept saying how bad it hurt and kept closing her eyes.

The rotary cadence of the helicopter thumped louder as it landed on the road at the top of the driveway between the flares. Three people came hurrying toward us with an aluminum stretcher type thing with three straps on one half and a tubular scoop like thing making up the other half. Apparently that was the apparatus they would be strapping Lucille to so she wouldn't move.

I stood and got out of the way, watching the surreal scene play out in front of me. There was a flurry of activity around her and I couldn't really see what they were doing, didn't really want to. I never heard her scream, but the noise of the helicopter could have drowned it out. Or, she might have just been unconscious, which was what I hoped for. Within minutes Lucille was safely onboard the helicopter and in flight to Redwater Falls.

I wanted to go with her, of course, but they wouldn't let me. They'd also rejected my suggestion that they fly her on to Dallas where the odds at competent medical care were considerably higher. As I watched the helicopter disappear, I kept reminding myself that Jerry and I had both survived trauma care at the General Hospital so there was a glimmer of hope that she would too. My shoulder twitched its own reminder. To be fair, my arm had healed miraculously well, and my doctor in Denver said he couldn't have done a better job himself. He could have just been lying to me, but I chose to cling to that statement.

Chapter Twenty-Seven

I was almost back to the Expedition when Jerry hurried up beside me. "Jolene, I can't go with you to the hospital right now. Bob Little's in the crappie house. I have to stay here for a while."

I processed his words a bit slower than usual, but eventually came up with the obvious conclusion. "He's dead."

Jerry shook his head to stop me from asking questions. "Later. You have enough to deal with. Fritz is already headed to the hospital and Leroy's coming to take you. He should be here any minute. You need to go with him, understand?"

"No, Jerry, you have to take me," I said, hearing the pitiful tone of my voice even as I said it. This time, I couldn't stop my mind from dropping into all the old programming. Jerry was going to abandon me when I needed him the most. Tears welled up in my eyes and a sob lodged in my throat. He couldn't leave me, not now, not like this.

"Jolene, you need to get out of here, okay? I'll be there as soon as the forensics people get here to process the scene." He took me in his arms and kissed my forehead. "I love you, Jolene," he whispered. "I'll be there for you. I will."

Why would he? Not one man in my life ever had. Danny certainly hadn't. Something—anything—was always more important than me. Even when the kids were born. He was there during both events, but he made sure he never missed a full day of work because of it. And I always made excuses for him. Of course, Mr. Nameless who came after him was even worse. I don't think I could have felt less valued, and the excuses I made up for him and how he treated me were beyond ridiculous.

"Go on and sit in the car," Jerry said, giving me another quick kiss. "It won't be but a few minutes."

I unwrapped my arms from around Jerry's waist as three more pickups pulled up along the road. Two had the red flashing lights of volunteer fire fighters on the top. The third truck only had a row of yellow lights across the top of the cab. That particular truck also had A-frame poles on the back and a very large man climbing out of the driver's side. I wiped my hands over my face and composed myself then nodded toward Gilbert Moore. "What's he doing here?"

"I have no idea," Jerry said.

"Well, I want to talk to him."

Gilbert Moore must have read my mind because he was already walking down the hill toward us.

Something about the guy just rubbed me the wrong way. I had nothing specific to call him on, but it seemed like he was guilty of something—or would be if he got the chance. Whatever the case, I had plenty of questions for him, starting with why he always showed up whenever some kind of drama was in play. Like tonight. I stepped away from car and marched up the hill toward him, figuring now was as good a time as any to get to the bottom of all of it.

Pop. Pop. Pop.

Gilbert Moore jerked forward. "What the hell?" he yelled, grabbing his left shoulder. He hesitated for only half a second then crouched and ran toward us. Jerry grabbed me, dragged me to the far side of the Expedition then pushed me to the ground. As Gilbert Moore stumbled toward the back of the car, Jerry grabbed him too and shoved him toward me then pulled out his gun as he scanned the area.

Gilbert slumped down beside me. "I've been shot," he said, leaning back against the tire and panting. "Who the hell would do that? What the fuck's going on here?"

"I have no idea," I said, my breath still coming in quivery gasps. I scooted around to where I could reach his shoulder better. His tan tee shirt was already soaked with blood. A lot of blood. "We need to get some pressure on that," I said, trying to sound as calm as possible.

Jerry opened the car door, grabbed a first aid kit and tossed it to me. "Use the gauze packs." He then grabbed the radio and began issuing more orders.

I didn't need a close look at Gilbert's shoulder to see that major damage had been done. There had been three shots, so it was possible there were three wounds in the same area, which could be why there was so much blood. Whatever the case, I had to deal with it, like it or not. My hands were shaking, of course, but so was my whole body. Still, I managed to open the kit, put on the gloves then open the packages of gauze so they'd be ready to pack the wound once it was exposed. "Can you take off your shirt?"

Pain was etched on his face, but he still managed a fake little grin. "I will if you will."

"Oh, for godsake."

Pop. Ping.

Jerry ducked out from inside the car and crouched beside Gilbert Moore, giving him a quick assessment. "Get pressure on that. Right now. Ambulance is on the way." And with that, Jerry raised up, moved toward the front of the car. He fired in the general direction of where the shot had come from, which was down toward the lake and to the left of where we were. Whoever it was had probably been in the trees between the properties when he shot. But now he was on the move and we were easy targets. Other than on the property line, there was only one small cluster of trees on Lucille's property. Jerry eased out from behind the car and ran toward it, firing.

I waited for more gunshots, fearing the absolute worst was coming for all of us. I felt myself starting to panic for about ten thousand reasons.

"Calm down, he knows what he's doing." Gilbert paused for a moment, panting a little and swallowing down a wave a pain. "Besides, if you hurry," he said, trying to grin, "we can get naked and fool around before he gets back."

What'd he say? I shook my head as his asinine suggestion captured my attention, which I figured was the point. It was far better for me to be annoyed than panicked and hysterical. "You really are an ass," I said, reaching for his shirt and tugging it out from his pants as fast as I could. "Just sit there and shut up."

"That's what I'm talking about," he muttered, trying to be funny but looking very near to passing out. "A woman who knows what she wants."

Nothing that was occurring was what I wanted. "Alright, Smartass," I said, keeping the banter going as much for myself as for him. "I'm going to pull your shirt off over your right side and head first," I said, doing exactly that as quickly as I could.

He sucked in his breath and clenched his jaw.

"Now, lean up just a little."

He did, moving just enough to where I could get the shirt the rest of the way off, pulling it quickly off his left shoulder. He cursed through gritted teeth and beads of sweat broke out across his face as I pulled it the rest of the way off his arm.

I hurriedly put one large stack of gauze against the wound on the front side of his shoulder and had him hold it with his right hand. He wasn't doing a great job, but it was good enough. He was slumped so I could access the back side, which was probably worse than the front although I was really trying hard not to really think about it. I put two stacks of gauze there then folded his tee shirt behind that and had him lean back against the car to put pressure that way. It wasn't fully effective so I put one hand over the top of the wound on his back and took over holding pressure on the front as well. As I did, his hand dropped to his lap with a thud.

"That'll ruin your day," he muttered.

"You're going to be okay," I said, hoping it was true. Then, realizing that if I went soft and coddling on him he'd probably crack, I added, "But I'm guessing it's gonna leave a scar."

"I've had worse," he muttered, closing his eyes, "on my heart."

"Oh, please," I said, trying to sound nonchalant. "I wouldn't have figured you for having one of those things."

He didn't even try to respond to my comment, which was not a good sign. He'd lost a lot of blood and I could only hope that I had stopped the majority of the flow. I knew I had to keep him conscious if I could, so conversation was essential. Only a few minutes ago, I'd had a whole list of things I wanted to chat with him about. Now, I couldn't remember any of them.

I caught a glimpse of movement up on the road. From where I was sitting, I could only see two pickups off to the left at the top of the driveway. Red lights still flashed on both and I could see someone moving behind and between them. I figured the volunteer firefighter guys had wisely retreated from the line of fire and had no idea that anyone else down here needed help.

The faint sound of a siren in the distance told me some kind of emergency vehicle was on the way. I sincerely hoped it was an ambulance since Gilbert Moore needed to be heading to a hospital very soon. He was trying really hard to be tough, but he was wearing down fast and I knew he could easily slip into shock. He wasn't my only worry, of course, since I'd just watched a helicopter speed away with my badly injured mother, and the man I loved was out there in the dark somewhere with a killer. I also conveniently glossed over the fact my hiding spot was in no way a safe zone and kept my mind on the task at hand, which was keeping the big man next to me conscious.

"My mother says you're a liar," I blurted out, the words coming without thought.

That got his attention and he cracked his eyes open a little. "So do my ex-wives and former girlfriends."

"Then I'd say there's probably some truth to it, Mister Moore, your character being the common denominator in the equation."

"I'm fine," he snorted. "I just have a bad picker, that's all."

"Oh, I see. Your only fault is that you choose defective women. If your picker worked, you'd be able to find one that believed your lies and would let you get away with whatever it is you want to get away with. If only you could pick the right woman, there wouldn't be any problems."

He scowled. "I don't think I like you."

"Well, then you better hope you don't die because you'd like Doctor-Doctor-Doctor Travis even less. He wouldn't be nearly as nice about pointing out your character flaws as I am."

"What?"

"Never mind." My arms were getting tired from the strain so I tried to shift around to make myself more comfortable and keep pressure on his shoulder at the same time. I kept my fingers as steady as possible as I moved, but he groaned a little anyway. "Sorry," I said sincerely. I hated anyone having to be in pain, even a jackass.

"So your mother says I'm a liar." He closed his eyes again. "I don't even know who your mother is."

"That makes one person in two counties," I muttered. "Lucille Jackson. She owns what's left of this cabin."

"Oh. Her." He frowned but kept his eyes closed. "She's probably the one who shot me. She threatened it often enough when we were working out behind her house. Bob just said to ignore her so we did."

"I'd blame her too except that she was on that helicopter that just left. The cabin blew up and nearly killed her."

"So that's what happened," he said. "She gonna make it?"

In medical terms, I couldn't say for sure, but in Lucille terms I could. "Oh, she'll make it. She's gonna be really pissed off if her hip is broken, and someone may very well die because of it, but it won't be her."

He snorted a little, understanding exactly what I meant. Then the reality of the situation dawned on him. "Where's Bob?"

"I haven't seen him," I said truthfully.

"Was he in the cabin?"

"I don't think so," I said, again, truthfully. I didn't like holding back what I knew, but in this case he had enough to worry about. "So why are you here?"

"I've known Bob for years," he said. "I knew he was staying out here for a while so when I heard an explosion then a helicopter over this direction, I figured I'd better come check on him."

"What were you doing for him out behind my mother's house?"

"Test well," he said, his voice getting softer. "Gas pocket. Big one."

The faint siren had turned into at least two loud sirens that were getting very close. Of the pickups parked along the road, the two that I could see had backed up, clearing the driveway. A sheriff's car with blue lights flashing and siren blaring wheeled off the road and zoomed down the driveway toward us. He stopped a few feet away, sandwiching us between the two vehicles. Leroy jumped out and crouched down beside us, eyeing Gilbert. "Ambulance is right behind me. Lucky it was already headed out here after the first call. Couldn't have gotten the helicopter back here that fast."

Yes, it was very lucky, and I was incredibly relieved about that part.

Leroy jumped back in the car and made a call to the guys up on hill, telling them to get down here to us when the ambulance came.

"Leroy, the guy who shot Gilbert is still out there. Jerry's gone to look for him. There were gunshots at first, but not in the last couple of minutes. You've got to go help him."

Leroy nodded, his jowls jiggling with every bob of his head. "Which way?"

I told him where the shots had come from and he scurried back to his car and grabbed a shotgun. As he headed out, I felt compelled to urge him not to shoot Jerry. He seemed to take it okay, just nodded and scurried toward the same patch of trees that Jerry had. They did not provide as much protection for Leroy, but no shots were fired so he made another run for it and was out of my line of vision.

Other sirens wailed and as I looked up the road, I saw that an ambulance had turned down the drive and was now backing in behind Leroy's car.

"Looks like your ride is here," I said to Gilbert.

"Good thing," he said. "Because you ain't worth shit at comforting a man who's dying."

"And here I thought we'd sort of bonded, kind of a 'Beauty and the Beast' thing."

He grunted and turned his face toward me then reached up and squeezed my arm. "Thanks for helping me." He stared at me, or maybe through me, for a few long seconds. "You tell Sheriff Parker that he's a lucky guy to have you. You tell him I said that."

"I will," I said, smiling. "It will be a refreshing change from what he usually hears."

Chapter
Twenty-Eight

wo EMTs, a man and a woman, jumped from the back of the ambulance and knelt down beside us. Once again, I told the professionals what had happened. They checked Gilbert over as I talked, letting me continue to hold the pressure as they did what they needed to otherwise. They were moving so fast I really don't know what all they did, I just saw a pads and wraps coming toward his shoulder and then they told me to move away. I did and they somehow had him trussed up and ready to move in mere seconds.

From out of nowhere, other people appeared, including the volunteer firefighters who'd been at the top of the road. Apparently, once the ambulance arrived they had gotten word on what was going on and took the chance to come down as well.

"We're going to get a stretcher for you, Mister Moore," the female EMT said.

"Like hell you are," Gilbert said, shaking his head. "There's a sniper in the trees ready to pick us off. I can walk."

I had doubts about the walking part, but he was definitely right about the exposure. The less time anyone was between the car and the back of the ambulance, the better.

"You're to come with us," the man said to me as he helped Gilbert to his feet. "Sheriff's orders."

"No," I said automatically then I realized that if I did, I could be with my mother. I also realized I would be leaving Jerry in the woods with a killer. I knew I couldn't really help him, but I wouldn't leave him either. "No, I'm staying here. Now hurry."

The woman ran to the back of the ambulance and jumped inside. The other EMT and the two firefighters helped Gilbert to his feet. Technically, they didn't seem to need me anymore, but I wanted to stay close just in case. If he did start going down, having an extra set of hands would still help.

Once he got his balance, he seemed to get a burst of energy and hurried toward the ambulance. I followed, but stayed out of the way as the three men climbed with him inside.

Pop.

I heard and felt the trace of the bullet as it whizzed past my ear. I automatically dropped to the ground and scuttled back to my hiding spot beside the Expedition. The EMTs and firefighters stared at me for a moment, as if they wanted to grab me and hurl me inside with them. I shook my head and motioned for them to go on. One guy jumped out and ran toward me as the other slammed the back doors on the ambulance. Within seconds it was zooming up to the road.

Bam. Bam. Bam.

"Get in the car," he yelled.

That was exactly where I was headed and I didn't need him to tell me. I jerked open the passenger door and crawled inside, another burst of adrenalin sending my heart racing.

The firefighter climbed in beside me. "Stay down."

I crawled forward and scooted myself upright where I could pop my head up and see out the windows if I needed to. "Hi, I'm Jolene," I said. "Come here often?"

He shook his head and shushed me.

Fine. I can be quiet if I need to. I hugged my knees to my chest, letting my thoughts go where they would.

The last three shots had sounded different—distant, not directed at me, and maybe even from a different gun. But who had fired them? Jerry? Leroy? The sniper? I had no way of knowing. Maybe it was because of all I'd been through in the last two days or maybe I was just tired, but I didn't panic. I had plenty of reasons to, I just didn't. I also, for once, didn't consider mounting a rescue for Jerry. Adding my unarmed and unskilled presence would be a liability to him not an asset, so I stayed put, trusting that he could take care of things just fine without me.

A flash of light bounced off the windows inside the car. I sucked in my breath as fear shot through me yet again. So much for my bold statement about having panic under control.

"Jolene!"

"Jerry!" I peeked up from between the seats so I could see out the window to my left. There, in the glow of the mercury vapor light was the sheriff, walking toward the car. He held a rifle in one hand and a small statured person with the other. Leroy followed behind, carrying his own shotgun. I jumped out of the car, realizing that the unfriendly firefighter had already vacated his spot.

As Jerry came closer, his captive's face became clear. It was Damon Saide. The weasel held a bloody hand close to his chest and hopped on one foot, howling and crying.

So Saide was our shooter. On the one hand, I wasn't surprised at all. On the other, I couldn't see how it made any sense. Why had he shot Gilbert? He'd only barely missed me... I'd been marching up to confront Gilbert as the shots were fired. Same thing had happened at the ambulance. I'd just stepped back when the bullet whizzed past. "Oh, my God," I muttered. "He was after me." I ran toward Jerry and Saide to demand an answer.

As it turned out, I didn't have to demand anything. The second I cleared the back of the car, Saide started screaming. "I should have killed you when I had the chance. If I'd known you were going to get everything I would have. It was perfect. And you ruined it, ruined everything!"

Jerry jerked him up the driveway and kept walking, Saide hobbling and hopping along beside him.

"What are you talking about?" I said, following along.

"It's not right!" he howled. "This deal was going to work. I'd done everything exactly right. There was no way anybody could screw me over this time. I had a contract! And then you ruined it, you... you... greedy... bitch."

Okay, the bitch part I get, but greedy? How? Once again, I was talking to a crazy person who made no sense, so I quit. Damon Saide, however, did not. He just kept repeating that it was his deal and he deserved and things along that line. Maybe at some point it would make sense, but it sure didn't at the moment. And, I really didn't care. I just wanted this all to be over with.

Walking up the hill behind Jerry and his wailing captive, I realized that another ambulance had arrived at some point.

Several other vehicles had as well since there were more cars with flashing lights and armed people in all kinds of different uniforms positioned along the road, and those were the ones I could see. I glanced around behind me and saw several more uniformed types with weapons still drawn coming out of the trees behind us.

The back of the ambulance was open and Jerry shoved Saide toward it. He told Leroy to keep an eye on things as the EMTs worked with the still-howling weasel.

Jerry turned around toward me just as a woman stepped out from behind a black vehicle. "Why thank you, Sheriff," Iris said. She flashed him a badge and ID with what looked like the letters F, B and I prominently displayed. "I believe we can take it from here."

"You'll have to do better than that and you know it," Jerry said, not acting at all surprised.

The woman I knew as Iris was dressed in black, something between a cat suit and a business suit. She nodded to his phone on his belt. "Call Perez."

Jerry did and confirmation was swift and not to his liking. He snapped his phone closed. "I want answers. I have several open cases that I want closed, and obviously I need Saide to do that."

"You'll get your information, Sheriff, but we get him first. The ATF boys will get a go as well."

"All right then. You get Saide and you get everything that goes with him. The entire situation is yours. Bob Little is down in the crappie house. Take a body bag and a winch."

Iris crossed her arms but kept her face just as flat and blank as ever. "Are you telling me that Bob Little is dead?"

"No, Bob was just fishing and caught a big one," I said. "Needs help getting it up the hill."

"I don't like you," Iris said, cutting her eyes toward me.

"Take a number," I said, not caring who she was or what she could do to me if she wanted to. "I don't like you either."

"Jolene, honey, it's okay."

Oh, it was anything but okay. I'd said that phrase no less than a hundred times tonight and I could no longer convince myself of the lie. If you find yourself in the same vicinity as any three-letter government-sanctioned mafia group, you can be assured that nothing is okay. You may think you live in the home of the free and the brave, but you do not. These people can and will do whatever they want and there is nothing you can do about it. Unfortunately, I didn't care about any of that at the moment. I knew they would insist on interrogating me tonight, but I was just not in the mood. "Here's the deal, Iris, I know very little, if anything, about the reasons for anything that happened tonight. The squealing weasel did admit to kidnapping me and expressed regret at not killing me when he had the chance, which he apparently intended to rectify tonight but missed. Twice. I have no idea why he wanted me dead or why he wasn't a better shot. I have nothing else to say and I am not going anywhere but the hospital to check on my mother." That said, I turned and walked back down the hill toward the Expedition.

I had been near exhaustion hours ago, and the adrenaline I'd been running on had long run out. I was very close to the crash and burn point, and I needed far, far away from any temptation to tell anyone anything. They could make me stay, of course, but I was going to make them work for it.

I did not hear Jerry following along behind me and figured he'd stayed behind, making promises about what I would do tomorrow and how it would be better for the FBI if I were rested when they talked to me. It would be better if I never ever had to talk to them at all, but even Jerry couldn't pull that off.

I was just about back to the car when one of the firefighters walked up to me and handed me a rumpled piece of paper. "The guy made them stop the ambulance on the road. Told me to give you this."

I took the paper and opened it up.

"Said he'd been a lucky guy once too, but he was an ass." The man shrugged. "He said you'd understand."

The paper had a woman's name and phone number scrawled across it. I really didn't understand, but I nodded to the firefighter and smiled, telling him I'd take care of it. Not knowing what else to do, I grabbed my phone and dialed the number.

A sleepy woman answered and I gave her the details on Gilbert Moore and told her that he'd asked me to call her. She seemed a little surprised at first, but then scared once it sunk in what I was saying. I was just finishing the call when Jerry walked up beside me.

"What was that about?" he said, leaning on the passenger door.

I showed him the paper. "Gilbert asked me to call her."

"Ah, a woman. I suppose nearly getting killed will do that."

"Now, exactly what do you mean by that?" I said, wondering if his own near death experience had influenced his feelings about me. "Gilbert may really love her and finally realized he's been a fool and wants another chance."

"Or, he may just want her when it's convenient for him, like now, when he's scared. When he's feeling good again, she'll just be something he thinks about when he's not amusing himself elsewhere." Jerry saw my questioning look and sighed. "If you must know, he dated a very good friend of mine once, and I saw the fallout from it. There are always two sides to every story, of course, but in this case they both include him being a narcissistic jerk. It's not likely that's changed."

"Oh," I said, a little disappointed.

"Still, having you as his guardian angel while he thought he was bleeding to death could have put the fear of God in him. Who knows, you may have completely reformed him into a compassionate, considerate and honorable human being."

When he put it that way, even a hopeless romantic like me couldn't get behind it. "I think I'll still hang on to my delusions of a happy ending."

"Happy endings are for people who want them, Jolene," Jerry said, leaning down and giving me a quick kiss on the forehead. "Let's go to the hospital and check on your mother."

"We can go?"

"Yes, apparently Agent Bedford doesn't want to deal with you tonight. I think you scare her."

"The devil wouldn't scare her," I muttered. "I don't suppose she was really worried about the horny toads either, and her name probably isn't even Iris."

"No, Irene Bedford," he said, buckling the seat belt around me as if I were a three year old.

As he closed the door, I laid the seat back and curled up like one.

Chapter
Twenty-Nine

"**J**olene."
Was someone calling my name? I heard a dinging of some sort.

"Jolene."

Jerry. It was Jerry calling. He'd just have to call back later. I didn't even know where I'd put my phone. Something touched my shoulder and I swatted it away.

The next thing I knew I was being scooped up out of the seat. I instinctively knew that Jerry had me so I wasn't afraid. I managed to open my eyes enough to realize that he was carrying me through automatic glass doors into a brightly lit room. As he lowered me into a chair, I managed to wake up enough to realize we were in the emergency room of the General Hospital. I rubbed my hands over my face and tried to clear the fog from my head. "Oh, God, I don't think I can wake up."

"Jolene, I checked on your mother on the way here. She's in surgery now and will be there for a while. She has a broken hip. It is serious, but she'll be okay. Did you understand that?"

"She's okay. Broken hip," I muttered. "She is not going to be happy about that."

"I have to go to the police department right now, but I have some people here to stay with you."

You're leaving?" I said, hearing that pitiful tone in my voice yet again. Catching myself, I sighed, "I don't need a keeper, Jerry. I'll be fine."

"Fritz is up in the surgery waiting room. You can all go up there in a few minutes."

"What? You called Rick in for this?" It was not a psychic revelation or even a lucky guess. My eyes had begun to focus again and I could see Detective Rick Rankin, aka Surfer Dude, standing behind Jerry.

Amidst previous murders and investigations, Rick and I had become well acquainted. In fact, I liked him a lot. When we weren't busy with dead bodies, the three of us had really had a good time together. But he'd moved down near Dallas and it made no sense that he was conveniently in town when I needed a babysitter. "What's he doing here?"

"Remember me telling you that he's engaged?" When I nodded he continued. "Well, some of his soon-to-be wife's family lives around here."

"Oh, that's nice. So why are you punishing him by making him stay with me?"

"Actually, Miz Jackson," Rick said, stepping forward. "My fiancé is here at the hospital visiting a relative anyway."

Jerry leaned over and whispered "I love you" in my ear then gave me a quick kiss. "I'll be back as soon as I can. Call if you need to," he said, almost running toward the door.

Rick sat down beside me in the chair. "Long night?"

"You called me Miz Jackson? What's that about?"

He shrugged. "Do you want to go up to the surgery waiting room?"

"Yes, but give me a minute. I'm still trying to move into semi-consciousness." I rubbed my hands over my face several times then tried to slap myself awake.

Rick handed me a bottle of water. "Here, you probably need to drink something."

Now that he'd pointed out my need for intake, I also realized my need for an outflow. "Hang on to that. I need to run to the restroom."

He pointed me in the right direction but I declined his offer to walk me there. I stumbled my way across the waiting room, but I made it. I was walking and considerably more alert on the way back. I was also covered in water from splashing it on my face. I sat back down, took the bottle and swigged half of it. "I think I'd like to sit here for a few more minutes. While I do, why don't you tell me about this girl of yours. Is she cute, where'd you meet her, what does she do, when are you getting married, all that stuff."

Rick Rankin, the former Redwater Detective who'd run me through the ringer on a number of occasions, was shifting in his chair and sweating like he was on the other side of the interrogation table. "Well," he said, clearing his throat. "Yes, she's cute." He cleared his throat again. "Pretty actually, really pretty." He looked as nervous a high school boy on his first real date. The man could not speak. It was kind of endearing. The tough talking detective seemed at a loss for words. He must really be crazy about the girl.

"Hey, stop being so nervous about it. I'm not jealous." I reached over and punched him in the arm. You weren't quite young enough for me anyway."

My joke did not seem help lighten his mood; in fact, he even looked a little sick. His blond-tipped head tilted to the side and his mouth worked up and down, but no sound came out, kind of like he had a really big hairball caught in his throat. "I...I..."

I pushed myself upright in the chair and leaned toward him. "Rick, what is wrong with you?"

He took a deep breath, closed his eyes and said, "I met her here at the hospital. She's beautiful and smart and I'm crazy in love with her."

I couldn't help but chuckle. He'd spit it out as if it were a confession. "Now, see, that wasn't so hard." I stretched my arms and stood. "You are definitely a smitten man, Detective Rankin, and I am happy to see it."

He eyed me cautiously, his face still pinched.

"I'm feeling better now. Mother's going to be in surgery for a long time, so if your sweetie is here, maybe we can go meet her before we go to the waiting room."

"Yes," he said, nodding his head. "That could work."

Rick and I walked down a long hallway to the elevator and he pushed the button for the third floor. As we stepped onto the elevator, he said, "Before you meet her, promise me that we can still be friends."

What an odd thing to say. I looked at him and frowned. "Of course, why couldn't we?"

"Just promise."

I shrugged. "Okay. I promise."

"Good."

The elevator door opened and Rick guided me down yet another hallway. The small sign on the wall beside the door said "Orthopedic Surgery Waiting Room."

"Mom!"

My head snapped around the doorway to look inside the room as Sarah came running toward me. I grabbed her and hugged her. It was so good to see her, but I couldn't tell her so. I couldn't say anything. A bubble of emotion I didn't even know I had suddenly burst, and I couldn't stop the tears.

"Oh, Mom, I'm so glad you're okay," Sarah said, giving me another hug. "They just came out and said Gram was doing fine. And now you're here and you're okay, and you're here with Rick and that must mean everything is okay there too. Oh, this is so good."

The words she's just said in rapid-fire succession began to sink in, and from the glossy blur of my vision, I saw Rick Rankin shaking his head and waving his arms at her. I was exhausted and emotionally unstable, but I was not stupid.

I pushed back from Sarah, but kept my arm on her shoulder as I guided her closer to Rick. When the light bulb had come on, my tears turned off, but I was still sniffing so Rick grabbed some tissues from the box on a table and handed them to me. "Why thank you, Richard," I said, in a tone that said far more than the words.

"Oh, no," Sarah said, her eyes wide and darting between us. "You hadn't told her?"

"I was building up to it," he croaked.

"Children," I said, condescendingly because that was exactly what the situation called for. I slid my arm off Sarah's shoulder and motioned for them both to sit. "You two have a seat. I'll stand for a while."

"You were supposed to take care of this," Sarah hissed at Rick.

"She's your mother," he snapped back.

"Now stop that!" I said, hearing a replay of Jerry's same exact words about Lucille to me. With that little revelation, I wasn't sure which of us was going to have a meltdown over our mother first, so I grabbed a chair, pulled it up in front of them and plopped myself in it. "I think I will sit down. Now you two start talking."

Thankfully, the waiting room was small and otherwise unoccupied so we could have an open dialogue, which would be a new experience for us all, apparently.

"Well, actually, Rick and I met in this very hospital a few months when you were recovering after getting shot." She glanced at Rick and smiled the smile of a girl in love. "We just started talking and well, one thing led to another."

"The long distance part has been really difficult," Rick added. "But we've made it work."

Well, I guess they had. And they'd had help with it too. "Your grandmother knew about this, didn't she?"

Sarah squirmed in her chair. "She's been very supportive."

While they chattered about their romance, several things began to make sense, such as Sarah being in Texas and Lucille renting a hotel room that Sarah didn't actually stay in. Because, I'm guessing, she'd been either at the Hilton with Rick or driving back and forth with him to his home in Dallas. She was at the courthouse rally though, and with Jerry the next morning. But she certainly was never in Tiger's room. In fact, as best I could tell at the moment, there were only tiny shreds of anything that resembled truth in the stories I'd been told up until now. I looked up from my thoughts at my lying daughter. "It's my own fault, for letting you spend summers with your grandmother."

"What?"

"Jerry knew about this too, didn't he?"

"Now, don't be getting mad at Jerry over this," Rick said. "None of it is his fault. He tried to get us to tell you, we were just afraid to. And then with all the other things that started happening, well, there just wasn't a good time."

"Jerry didn't know what was going on at first," Sarah added. "But when everything kind of blew up, well, we had to tell him. I begged him not to tell you."

"It's not his fault," Rick repeated. "We put him in a tough position."

274

"Mom, don't get mad at him about this," Sarah pleaded. "I really like him and he seems to like you, and well, we don't want do anything to mess that up."

"This is crazy," I said. "I do not understand why you people can't just tell the truth and be up front about it. Am I really that scary?"

"Yes," they said in unison.

I frowned. "I haven't burned anyone at the stake since the nineties and my last beheading was a good five years ago. What is it that you can possibly fear about telling me these things?"

"I'm moving to Texas when the semester ends," Sarah blurted out. "And I'm changing schools."

"That didn't exactly answer my question, but okay," I said simply. "And really, after everything that's happened here in the last few days, you moving to Texas and changing schools doesn't even flicker the dial on my anxiety meter."

Sarah frowned, either confused because I wasn't mad or disappointed that she didn't have to fight with me for acceptance of her decisions.

"We're getting married," Rick added, eyeing me to see how I'd react to that one.

"I kind of guessed that one at this point, Richard. And a hearty congratulations to you both. I'm thrilled. Now, what else is there you've neglected to tell me?" I asked, wondering if there was a grandchild in my future.

"I'm not pregnant if that's what you're fishing for," Sarah said. "I don't even know if I ever want kids."

"Then pray tell, what is the big problem with talking to me about this? Did you think I'd say no?" I stared unblinking at my daughter. "And so what if I did? It's your life, not mine. You get to make your own choices. Whether I am happy about those or not isn't your problem. And, by the way, aside from this little undercover operation, you make great choices."

She had a deep frown that said "well, when you put it that way" then an obvious "but" occurred to her.

I knew right where she'd gone. "Nope, being afraid that I would get mad isn't an excuse either. If, as your mother, my love is conditional on you doing what I want you to then it isn't really love, now is it?"

I let them both stew on that for a few long seconds then added, "Right." I pushed myself up out of the chair and slid it back to its place then gave them each a hug. "I'm happy for you and will no doubt be ecstatic after I've had a few hours sleep, which I plan to take care of over there in that corner. Wake me if there's news on your grandmother."

"That's it?" Sarah said, standing.

"That's it. I can see that you two are head over heels in love and I'm thrilled. I'll admit I'm not crazy about his occupation," I said, nodding toward Rick, who'd also stood. "But I have my own issues in that department so we can all just deal with them together." I walked over to the corner and began arranging myself a sleeping spot. "Besides, Sarah, I knew him and liked him before you did. He was really sort of pre-approved."

"I think she's delusional," Sarah said to Rick. "She's not going to remember any of this and then we'll have to go through the whole thing again when she's back to her old self."

"Oh, for godsakes, I can hear you." I sat down in the corner, propped my feet up in the chair across from me, crossed my arms and leaned my head back. "I am not sleepwalking and I don't have dementia. And Sarah, I'm not the same person I was when were kids together." She looked confused, of course. "I was a kid even in my thirties. I think I've grown up some now." I grinned a little. "I will, of course, insist on sharing my hard-earned wisdom with you both."

"Okay, then," Sarah said, eyeing the door and plotting escape. "We're going to go get a bite to eat. Can we bring you something?"

At the mere mention of food, I realized I was starving. But I wasn't likely to know it in about thirty seconds when I passed out. "No, go on. I'll get a bite later."

"I love you, Mom," Sarah chirped, grabbing Rick's hand to drag him out the door.

Rick waved then said, "Fritz is here. He's been walking the halls. He'll probably be by before long."

I nodded and let my eyes close.

Chapter Thirty

"**J**olene? Is that you, Jolene?"

"Yes, Mother, it's always me," I muttered.

What did she want now? Couldn't the woman let me sleep just this once? Whatever stupid thing she wanted me to do this time, I wasn't going to do. That seemed like a really good policy that I should have instituted a long time ago. I growled and turned over, my face smashing into something.

"Jolene," she called again. "I need help. Help me."

Help? What? Reality slowly crept in through my delirium, and when it did, I automatically jumped to my feet. "Mother?"

Once I got my bearings, I realized I was in a hospital room, one with glowing lights and beeping noises coming from a bank of monitors. Other bits of memories drifted by and I vaguely recalled Jerry leading me here and putting me in some kind of reclining chair. I stumbled to the side of her bed and grabbed the rail. "I'm here, Mom. I'm here."

Tubes and wires connected her to a variety of machines that monitored blood pressure, pulse, oxygen level and about five other things I had no idea about. They didn't seem to be flashing warning signs, so I figured she was at least stable. She was also asleep so I guess I'd just dreamed that she was calling to me.

She'd indeed broken her hip and a bone in her foot, and her shoulder had a hairline fracture as well. But there had been no internal injuries, which was amazing, and she'd only come away with a mild concussion. She really was going to be okay.

As I stood there, staring down at her, it hit me again how very close she'd come to being killed. The only reason she hadn't been was because she'd still been behind the door, not in the doorway, when the blast went off. If the door hadn't taken the brunt of the blast, she'd have been in pieces across the grass.

She made me crazy without even trying, I wouldn't deny that. And when she'd done it on purpose, I'd entertained thoughts of killing her myself. And now, standing here facing that reality, the thought of losing her shook me to my very core.

I didn't want to lose my mother. I actually loved her. And no matter how I might wish it to be true, my twisted little psyche wasn't going to automatically untwist, according to whether or not she was breathing. My mother might have been the architect of some of my issues, but they were mine now and mine to dismantle. And, as she'd said to me before "everybody has a bad childhood, that's what childhood is for." I think some comment about me "sucking it up" had been involved as well. "You know, Mother," I said softly. "Just because you got yourself wounded in the line of duty doesn't get you off the hook for anything. You've still got a lot to answer for."

She didn't answer, of course, but I kept talking anyway.

The light was dim, but I thought I saw her lips move slightly. I also thought I heard a faint whisper that sounded like "I'm sorry." One of us was delusional, and I figured it was me, so I went with it and reached over and squeezed her hand lightly. "It's okay, Mom, you're okay."

I don't' know how long I stood there, staring and thinking, but a hand on my shoulder broke my trance.

"Come on," Jerry said, gently patting my shoulder. "I'm taking you to get something to eat. She's stable and on high dose pain medicine. She probably won't wake up for a while."

Jerry led me through the maze of hallways and elevators to the hospital entrance. "Lucille didn't tell you, did she?" he asked, guiding me out the door and toward the parking lot.

"Tell me what?"

"Anything. Did she tell you anything at all?"

"No, nothing. Well, I thought she said she was sorry, but I think I just imagined it."

Jerry sighed and groaned all the same time. "Wow, where to start," he said then didn't say another word as we walked across the parking lot. When we got to the Expedition, he opened my door and I hopped inside. He stayed there for a few minutes, just looking at me. "People do crazy things, Jo. They do really crazy things for love."

Did he mean him, or me, who? I waited for him to respond, but he didn't, he just shook his head and closed the door. Once he was seated behind the wheel and the car was running, he said, "Let's start with the land behind your mother's house. You were right. There is toxic waste buried there."

"That can't be good."

"No, it isn't. But it is why Tiger, Bobcat and Lily were in town—to try to fix it."

"I was really rooting for the horny toad excuse."

"Tiger worked at Bob Little's plastic factory and was one of the ones who buried waste there years ago. He believed the chemicals he was exposed to at the factory, which are what's buried in the drums, to be the cause of his cancer so he came back to right a wrong. He left a pretty good map of the locations with your mother. It won't be cheap to clean up, but Tiger's work will help a lot."

"Wow. So there is groundwater contamination?"

"Not sure yet."

"So I get that Tiger was on a mission, but what about Lily and Bobcat?"

"Lily was his daughter," Jerry said, "which is why she was crying most of the time. Bobcat was an old army buddy just here for support. Tiger got the FBI interested, and Iris, AKA Agent Irene Bedford joined the group."

"My God, what a mess," I said. "Well, I guess that puts an end to the park plans."

Jerry sighed. "Probably, although it was actually Bob Little who was behind that to begin with."

"What? How could he be behind it? He was fighting it, along with Mother."

Jerry put the car in gear and backed out of the parking space. "That was your mother's version of the story."

"Yes, well, there would be that."

As we drove, Jerry said, "Apparently Bob hadn't directed the dumping, but found out about it and knew it was going to come back to bite him and your mother since some of it is on her property. He thought if he could sell all the property, including your mother's, he could relieve them all of the liability."

"That seems doubtful," I said, the words "Superfund site" jumping to mind. "I'm guessing Mother knew nothing about any of it."

"Nope. And Bob was trying every angle he could think of to generate cash from the property."

"Why? Was he in debt?"

"Quite the opposite," Jerry said. "Best I can figure, it was just his way of estate planning. He was trying to get your mother set up for life financially and make arrangements for his heirs before he died."

"Interesting approach, I guess."

As we came to a familiar intersection, Jerry pointed to the Settler's Restaurant where we'd had our incident with Damon Saide. "It could be fun."

I laughed. "I think I'd prefer a quiet corner somewhere."

Jerry pulled in to a Denny's just down the road, which was a good thing since I was absolutely starving.

Luckily, we were seated immediately and within minutes had ordered and were sipping coffee and hot tea. After the gassing incident, I was pretty sure that water and tea would be the only two beverages I would ever touch again. "So how does Saide figure into this?" I asked.

"Bob hired him to front the deal, make it look the way he wanted it to for appearances. Once Saide learned about the potential gas field, he pushed Bob to drill. Bob did, of course, for his own reasons, and they both realized there was way more potential in gas profits than liabilities in cleanup.",

"Only Bob had already signed papers, agreeing to sell," I said. "But surely he hadn't included the mineral rights too."

"No, he hadn't, which is why Saide was after your mother. He thought he could trick her into selling her part."

Okay, that much made sense. "Wait a minute," I said. "Didn't we find out that Mother owned mineral rights on Bob Little's property too? Is that what Bobcat told me?"

Jerry shook his head. "No. Since the property she owned looked like it was still part of the ranch—and she does own mineral rights on that—it could have been misinterpreted. And that really wasn't Tiger's concern anyway. He was here to force Bob Little to clean up what was buried there no matter who owned it because his company was responsible for putting it there."

"And if that happened, there wouldn't be any gas production for quite some time. So Saide had to push things through. But he couldn't get Mother to sell." Something still didn't fit. "All that's well and good, but why kill Bob Little?"

Jerry took a deep breath and sighed. "We think he went to force Bob to sign over the mineral rights to him. And when he couldn't, Saide killed him."

I frowned. "Couldn't or wouldn't?"

"Couldn't. Seems Bob had transferred everything he had besides the ranch, including the mineral rights, into a trust for his heirs."

I tried to pull together the bits and pieces of things people had said and who had done what to whom, but the thread was just out of reach.

Jerry realized that I was trying to make sense of the nonsensical and reached over and squeezed my hand. "Saide intended to force an heir to sell to him."

"Dumb plan."

"True enough. But he thought if he could kill you, Sarah would be easily swayed to sell."

"Say what?"

"There are papers in that box your mother had that will clear all of this up for you."

"Then I'd say now would be a good time to trot them out because I'm a few steps behind in this dance."

"Yes, Jolene, Bob Little left everything he had to you."

I shook my head. "Jerry, I don't even know the man. Why would he leave me anything?"

He sighed again, pulled his hand back and took a swig of coffee. "Lucille was supposed to have told you this at the cabin." He let out another heavy sigh. "The thing is Jolene, your mom and dad couldn't have children. Don't know why, they just couldn't. So, when Glenda Little died after giving birth, they adopted you. Remember, you saw her death certificate and it was only a few days after your birth."

I bobbed my head up and down, or think I did. It's hard to tell what's real and what's not in moments like these.

"Bob's grief over Glenda's death nearly killed him. He couldn't take care of himself, much less a baby. Your mother stepped in."

Wow. On the one hand I was stunned speechless, on the other, like so many moments before this, it was so surreal it couldn't possibly be true or apply to me. Even though I still had some small measure of objectivity in my thoughts, I had nothing leaping to my tongue to say except, "Wow."

Breakfast arrived and Jerry made me eat it. He filled in what he could, but most of the details were lying with my mother in a hospital bed a few blocks away. At least some of her words made sense now. She'd gone to great lengths to be sure that I never learned that I was adopted until after she'd passed. But when Saide found out about the gas reserves, he also found out who owned what and started trying to find a way to get control of it all. Lucille knew her secrets were about to get out and tried everything she could think of to stop it. Then an odd thought occurred to me. "How is it that everyone in town doesn't know about this? She couldn't have had an imaginary pregnancy, remained slim and trim, and came home with a baby one day."

"A lot of people knew they adopted a baby. They'd been trying to for quite some time. No one knew it was Bob Little's."

"So maybe that's why she didn't tell me. She didn't want me confused since Bob literally lived next door."

"Could be," Jerry said, "but only your mother knows why she does what she does."

"And I think it's about time she enlightened the rest of us," I said. "Let's go back to the hospital and wake her up. We've got a lot of catching up to do."

"Jolene, Jolene, Jolene," Jerry said, shaking his head then taking another sip of coffee. "She might not be quite ready for the Inquisition just yet."

"I know that," I said, confusion, irritation and compassion taking turns in my thinking. "Besides, the whole thing seems pretty unbelievable, so I could just wake up and realize it was all a dream. Then I wouldn't have to deal with any of it."

"It isn't a dream. And you have quite a bit you're going to have to deal with."

I took a sip of tea and stared for a minute then said, "That would be the toxic waste dump."

Jerry nodded. "And the oil and gas wells."

"Right, Mister Barnett Shale is my new best friend."

He chuckled. "Owning a big pocket of natural gas can't be too bad."

"Yeah, well, that remains to be seen."

"Then there's the house the hill too. Nice, but needs a lot of updating. Rumor is that it's haunted."

"Perfect. This just keeps getting better and better."

Jerry squeezed my hand. "Hey, come on, smile. You own a ranch in Texas. You're an heiress."

"I think we've circled back around to the toxic waste."

"It's not anything you have to deal with today. Besides, I have no doubts that you'll have everything lined out in no time." He stood and held out his hand to me. "I'll be there whenever you need me, Jo."

I smiled suggestively, or perhaps deviously. "And what about when I just want you?"

He pulled me up and tugged me toward him. "I am always on call for you."

Chapter
Thirty-One

When we arrived back at the hospital, Lucille was still out of it. Jerry convinced me to go to the hotel, which was nearby, and sleep in a real bed for the rest of the day. He'd had work to do for a while but he came back and spent the night with me. And with no immediate dramas hanging over our heads from anyone anywhere, it was a glorious night, one I could get used to experiencing on a regular and routine basis. One might say I was glowing when Jerry dropped me off at the hospital the next morning.

I was also a little more grounded in reality since I'd had some time to review some of the paperwork regarding my surprise inheritance. The call from Bob Little's attorney had cleared up any lingering questions about the situation being a mistake. It wasn't. And furthermore, I had urgent situations that required my utmost and immediate attention. Mr. Attorney did not appreciate my pithy comments as we went along, so I just quit listening to his rambling about the list of things I had to do. I did perk up when he told me that the toxic waste police were already onsite at "my" ranch and would be getting with me very soon to let me know what I was going to do about my pesky little dumping problem. I informed him that he was the attorney of record and that he could just handle it. He informed me otherwise. I did not foresee a warm and chummy friendship with Mr. Attorney.

When I arrived at Lucille's room in intensive care, she was gone. I might admit to a brief moment of panic—okay, it shot through me like a knife—but it was only for a second. I went to the nurses' desk and found out that she'd been moved to a regular room one floor up.

They'd given me the room number, but I wouldn't have needed it. I could hear her the minute I rounded the corner. She was definitely wide awake now.

"Jolene!" she screeched as I walked into the room. "Did you put them up this?"

A male nurse in purple scrubs stood beside her bed, adjusting the IV. "I'm Phillip. I'm the nurse on duty." He did not sound excited about it. "She's been a little agitated since she got here. We've called the doctor to get her something."

"That's my daughter, and she'll put a stop to all this nonsense." She waved her good arm at Phillip. "She won't let you drug me!"

Phillip finished his work and walked out. I knew I'd be talking to him shortly in private, not that he didn't already know all he needed to know about what he was dealing with.

"Do you know what that doctor said before he moved me down here?" she said, bypassing any social niceties such as "good morning" or the obligatory "how are you." "He said they're going to send me to the nursing home in a few days. I never heard of such a thing. I suppose I ought to be glad I'm not a horse or they'd have already shot me dead."

"Yes, good thing you're not a horse," I agreed.

"You're not going to let them put me in the home, are you, Jolene? You wouldn't do that to your own mother, would you? I am your mother, you know, and I don't care what anybody says. And I'll shoot the first one I hear asking you who your 'real' mother is, that's what I'll do. I just dare somebody to say that. Real my hind foot. I'm as real as they come, that's what I am."

"Yes, Mother, dear, you absolutely are as real as real can be and then some."

She scowled at me. "Well, don't you forget it."

"How could I? My damaged little psyche is not about to let you off the hook simply because we don't share the same blood type. And furthermore, it's not a nursing home, it's a rehabilitation center, and God knows you need rehabilitating."

She huffed and sputtered. "You make it sound like I'm some hopped up druggie being sent off to get clean."

"Pardon me. I did not mean to imply that you were a druggie. It is a physical rehabilitation center that, and yes, you are definitely in need of it."

She crossed her arms and huffed again. "I suppose I should be honored that you're still treating me just as hateful as you always have, even knowing the truth. I suppose I should be, but I'm not. I don't care what you call it, that place is a home full of old people, and I'm not going there. You can't do this to me."

I stood at the end of the bed, resisting the urge to point my finger at her. "First of all, I am not doing anything *to* you. You need specialized help so you can get back to walking again quickly. That isn't a special Hell I dreamed up just to make you miserable. It's just what you have to do. There is no choice. So, as you've told me before, just suck it up and do it. Besides, it's only for a few weeks, not the rest of your life."

She stuck out her chin and tipped her nose up. "Well, then, I suppose since you've got me all penned up, you'll run off back to Colorado and just leave me here to go through it all by myself."

"Merline and Agnes will be here every day, I'm sure. And so will Fritz."

"You *are* going to leave!" she shrieked.

"Yes, Mother, I am. This afternoon, in fact. The sooner the better even."

Her mouth dropped open. "Well, that is just the most hateful thing I've ever heard of. That is just the meanest thing you've ever done. Ever!"

"Yes, well, it may be, but I still have to go find something to do with my home since I will apparently be here in Texas for quite some time. Seems there are lengthy dealings with the estate of a man I never really met, not to mention your home that needs tending, and last, but certainly not least, there's the always-pressing need to try to limit your access to trouble. Actually, that last one is impossible, and yet it will somehow cause me more grief than the all the other problems combined."

She frowned as she processed what I'd told her. "Well, what about me? You didn't say one word about me other than having to come back and board up my house and find some place to put me where I can't escape. Are you even going to come visit me in the home?"

"Mother Dearest, in case you haven't noticed, this is *all* about you."

She puckered her lips and stuck out her chin again, somehow looking relieved and annoyed all at the same time. "So you're coming back here then?"

"Afraid so."

"When?"

"A week."

"A week! They'll have put me in the home by then!"

"You'll be in rehab, and quite well taken care of, which is why I'm going now. It's when you get out of rehab that really concerns me."

She stuck her nose higher in the air. "Well, don't you be worrying about that. I can take care of myself."

"Uh huh."

"Don't you be talking down to me, Missy. That's what all you young people do, just let us seniors show the least little bit of weakness, and then you start treating us like senile invalids who can't do a thing for ourselves. Well, I won't have it! My leg might be hurt but my mind is working just fine." She scowled at me to see if I was going to challenge her statement. "That's right. I can take care of myself as well as I ever could. I'm the mother here and you won't be treating me like a child."

I walked over to the bed, leaned down and kissed her on the forehead then squeezed her hand. "I'll be back before you know it. I love you, Mother. Behave."

"Don't you be telling me to behave. I am not a child!"

She was still scowling and grumbling as I walked out the door, but I considered it a good thing. Our relationship hadn't changed one bit, which was not necessarily a good thing, but it was the best thing at the moment. I couldn't say that I'd really dealt with much of the emotional aspects of what I'd learned because I was busy with the very real world details of it all.

My whole life people had always commented on how much I looked like Lucille. Until now, it had just been annoying. Now, it made me curious. Glenda must have had similar features, because I didn't look anything at all like Bob Little. I supposed

I'd find out about all of that soon enough, not that it really mattered. Right now, all that mattered was that the people I loved most in the world were okay. Really okay.

Jerry met me in the hall as I walked out of the room. "You're not even gone and I already miss you."

"Me, too," I said, smiling up at him. "I've been spoiled, having you around like this."

He put his arm on my shoulder and covertly ran his fingers up my neck. "Don't forget me."

Tingling heat flashed through me and I sucked in my breath and gritted my teeth.

He laughed then moved his hand down to hold mine.

I recapped my plans as we made our way out of the hospital. At the front entrance, a truck with yellow lights across the cab made me think of Gilbert Moore. I'd checked on him earlier and learned that he'd made it through surgery and was going to be just fine. I wondered if the woman I'd called had come to be with him. She'd sounded genuinely concerned so I figured she had. But she'd also sounded afraid, and not just for him, but for herself. She had reason to be. By his own admission, he'd hurt her before. And she obviously knew that if she let him, he could do it again.

I understood it only too well. My own fear of being hurt again had caused me to put up walls with everyone, even Jerry. I'd loved him for most of my life in some capacity, and yet I'd held back. Now, however, I was beginning to feel safe enough emotionally to maybe start thinking about possibly letting down my walls just a little. I hoped Gilbert's brush with death would change him for the better, would help him recognize and fix whatever was keeping him from really loving and trusting someone. I hoped my own journey had gotten me to the place where I could do the same.

At the car, Jerry opened my door and I climbed in. He didn't shut the door, however.

"Fear makes people do stupid things," he said, as if he'd been reading my mind. "We both did stupid things when we were kids, Jo, and we can't go back and undo those."

"No, we can't."

"But we can do things differently now." He leaned in the car and put his hand on my cheek. "I can't promise you there won't be problems. In fact, I promise you there will," he said, his eyes soft and his voice a deep rumble. "But I also promise you that I love you and that you can trust me."

My heart seemed to burst open and tears pooled in my eyes. I reached up and squeezed his hand with both of mine then pulled it against my chest. "I know that, Jerry. I really do."

He brushed his lips against mine. "Then marry me."

TO BE CONTINUED

in the Fourth Jolene Jackson Mystery

KILLER MOVES